BEAU

In the Company of Snipers

Book 18

Irish Winters

COPYRIGHT

Beau; In the Company of Snipers, Book 18

Cover design: Kelli Ann Morgan, Inspire Creative Services
Cover image: Paul Henry Serres Photography, www.paulhenryserres.com
Cover model: Simon
Interior book design: Bob Houston, eBook Formatting
Editor: Linda Clarkson, Black Opal Editing and Proofreading

ISBN Paperback: 978-1-942895-64-0
ISBN eBook: 978-1-942895-65-7
Library of Congress Control Number: 2018957237

DEDICATION

To one of my greatest fans

Captain Robert Dean

Former Commander, US Army 5th Division

1/61st Infantry, A Company

It's true.

"Rangers lead the way."

In the Company of Snipers

You can find Irish Winters on Facebook: https://www.facebook.com/author.irishwinters

On Twitter: https://twitter.com/irishwinters1

For news on upcoming releases, sign up for Irish Winters' Newsletter at IrishWinters.com.

For more information about all my books, visit IrishWinters.com.

IN THE COMPANY OF SNIPERS

This series revolves around former Marine scout sniper, Alex Stewart, and his covert surveillance company, The TEAM, home-based out of Alexandria, Virginia. An obsessive patriot and workaholic, he created the company to give former military snipers like him, a chance at returning to civilian life with a decent job, security, and a future.

This is not a serial with each book ending at a cliffhanger. *In the Company of Snipers* is a collection of passionate love stories involving strong women and men who are tough enough to take on the world alone. Each is a stand-alone read, complete in itself.

Spoiler alert: Every story contains adult scenes including sexual situations (some explicit), language, and violence. I don't write sweet romance, so be forewarned.

Book 1, *ALEX*, reveals how The TEAM came to be, as well as how Alex met Kelsey, how they fell in love and fought all odds to stay together. Each of the following books is a complete romance in itself, where, in the course of an active TEAM operation, one agent comes face to face with his or her demons. The men and women I write about are all patriots and warriors, dealing with what they've lived through or mistakes they've made.

It's my hope that you will come to realize along with my heroes...

Love changes everything.

Prologue

On her hands and knees in the early morning Virginia sunshine, Catalina Montego worked hard to make her latest rose garden worthy of America's notice. To blend in, she'd chosen simple attire for the day. Stonewashed denim jeans. A garish black t-shirt with the red, white, and blue symbol of America in the center of her chest. People here liked that emblem. They identified with it. The plasticized symbol of capitalism had nothing to do with her heart, though. Never. The outfit merely lent the appearance of belonging in this deceitful land of the free, something that would never happen. She was only here on a mission. A gardening mission, so to speak.

But enough of that. Creating new flowerbeds was backbreaking, dirty work, and she was tired from her late night—make that all night—escapades. *So much to do and so little time!*

But that was the way it had to be. Only with enough blood, sweat, and tears would prize-winning roses be nourished the perfect way Nature intended. The right way. *Organically.*

A deep purr rumbled at the back of her throat at that delicious word. No one ever said the blood, sweat, or tears had to be hers.

Smiling, she stuck all ten fingers into the newly loosened soil and wiggled them. Ah, yes. America! This was the only place to plant these particular rose bushes. Right under his nose.

Soon, they'd root and thrive and thrive... until the overpowering fragrance from her dearest loves filled the air. Fed by the blood of the so-called righteous, that scent would soon conceal the other odor that accompanied such single-minded work. Like a benediction of sanctified Catholic holy water, she sprinkled two handfuls of dirt over the fresh grave, *ahem, hole*. Satisfied, she sat back on her haunches at the mere thought of this unique mingling of dirt, soil amendments, and, oh yes, root balls. Every horticulturalist knew the flower was only as strong as the root. But planting balls was... *Orgasmic! Simply orgasmic!*

Glancing at the lavish home two doors down the road, she allowed another smile. Alexander Stewart would be home soon. Her Spidey senses tingled with the thrilling knowledge of her firm hold on such a fine, brave man. Of all her lovers, he would never let her down. He'd have no choice. Not that he knew the power she held over him, or the very special place he held in her heart. Not yet. But soon.

She literally loved him to pieces. A piece here. A piece over there! Ha! What a noble burial he'd have. Precisely what he deserved! But not right away. Oh, no. Only after enough time and torturous worry, would she allow him to go to his grave. Catalina intended to love Alex Stewart a long, long time...

For years she'd been forced to study him from afar, had even searched for and chatted online with those other fellows who'd been with him that night, Vic What's-His-Name and

Rodney Whoever. They hadn't known much, but she'd gotten just enough information to bring her to this spot today. And here she was, nearly in the proud man's backyard.

One thing she now knew for certain, the mighty Alex Stewart was not immune to persuasion. He might think he was, but she was here to prove him wrong. Sacrifice. It all came down to sacrifice. If you loved someone, you took exquisitely good care of them, right? You never—ever—let them, or the hope that they still lived, go. You willingly sacrificed yourself, your time and ultimately, your life to protect them, right? Like a beloved wife. Or a precious child. A dear, dear friend...

Turning to the tightly sealed container at her side, the one marked BIOHAZARD like the rest of the *meat* she shipped all over the world—prime cut only—she surveyed her early morning effort. At last, the soil was ready. The warm, wet nutrients in this container would decay quickly. Perfectly. Without a trace. Just like the greatest serial killer of all, Mother Nature, had always intended. The circle of life was a stunning concept.

"My heavens are you at it again?" the pretty brown-haired woman asked. She seemed such a startling ray of sunshine for so early in the day. Catalina nearly straightened her dark glasses to block the glow from that welcoming smile. This friendly neighbor brought her pretty little daughter along with her. What a yummy, scrumptious pair.

"I don't mean to interrupt, but you were out here late last night, too. I saw your light through the trees. You must really like gardening."

Catalina brushed the back of one gloved hand over her forehead in feigned exhaustion. Nosey neighbors were the last things she needed, but this one in particular deserved special handling. Almost as special as these nutrients, so primed and ready to dissolve.

"You know what they say. No rest for the weary, and the wicked don't need it." *Or something just as idiotic as that.*

Rising to her feet—just to lend credence to the charade—she tugged one glove off and extended a hand in what people in America termed neighborly friendship. Catalina called it calculated guessing. Sizing up one's intended mark. Measuring the fit, weight, and dimensions of her quarry for her specialized—equipment. "I'm sorry if my late night gardening disturbed you. My name is Ca… Ca… Ahem!" She coughed at her near misspeak, then said as graciously as she could muster, "I'm Athena, and you are?"

"Kelsey Stewart," the pretty woman replied graciously.

Of course you are. My word, your tiny hand is warm and smooth, almost childlike compared to my practiced grip. But that's what working every day of your life will get you. Stronger. Harder. Better than simpering females like you every single time.

She took firm hold of this innocent's grip, debating the challenge of prey so easily captured. This one would go quickly into the auger, her bones so fragile and her skin smooth. No doubt saturated with any number of the rich emollients American women utilized every day of their pathetic lives. Nine to one, this dainty little hand had never done more than pamper her silly daughter's curly locks. *Too bad my equipment is already, shall we say, engaged?*

Catalina suppressed the urge to act impulsively. Her wickedly cruel but delightful brother had always said—before he'd been murdered in cold blood—that good things came to those who waited. But Kelsey's long, silky hair was a definite plus. The longer, the better. It made good handles. As did arms. Feet. Twisted fingers. Speaking of fingers... *My how the stunning solitaire on this woman's finger gleams like a veritable beacon of the wealth and arrogance of America's upper class. Or is that crust?*

The stark contrast of the handhold, the difference between Kelsey's fair Caucasian lack of pigment against the sun-blessed skin of Catalina's rich Cuban heritage, curved the corners of Catalina's lips. Just a tiny bit. Not enough to pass for a real smile, but enough to acknowledge she was and always would be the winner. Even at the most basic societal stratification. Ah, yes. She already had what every pasty white woman in America wanted—a year-round tan. Didn't that make them the pitiful ones?

"I'm just next door if you need any help," Kelsey said with a bright smile, returning Catalina's grip with unexpected strength. That was interesting. Not necessarily a game-changer but worth noticing. Maybe even accommodating. "It's no trouble. Honest."

What an odd woman. So eager to please. So obtuse. So, so—nice. But why? "Have you been watching me?" *Do you already know who I am and why I'm here?*

The silly woman's smile only brightened further at that subtle accusation. Which was further proof that Alex Stewart had married for looks, not intelligence. The dolt. His whimsical, cutesy little wife wasn't smart enough to realize when she'd been insulted.

This next abduction will be so easy.

"No, but you're my neighbor now, and I'm here to help unpack or haul boxes or whatever you need. Just ask, okay?

Lexie goes down for her nap right after lunch. We'll have you completely settled in by nightfall."

How droll the elite's tendency to overuse the word 'we,' as if Catalina had ever—ever—strived to be included in the pretentious minority that took whatever they wanted from the rest of the world. But this friendly neighbor was dressed to *'help,'* as she'd put it. And her husband would be home soon. The timing couldn't be more perfect. If only…

Suddenly perturbed at her impulsive actions of the previous evening, she cast a sharp glance over her shoulder at the general location of her new, *ahem,* workplace. She'd acted rashly. Too much. Too soon. That error in judgment had already cost her hours spent on the road. First from the heart of Washington D.C. to this quaint little bastion of greed, then back to her hotel room near the District. Just because... Alex Stewart needed to remember that actions had consequences. Even the proud eventually fell, and his fall would be stupendous.

Damn. Damn. Oh, bloody damn. Catalina had no choice. She hadn't yet finished with her previous *guest.* He was still in there. Might even be awake by now. Normally, she had no trouble handling two guests. She was the stronger one. Survival of the fittest, you know. But Alex deserved so much more attention to detail. As in gruesome, gory Technicolor detail.

The best revenge—the kind where a woman could dance and sing on her enemy's very fresh grave after she'd made him suffer for years—was, unfortunately, in those details. She let Kelsey's fingers slip from her hand, sure there would come another opportunity and another day. Soon. But for now… *Alexander Stewart will just have to wait his turn.*

"You're too late. I didn't bring much with me, and it's already unpacked. I'm just planting a few roses to brighten this drab yard." She pointed to the ugly saguaro cactus in the corner behind her. "That has to go."

"Me yikes fwowers," the little girl babbled.

Standing there with the first rays of morning sun glowing on her face, the child had to be as mentally deficient as her mother. Lexus, was it? Named after a car. How utterly American.

"And you'd attract the cutest baby worms," Catalina told the child, her tone dripping with affected adoration. She wasn't into pedophilia and its eventual need for a quick but oftentimes messy and noisy resolution. Her roses required a more robust fertilizer, the sort that came with a youthful spike of male vigor and testosterone.

"Well, enough of this chit-chat. I must get these babies planted. I'll see you around." *Or not. Either way works for me.*

Kelsey turned aside, but not until her gaze scrolled past Catalina to the twelve thorny plants lined up in their black plastic buckets like brave little soldiers on the brick walkway behind her. "You're planting all of them today? Come on. Are you sure you won't need help?"

Catalina arched a brow at the woman's naïveté. "Don't be ridiculous. I love these roses to pieces." *And I do mean pieces.* "For them to thrive, I must execute, *ahem, ahem...*" Pressing her wrist to her nose, she let loose several more faux-feminine coughs. "I must plant these flowerbeds with sufficient forethought. One can never be too careful."

The sudden light in her neighbor's dark eyes struck Catalina as either extremely odd or exquisitely intelligent. For a moment, an actual shiver skated over her stronger-than-anyone-else-in-the-world's shoulders that this Kelsey person might possibly be able to read her mind. Or at least, to deduce more than Catalina had originally given her credit for.

But no. Banish that silly thought. Americans weren't bright enough or traveled enough to see beyond the end of their self-entitled noses. Privileged, yes. But smart? Experienced? Wise to the ways of the big, scary world with all its pains, injustices, and untold miseries? That would be everyone on the planet *but* a United States citizen.

"Okay, well, let me know if you need anything," Kelsey offered, slanting her shoulder like a barrier between Catalina and that delectable child at her knee. "I'm in the stone and log home two doors down. Use the intercom at the gate if you need anything, and I'll let you in."

Let me in? Catalina tossed her head at that inane invitation. *Like you could stop me.* "Yes, yes, well, back to work. The early bird, you understand."

"I yikes birds," the lovely morsel now scooped up into her adoring mother's arms mumbled as she stuffed all five fingers in her tiny face.

"Yes, Lexie, and you like puppies and kittens and…" Kelsey's motherly words were lost as she hurried away with her child.

Just as well. Catalina knelt, admiring the row of graves, *ahem,* rose beds she'd dug with her own two very capable hands in the wee, wee hours. How she loved the smell of dirt, Mother Nature's delectable, all-in-one morgue and cemetery. The musky, musty fragrance of life undone alone restored a sense of balance to one's ragged nerves. *I must bottle this!*

But first…

Tugging her nitrile gloves back on, she stretched forward and once again dug all ten fingers into the lush, rich soil. Gloves gave her the perfect amount of tactile sensation without fear of contracting AIDS, Ebola, or any number of disgusting contagions that came from handling bodies. Plus, gloves kept her nails clean.

This was why she loved planting roses and things. *The outdoors. The fresh air. The absolute surety that nobody in America knows I'm here!* Better rephrase that. After all, a few bodies did know she'd arrived, and soon another would understand the meaning of her presence as well. There'd be no need for gloves then. The touching of skin on skin was important in this next step. Like her roses needed the sun, she needed the tactile sensation of a man's rugged body writhing beneath her. The bleeding. The screaming. And ultimately, the begging. But until then…

The lid to the container came off. The most potent soil amendment in the world spilled a crimson cascade into the grave. Catalina Montego growled with deep throated glee, "I have loved each of you to pieces my dear, brave boys. A piece over there. Another there, and, oh yes! One. Right. Here."

Chapter One

Like so many times before, Alex stood at his office window with one foot on the low sill. Dressed in his uniform of the day, a charcoal-gray business suit, a red power tie that never failed to constrict his throat or his temper, he glared down at the pleasant streets of Alexandria, Virginia. This solitary watch had long ago become his thinking place, his chapel. It was here more prayers than anyone could ever know were flung heavenward in his struggle to understand and accommodate the Almighty Man Upstairs, and the problems He bestowed on the few, the brave, and the proud.

There was a time Alex cursed God, and rightfully so. He could've saved Sara and their darling daughter, their only child for Christ's sake. Could've had Alex's six like a true friend back then. Yet He hadn't been there when Alex needed Him most. No. Years ago, He'd let the two people Alex loved more than life itself, die in a senseless traffic accident. A son-of-a-bitchin' car wreck. A world away in service to his country, Alex lost everything that had truly mattered. His soul. His breath. And all because God turned a blind eye on him.

Or so Alex had thought.

But in a bizarre twist of fate, along came a battered and betrayed woman. Kelsey's loss then had been tenfold Alex's. Yes, his had been thoroughly tragic, but the accident that claimed his family was a freak happenstance of nature. His wife and daughter were in the wrong place at the wrong time. It sucked, and it hurt, but accidents happened.

Kelsey's loss was so much worse, if one loss could truly be measured against another. She'd lost her two young sons to the man who should've fought the hardest to protect them—her first husband and their father—their murderer. She should've hated the world as much as Alex did then. She could've railed against God every day since. Her sons were just babies when they'd been brutally killed. If anyone should've hated God, it was Kelsey.

But she hadn't. Not even once. Made of better stuff than most people, she'd found ways to forgive the bastard who'd stolen her children instead of damning him to outer darkness. Not right away, but eventually, she'd understood how his twisted childhood and his psychotic mother had driven him to murder. How day after day, Edith had manipulated and convinced her only child, Nick, to end her grandchildren. Then to murder Kelsey.

But the jealous bitch was dead now, thanks to that tiny mother bear who kept Alex's bed warm at night. At first blush, Alex had once thought Kelsey weaker than him. After all, who in their right mind forgave her children's murderer? But when Kelsey also forgave him, Alex Stewart, for what he'd done to her? For being a damned, obnoxious know-it-all and a prideful ass? For telling her to get out of his life when she was the only thing holding him together? Yeah. Damned humbling.

Instead of railing against the Man Upstairs, Kelsey was one of those rare individuals who embraced the freedom wrought by forgiveness, a trait Alex was still learning. It sure as Hell didn't come easy. Yet with that one simple act of forgiveness, she'd taught him to remember the gentle man he'd once been. The father. The loving husband. The gentle warrior.

Like an innocent lamb leading one pissed-off, cantankerous wolf by the scruff of his stubborn neck, Kelsey's patience with the world, combined with her love for him had eventually brought Alex back from the brink of self-pity and destruction. Eventually, he forgave God, then forgave himself. But he'd never take credit for the better man he was today. He'd never been that kind of strong. No. That would be the petite brunette who ruled his world and his night times. She was the strong one. He was the pretender.

Kelsey might've needed him those first few days they'd met. Barely alive, she hadn't the skills to defend herself. But Alex knew the truth. Yes, he'd saved her life when he'd found her nearly dead at his remote cabin in far-off Washington state, but she'd saved his soul. In the process, God had become more than a bitter curse word. Better yet, He'd become a friend, and Alex was going to need Him in the next days and weeks. Possibly months.

His agents' recent unauthorized excursion into Cuba hadn't gone unnoticed, not by the State Department or the SECDEF, Secretary of Defense Arthur Turner. Not that Alex had anything to fear from Art. He'd worked closely with the SECDEF on many clandestine operations, but this one was different. Eric Reynolds, Cassidy Dancer, and Seth McCray, three of Alex's best, had returned with concrete evidence that Roland Montego, a known and extremely sadistic human trafficker, was dead.

Cassidy had nearly died on that operation. Captured during an ambush, she'd been taken prisoner by Montego. But before he'd beaten her nearly to death, she'd managed to activate the miniscule camera hidden within the golden threads of The TEAM logo on her shirt. Smart woman. Through the miracle of technology, she'd taken enough evidence in that basement prison on Isla de la Juventud to nail Montego's ass to the wall. Not that he'd lived long enough to be prosecuted. No. Agent Seth McCray had ended the bastard right there in his own prison.

Alex shifted his weight, watching the orderly weave of traffic on the street below. Little had Cassidy realized that she'd also filmed a woman from Alex's past, Roland's sister, Catalina. Prior to the day of Roland's death, she'd visited her brother's lair often, and participated in the atrocities committed against the women and children held prisoner there. Alex rolled his neck at that disquieting fact, never more certain that Catalina had left bodies wherever she'd traveled. Including Virginia.

Years earlier, prior to his first deployment, he'd been out with a handful of his USMC buddies one evening, throwing back a few beers before they left home and family for a six-month tour. Aaron Pope, Vic Irvinson, and Rodney Barr, all good guys a man trusted.

They'd just ordered their last round, when a buxom blonde, whom no red-blooded American male could miss, slithered into the Norfolk bar. Six-inch stiletto heels enhanced her long tanned legs as much as the seductive tangles spilling over her shoulders enhanced the depth of her cleavage and the swell of her plump breasts. Wearing painted-on black jeans and a slinky, green sequined tank top, the woman Alex now knew was Cat Montego, had stalked past the lookers sitting at the bar as she aimed for the table in the farthest corner. His table. His men. His friends.

"Hey, hey, hey, don't look now, boys, but trouble's coming our way," Rodney had murmured. He'd just pinned on Lance Corporal. Thought he was a big man. Also thought he'd get lucky.

"God have mercy," Vic hissed as he'd leaned back into his wooden chair, his stubby fingers drumming the tabletop in time to the samba beat of her full hips. "Come to daddy, baby girl. Ah-huh, I got what you want. Keep walking this way and you can have it."

That night married men hadn't shown up on Cat's radar, so she'd walked past Alex. Good enough. He wasn't looking for trouble. He had a woman he loved waiting for him. But Aaron had said nothing. He'd just sighed, and that was the clue Alex missed.

He remembered thinking then that Cat had more nerve than brains the way she'd come onto Aaron like they were already best friends. Running her fingers through his short, blond hair. Rubbing her hip against his thigh. Whispering in his ear. Kissing him full on the mouth. What kind of woman did that to a stranger? A predator. That's who.

Back then, Rod and Vic snickered at the overt attention they'd missed, but Aaron was already lost. Balls deep in lust for the sexy body pressed up against him, his hands moved to places they shouldn't have. Like a horndog, he'd shared his drink with the sultry vixen. They laughed. They whispered. They kissed.

The last time Alex saw Aaron, he'd called, "Later, guys!" over his shoulder as he'd led Cat outside. Supposedly to his car, an economical POS that looked like an orange toaster.

"Don't stay up all night," Vic teased, while half the men in the bar grunted like the apes they were. "We're leaving at oh-five-hundred! You can't miss it!"

"Yeah, big guy," some jerk shouted in a sweet falsetto, while the guy next to him feigned a swoon and squealed, "Oh, you handsome piece of meat. Kiss me now!"

Raucous laughter erupted. But as Aaron disappeared into the night, a premonition skated over Alex's shoulders, urging him to call his buddy back. To do something—anything—to make Aaron stay. It was wrong, him leaving like he did. He didn't know Cat, and he surely shouldn't have trusted her, not so fast. Yet that was the way of unmarried guys in the service. They took chances on and off duty. Besides, Cat was a tiny thing, barely five feet tall. Surely a six-foot -our basketball rookie who'd forsaken the NBA to serve Uncle Sam, could handle one quick night with her.

Not a day went by that Alex didn't wish he'd stopped Aaron from leaving. Because Aaron didn't make it back to the barracks, he didn't report for revelry the next morning, and he didn't deploy with his buddies. Quite simply, he was never seen again. His car was still parked outside the bar when Alex, Vic, and Rodney bailed. To this day, the local authorities hadn't found a trace of hard evidence that Aaron had met with foul play. Not a fingerprint. Not one solid lead. He'd vanished. His mother and father, his brother and two sisters still waited for him. Still grieved. Still hoped against hope.

Alex glanced over his shoulder to the phone on the corner of his desk. Beyond that sat the latest portrait of Kelsey and his daughter, Lexie Rose, two brown-haired beauties he'd die for. Always bright-eyed and smiling, Kelsey's love for him reached out from the simple wooden frame and enfolded him. Warmed him. Reminded him. Told him to do what he believed he needed to do. Promised she'd stand by him no matter what came their way.

"I love you," he told her truly, "but I know she killed him, sweetheart. Aaron Pope is dead because of Catalina Montego. I can't let her get away with it. Not now that I know where she is."

'And I'm sure she remembers me,' a disquieting thought Alex wouldn't share with his adoring wife. She didn't need to know all the burdens he carried. Kelsey's primary job in this crazy world was to take care of Lexie. His was to make certain his women stayed safe.

Walking back to his desk, he pushed his chair aside as he hit the intercom button on his phone. His newest recruit, Benjamin 'Beau' Jennings, a former Army Ranger and a crack shot, was about to get his feet wet in the risky world of covert ops.

Mother intercepted the call before it rang twice. "Sorry, Boss, but Beau hasn't come in yet."

"Why not?"

"Not sure. Still waiting for his call. You do know I'm still tracking your Cuban friend, Catalina Montego, as you requested, don't you?"

Alex's gut clenched tight with a burst of acid. "And...?"

"And you were right. She arrived last night at Dulles. From there, she grabbed a taxi and checked into the Marriott in Crystal City." The Marriott was a five-star hotel with underground access to the District's Metro, and too damned close to TEAM headquarters for comfort.

But that saved Alex the trouble of sending Beau to Cuba after her. "And...?"

"She's not in her room," Mother replied softly, an odd tremor in her tone. "I asked Justice to personally check for me. He just called back. There's no sign she slept there, no suitcase or anything, but she left a message for you. The police are there now."

Justice was her live-in companion and soul mate.

"For me? What message?"

"She left a man's bloody finger wrapped in a plastic bag on the bed and a written note that said: *'I know where you live and work, Alex Stewart. Give me what I want, and you can have the rest of him.'*"

"Him who?" Alex asked though he feared he already knew. But how could she still have Aaron after all these years? What had she done to him?

"Not sure. The police are running the print now."

"Was she alone when she arrived?"

"Yes, I recorded the footage from Dulles' surveillance cams if you want—"

Son-of-a-bitch! Could she somehow be behind Beau's absence? "Send two agents to Beau's place. Do it now."

"I already sent Mark and Harley. Beau's not there and his motorcycle's gone. Hold on, I'm getting another call. Sasha Kennedy, The TEAM. Yes. Say again?"

Alex's gut twisted as he waited on Mother. That couldn't be Aaron's finger, and it had better not be Beau's. How could Montego have known who he was or who he worked for?

"Understood, and thank you for the courtesy call, Detective Oberg. He'll be right there," Mother replied evenly.

"Yes?" Alex asked to hurry her along.

"Boss." With that one word, her tone changed from professional to panic. "Get over there right now. God, it's... it's Beau's finger."

Chapter Two

Sweating profusely, Beau strained against the stout wooden table at his back. He needed to be on his feet and gone, but the bloody stump on his left hand where the first two sections of his smallest finger used to be, screamed at him to, *'Stop moving, asshole!'*

Like hell. Whoever'd committed this atrocity would be back, and he meant to be gone. If only his head would clear. If only he could remember. A drink. He'd just settled his ass at the bar for one damned drink, when... *Think, Beau! Think!*

The cold chill of dizzying panic settled in, choking him. A man on his back was a dead man, but a man in cuffs on his back was a damned fool. *How the hell'd I get here? Where is here?*

Ducking his head to shake the fright climbing up his spine, he took quick stock of the place he'd woken up in. Just your every day, ordinary rich folk's dining room. Blinds covered the floor-to-ceiling bay windows at his left, leaving barely a hint of sunshine at the edges. A black granite countertop stood tall at his right. Bright, blinding chandelier lights glared down from overhead, the chandelier itself was wrought iron. Glittery, spackled ceiling beyond that. Brick and plaster walls. No big deal except for the massive worktable he was restrained on, cuffs binding his wrists and feet to the corners, and the industrial-sized meat grinder on that countertop. Wait. Were those drops of blood on the blades?

"Jesus!" he hissed at the ceiling. "A little help here?"

Whoever did this had tied off what was left of his finger with a single piece of string. Looked like baling twine. That was the only thing keeping him from bleeding to death, which, as kind as it seemed, was anything but. All staying alive meant was that more torture was headed his way. *Shit!*

Taking a deep breath, he willed his body to relax even as his heart hammered in his ears. A frightened man was a frantic man, and Beau didn't intend to be that guy. Sucking in another slow inhalation, he forced his panic off. These cuffs were nothing to a kid who'd spent plenty of time cuffed in the rear seat of too many police cruisers off the wild Las Vegas Strip.

"You can do this," he told himself as the first reality settled into his gut like a rock. Back then, he'd been a skinny teenager out for big thrills in a city that never slept. He'd been tough and reckless, but a kid nonetheless. A skinny, malnourished kid. Now he was—bigger. Wider. Thicker. Hope to Jesus, smarter.

But damn, his body had filled out. Packing hundred-pound gear bags, ammo, weaponry, and sometimes other men, tended to do that to a guy. Still... it was all in the way most cuffs were designed to work. Too bad they weren't the zip-ties some cops liked to use. He'd already be gone.

Voices. His pulse skyrocketed. *Shit, someone's coming! Get it done, Jennings. Move it. Move it. Move it!*

Once again, he stilled his breathing and let his better senses re-engage. That was what it took. *Relax. Breathe evenly. Think smart. Twist your wrist. Angle it just right and...*

Nothing happened.

Swallowing hard and blinking the sweat out of his eyes, he started over. Just one wrist freed was all he needed, but unfortunately, it had to be the one spurting blood every time he flexed. Talk about pain. But he could count on his bleeding to also make that cuff slippery. He tugged, twisted, pulled, and… *Jesus H. Christ, this hurts!* Until slowly. Gradually. So damned excruciatingly slowly that he wanted to cry, his left wrist slipped free of the bloody metal bracelet.

There was no time to rest. Reaching across his body to his right wrist, it took less than a few, extremely painful minutes to manipulate the locking mechanism. Yeah, a kid on the streets learned more tricks of the trade in the dead of night than most petty thieves, and these locks were right up Beau's alley. Put him inside a locked police cruiser, and even with one missing digit, he'd be back on the street in seconds. *Time me.*

With his heart jackhammering up his throat and sweat stinging his eyes, Beau was two cuffs down, two to go. Not good. Not good at all!

Ignoring the knots twisting his already twitchy back and neck muscles, Beau straightened, then cocked his head. He'd detected two distinct female voices outside. *What the hell? Was that Kelsey? Alex's sweet wife? Say it's not so. Couldn't be. What's she doing here?* A smaller, higher pitched voice murmured. *Is that Lexie Rose? Jesus, no!*

Panicked beyond belief, he nearly bellowed at them to run, but thought better of it and closed his big mouth instead. There was no sense alerting his killer that he'd come to.

Gotta move. Gotta run. Gotta get them the Hell away from here!

Shaken more than ever now, he jerked at the cuffs on his ankles. The good news, he was still wearing the jeans and TEAM polo he'd worn last night. Waking up nude and bleeding would've been so much worse. The bad news? The imminent danger to Kelsey and Alex's only child rattled Beau so much that he couldn't concentrate. His fingertips slipped over the cuffs, rattling the chains against the wooden tabletop. He couldn't get a grip. Like a fool, he hunched over his knees and jerked at the chains. Nothing budged.

Not smart, wise guy. Settle down. Keep your head. You've done this before. You can do it again. It took seconds to remember that cooler heads prevailed, that clear thinking was the best tool in a guy's arsenal. Not guns. Just brains.

So use 'em!

He settled down. Manipulating the connection where the locking mechanism joined the cuff on his right ankle... exerting the right amount of pressure... at just the right angle... he bit his lower lip and concentrated like a son-of-a-bitch. Then chewed the inside of his cheek, still focused as Hell. Then hissed a vehement curse against the people who designed these damned cuffs! What motherfucker had improved them?

Son-of-a-bitch, this won't give. But just when he thought he was screwed... *Pop!* The cuff on his left ankle sprang open, and freedom was just a pounding heartbeat away.

"Run, Kelsey," he muttered, truly frightened and fumbling the last restraint between his slick fingers. "Grab that baby girl of yours and run as fast as you can. Get away from here. This place is a deathtrap."

By then, the last cuff was slick with blood. His fingers slipped instead of gripped, and time was running out.

Whoever'd done this to him was one twisted son-of-a-bitch, and they'd be back. He had to be gone by then. Had to!

Fighting his rising panic, he tackled the final cuff with all he had. He was so close! He only needed another minute. He could escape this cuff, too. He could!

Until the door burst open and morning sunlight spilled into the room, blinding him. Scaring him. "Where do you think you're going, Benjamin Beau Jennings?" the Hispanic bimbo standing in the doorway shrieked.

"To hell!" he roared back at her, his heart pumping like artillery in his chest. "With you!"

Jesus Christ, get me outta here!

Chapter Three

While waiting in Detective Oberg's cramped, city-budget-sized office, Alex's phone vibrated from deep inside his suit jacket. Damn, what now? Kelsey? That was odd. She rarely called during office hours. She knew how busy he was.

"Hello, sweetheart. What can I do for you?" he asked, his eyes skating over the forensic report Detective Oberg had just handed him. The print was a positive match. That single digit was definitely Beau's baby finger, left hand. Severed and crushed above the second joint. Wherever he was, Beau was in danger of bleeding to death if Alex didn't get to him soon.

"I know you're busy, but I just had the oddest talk with our new neighbor."

"Ah-huh," he replied, pissed that Cat Montego had targeted his TEAM. *My team! How does she know Beau? Barely moved from the Army base at Fort Hood, he's only worked a few months for me. Has she been stalking us? Me?*

"Anyway, our new neighbor was up really early planting roses. I saw the light in Congressman Ringer's yard when I was up with Lexie in the loft, rocking and reading to her…"

Kelsey called the third story alcove he'd built just for her a loft. Alex called it a sniper hide. *Tomatoes. Tah-matoes.*

"As you can see, this is definitely your man," Detective Oberg pointed out. Dressed in a rumpled black suit, his tie missing, Oberg's strained voice betrayed his worry that

Alexandria might have a serial murderer on the loose. "If he was alive when he lost that finger, he's in damned bad shape now. Could be dead."

"Could be." Alex nodded even as Kelsey asked, "Are you too busy to talk now, honey? I can call back later, but I think I'll call Howie now just in case."

Howie Prince, Chief of the sheriff's department that patrolled Alex's gated community.

"Hold on," Alex bit out at Oberg. "This is my wife and…" He offered his index finger to get the detective to hush. "What'd you say? We have a new neighbor? Since when? Why do you need to call Howie?"

Oberg rolled his eyes, not that Alex cared. Kelsey always came first, even now with one man missing. She just needed to make it quick.

"Yes, Athena. Her name's Athena. I'm sorry I didn't get her last name, but I believe she's from South America. She's… I don't want to jump to the wrong conclusion about someone I just met, but she's, for lack of a better word, off-putting. Does that make sense? I can't put my finger on it, but there's something not right about her."

Alex caught the odd tremor in his wife's tone, but Kelsey saying that she couldn't put her *'finger on it,'* while he was staring at the first two joints of Beau's disembodied baby finger, lent a peculiar vibe to the conversation. "Hold on a sec," he said as he activated the security app on his cell that provided a twenty-four-seven birds-eye view of his home via his CCTV security system. Sliding his fingertip from pane to pane, everything looked normal. Residential traffic was light at the moment. The morning sun obstructed one view, but the others relayed nothing out of the ordinary.

Switching back to his wife, he asked, "Are you sure it was Ringer's?"

Alex had recently moved his small family west from quaint Alexandria, Virginia, to a gated-community just east of the Shenandoah Valley. Kelsey deserved the lavish stone and mortar home he'd built for her. Actually, she deserved more, but she'd stopped his grandiose plans and settled for the three thousand square-foot home they currently lived in, instead of the rustic mansion he'd planned. Which was part of her charm. Kelsey knew how to get along with less. Like him, except when it came to her. If he lived to be a hundred, Alex knew he'd never deserve her.

"Yes, Ringer's, two doors down from us. You know the one with the xeriscape in their front yard that everyone hates? The one with that poor, dead saguaro cactus in the yard?"

Ah, yes. That eyesore. "Hold on again," Alex said as he fingered the app to locate the camera lens pointing westward. Again, no problems were visible at the five-acre estate of Congressman Bruce Ringer, the latest congressional casualty whose constituents hadn't liked his politics enough to reelect him. Damned shame that. Ringer was one of the few men on the Hill that Alex respected, which had probably jinxed him. But Virginia was no place to dabble in arid landscapes. Too much humidity killed the effect. Might've killed Ringer's chance for reelection, too.

"Listen, Stewart, if you've got better things to do…" Oberg grumbled sarcastically.

Alex glared at him while Kelsey went on. "She said Lexie would attract the cutest little worms. Isn't that creepy?"

The hairs lifted up the back of Alex's neck. "When did Ringers move?"

"That's the thing, Alex. I don't think they did. The last time I talked with Eloise, she said they were taking a break from the stress of working in the District. They planned a cruise to Australia and New Zealand. That was all."

"Make sure the alarms are on and engaged, that all are working properly," Alex told his wife, trying not to scare her. But with Beau missing and Montego's baby sister on the loose... It couldn't be her in Ringer's house, could it?

"The system's always on when you're gone. You know that."

Oberg cleared his throat, no doubt bored with this mundane, domestic conversation, but who the hell cared? Not Alex. His gut wasn't roiling with acid for nothing, and something in his neighborhood off-putting enough to catch his very intelligent wife's suspicions deserved his attention.

"And another thing," Kelsey said, her voice hesitant. Lower. As if afraid he'd think she sounded foolish. "I got the oddest sensation when she shook my hand. It's like she didn't want to let me go, and the way she looked at me—"

CRASH!

"Oh, my God! Alex!"

"Kelsey? Kelsey!"

The phone went dead.

Chapter Four

"Shhhhh," Beau hissed, his index finger to his lips to keep Kelsey Stewart from screaming. She'd dropped her phone when he'd barged through her side door into her mudroom. The poor thing looked like a trapped doe, her brown eyes wide and bright with terror, her feet positioned to run, and her mouth opened wide in shock and fear.

"Sorry, ma'am. It's just me, Beau Jennings. You remember me, don't you?" He pressed his back to her doorframe, so damned weak from blood loss and the adrenaline kicking his ass that he wanted to drop where he stood. "Sorry I scared you, but I'm... I'm..." *About to fall down.*

She was on him in an instant, her fingertips so damned gentle on his elbow, tugging him toward her kitchen table. "Of course I remember you, Beau. Come sit. You're hurt. What happened?"

"No," he ground out as he resisted her gentle change of direction and slanted the blinds at the kitchen window to see precisely where Lexie was. His missing finger could wait. He'd been followed, or soon would be. He was sure. That bitch was still out there. "Can't rest. Not yet. Where are the dogs? Where's Lexie?" *Jesus, please let them be inside. Let her be safe.*

"She's outside playing with them, Beau. You're scaring me. What's going on?"

"Where is she, on the swing set?" he asked, moving to another window and glad he hadn't frightened Lexie like he'd scared her mother. Kids deserved to grow up safe and happy, certainly not scared of him.

Alex owned two of the fiercest canines on the East Coast, but Beau wouldn't take chances. He'd jumped two fences and run barefoot through the next yard to get to Stewart's. No wonder he hadn't seen the dogs. They were out back.

Kelsey nodded. Her gaze drifting to the bloody stump and the red stream dripping down his pant leg. "You're why Whisper and Smoke barked a couple minutes ago. Wait here. I'll go get her and—"

"No!" snapped out of him. *Jesus, no, don't go out there.* "Gun. I lost mine." Said no Ranger worth his salt—ever! "You got an extra pistol around here that I can—?"

"Here. Use mine." Reaching behind her back, Kelsey withdrew a tiny black pistol from her waistband.

Thank fuck! Greedily, Beau accepted the firearm, trying not to get any of his blood on her clean fingers. Trembling like a sissy, he checked the chamber. Nine mil, good enough. Not his first choice, and not what he'd been carrying last night before everything went south, but sufficient. A nine mil had decent knock down power. It'd send the witch who'd cut his finger off, back to Hell where she belonged.

"Hate to tell you this but your neighbor's psycho," he muttered as he scanned the yard and located Lexie. Thank you, Jesus, the little tyke was out there on the concrete patio. Laughing. She had her butt planted on a pink three-wheeler with a smiling blue *Smurf* face between bright yellow plastic handlebars.

That sight alone made Beau's knees even weaker. Kelsey and Lexie were safe. Beyond her, one of Alex's former EOD dogs, a massive black German Shepherd, stood with his head cocked, watching her, but with his nose high, scenting the air. Yeah, Whisper was no dummy. He knew something foul had gone down in his neighborhood.

With one floppy ear, he gave the impression of being a big, happy pup. The gentle way he played with Lexie reinforced that lie. Not so. There was nothing sweet, silent, or forgiving when Whisper flipped into attack mode. Jesus bless the idiot who so much as looked sideways at that little girl without Whisper's blessing. They'd lose more than a digit.

Smoke, the silver Malinois and Whisper's kennelmate, trotted the six-foot high fence, his tail waving like a flag and his nose in the air as well. Damned straight. Both dogs knew he'd breached their perimeter. Nine to one, they would've ripped him to shreds if he'd landed inside that fenced yard with them, bleeding like he was.

Beau's heart slowed its frantic beat, but he'd heard that insane woman's shriek when he bolted out her side door, hell bent on escape. The lunatic had put her faith in a wooden hollow-core door. Not smart. Bitch should've invested in steel. That's what kept folks safe. Steel. Not wood. Definitely not store-bought locks.

But vaulting the two fences between her house of terror and Kelsey's, had taken more energy than Beau had to give. He sagged against Kelsey's wall, fading fast. Jesus H. Christ, the floors and walls were breathing as hard as he was. "I need Lexie in here now," he wheezed, worried he might not survive confronting the two meaner than shit K9s, but… *Here goes.* "Hold the door while I run out and grab her and—"

"No, Beau. Stay. Watch." Opening the slider that led to the patio, Kelsey called, "Whisper. Bring Lexie. House. Now."

Well, I'll be damned. The command had no more than rolled off her tongue than Whisper clamped onto Lexie's forearm and tugged her gently up from the trike. She squealed and slapped at his furry muzzle. Of all things, Smoke followed on Whisper's six like an Army Ranger, nudging his butt as if signaling him to move. It was obvious these dogs and Lexie had played this game before.

"I truly love your old man for teaching these boys to guard your little girl," Beau breathed. He hadn't dared put Kelsey in danger by ordering her to retrieve Lexie, and the dogs would've attacked him, but this? Bless Alex for being an overprotective, controlling ass.

"I love him, too," Kelsey replied as the dogs marched her babbling daughter through the backyard door and into the mudroom. Beau secured the door behind them.

Rather than startling Lexie by grabbing hold of her the instant she stepped inside like other women might've done, Kelsey directed Whisper and Smoke in the calmest voice. "Dollhouse, Whisper. Play with Lexie. You too, Smoke. Good boys."

"Hi, Mama. Bye, Mama," Lexie chortled as Whisper walked her into the living room with his tail wagging and Smoke still on his rear. The charming trio disappeared around the corner and beyond a burnished leather recliner, most likely Alex's.

"Is this house secure?" Beau asked, needing to be sure before he secured his weapon and fell on his face.

"Do you mean from Athena, the lady two doors west of here? Is that where you've been? In her house?"

"That's her name?" He cast a sideways glance at Kelsey as he reopened the exterior mudroom door and faced the direction he'd run from. "That's who did this to me. Now tell me, do you know for sure she can't hear us?" *Because she's sure as hell scared the shit out of me when she called me by my name.*

Kelsey nodded. "Alex installed counter-surveillance measures on this entire property. Audio jammers. Bug detectors. Bulletproof windows. She did that to you? She cut your finger off?"

He nodded, grimacing as reality struck. Kelsey's smaller weapon was a warm friendly in his palm, and until now, his pain came second to ensuring her safety. But shit Marie, the son-of-a-bitch throbbed like a mother. And the walls in Kelsey's tidy home really were breathing, weren't they? Beau slid to his butt to make the world hold still.

Kelsey knelt with him. "This home is more secure than you know, Beau. Now tell me what's going on while I get you up off the floor and onto a kitchen chair. You need a doctor, hon."

His head lolled to one shoulder. Damn thing was as heavy as concrete, but...*hon? Did she just call me hon?*

It'd been a long time since anyone had taken that tone or used that word on him. He was more like Alex, a wolf on the prowl. A cur. A man with so many ghosts on his six, it was a miracle he was able to get out of bed each morning. Only the wolf inside Alex had stopped gnawing his leg. He was calmer than Beau, as if he'd settled down. Had to be because of this tiny woman, the one with fire in her eyes, who looked like she expected Beau to hop off the floor and run to the chair at her kitchen table, just because she'd said so.

Beau wanted to do what Kelsey requested. Really, he did. Kindness was a rare thing in his life, but it took all he had left just to lift his sorry ass off the floor without moaning like a girl. If not for Kelsey's hand at his elbow, he would've preferred staying where he'd landed. Fewer things were moving that way.

But she said sit, so he dropped onto the first chair in his path.

"Lean back," she said, her gentle hand on his shoulder, pushing him into the comfortable leather seat. Man, Alex knew how to shop. The chair was softer than Beau's mattress at his bachelor pad. But somewhere between Kelsey tying a better tourniquet around the remaining joint on his throbbing little finger, the phone ringing off the wall, and the noisy buzz in his head, Beau pitched forward and…

He fell.

Chapter Five

"Yes, it's Beau," Kelsey whispered. It'd been a long time since she'd sounded this timid.

"But you're not hurt? Are you sure?" Alex demanded to know now that she'd finally answered the damned phone. "Lexie's okay?" Living near the Shenandoahs was great when he wanted distance between the demands of the District and his family. But it made for a worrisome helicopter ride when he couldn't get home quickly when he needed to.

"No, honey, we're both fine, but Beau's in rough shape. I thought I could help stop the bleeding, but all I'm doing is hurting him. I managed to get what's left of his finger bandaged, but he passed out. Right now, he's on his back on our kitchen floor. I spread some towels under his head, but he needs a doctor. I could call McKenna. She's just minutes away, but now that I know I've got a psycho in the neighborhood, I can't risk anyone else getting hurt. What do you think?"

"Where's Lexie?" Alex couldn't take chances. Not with his family. Never again.

"Relax, she's playing with the dogs. I can hear her giggling and bossing them in the dollhouse from here. They're probably dressed in drag by now."

Thank God. Not for the drag outfits, which were most likely just Lexie's doll's clothes, but that the women Alex held dear, were safe and accounted for.

The dollhouse, their euphemism for the steel-walled, vault-like safe room, had been decorated like a little girl's bedroom/playroom. When he'd planned it, Alex hoped he'd never have to use it. Complete with frilly curtains on windows that were really closed-circuit television screens, a locked weapon's safe that looked like a storybook tower, plenty of treats, and a chest full of plush stuffed animals, it would protect Kelsey, Lexie, and the dogs if needed. Better yet, to Lexie it was just another fun place to nap, play, or watch one of her kiddie DVDs. The safe room was all about keeping her innocent and alive as long as he could.

Alex took his first deep breath since Kelsey dropped the phone and hung up on him. "Don't take chances," he warned her.

"Understood, Boss. Now about McKenna. How can I get her or the paramedics inside without them getting hurt?"

"I'm not your boss. You'd never listen to me even if I were."

"Then how'd I learn to shoot and stand up for myself?" Kelsey's confidence came through loud and clear. "Who taught me that? I was listening then, wasn't I?"

There was that. Still seated in Detective Oberg's office, Alex refused to spar over the phone with his wife. Because she was right. Of course Lexie and Beau were safe. Alex was the hardhead, not her. "Listen, Maverick got in from Indonesia last night. He's at home with China today. I'll call him to collect McKenna. You stay put until they get there."

Another agent, Maverick Carson owned a horse ranch within miles of Alex and Kelsey's home.

"Copy that," she replied, mimicking his agents' responses. Still teasing him, damn it. "I'll just call McKenna then and tell her what's going on, so—"

"No!" This woman didn't know the meaning of the word obey. "This is serious!"

"Now, you listen to me, Alex. I'm not the pitiful little waif you found on your porch all those years ago. I'm not defenseless, and I'm not frightened of the world like I used to be. I may not work *for you*, but I've worked *with you* long enough to know how to protect my home and our daughter. You know I can do that too, admit it. Now call Maverick, while I let McKenna know what's going on. Once they arrive, I'll let them in through the garage, but only after the dogs check for the Boogeyman, understood?"

Alex would've retorted *'Copy that,'* if he hadn't been so damned far away and felt so helpless. He hadn't been there when Sara and Abby died, nor the times Kelsey was attacked. True, he hadn't met her until after her ex tried to kill her, but...

Son-of-a-bitch, this can't be happening again.

"Alex?" she asked quietly. "I'm sorry. I know you're upset, and I don't mean to tease, because nothing about this is funny. You know I love you more than life itself, but I'm being extra-cautious like you taught me. The house is locked down, and Howie's sending a patrol car over. If I know him, he's probably behind the wheel and rushing to my rescue just like you wish you were. Please don't be mad. I won't let anything happen to Lexie. Trust me, honey."

"I'm not mad, I'm just..." *Scared.*

The local sheriff, Howie Prince, was a good friend. The man was as honorable as they came, and Alex trusted him implicitly even as shame crept up the back of his stiff neck. He'd never meant to insinuate that Kelsey would ever let anything happen to Lexie. None of this was her fault.

Like Alex, she hadn't been with her two sons when they'd died, either. Not a day went by she didn't feel totally responsible for what they'd suffered. The curse of survivor's guilt sucked the joy out of the rest of your life. Every. Single. Minute.

Okay, then. "I love you, woman," he told her despite Detective Oberg's annoyed fingertips tapping his desk again. Still. Whatever!

"And I love you, Alex. Now come home to us. We've got work to do."

"On my way," he said as he disconnected what could very well be his last time speaking with his wife.

Shaken at all he stood to lose—again—Alex told Oberg, "Beau Jennings is at my house, and I have reason to believe Catalina Montego is inside my gated-community. The local authorities are in transit. Officer Howie Prince. He's a good man. I can give you his cell number." *Hell, I can give you the entire sheriff departments' numbers if you want them.*

Oberg scribbled down names, numbers, and addresses even as he kept lifting his head to level more than a dark stare on Alex. "So, you know the perpetrator."

"I believe I do, yes. Catalina Montego. Cuban. Thirty-five-years old. Blonde, least she was the last time I saw her in Norfolk. Brother was Roland Montego."

Oberg kept writing. "The human trafficker killed in Cuba last year? That was you who ended him?"

Alex shook his head. "One of my men, not me."

That seemed to impress the detective. For the first time, respect glimmered in his eyes.

"My wife spotted her two doors down from our place, at Congressman Ringer's home."

"Where's Ringer?"

"Supposedly he and his wife Eloise are on a cruise."

"You think Montego left the note." Oberg had an odd way of not asking questions.

"I'm certain. She's a predator, plain and simple. Her brother ran one of the most depraved human trafficking rings we've ever come across, and she helped him with every despicable thing he did." Alex's heart strayed to the little boy Seth rescued on that nightmare op into Cuba. Christopher had years of therapy ahead of him, but he was one of the lucky ones. He was now home with his parents. They loved him and would ensure he received counseling. But what about all the other missing girls and boys, young women, and young men out there in the world? Who was rescuing them?

Kelsey had better be extra-smart and extra-careful today. "Tell me, how many open cases concerning missing young adult males have you had over the last ten years? Specifically military members?"

A shadow darkened Oberg's smug face. "Dozens."

"Let me guess. All early twenties. None of them seen or heard from again." And all with families, moms and dads, wives and children, left waiting and worrying what had happened to these men.

Oberg nodded. "No suspects. No leads. And no evidence of foul play in any of those disappearances."

"Just missing men," Alex confirmed, his gaze back to the police photos of Beau's bloody finger. "So where are the bodies?"

Chapter Six

Dr. McKenna Fitzgerald, a pediatrician at the local family care clinic, had just finished monthly inoculations on the Bryce triplets. At three months, the terribly cute but bald little girls were thriving despite, or maybe because of, their mother's very weary demeanor. New moms and dads never got enough sleep, but the parents of triplets? McKenna couldn't imagine their harried schedule, and poor Carol Bryce looked beyond frazzled. Since her husband drove truck for a freight forwarding company, she usually came to these well-baby appointments alone and always at her wits end.

Today the woman wore faded jeans and a simple cotton blouse with burp stains on the shoulder. She'd cut her hair short when she'd gotten pregnant, but her dark roots were showing a good two inches. Poor thing.

On the other hand, Pamela, Penelope, and Pippa were immaculate, their matching outfits pressed, and sleeping like the well-fed little charmers they were.

"Penelope has teeth now. Two of them," Carol said as she massaged her left breast. "Can I stop nursing them? At least her. Please? She bites."

"You're breastfeeding?" McKenna had no idea. She scanned the girls' file for that missing detail, but no. There it was in indelible ink, in her handwriting: *Mother declined breastfeeding. Formula.* "I thought Rocks didn't want you to do that." Rocks Bryce, her overbearing but lovable hubby.

Carol scoffed. "He didn't until one of the guys he drives with told him it's the best birth control method known to man. Like he's an expert."

Yeah, about that... McKenna winced. "No wonder you're exhausted. Yes. At least start weaning them to formula. We can't have you depleted, while they thrive, can we?" She noted the triplets' medical chart before she shared the rest of the story. "I hate to tell you this, but women can still get pregnant while lactating. If you and your husband have resumed intercourse, you really need to be on birth control, at least for the first year, maybe longer. Your body needs time to heal, and you're not ready for another pregnancy. Nothing's foolproof, but that old wives' tale will only get you a bigger family every time."

Carol's mouth dropped open. "No…"

"Who's your ob-gyn? I can get you in to see him or her while you're here if they practice at our clinic," McKenna said, her fingers already on her handset.

Tears brimmed this poor woman's eyes, but the anguish on her face? Sad. Really sad. "I can't be pregnant. Not so soon. Not again. McKenna, what'll I do?"

"Simple. You'll run see your doctor right now, while we start these little angels on formula, that's what you'll do. Trust me, sweetie. The sooner you know, the sooner you can get on birth control." *I hope.* "Think positive, Carol. And if you need help at home, I've got the perfect helpers for mothers with new babies. Better yet, they work for free, and a couple of them will do light housework for you."

Carol snagged a tissue from the box on the counter and patted her teary eyes. "W-who?"

"First, let me make that call. Do you have time to see your doctor today?"

"No way. I've had it. Maybe tomorrow morning after the girls' baths."

McKenna rang her front desk. "Margo, could you make a morning appointment with…" she looked to Carol for a name.

"Filbert."

"With Dr. Filbert for Carol Bryce. Thank you."

"So tell me about these helpers."

"Have you heard of Golden Horizons?" McKenna replied as she settled the phone on its cradle.

"The senior center down the road?"

"That's the one. Three times a week, some of those dear people volunteer to help my new parents. They'll come to your home for a couple hours, and they'll rock, feed, or bathe your babies, anything to help. If the babies are asleep, they've been known to watch TV while you take a nap. Here's their number if you're interested."

Carol took the card from McKenna's fingers and stood, casting one eye on her sleeping trio, blissfully unaware of the chaos their births had caused. "Did you come up with this idea?"

"Senior citizens helping new moms and dads? Nah." McKenna shrugged that notion off. "I just made the suggestion one afternoon while I was over there playing Parcheesi with Dad. They're the ones who volunteered. As my dad says, it's better to be seen than viewed."

A knock at the door preceded Margo's bright smiling face. "Here's your appointment card, Mrs. Bryce. Ten am sharp, tomorrow morning. Aw, look how sweet those little angels are."

Carol finally smiled. "Yes, they are my angels. And they might get a sister or a brother before we know it."

"You're pregnant?"

"I hope not." This time, Carol chuckled. A little. She wasn't ecstatic over the prospect of motherhood so soon after delivering triplets, but she seemed in a better frame of mind than when she'd first arrived.

"Dr. Fitz, you've got a call on line one," Margo said. "Kelsey Stewart's waiting for you."

"Are you going to be okay?" McKenna asked Carol before she dismissed this poor mother. People who believed stay-at-home moms didn't work were morons.

"I am now," Carol replied as she gripped one baby carrier while she slung her purse and diaper bag over her shoulder. Margo knew the drill. She lifted the other two sleeping angels in their carriers to give Carol a much-needed assist out to her family van.

McKenna squeezed between the baby carrier and Carol's purse to hug her. "You call me if you need anything, understood? I'm always here for you, day or night."

Carol squeezed back. "Thank you so much. I'll be okay. I promise."

"I know you will," McKenna whispered before she eased out of her patient's arms. She didn't hug others often, but this one needed a rope to hang onto, and McKenna was that rope. At least, she was the knot tied at the frayed end of it. Children, all children, needed a healthy, balanced emotional start in life and usually a happy mother was the one who made it happen. "See you in one month."

As the door closed, McKenna answered her phone. "Hi, Kelsey. What can I do for you today?"

"I have an emergency, McKenna, only it's not Lexie, and I can't explain over the phone. Can you make a house call? Please? Now?"

"Sure. I've just said goodbye to my last patient for the morning. What's happened?"

"I'll tell you when you get here, but I'm sending an escort. Don't leave until Maverick Carson arrives. He'll be there in a minute."

"China's husband?" *How odd?* "Since when do I need an escort to your house? You're like eight, maybe nine miles away. I'm pretty sure I know the way and…." She jingled the keys in her pants pocket. "Hey, look, Mom, I've got my very own car, and I know how to drive."

"Please, don't ask. I need you to be safe. Hurry."

The connection ended just as Margo peeked her head back into the exam room. "Have I got a patient for you," she breathed, fanning herself. The slender brunette had a way of making fifty look like the new thirty. "Puh-leeeeze, I mean pretty puh-leeeeze let me assist while you examine him. Pretend I'm your nurse, okay? I just want to touch this guy, like all over."

This day was becoming just plain weird. Her secretary was acting like a hormonal cougar, and her best friend had gone spooky only seconds ago. Was there a full moon?

"Would his name be Maverick Carson?"

Margo rolled her dark eyes and licked her lips. "That's the one."

"Calm down. It's not like he's here for a well-baby visit. Where is he?" McKenna peered past her flirty office helper, and... *Well hello, baby.*

McKenna hadn't yet met China's busy hubby but talk about one tall, lean, rugged-looking cowboy right out of the wild, wild West. Rider jeans, worn thin at the knees and frayed at the hems, hung over scuffed, dusty work boots. A tight black and gray checkered shirt, complete with metal snaps in lieu of buttons, stretched over a wide chest that looked chiseled and taut and downright delectable. Best yet, he fingered a dusty brown Stetson that cinched the look.

Most guys wouldn't have taken their hats off indoors for fear of hat hair, not that this guy had to worry about that. Short but thick and rich, dark chocolate waves hung over his forehead as he stood there with his back against the wall, watching the waiting room like a soldier on guard duty.

"Isn't he yummy?" Margo whispered. "Don't you want to eat him up?"

McKenna couldn't answer the woman who was old enough to be Maverick's mother, but yes. China's man certainly looked downright lickable. Like an all-day sucker. Just the idea of him *coming* for her, kickstarted McKenna's nearly dormant libido.

He's married. Get your mind out of the gutter.

She pressed a palm to the door, breaking hers and Margo's views, while hoping this tall, handsome fellow hadn't spotted them making fools of themselves like a couple teenage girls.

"Umm..." *What was I going to say? Oh, yeah.* "Grab my medical bag for me. It's in the closet behind my desk. I've got a house call."

"Can I go, too?" Margo nearly squealed. What was it with older women? Did they all turn into horny old ladies after menopause hit?

"Will you stop? Get my bag while I sign out the drugs I need. Go."

Margo cracked the door, still peeking. "If one of them's Viagra, I don't think he'll need it."

"Now," McKenna said sternly as she put her hand on her friend's shoulder. "This house call is an emergency, and I need to run. Meet me at the front desk. Hurry."

Not certain exactly what Kelsey might need, McKenna signed for a painkiller, then grabbed a few generic supplies to restock her bag. Antibiotics. A suture kit. Another blood pressure cuff. By then, Margo was in the waiting room, bouncing McKenna's medical bag off her knee while she grilled Maverick. "You raise horses?"

He nodded, his gaze straying over her shoulder to McKenna. "Yes, ma'am, I do. Dr. Fitzgerald?" he asked as he extended his right hand and straightened his shoulders. "Pleased to meet you. Maverick Carson at your service. I'll be escorting you to Kelsey Stewart's."

She nodded, intent on acting professional. Kelsey's husband was a looker, too, but this guy radiated enough testosterone to bottle, sell, and make a fortune. She'd call it *"Cowboy,"* then sit back and watch the money roll in.

"Mr. Carson," she returned. "Nice to meet you as well. I've treated your daughter, Kyrie in the past. I'm not certain why I need an escort, but let's get on with it."

"Are you sure you don't need—?"

"Anyone to finish transcribing my dictation? Why, thank you, Mrs. Heller. It's so kind of you to ask." McKenna poured the sugar on poor, panting Margo. "I shouldn't be long, but just in case, would you clear my schedule for the rest of the day? Tomorrow's my day off, so apologize to my patients for me. Thanks, hon. See you in an hour or so. Bye, now."

Maverick held the door as she marched out of the clinic, intent on grilling him during the five-minute drive to Kelsey's. "What's so important I can't drive myself?"

"You'll see, ma'am," he replied evenly. "May I take that bag for you?"

"Ma'am? Me? You do know that makes me sound ancient, don't you? And no, you may not take my bag."

"As you wish." Maverick answered as if he were Wesley from *"The Princess Bride."* Very courteously, he opened the passenger door of a sleek, black Infinity and gestured her to slide into it. "But Mom taught us boys that ma'am is the only way to address ladies, whether they're inclined to take it the wrong way or not."

"You're right. I was out of line," she breathed as she tucked her legs in and peered up at him. The way he handled himself and the way that cowboy hat perched low on his forehead… Gah. He was one hot *'well baby'* all right.

While he circled to the driver's side, she breathed evenly to get her pulse to slow down. Just because it had been a while since she'd had one, years in fact, Dr. McKenna Fitzgerald had studied too hard and too long to be reduced to drooling after a nice male ass.

But the minute he settled those long lean, denim-clad legs inside the vehicle…

As soon as he hit the ignition and flung one muscular arm over the seat while backing the car…

The second she caught a whiff of that delicious shaving lotion he'd doused himself with…

Her feminine receptors flared. Too much work and too little play had turned a dedicated doctor into a horny woman with illicit, inappropriate thoughts.

You need to get out more often and shack up with somebody. Anybody. Spread your legs, girl, and fly.

I'm busy.

Too busy to have a life? A quickie?

What is this, pick on McKenna day? He's married!

Then pick someone else. Anyone else. Just pick someone!

"So what's up with Kelsey?" McKenna asked as she corralled her wayward thoughts and fastened her seat belt. That didn't help. When she couldn't locate the belt receptor, she'd ended up facing her melt-in-your-mouth, let-me-lick-your-lips male escort. Where'd Alex Stewart get these guys? From a Chippendale catalog? "W-who's hurt? Lexie or one of her dogs, umm, Kelsey's dogs?"

Think woman! You are not post-menstrual or that hard up for a good time.

Skillfully, Maverick maneuvered the vehicle through early morning traffic, his head dipped low because, face it, even with his Stetson tossed on the rear seat, the man was a tight fit for this car. It had to be China's.

Focus!

McKenna smoothed one hand over her knee on her way to the medical bag at her feet. That was what was important, her medical expertise and the lifesaving items in that bag, not some married guy with an irresistible cowboy vibe and an incredibly hot bod. Nope. Nada. Dating and marriage didn't matter in the grand scheme of all things Doc Fitz related.

Only the children she could save mattered. The mothers she could keep from hurting or killing their children. They were the important ones. Only them.

When Maverick pulled through the guard shack at Kelsey's gated community, he let out an intensely masculine growl. Emergency vehicles blocked the street for the next two blocks west. An ambulance. Fire engines. Police vehicles.

"What's going on?"

He parked alongside the nearest curb, then turned to her without answering. "This is what'll happen next, Dr. Fitz. I'll come around and open your door. Once you're on your feet, you and I are going directly into Stewart's side garage door. Got that? Stay right with me and do not bolt. Keep your head down. Don't look around and don't talk to anyone."

"But the police—"

"Focus on me. Just me. Anything happens, you run for that door and don't look back."

"What on earth is going on?"

Maverick glared out the windshield. "There's a murderer on the loose. You ready?"

Clutching the handle to her bag, McKenna pulled it close to her chest. "Always."

Chapter Seven

Beau came to in groggy, disjointed stages of flickering lights, sharp staccato gunfire, and a banshee with a wicked blade in her gnarled fist. Peeling his eyelids back, he took a deep breath and—*It's her! The bitch who cut me. She's here! Right now! In my face! The nerve!* He shoved her back, ready to roll and run, his heart thudding a mighty, "Fuck off!"

Strong hands muscled him back to her table, and...

Shit, no. She's got help. Get me out of here!

"Beau, honey. Beau!" All at once, the bitch morphed into pretty Kelsey leaning over him, her brows furrowed and concerned and...

That was just plain weird. But those *were* Kelsey's brown eyes smiling through the fog in his head. That *was* her dark chocolate hair spilling into his face. She was patting his cheek. Kneeling on the same table with him. Ah, no. Make that the floor. *I'm lying on her kitchen floor. What the hell?*

He forced a swallow, blinking to clear the muddled haze in his head.

"Wake up, hon. It's just me. Take it easy and breathe."

Okay. I can do that. I think. For you, I can breathe. Eventually. Once my heart stops climbing up my throat. It'd be nice if she stopped touching him, though. Kelsey's hands were clean and pure. She should know better than to touch someone like him.

Gradually, the room came into better focus. Kelsey was leaning over him, and yes, he was on his back on her floor. The hulking shadow leaning over the top of him, pressing him down to keep him from hitting his wife was—

Oh, shit. Alex. Another woman, a much prettier-than-the-bitch-who'd-cut-off-his-finger knelt alongside Kelsey, but nearer Beau's head. Wearing scrubs and a stethoscope like a nurse or a doctor or—

"Where the fuck am I?" he demanded, searching out the stern, upside-down-glare of his no-nonsense employer. Not wanting this to be happening to him in Kelsey's kitchen. "How, how'd I get... here?"

"Settle down," Alex replied, his tone uncommonly gentle despite those laser-sharp eyes boring holes in Beau's forehead as if he were reading his mind. Beau wouldn't put it past Alex to be able to do that. The guy had a photographic memory or something. Maybe x-ray vision, too. With one scathing glance, he could make grown men wet themselves. "You're hurt and you're at my place, but you're safe now, Beau. I've got you."

"Th-that's my line. Course I'm safe. I'm A-Army, b-but..." He sucked in a long breath to calm his heart rate and get his bearings. His head, which at the moment felt like a bag of marbles with a hole in it, the marbles scattered to who knew where, pounded like a mother. Waking up in Alex's house was—weird. Damned unsettling. And the last place Beau wanted to be.

But with a snap of his wrist, and all the pain that came with it, he remembered. "Son-of-a-bitch!" hissed out of him as he tried, unsuccessfully, to curl that wounded, throbbing limb into his chest. "What the fuck's wrong with my hand? What happened to me?"

The unnamed woman, who now held one damned long hypodermic needle in her fingers, also had a firm grip on said throbbing wrist, and he didn't dare struggle too much. Damn, what a bloody mess his finger was. Made a guy's innards roil looking at what was left of it.

"You have got to hold still, sir. I can't help you if you fight me. Now please. Relax and let me do my job. You want to feel better now, don't you?"

Fuck, yeah. "Who are you?" he asked because he damned well needed to know who thought she was in charge of his fingers this time.

Her head lowered as soft green eyes focused intently on his wounded hand. "I'm Dr. McKenna Fitzgerald." Of course, she also inserted that needle into his bloody stump, when she spoke and—

"Ow, ahh, shit! Damn it, Jesus!" he cussed, fighting the urge to knock both these women on their butts, so he could get the hell out of there and make the pain stop. "You're killing me!"

Kelsey kept patting his stomach like she needed something to do with her hands. "It's okay, Beau. It'll be okay."

'In which fuckin' universe?' he wanted to scream, but he didn't. He couldn't. Not at Kelsey. Sucking in a deep breath, he forced his rank, foul, other self, back into its corner. Just because he was hurting—like a mother!—he couldn't hurl obscenities at one of the sweetest women he'd ever met. But that other gal... She'd better knock it off.

"Another pinch," Dr. Fitzgerald said in that annoying professional tone she no doubt used on other helpless victims. Her hair flipped over her shoulder when her head tilted. It caught his eyes. Pretty hair. Blonde, but streaked with raspberry red highlights. For a second, he lost track. It looked like rays of pink sunshine were caught in those shimmering strands. As if the sun couldn't help kissing her. Like he wanted to kiss her. Beau reached out to run one of his not bloody fingers through it when—she stabbed that son-of-a-bitchin' needle into his finger again!

His back turned into McDonald's golden arches. "Jesus Christ! Will you leave the fucker alone? It's gone already!"

"Settle down, Beau," said the man with All. Ten. Fingers!

"*You* settle down!" Beau hissed at his employer. "You're not the one she's stabbing, are you?"

Alex stopped talking. Damned good thing.

"Another sting. Sorry. I know this hurts."

You think? Beau bit the inside of his cheek, ashamed for acting like no Army Ranger ever and in front of his employer no less.

"But it'll all be over in a few seconds. Can you hang tight for me, big guy?"

Big guy? Now she'd made him feel like a baby. Despite having cursed at her, he snapped, "It's nothing." He wasn't used to being the one on his back. But he remembered more and more. It hadn't been a dream. That digit really *was* missing.

His narrow escape from that wooden table came back to him in an adrenaline-powered hot flash of awareness. Tilting his chin up, he stared at Alex. "I was in Boxster's Pub. Alone. Last night. After work. You know the one, and... Shit. That's all I remember. When I woke up this morning, the bitch, ah…" He glanced at Kelsey. "Sorry, ma'am. Don't mean to cuss so much, but… Holy Christ!" His head came off the floor as Doctor Pain-In-The-Ass stabbed him yet again. "Are you done torturing me yet?"

Withdrawing the needle, she leaned back on her heels with a sadistic, satisfied smile. "I am now. You'll be numb soon. In the meantime…" She set the damned thing aside—*thank you, Jesus!*—and removed the stethoscope from around the slender neck he wanted to wring. Her hair swished again as she pressed the cold flat disc under his shirt to his sweating, heaving chest. He felt like a racehorse gone lame on the track, slathered and about to be put down. "Let's have a listen, shall we?"

"Yes, let's! And while we're at it, how 'bout I stick you?" Instantly, Beau's gaze flickered to Kelsey in shame. Okay, that hadn't come out like he'd meant. Not exactly. But the thought of *sticking* this annoying doctor offered a pleasant distraction.

Alex's grip lessened. "Do you remember anything else?"

"Yeah," Beau muttered, breathing hard through his nose and hating being the center of attention. "No. Maybe." Shit! He couldn't remember Jack!

He focused on his breathing and on his boss's stern glare, not the woman running her fingers over his chest checking him for a heart. Yes, he had one. Least, he used to a long time ago. With the soft pitter-pat of her fingertips on his chest, the urge to run a comb over his head came out of nowhere. This was so not his best day. *I look like shit, and I'm disgusting. Please go away. Leave me alone.*

"She was nothing like you, the bitch who did this, I mean," his big mouth told the doctor for some inane reason. "She wasn't pretty." *At least I don't think she was.* He couldn't sound intelligent to save his life, and trying to recall what went down this morning or last night? Not happening.

"That's nice," the doctor replied, her tongue in her cheek like she knew he was making a fool of himself.

Great. Go ahead and laugh at me. Everyone else has.

Focus! Oh, yeah. Beau turned back to Alex. "She had l-lots of jewelry. Rings, bracelets. Junk like that. I could hear them jingling. Like wind chimes." *I think.*

"Was she blonde?"

"Maybe. Couldn't tell. Only saw her standing in the doorway."

"Then how do you know she wore jewelry if you're not certain what she looked like?"

Beau shrugged. *Maybe because I heard it?* Why'd Alex have to ask such hard questions?

"That's better," the doc purred, her long fingers once again fluttering on his pec like he'd been a good boy just because she'd found his heartbeat.

Beau shot her a covert glance. She was pretty for a physician. Her nose was what they'd call pert. Cute. Turned up at the end. Dots of cinnamon freckles ran across her cheeks. He liked the combination. They reminded him of those sugar sprinkles on cupcakes. Sweet extras not every kid came home to. They were what good mothers put on after school treats they made for their kids. Other mothers. Not his.

Fidget Jennings never baked anything but crap in her life. Even that wasn't baking. You don't bake heroin. You want to get pinned real good, you cook it. In a spoon. Over a Bunsen burner flame, or if you're too broke, a cheap candle'll do the trick. Not the nice smelling candles rich folks bought. Just the dollar store chunks of colored wax. The ninety-nine cent specials with three wicks. Every kid with an addict mom knew to buy those, cuz guess who got sent to the corner store when mom ran out of juice?

"Hispanic?" Alex asked gently.

Beau blinked up at his boss. "Huh?"

"Was the woman who did this to you Hispanic? Did she say anything else? Did she speak with an accent?" Why was Alex talking so slowly and enunciating like Beau was an idiot?

"This morning, fuck yeah." Not that Beau could remember much. He shifted his gaze to Kelsey, hoping she'd forgive his language, then onto the Doc, not sure he cared what she thought. "Sorry, but you're... who?"

"Doc-tor Fitz-ger-ald," she enunciated just as slowly as Alex had, smiling down at Beau like he was a five-year-old. "But you can call me Doc Fitz. Most of my patients do, if they can talk, that is."

What other kind of patients were there? Mutes?

"Was she Hispanic?" Alex asked again, a hint of exasperation in his tone.

Beau nodded. "Think so. Yeah, okay. Hispanic."

"Does that sound like the same woman?" Alex asked Kelsey.

She nodded. "Yes, Athena is Hispanic. I'd put her at five feet tall, maybe one hundred forty or fifty pounds."

Both Kelsey and Alex looked expectantly down at him, making Beau feel like he was in a tennis match. Who to look at first? No contest. Kelsey won. "I didn't get her name, ma'am. It's not like I had time to chat. I was kinda busy getting away."

"No, of course not, but she was very intense, wouldn't you say?" Kelsey asked, her eyes wide and her brows arched encouragingly.

"Most killers are," he murmured, trying to keep his eyes open. Trying hard not to look weak in front of his boss. Doc Fitz, either. For some reason, it was okay that Kelsey was there, helping him. Not that it made sense, but he didn't mind looking weak with her. She was different. Always kind. Forgiving. A guy didn't have to pretend who he was with her. He could be broken, but she had some kind of invisible super glue that had put him back together after their few meet-and-greets. Everyone liked Kelsey.

"Focus," Alex reminded him, tilting Beau's chin up to maintain eye contact. "Tell me what else you remember. What'd she say? Specifically."

"Oh, yeah. Sorry." Beau lifted his wounded arm. At least, he tried. But Doc Fitz now had it strapped to a board that extended under his shoulder blade. He didn't remember when she'd done that. Not like his hand hurt any longer, but his head did. The room was back to spinning like a giant carousel—or else he was. To catch his balance before he flew off, not like he could, but still, Beau slapped his free palm to the floor and spread his fingers. That slowed the spiral he seemed to be riding.

"Beau?" Alex reminded him.

"Umm, yeah...?"

Doc What's-Her-Name's stethoscope had just dropped to her chest. It dangled there, nonchalantly bumping the lush mounds hidden beneath her baby-blue scrubs like he wished he were capable of doing. She canted her head, studying him, her smiling green eyes exact replicas of the hidden pools he'd stumbled on in that desert oasis a few years back. Mysterious. Refreshing. Hiding secrets while saving his worthless life.

Complex thinking got crazy difficult. His entire body hardened as if she'd just put on a striptease act instead of simply checking his stats. Beau licked his lips, not able to make his eyes move off his attending physician and those luscious—scrubs. If she'd lean over just a little bit farther...

All at once, a tray of surgical instruments, tape, scissors, shit like that, appeared beside him. Some kind of surgical drape covered his left arm up to his shoulder. Blinking, Beau took in details he should've noticed earlier, like the bath towels under his injured arm and hand. Like the pillow under his head. The step stool propped under his feet. Okay, that was thoughtful. They were treating him for shock. Good thinking.

"Beau?" Alex asked again, his fingertips squeezing Beau's shoulders. "Are you still with me?"

"Ah-huh. Yeah. Sure..." Beau answered, but he wasn't. He wasn't even in the same room or on the same floor any more. Not unless floating above it and looking down at himself counted.

Across from him, Maverick Carson leaned against the closed mudroom door like an angry ghost. Maybe the Grim Reaper, with his arms crossed over his chest, and his eyes always so, so black. Unpleasantly dark. Glowering. Hovering. The only things missing were the black robe and scythe. But that was Maverick for you. Never overly friendly. Never approachable. Beau had yet to understand what made him tick.

He startled, his damned heart pounding up his throat, ready to jump back into action. "Where's Lexie? Is she safe?" *Jesus, please say yes!*

"Don't worry. She's still playing with the dogs," Kelsey supplied, her fingers gentle on his stomach again.

Oh, yeah. I remember now. "In the playroom, r-r-right?" He nodded, needing Kelsey to agree with him.

"That's right. In the dollhouse, now what did Athena say to you, hon?"

That word again. Spoken with such care and concern, it brought tears to his eyes. "Nothing much," Beau huffed, not sure who was who anymore. "Just a bunch of Spanish bullsh… um, cursing. You know. Stuff."

He looked at Kelsey when he answered, but her eyes weren't hers anymore. The soft browns had morphed into worried greens. How very odd. Kelsey was suddenly Doc Fitz and shouting from the other end of a long, dark, swirling tunnel. "I'm losing him! Beau! Stay with me!"

Sure wish I could…

Chapter Eight

"Start him on a saline drip, monitor his heart, and make it quick! He's dehydrated," McKenna barked at the EMTs transporting a still unconscious Beau through the Stewarts' door and out to the waiting ambulance straddling their front lawn. She would've had them begin transfusions, but EMTs weren't authorized to do that. "I've alerted my people at GWU. Dr. Decker's on standby."

That would be the orthopedic hand surgeon who specialized in reattaching severed hands and fingers at the prestigious George Washington University Hospital in Washington D.C. "Hurry people. This man already coded once. It will *not* happen again."

EMTs hadn't been allowed to enter until Sheriff Howie Prince and his officers cleared the area, and by then, McKenna had Beau Jennings' heart beating again. But he'd scared the bejesus out of her, going into cardiac arrest like he had.

"Understood, ma'am. You wouldn't happen to have the rest of this guy's digit, would you?" one of the EMTs asked as the gurney cleared the doorway. "Or do we need to look for it?"

Alex took over. "It's already on ice at GWU. Maverick, go with Dr. Fitzgerald. I'll be in as soon as I can."

"Copy that," Maverick murmured as he tipped his hat to Kelsey. "Ma'am. You take care and let China know if you need anything, you hear? She's just minutes down the road."

"Call her back," Alex ordered. "Tell her to keep Kyrie inside until we know where Montego is."

Maverick nodded. "Already called everyone, Boss. China's got the place locked down, and Mother's getting the word out to all other agents to keep their wives and children indoors and safe. Don't worry. We'll get Montego."

"Thanks," Alex muttered. Usually, he had the glow of a commander. Calm and rational, there was always a sense of balance to the man. Like the bow wave of a mighty ship, it preceded him before he entered any room. It was as if he were a massive aircraft carrier in just another storm. As if nothing dared rattle him. But not today. The man was a ticking bomb, the cords in his neck wound tight and his shoulders square.

McKenna paused at the open doorway when Maverick stepped to her side. "You guys really think the woman who did this will strike again? While the police are looking for her?"

"Not taking chances," Alex replied, his normally icy blues gone dark and stormy. "I'll call in another agent to stand guard with Maverick while Beau recovers, but you need to watch your step. If Montego is behind this, she prefers to victimize men, but don't trust her. You own a weapon?"

She shook her head. "Sorry. Only gummy vitamins. Lollipops. Stuff kids like." And, oh yes, an ulcer since Beau pulled that flatlining routine. She should've seen it coming. Dehydration, shock, and blood loss compromised the heart every time.

Alex stuck his chin at Maverick. "Don't let her out of your sight."

"Didn't intend to," he replied, his gaze already out the door and his hand cupping her elbow. "You're with me, Doc Fitz. There won't be enough room for you in the ambulance, so we'll follow in my vehicle."

"I'll call later," McKenna promised Kelsey before she was forced to accompany her bossy escort to where he'd parked several houses down the block.

This whole bodyguard-the-doctor routine was stifling, on the verge of claustrophobic. What'd Alex and Maverick think she was going to do, go looking for trouble? Hardly. McKenna was more the type who hid under her bed after watching a scary movie. Not like she did that, either. People who survived their own horror shows weren't inclined to enjoy gruesome box office thrills.

"Or I'll call you," Kelsey called out before Alex shut the door on her.

Man, these guys were bossy!

The trip to GWU was uneventful, but McKenna couldn't relax, not after the brutality she'd witnessed. Whoever this Catalina Montego person was, she'd cut off the distal and intermediate portion of Agent Jennings' digitus minimus manus—his baby finger—with a sharp, but blunt, instrument. One that easily severed skin and tissue, but crushed bone. McKenna had sutured what veins she could on the exposed proximal phalange to control the bleeding, and she'd packed his entire hand and arm in ice.

But she doubted even Decker could reattach that finger. There was too much tendon and bone damage. She wasn't up on all the latest whiz-bang advancements in reattaching damaged limbs and fingers, but she knew enough. The second interphalangeal joint had been severely compromised, and unless Dr. Decker now attached bionic digits—which was entirely possible these days—Agent Jennings would soon join the ranks of all those who'd come home damaged from war. Or who'd stuck their fingers in lawnmowers and augers.

The poor guy. Even as sweaty and confused as he'd been, Beau was one of those gloriously handsome Hispanic males, the kind that melted panties and made millions at the box office. His brows were black, but not bushy. More elegant. Refined. A definite five o'clock shadow graced his cheeks, jaw, and neck, but on him, it looked sexy. His hair was lush and thick, trimmed at the sides, yet longer on top. When she'd first seen him, she'd barely managed to not brush through the strands hanging into his eyes.

Olive skinned, the man had the most incredible lashes. Thick and long, they'd sucked her gaze into eyes so black and hostile, she'd been half-afraid to treat him at first. He'd looked like he might bite, and the words out of his mouth? Atrocious, vile, and—her heart fluttered—again, Beau Jennings was fiercely sexy. In a roundabout way, he'd even implied that she was pretty. Not many of her patients ever told her that.

Beau was also built like a tank, his abs washboard hard, his chest wider than Maverick's, his thighs overworked and as thick as tree trunks. Long-legged and belligerent, he wasn't her type. At all. Yet she hadn't been able to force her gaze off him once she'd knelt at his side. Lethal danger shuddered off him, but once she'd touched him and found him trembling beneath her fingertips, her heart told her true. This god of thunder and death was scared. Hence the bad language.

Not that she found foul-mouthed men attractive. She didn't. But most doctors, nurses, and others in the medical fields tended to be overly refined, even reserved. Often stuffy. Boringly intellectual. Full of themselves and proud of the letters after their names. Trimmed, clean, and—sterile. They were more white-collar than blue, though she knew a few who hiked, skied, and scuba dived. Not like that put them in the same category as truckers, farmers, or Alex Stewart's snipers. Beau Jennings was just—different—in a deadly, irresistible way. He was raw. Rude. Volatile. One look at him and the tiny hairs on the back of her neck lifted as if she'd come way too close to a lightning strike.

McKenna hadn't failed to notice Beau's bare feet, either. Dirty, yes, but rugged, his toes were straight, his nails trimmed, and the metatarsals long. What was it about a man's bare feet that made her heart somersault? Probably because she seldom saw them. Guess that made all things male and bare enticing.

She'd detected more than his fierce masculine pride when she'd wrapped that poor callused hand in ice prior to transport, though. His poor injured hand had also testified of a prior injury. A nasty burn. The scar itself was massive but old and smooth, as if he'd grabbed something hot when he was younger. Maybe an overheated weapon during his Army time? She wondered if Alex knew.

And that tattoo covering his massive left arm, what was that about? Comprised of a hooded demons' skull that reminded her of Death, it encompassed his entire shoulder, then wound down and around his arm like a coiled pet dragon, complete with scales, until it ended with a wicked, toothy face on the back of his poor hand. A tat that size had to have hurt when he'd gotten it.

But wasn't it interesting how Beau had deferred to Kelsey every time she spoke to him? What was that about? Kelsey was everyone's darling, but he'd looked positively star-struck whenever she'd leaned over him. Like a little boy who wanted to please her. It was almost comical. Yet the glow in his dark eyes when she spoke made him—endearing.

Several hours later, McKenna still waited for news on her patient. Dr. Decker hadn't yet taken a break to update her on Beau's progress, which hopefully meant all was well. She thumbed through what few magazines she'd found, and she paced.

Her opinion of Maverick deflated as the afternoon dragged on. He'd grown moody after he'd called home and talked with his wife, China. Whatever transpired during their conversation hadn't set well with him. McKenna assured him that she'd be fine by herself if he needed to run home to secure his family.

But he'd flatly refused and ended up telling her to knock it off after she'd encouraged him one too many times. "I don't cut and run," he'd said with something akin to disgust in his tone, like she'd accused him of shirking his duty, which she hadn't.

She quit asking.

Now he sat sullen and quiet at her side in the hospital's family counseling/consultation room just outside trauma surgery. Thankfully, another agent showed up with two Starbucks and a couple sandwiches from the Fresh Grill cafeteria on the first floor. Gabe Cartwright seemed a more even-tempered man. With short mahogany hair, he was quick with a smile, and the complete opposite of prickly, brooding Maverick.

McKenna craved the coffee Gabe brought, but her nervous stomach wasn't up to handling solid foods. Not until she knew how Beau's surgery went.

"Is there someone I can call?" she asked, holding the Starbucks venti in both hands. "For Mr. Jennings, I mean. A wife? Parents? Anyone we should notify?"

Gabe shook his head. "He's got no family, ma'am."

"Just us. Not like he cares about us," Maverick added with a snort.

No matter what she said or asked, he rained on her parade.

Gabe winked. "Don't let him get to you, ma'am. You know how brothers are. Some of us don't know when we've got it good."

Maverick turned and glared at Gabe. "And some of us don't know when to shut it."

Which made Gabe grin wider at McKenna. "See? What'd I say? Am I not the more handsome man sitting here? Does not a frown turned upside down bring a ray of sunshine to a cloudy—ouch!"

Maverick landed another solid punch to Gabe's bicep, pushing him over the armrest. "Who the hell are you today, *Mister Rogers*? A frown turned upside down? Really? You've been watching too much TV with Suzette."

McKenna had the urge to make them sit in different corners.

"Then why so glum?" Gabe asked his buddy. "It's not like the world's ending. We've been through shit like this before. This is just one more mean chick with a vendetta."

"Yeah, but…" Maverick ran a hand over his head. "It's Gorgeous. She's foaling again. Last one came breach. We lost it."

"Ah, it's springtime in the Rockies. I forgot." Gabe swallowed the rest of his Starbucks and tossed the cup into the trash receptacle across the room before he turned to McKenna and explained. "Maverick and China own around thirty Percheron draft horses. The mares drop their foals in spring. It's a big deal, I mean" —he held his arms out wide, his fingers fluttering— "a Percheron foal is a really big deal."

"Will you stop?" Maverick hissed. "You make it sound like she's foaling a mini-truck."

"I forgot that you raise horses," McKenna said, thankful for a neutral path to Maverick. No wonder he was anxious. He wanted to be home helping that mare deliver her baby, something McKenna could relate to.

He met her gaze from beneath dark, threatening brows. "Yes, ma'am. Thirty-two at last count. The Wild Wolf Ranch East is just down the road from Alex and Kelsey's place. Ten miles past the truck stop if you're coming east."

She cocked her head. "Those are yours? Oh, my gosh! I pull over there all the time just to watch them. I've loved horses since I was little. But I thought they were Clydesdales."

He shook his head. "Every last one's a registered Percheron, born and bred. China keeps their pedigree charts. She's the expert. I'm just hired help. You ought to visit us sometime. They're really quite gentle."

An invitation was the last thing McKenna expected. He really was a handsome man when he wasn't scowling. "I'll do that, thanks."

"Do you ride?"

"No, but I've always wanted to. Do you?" She could imagine him sitting tall in the saddle, his cowboy hat pulled low as he galloped into the sunset, or something equally as romantic. China Carson was one lucky woman.

"Yes, ma'am. Every chance I get. When I'm not traveling, I run *Everyone's a Cowboy*."

"No, really!" Okay, now that was just plain weird. "I refer patients to you all the time."

Everyone's a Cowboy was a local therapeutic riding program for special needs children. Affiliated with the Professional Association of Therapeutic Horsemanship, internationally known as PATH, *Everyone's a Cowboy's* reputation for reaching out to all children, no matter their disability, exceeded others in the region. It made sense now. The woman behind it was a Ms. Wolf. Probably also how Wild Wolf Ranch got its name. Hmmm.

Maverick nodded. "That's good to know. It keeps my head in the game."

"Instead of up his ass," Gabe quipped, which earned him another hard glare from his buddy.

The door opened and both Maverick and Gabe lifted to their feet as Dr. Decker ducked inside the room and inclined his head to McKenna. "Are these family members?" he asked, ever conscious of the HIPAA mandate to protect patient confidentiality.

Before she could speak, Maverick stepped forward, one hand extended. "No, sir, we're not, and if you need us to leave, we will. But Beau has no living family that we know of. Name's Maverick Carson and with me is Gabe Cartwright.

We work with Beau, and we consider ourselves his brothers more than just his friends."

"Thank you for understanding, but rules are rules," Dr. Decker said as he returned the shake. "I can't divulge patient information until he gives me written consent. If you don't mind, I'd like to speak with Dr. Fitzgerald in private."

No sooner said than done. With an obedient, "You bet," Maverick and Gabe retreated to the hallway and closed the door behind them.

"How is he?" McKenna asked.

"He'll survive, but he's looking at a couple more surgeries and months of rehab. He's lost the use of that joint. I couldn't save it. Give him another hour and you'll be able to see him."

"You were able to reattach it then?" Amazing.

"Absolutely. It'll be the slightest bit shorter than it was, but in order to reattach the bone, I had to clean the tissue, and..." Dr. Decker launched into a complex technical explanation of what he'd encountered reattaching the nine muscles, the bones, as well as the veins and nerves in Beau's pinky finger. Lost somewhere between the two intrinsic flexor muscles and the dorsal digital nerves, McKenna stood in awe of Dr. Decker's incredible skill and knowledge. He made the last several hours sound like just another day in the life of.

"Good job suturing those dorsal arteries by the way." Dr. Decker cocked his head. "That probably saved his life. But why you? You're a pediatrician. How'd you get involved?"

"I was just nearest the scene at the time."

"Who did this to him?"

She shrugged. "Some psycho named Athena or Catalina Montego. Yes, I've never heard of her either, but Alex Stewart thinks she's after his agents."

Dr. Decker's gaze narrowed. "Alex Stewart, as in the owner of that security business over in Alexandria?"

"The TEAM, yes. Do you know him?"

"I know his wife. Kelsey talked my fourteen-year-old son into returning home a couple months ago. Thought we'd lost him for good. She's an unbelievable force in our community."

"She's my very best friend," McKenna beamed. "Everybody loves her, and she does so much for runaways. I'm thrilled you know her."

"She does good work." Decker paused, his salt-and-pepper hair cut so close she could see his tanned scalp. Glancing at the door, he asked, "Those men are guarding you and Mr. Jennings?"

"Yes. It was rather crazy. Maverick escorted me from my office to Kelsey's home where I treated Beau. He's been with me since." *But he'd rather be home, and I wish I were at my office.*

"I don't usually do this, but..." Decker withdrew a business card from his pocket. "If either you or the Stewarts need me, call. Understood? For anything. I owe them."

She tucked it into her hip pocket. "Will do. Thank you for taking this case on. You could've turned me down. I really appreciate what you've done."

"I'm glad I was on call." He nodded toward the closed door. "Why don't you go wait for Mr. Jennings? It shouldn't be long before they transfer him from recovery."

Which made her stop to think. She had no business waiting around any longer. Beau had Maverick and Gabe.

They were his brothers. His family. Not hers. Besides, what were the odds that Montego, whoever she was, even knew about McKenna Fitzgerald or where to find her? This might be a good time to cut and run back to the land of runny noses, whooping cough, midnight earaches, and monthly inoculations.

Just as soon as she could.

Chapter Nine

"I told you we needed a bigger house," Alex grumbled at Kelsey.

"You're just a poor loser," she shot back at him.

In an effort to thwart what he believed was Catalina—*aka Athena, the liar*—Montego's demented plan, Alex had ensured all of his agents, their wives, children, parents, and grandparents were safe. He'd alerted Murphy Finnegan, the chief of his Seattle office, that Beau had been compromised and to take protective measures, though Alex doubted those measures were necessary at his second office. Still, a smart man didn't take chances. Those agents all had families, too.

At the moment, his pride and joy was busy bossing Mark Houston's three girls, JayJay, Faith, and little Markie. Lexie thought she ruled the roost, but it was easy to see Mark's wife's influence on her girls. Lexie adored JayJay, the oldest, and JayJay, in her gentle way, could get Lexie to agree to anything. Cute to watch. If a man had that kind of time.

Since Mark was out of the country, Libby and her family were staying with Kelsey until this debacle was over. Eric Reynolds and his wife Shea were, at this moment, escorting Hunter Christian's wife, Meredith and their son Courtney to join the group now sequestered in the smaller-than-it-should've-been Stewart enclave. With Hunter on a mission in

South Africa, Alex would make sure his family stayed safe while he was gone.

"But we could've had six more bedrooms. Think about it. Six. Everyone would be comfortable then."

Kelsey chuckled as she cleared the corner of one of the two queen-sized beds he was helping her make. "Relax. The kids love sleeping on the floor. They think they're camping out, and we've got two sofa couches downstairs if more show. Have you heard from Mother yet? What's she doing?"

He tossed the pillows to the other bed. "She said she and Justice will be fine, but I told her to bring Dempsey here to play with the kids. God knows she spends too much time with that brainiac mother of hers."

"Aw, you old softie," Kelsey murmured, tugging the fitted sheet over one corner of the mattress. "Dempsey's such a doll. Do you notice how closely Whisper follows her when she's here? He's turned into a regular babysitter."

Alex nodded as he kept up with his wife and tugged his corner extra tight, military-style like she did. "He's a born service dog, that one."

"He's always been my guardian angel," she agreed as she floated the flat sheet over the mattress.

Remembering the dark day when Whisper had first encountered Kelsey, Alex came around the bed and caught her in his arms before she had time to protest. Which she would have, had he not spun her off her feet. "I need all of you to be safe," he growled, something as simple as the scent of her hair was ambrosia to a hardened warrior like him.

She melted into him, her head under his chin, her ear over his heart, and her fingertips tapping his collarbones. "I can't believe what Howie found in our little neighborhood. The poor Ringers."

"We don't know for certain it was them." Alex said even as he steeled his heart.

The DNA evidence in the square container Catalina left behind had gone straight to the FBI lab. Right now, the rose plants, meat grinder, as well as eight more plastic containers and the various body parts Chief Prince had found in Ringer's kitchen freezer, were undergoing thorough analysis. But DNA results weren't spontaneous like Hollywood made everyone believe. It could take months, even years, before the FBI reported what comprised the bloody mixture Catalina had prepared as fertilizer.

If they were in the mood to report their findings to a private contractor, that is. Which the FBI often was not. The only person keeping the Bureau in Alex's good graces was their director, Zachary Strong. If not for him and his stand-up policy of running a tight and honest ship, Alex wouldn't hold his breath waiting. Most federal agencies were sucking black holes of bullshit and bureaucracy, more intent on covering their asses than in serving America. But Strong changed the Bureau's way of doing business when he took over, and Alex trusted him, enough that he'd volunteered two of his best agents, Ky Winchester and Tate Higgins, to work for the FBI's Deuces Wild Team.

But the fact remained. The Ringers hadn't boarded their flight to New Zealand, and the national news hounds were, even now, filling every available second of airtime with their style of investigative reporting: theories, holier-than-thou suppositions, and downright ugly innuendos as to who murdered who, who cheated on who, and—the usual.

Spinning what could tragically be two gruesome deaths for increased ratings instead of seeking something as noble as justice. Hell, just for the sake of good old-fashioned truth. Alex hated most everyone connected with the press. Not all. Only those who'd proven themselves to be predators instead of reporters.

"I feel so bad for Eloise. She was excited for this chance to get away."

"It has been a helluva year for Bruce."

"Every year is hard in his business," Kelsey murmured. "Have you heard from Maverick yet?"

Alex shook his head. "He won't call until he has something to report."

"China's got plenty of room if anyone would rather bunk there."

Alex agreed. China Carson knew how to handle a rifle, too. She'd had no trouble ridding her land in Wyoming of varmints. Catalina wouldn't stand a chance against her.

"We need another vacation, just you and me," Kelsey whispered, her lips moving soft and warm up his neck, forever reminding Alex that he might be scarred, battered, and tossed aside by the rest of the world, but he had survived, damn it. And somewhere during that survival, he'd been blessed. He wasn't about to apologize for finding Kelsey.

"Let me guess. Hawaii again." Her favorite touchdown after some of the hard-fought wins they'd scored these past years.

Her breasts flattened against his pecs, firing his blood. "You know me. The sun. The surf—"

"Sipping mimosas." His hands slid down her back to cup her bottom. Damn, he loved this woman. Kelsey alone had the power to make him forget and to remember at the same time.

"There is that. I do love a good mimosa," she whispered, nipping his jaw while her warm breath skated across his neck. Enticing him. Inciting every last hormone in his all-male body to stand up and pay attention. To take her now, undress her quickly and make love, while the house was full of friendlies and their daughter was preoccupied.

But the moment he fingered the bottom hem of her blouse, his cell vibrated in his pocket. Not the vibration he was going for. "Hold that thought," he said as he palmed his phone in one hand, her ass in the other. "Maverick?"

"Beau's awake, Boss. He's talking."

"I'll be there as soon as Zack and Jake show."

"Copy that."

"How's McKenna?"

"Unhappy. She's got patients. Doesn't like having her wings clipped."

"She'll get over it. See you in an hour. Tops." Alex tilted into Kelsey's warm body as his phone slid back into its assigned pocket.

"I'll be okay if you have to go," she reminded him for the hundredth time. "I've got my pistol back from Beau. It's loaded. Libby brought hers too if you want to leave now to beat rush hour traffic."

At close to quitting time in the District, traffic was about to get thick, congested, and faster than speed limits allowed as people raced out of the city for home. But old habits died hard. "I'm not leaving you until I've got trained men here." *I won't risk losing you again. My heart can't take it.*

Instead of arguing, Kelsey snuggled, her ear against the middle of his chest, listening to that very stubborn heart. There was a time that pesky organ hadn't worked so well. A time when it had seemed broken beyond hope and repair. He'd been furious at the world back then. Pissed at himself for living when the best parts of his family hadn't. But with Kelsey and now Lexie in his corner, he was born again. Saved. Might sound corny, but every man should be so blessed to have a good woman to come home to at the end of a hard day. Hell, at the end of any day.

"I love you, Alex Stewart," she told him truly.

Inhaling, he knew without a doubt. Kelsey was saving him all over again. "I'm staying," he told her. "Get used to it."

She lifted her chin, her eyes glowing. "I wouldn't have it any other way."

Chapter Ten

He was *not* staying in this hospital one more day. Groggy or not, injured or not, Beau Jennings was no slacker. It had been two long days of waking up, only to be given, against his will most of the time, something that put him right back to sleep. Hell, he could barely remember what he'd told his employer during that terse visit. Alex seemed pissed then. Who the hell wasn't?

Finally alert when the nurse offered another round of pain meds last night, Beau refused the shot. A man needed a clear head to work, and those drugs were messing him up. It was past time to move out. While he lay flat on his back, the bitch was getting away.

If only Maverick and Gabe would listen. All he needed was a little help getting to his feet, and losing the catheter some busybody thought he needed, which he did not. How hard could it be to yank one of those things out anyway? He meant to find out.

Until the woman trapped with him, namely Doc Fitzgerald, canted her lovely head at an extreme angle like she knew precisely what he was thinking. She'd been with him when he'd first come to, and she'd looked so worried. For a moment, he'd basked in her presence like a drug addict in the afterglow of a solid score, but that hadn't lasted. She'd become just as big a watchdog as Maverick and Gabe. Twice as bossy. And she knew what she was talking about, damn it.

"Stop it, Agent Jennings," she murmured, her elbow on the armrest and her chin in her palm. "If I have to stay here, so do you. Especially you. You just underwent extremely delicate surgery to attach a severed finger, that, oh by the way, your boss was smart enough to put on ice until he caught up with you. One wrong move could disable your hand for life. You don't want that, do you?"

He offered her his chin, impatient to be gone. Hospitals didn't agree with him. "You can't keep me here against my will."

"No, but Dr. Decker can," Doc Pain-in-the-Ass volleyed back at him as she straightened in her chair. "Do I need to call Alex Stewart, too?"

Didn't that take the piss out of Beau's vinegar? Alex would do it, too. He'd fly in on that fancy helicopter of his and he'd have no problem telling Beau to shut up, lay down, and stop whining. Her threat was nearly enough to keep him flat on his back. But nearly wasn't good enough.

Fighting a dizzying wave of determination, he swung both feet over the edge of his bed just to prove he could. The extreme nausea crawling up his neck like a chilly centipede was nothing. It'd fade in a few minutes, but he didn't want her to help him get to the head and take care of his business. And she would. Know-it-all doctors did personal, private, embarrassing stuff like that. They fussed, and they bossed as if a guy were a two-year-old. This doctor in particular, had a way of talking to him like he'd better listen to her.

"You're not getting up," she told him. Like she could stop him?

Just watch me, he thought, his dander up and both palms now flat beside him, what was left of his fingers gripping the mattress. He'd had surgery on his hand, for Hell's sake. Not his head or his ass or either of his very capable feet. There was no reason to lounge around and feel sorry for himself. Wounds healed. Soldiers reengaged. That was what they did, by hell, and he needed his ass back in the fight to do what he did best. Find the bitch who'd cut off his finger and end her sorry ass before she hurt someone else. That was her MO, right? Well, this was his.

Once Beau wrapped his head around a mission, he didn't give up, and he didn't fail. This mission, though self-proclaimed, was no different. Up and on his feet now, he took it slow and easy to make sure he had solid footing. There was no need to hurry or fall on his face and end up making a fool of himself.

Of course, Doc Fitzgerald jumped to his side, but okay. She could tag along. Until he hit the head. Baby steps. Like an old man, he inched forward. She followed with that damned IV tree and his pee bag. Finally at the door to the head, he grabbed hold of the tree, pulled the embarrassing bag out of her hand, and bit out, "Do you mind?"

She shrugged. "Trust me, I've seen it all before, buster, and you are not going one more step without me."

Buster? Squaring his shoulders, he straightened to every inch of his six-foot-five height. "Trust me. You haven't seen this equipment, cupcake. Now back off and let me do my business in private."

Her gaze narrowed up at him like a sniper, because, yeah. She was a short little thing. She had no choice but to look up. Tiny, but fierce in a cute sort of way. The left side of her upper lip lifted. Her nostrils flared. She narrowed her brows. *Oh, my hell, she's trying to intimidate me.*

He gave her his chin again to get her to step back and climb down. "I'm a big boy, Doc. I can wipe my own ass. Been doing it for years."

Damned if she didn't lift to the tips of her toes and get in his face, glaring at him like a five-foot-nothing drill sergeant, her hands on her hips like he should be afraid of her. Seriously? Not happening, sister. Yet something like a double somersault flipped in Beau's chest. Might have been his heart. Sure felt like it stuck a perfect landing. Had to have been indigestion.

But the woman was on the light side of a hundred and ten pounds, tops. A delicious hint of sugar cookies struck his nose, tempting another long inhalation—just because. Not that she smelled good, but that soft feminine fragrance was a helluva lot better than the antiseptic taint. Beau took another deep breath—also just because.

Doc Fitzgerald didn't have a dog in this fight. It took her a minute before she licked that lush bottom lip, gave him one last impertinent nod toward the head and growled, "Keep it quick. I'm here if you need me."

Then, because his eyes needed an assist in looking away from that tender bottom lip, he stepped back with his handy-dandy IV tree, his bag dangling off his fingers, and he snapped, "I don't."

Quickly, before he changed his mind, Beau crossed the distance and shut the door in her face. For added measure, he growled, "Good riddance," loud enough she had to hear it.

"Don't make me come in there," she threatened.

That'll be the day.

By the time he got rid of his IV and the catheter—which was not fun!—Beau was worn out and verging on the light side of exhausted. But he'd lived with being dog-tired all his life. Growing up on the hard streets of dusty Las Vegas taught a kid quick. You caught a few Zs when and where you could. If you could. If not, suck it up, crybaby, and keep moving.

Army life was no better. Cleaner, yeah, but none of the deployments he'd ever worked involved what Navy SEALs termed 'easy days'. There was no easy day in his book. Some were longer than others, but days were just days.

Besides, he'd grab a power nap once he was out of the hospital and back on the street. After he caught up with the woman who'd snipped his finger off like he was a tree that needed pruning. Catalina Montego, a known murderer, and the sister of the human trafficker Seth McCray had ended less than a month ago in Cuba. She was on the FBI's most wanted list and she was here in the States, damn her to Hell.

Well, she's on my list, too. Want to guess who'll get to her first?

Sure of himself and his way forward, Beau finished his business as quickly as he could. He brushed his teeth, ran the hospital issued comb over his thick, wavy hair, then ran a warm washcloth over what he could reach of his body. At last, feeling like a man in control instead of a gutter rat, he jerked the door open and—

There stood two pissed off former Marines who might could put him back in that bed. Gabe Cartwright's usually mischievous green eyes weren't smiling. Neither was his curled lip. He stood there with both hands on his hips like he thought he was a door Beau couldn't get through.

Maverick Carson stood beside Gabe, his expression blank, which was never a good thing. Maverick tended to explode into action when a guy least expected. He'd been known for taking down a fellow agent in the middle of TEAM headquarters and beating him bloody.

Shit. This might not work. "I've got things to do," he told them instead of, *'Fuck off. I'm outta here.'*

"I don't have time for this, Jennings," Maverick growled. "It's been a long day. Get your hairy ass back to bed."

"And do what? Lay around and pick my nose while that bitch gets away? Not happening."

Gabe shot him down with, "Pick whatever you want. Doctor's orders, Beau. You're on blood thinners and heavy antibiotics. You flat-lined, you moron. Son-of-a-bitch, where's your IV? Do you see that, Maverick? This shithead tossed his cath, too."

Beau shifted his weight, positioning his heft for the knockdown, drag-out that was sure to come. "I don't need that stuff, boys. Let me pass."

"So you're a physician now? Been to college, did your internship, and know your blood pressure's been out of control since you arrived? By ambulance, you dick," Maverick hissed as he stabbed a finger at the bed. "Stop being an ass, Jennings. Heal first. Fight later. 'Sides, you've got no clothes. Were you going to stroll out of here with your ass showing?"

Shit, this was going nowhere, and Beau had the sneaky suspicion that tattletale, Doc Fitzgerald, had already ratted him out to Alex. That'd be her style. She'd called out Maverick and Gabe, why not Alex?

Speaking of the nosy woman... "Where's Doc Fitz?" Beau asked his two over-protective mother hens.

Gabe looked at Maverick. Maverick glared at Gabe. Then both roared, "Son-of-a-bitch!"

"You guys lost her," Beau crowed. "While you're squaring off with me, a woman eluded you. A tiny, stubborn woman! Alex will be so pissed."

Chapter Eleven

McKenna hadn't intended to walk away. She'd simply stepped to the nurse's station outside of Beau's room to check in with her office, while Gabe and Maverick confronted him. One call, that was all. But then the yelling started. By the sounds of it, Beau wasn't backing down. Neither were Maverick and Gabe. They had their hands full, and well, when opportunity knocked, what did a smart woman do? Simple. She headed for the stairs.

By the time she hit the ground level, heavy footsteps pounded behind her. Might have been Maverick or Gabe. Could have been someone else. She didn't wait to find out, just walked a little faster. But really? Think about it. Protective custody was for someone who needed it, not her. She had patients to visit. A father to call. A life!

With her heart pounding, she ducked out of the stairwell and into a nearby corridor that led to one of the private staff exits. Patients and family always came through the front doors or the emergency room. Not doctors.

At last on her way to freedom, McKenna called for an Uber driver, and that was that. In two minutes, the closest available driver picked her up at the curb and whisked her away. She never caught sight of Agent Carson or Cartwright if that had even been them in the stairwell.

Whew! Ducked down in the back seat where no one could see her, she blew out a deep breath of freedom. Alex Stewart might not be happy with what she'd done, but she didn't work for him, did she? Besides, facts were facts. Catalina Montego didn't know who Dr. Fitzgerald was. They'd never met. How could she?

Feeling back in control of her life for the first time in days, McKenna contacted Margo and caught up on which doctors had covered for her during this forced hiatus, who they'd seen, which patients needed follow-up calls, and so forth. By the time Margo filled her in, McKenna's heart rate was back to normal and her outlook was sunny.

"Hey, listen. I'm taking a couple more days off. Would you inform my associates that something urgent came up? Yes, I'll gladly cover for them once I'm back, but until then" *—because I don't want Alex to know where I am—* "I'm out of contact. I'll explain when I return."

"Is your father okay?" Of course, Margo translated that vague request into a possible family emergency that involved Sanders Fitzgerald's health. Come to think of it, she always inquired after him. Maybe it was time for a little matchmaking.

"No, Margo, he's fine, so don't worry, okay? There's something I need to deal with. Just business. Nothing too serious. Trust me. You'll be the first one I call if anything happens."

"You do know I'm here for you, Dr. Fitz. If you ever just need to talk—"

"Oh, stop," McKenna gushed, relieved to be discussing work and life instead of intrigue and danger that simply was not happening. Not to her. "You act like I'm dying. But honest. It's just a business deal…" *Sort of.* "…that I need to straighten out. It's a timing thing. No worries."

"Well, if you're sure." Margo hesitated, then added, "It's not about that guy you left with the other day, is it? Are you and he seeing each other? Are you—Oh, my gosh, are you and he running away together?"

Ha! That'd be the day she had an interest in a man. Any man. Even if she did, it wouldn't be Maverick Carson. Not now that she knew what a brooding, bossy, totally-devoted-to-China man he was. Beau, maybe. But, on second thought, not him either. And that was just plain sad, because he was handsome.

But McKenna had built her life around her profession and the children and mothers she served. Ever since she'd been a battered child, she'd been driven to never let abuse happen to other children. Mothers in this crazy world needed more resources, especially stressed-out moms like Carol Bryce, who burned the candle at both ends until they woke up one morning in complete mental darkness. If anything frightened McKenna, it was that kind of dark. Dark days. Dark moods. Dark closets.

"You're making me laugh. You know me, unlucky in love and not looking for Mr. Right, because he's not out there, remember? Quit worrying, and, oh yeah, if anyone asks, you know nothing, all right?"

"You got it, Fitz. My lips are zipped, and I'm throwing away the key." Margo mumbled as if she'd done just that.

What a good friend and a truly funny lady. McKenna was lucky to have her on staff. "Thanks, you're a peach. I'll be in touch."

"Tell that father of yours I said hello!" Margo called out as McKenna ended the call.

That woman. If anyone needed a man in her bed, it was Margo. Not McKenna. She'd settle for getting her life back.

The next call she placed was to the unflappable Sanders Fitzgerald himself. Now there was a man who knew what trouble was. At five feet, nine inches and with a full head of premature gray, make that silver, he was a looker. How he maintained an upbeat personality given his past and the anguish he'd dealt with, amazed McKenna. But that was her dad. He was one of those glass half-full kind of guys.

He'd survived a broken marriage to a severely unbalanced woman, McKenna's mother, Aurora. From the start, he should've known all was not well with the family he'd married into, since all six girls were named after female Disney characters. What kind of parents did that to their kids? *Unstable parents, that's who.*

But Sanders was one of those truly good guys, always seeing rainbows instead of storms. The silver linings in the thunderclouds. He really should've looked closer at the cuckoos in the nest before he fell in love, though.

Because, not to be upstaged by their oldest sister's mental health issues, Bambi, Daisy, Minnie, Alice, and, oh yes, Wendy, all suffered from the same bi-polar/mental disorder. Little did he know then the disorder had been passed from family to family like their very own private strain of Black Plague. It hadn't taken Sanders long to become protective of his only child. Hence, McKenna had never met her aunts or her maternal grandparents.

But the day he'd uncovered her most horrible secret still stood out with super high-density picture clarity, complete with Dolby Vision high dynamic range, HDR for the technically challenged. Sanders had been so outraged at Aurora. But so, so hurt for McKenna. Her cold fingertips slipped up to her throat at the recollection, as if she could stop the home movie forcing her to relive the past.

They'd been on the front sidewalk of their nondescript suburban home in South Carolina the day it happened. Back then they were still like everyone else. A small family where the father worked nine-to-five weekdays and had weekends off. A mother who stayed home to care for McKenna and the house. To have dinner on the table when Sanders returned from a hard day's work. Chores. Homework. They'd even planned a California vacation. One that never happened.

The day Sanders discovered McKenna's most horrible secret started out like so many other Saturdays. He was off work. They were supposed to go on a picnic at the new waterslide in town that afternoon. But first thing in the morning, in his cheerful, optimistic way, her father insisted on teaching her to ride her bike without training wheels. Little Dougie Morton down the block kept calling her a baby, and that just wasn't right. Sanders talked to McKenna, his one and only child, about bullies and how the best way to deal with them was to stand up to them. Little did he know...

When the bicycle wobbled, McKenna lost her balance and fell. She scraped her knees. What kid didn't do that? But the look of horror on her sweet father's face when he carried her into the kitchen to wash her knees, and instead, discovered massive, black bruises on her skinny thighs beneath her ripped jeans. That led him to the tender, raised welts on her backside. The angry red stripes on her back and shoulders. A line of ugly bruises on her vertebrae. The telling crescent patterns left by Aurora's sharp fingernails on McKenna's upper arms.

Sanders didn't ask who'd hurt her. Neither did he raise his voice or scream for Aurora to come see what he'd found on their—THEIR—daughter. He didn't curse, and he didn't accuse. He simply wrapped McKenna up in his arms and sat her on his lap at the kitchen table. He pressed her sweaty head against his chest, and he held her there as if he'd never let her go. She surely hadn't wanted him to, when over and over he murmured, "Never ever again. I promise you, baby girl. Never. Ever. Again."

She had only to close her eyes today to conjure the same comforting scent of fabric softener from his shirt. The spicy, tingle of his shaving lotion. The scrape of his just shaved chin against her sweaty forehead. Sanders saved her life and her soul that day. He would forever be McKenna's first true love.

He was the tenderhearted father who wouldn't even kill the spiders that invaded their house every autumn. Instead, he'd carefully scoop them up with a towel and tell them, "Not in my house, kids. Go play outside where you belong." And out they'd go to creep back in on another, chilly day.

She'd cried there on his lap, but only because he'd cried, and that was her fault. Daddy wasn't supposed to ever find out what Mom did, because it would hurt his feelings. That was what Mom said, and why McKenna *must never tell him what a bad girl she was.'* Of course, little girl McKenna had totally believed she was the cause of his tears. That everything was her fault. If he'd never found her sores and owies, he never would've cried.

She cried with him, not because of what her mom would do to her, but because his feelings were hurt. Like any child of an abusive parent, she'd long since accepted her demeaning position in her family. How could she be a good girl if she couldn't keep one secret? She'd been so sure she was worthless.

But after he'd wiped his face, Sanders hugged her carefully and told her she was a good girl and that none of this was her fault. He promised no one would ever hurt her again. But she'd heard that before. Mom always apologized, too. Aurora cried after every beating and whipping she delivered. She always said she didn't know why she got so mad and lost control. She always promised McKenna she'd never, ever do it again. Until the next time...

"Talk about crazy," McKenna whispered to herself as she thumb-dialed her father at Golden Horizons. When he didn't answer on his private room line, she dialed his cell.

"Hello there, Lamb Chops!" he answered brightly. "How's my best girl and my favorite doctor? Still planning on dinner tomorrow night? You didn't forget your date with your old man, did you?"

"Hi, Dad. I could never forget you, and yes, I'm fine. But about tomorrow night... I have to give you a rain check. Something's come up."

"I hope whoever that something is, he's tall, dark, handsome, and ready to settle down."

McKenna smiled at her chipper dad. He'd been hinting she needed to get married quite a bit lately. Said he wasn't getting any younger. That he'd like a couple grandchildren before he kicked the bucket. Not that he was old.

Sanders had only moved into Golden Horizons when he'd had a minor stroke, and he decided he didn't want to live alone any longer. He needed a cane to walk, but since she worked long hours, he'd decided she needed her independence and stoutly refused to move in with her like she would've preferred. Something about cramping her style. *As if I have a style.*

The stubborn, dear old man. Out of respect for his wishes, she'd helped him move from his two-bedroom apartment above the coffee shop in upscale Adams Morgan, out west to the assisted living center closest to her practice and apartment. If there were a better father in the world, McKenna didn't know him. Well, except for Alex Stewart. He was almost as good and decent as Sanders Fitzgerald.

"No, Dad, I'm not dating anyone. I'm too busy to start a family, and I'm not looking. You know that."

"Well, darn," he complained. "Guess I owe Stu a root beer then."

"You've got to stop taking bets on me getting married, Dad. You lose every time."

"I know, I know. But one of these days, you'll surprise me. I can feel it in these old bones."

"Your bones are not old, and neither are you, young man," she scolded, loving the playful banter between them. He'd been in her corner from the moment he'd whisked her out of Aurora's reach, and through all the years of counseling to overcome the phobias inflicted on her by her unbalanced mother. To this day, McKenna still hated dark places and closets. She wouldn't be caught dead in one. Oh, the nightmares she had from being locked up. Yeah. Not going back there.

"So," he huffed. "Name me another day and time. I've got money in my pocket to spend and I intend to blow it on my best girl."

A thought sparked in McKenna's head. "Have you ever thought of dating again?" *Because I have a horny assistant in mind...*

"Me? Wouldn't dream of it. I've already got a barn burner in my sight, woman, and it's you. Now tell me when you can spare a couple hours for dinner and a movie."

"I love you. More than I can ever say. How about a week from today?" *Things should be back to normal by then.*

"It's a deal. I'm penciling you in. Hey, I gotta run. Stu's setting up the chessboard."

"Bye, Dad! Love you. Kiss Stu for me."

"Eww, never." He chuckled. "Stu's nothing but a dirty old man. His own wife won't kiss him. Love you, Princess."

McKenna settled back into the leather seat, at peace for the first time in days. She could hide out at home for the next week, and no one would be wiser. Right?

Chapter Twelve

"What do you mean, she's gone?" Alex hissed. "Do I have to do everything myself?"

"She split when Beau pitched a shit fit. We were distracted, what can I say? And you don't do everything yourself, do you?" Maverick volleyed back with a hefty slam dunk of sarcasm. "Gabe went after McKenna, while I was busy making sure Beau stayed put, but she's no dummy. By the time he hit the ground floor, there was no sign of her. How were we supposed to know she'd do something this stupid?"

Huffing through his nostrils, Alex closed his eyes and counted to ten. *Five. Ten.*

Not like that helped. "What the hell's Beau pissed about now? Is he in pain?" *Because he sure as hell will be if I have to leave my wife and daughter to fly all the way there just to set him straight.*

"Says he can't work like this. He wants out of the hospital to do his job."

"He doesn't have a job! He's confined to quarters, and those quarters are his damned bed!"

"I know, I know. Only thing keeping him here is his surgeon's refusal to sign him out."

"Smart man. What's his name?"

"Dr. Royce Decker." Maverick sounded as pissed as Alex felt, but shit. Doctors were supposed to be smarter than most people. Apparently, not Dr. Fitz.

"Tell him to call me. I'll be waiting."

"Copy that," Maverick bit out, his tone weary, which forced Alex to rethink his tactics. Blasting the guys who had his back was never smart business, and Maverick was as solid as they came.

"We'll find her," Alex offered by way of apology. "She can't have gotten far, and… You're right. This one's on me. I should've assigned more agents to this op. Can't expect you two to do double-duty."

"Yeah, well…" Maverick grumbled.

Alex could picture him standing in the hospital hall, facing the wall, raking a hand over his head, and still recovering from jet lag. His latest overseas operation had ended only a couple days ago. Maverick deserved a week off to unwind and reconnect with his family after that grueling schedule, not a twenty-four-seven assignment the minute his ass hit home plate.

"You're right, Boss. We'll find her, but you need to set Beau straight. He's hellbent on going after Montego by himself, and he's dressed, ready to walk out of here. Gabe's in with him now, but the bastard's not listening to a word we say. What's his problem anyway?"

Good question. What were any of their problems? Alex had seen it all. The men and women he'd hired all came home with PTSD, alcoholism, battle stress, and godawful survivor's guilt like what Maverick carried around like a cat-o-nine tails. Whipping himself on bad days for not being there when his only brother died, yet just as pissed at the world on good days, too.

He'd lost Darrell on a failed joint operation in Afghanistan a couple years back, and he hadn't forgiven himself yet. Might never. God knew it took Alex a helluva lot longer than that to admit that his first wife and daughter were gone, the key word being *admi*t. Not accept. Not endure. He still struggled with the harsh paradigm chance had forced on him. Who the hell didn't?

Alex cut Maverick a little more slack. "I'll send Taylor to relieve you. Go home. Kiss your wife. Play with that little girl. Call when you're ready to come back to work."

"I'm not leaving," Maverick ground out. "I said I'll do this, and I will. If you talk to Beau, I'll run out to Doc Fitzgerald's clinic and her office. They might've heard from her by now. No doubt that's where she's gone. This has been hard on her. I'll talk to her, get her to at least listen to common sense."

Okay then. "Thanks," Alex said quietly. He'd been right selecting Maverick out of the many applications who could have become TEAM agents that day. Like it or not, Maverick had needed the unique brotherhood The TEAM offered, he just hadn't realized it then.

"Listen, Zack and Jake are here. Eric and Shea are already here with Meredith Hunter and her son, Courtney. Harley's headed this way with Judy and the twins. Tell Beau to keep his ass in the hospital. I'm on my way."

"Copy that," Maverick replied more evenly. "Could you bring a couple steaks? Or something? This hospital food sucks."

"For you and Gabe, yeah. For Beau, no. He can eat that shit 'til I say different."

Alex hung up, not ready to leave his wife and daughter in another man's hands but going to do it anyway. Damn that Beau. The young man had been trouble from day one. Always arguing. Talking back. For a former Army Ranger who needed a steady job, he sure threw a lot of I-know-better-than-you bullshit back at the other agents. At Alex, too.

He'd seen guys like Beau before. Running headlong into trouble. Leading the charge when they weren't *in charge*. Picking fights. Seeking after the bullet with their names on it. But Beau seemed angrier than most. Alex just didn't know why.

After ensuring his wife and daughter were in good hands—namely Zack Lennox's and Jake Weylin's—Alex headed for the helicopter pad he'd convinced the city council they needed shortly after he'd moved to this town. Since he'd covered most of the up-front costs and provided a team of capable pilots, the council was easily persuaded. Not that this little community of horse ranchers and farmers really needed to fly into the city, but he did. So did Maverick.

Alex wouldn't have moved this far west without quick access to his office back in Alexandria and the District he served. Just wasn't smart.

The chopper was at the hospital's landing pad when his cell vibrated in his jacket pocket. Maverick.

"What now?" Alex bit out.

"Don't bother coming, Boss. He's gone."

"Son-of-a-bitch, we're hovering over GWU already. You let him leave?"

"Couldn't stop him. The man's possessed. Told us to fuck off, said you can take this job and shove it up your, well, you know."

Alex rolled the kink out of his neck that acted up whenever he lost control of an operation, or a stubborn, bone-headed agent who'd soon be looking for another job.

"Call when you catch up with Doc Fitz," he told Maverick. Then to the pilot he said, "Take me home," but he thought, *'I am going to kick Beau Jennings' ass!'*

Chapter Thirteen

Beau knew damned well Maverick and Gabe were tailing him, not like he didn't know how to lose them. But hailing a cab had taken longer than expected. And okay, he was tired, stupid, and hurting, not a good combination. But someone needed to end that bitch Montego before she hurt another unsuspecting guy, and he was the man for the job. He owed her. Big time. The woman had cut off his finger. Why couldn't anyone understand what she'd done to him? What she'd taken? How much that fuckin' hurt?

He'd never given anything away. Not his soul. Not his heart. Not so much as a crumb off his toast to a passing sparrow, yet she… *Shit!* She'd tied him down and mutilated him! The bitch wasn't getting away with it. What'd Alex think, locking him up in some hospital like a child pitching a temper tantrum? Beau Jennings had never been anybody's kid. He wasn't starting now.

"You decided where I'm taking you next?" Still keeping one eye on Beau in the rearview, the older gentleman waited patiently while the meter rolled. Tall, as black as night with short, curly hair and dark eyes that seemed to see through Beau, the cabbie was one of many immigrants who'd made his home in the District's surrounding neighborhoods.

He'd already taken Beau to his apartment, where Beau changed into black jeans, a plain black polo, black socks, and just as black work boots—for night work. Where he'd also strapped on his twin holster, complete with his two favorite pistols, loaded. He'd topped that ensemble off with a light—black, of course—leather jacket, more to conceal his arsenal than because of the cold.

"I'm thinking," Beau bit out, chewing the knuckle on his good hand. Whatever that nurse at the hospital had shot his injured hand up with had worn off. The damned thing throbbed like a mother. He was edgy, verging on mean. Maybe leaving the hospital so soon after that complex hand surgery hadn't been smart. Maybe Dr. Fitzgerald was right. *But what real man lies around in bed and heals, while everyone else does his job for him?* Beau wasn't made that way. He paid his dues up front and on time. Maverick and Gabe needed to back off. Alex did, too.

"Take me to this address," Beau finally said as he leaned over the front seat and handed the cabbie a card with Stewarts' street address. It made sense to go back to the scene of the crime. Yeah, Ringer's house would be cordoned off for sure. Police tape would be everywhere, but the sun was going down soon, and Beau planned on taking another look inside the house of terror. Catalina Montego, the bitch from Hell, had to have left a clue, and he planned on finding it. Then her. Then, double tap and problem solved. He'd rest easier. So would the rest of the world.

"You sure about that? It's a long way and it will cost you."

Money wasn't the problem. Stamina was. Endurance. Staying awake. "Yeah, I'm sure."

Beau rolled his shoulder, fighting the compelling urge to close his eyes for a minute. To rest, so he'd be ready to execute his plan the moment this cab's wheels stopped rolling. Maybe then his hand wouldn't ache. Yeah, right. "Wake me up when we get there."

The cabbie nodded. "You got it."

"And if you can lose the black Tundra following us, I'll double your fare."

The cabbie's brows lifted and promptly, the vehicle accelerated. "That I can do, sir. Hang onto your hat."

Beau fell asleep to the twists and turns of a man thirsty for cash. He himself had no use for the hefty paycheck Alex provided. It was more than he needed. Beau had long ago learned the benefits of living a frugal life, and of getting by. A man used to living in Army barracks or on the street, didn't need much. Just his pride and his damned finger!

Two hours later, Beau woke as the cab slowed on an off-ramp. Night had fallen and there was no sign of his teammates. Good deal. That'd make getting into Alex's gated community easy. Well, easier. The front entry had a guard shack, but Beau hadn't spotted any roving guards on the streets the time he'd been invited out here for a picnic.

Once off the interstate, he asked the cabbie to pull into the first all-night convenience store he came across. Scrambling inside, Beau purchased a prepaid phone, a burner. He'd left his cell behind in the hospital head, so Alex couldn't track him. Back in the cab, he tossed the plastic wrapping and plugged the new device into the portable power bank he'd snagged before he'd left his place. It'd charge that new phone in minutes.

Finally parked alongside the eight-foot, ivy-covered wall Alex lived behind, Beau handed over his American Express Platinum card and made an honest man happy.

"Want me to wait for you?" the cabbie asked as he ran the card and handed Beau his receipt.

Stuffing the paper into his jeans pocket, Beau shook his head. "No, but thank you, sir. I can take it from here."

The cabbie rolled his eyes. "I ain't no sir, but honest. I don't mind waiting for a guy like you, and I will give you a ride back to your place. Or wherever you want to go. For free. No charge. I'll be going that way anyway. Sounds like a good deal. I'd take it if I were you."

It was impossible to miss the blatant hope in the guy's voice. The older gent was kind enough. Maybe a little greedy, but Beau understood the hand-to-mouth rule that most blue-collared folks lived by. It was simply the law of the jungle. If you didn't make a buck, you didn't eat. But he didn't need witnesses, and he still had to get over the wall. That ought to be fun, him with a buggered-up hand that now ached like shit.

"You take care," Beau said by way of dismissal.

"If you say so, but..." The cabbie stalled, his gaze shifting to the thick gauze on Beau's hand. "If I may. Please, one word, just one. You seem like a nice young man, and I do not like to leave you out here, hurt like you are. It is late, and you're alone. You seem lost or sick, maybe. Are you? I can help. Trust me. I know people."

Beau shook his head. *Trust me.* The first thing everyone said before they walked out on a guy or stabbed him in the back. Yeah, he was plenty tired—of users. But he wasn't sick, not in the physical sense. Well, except for his hand. That hurt like a son-of-a-bitch.

"Don't worry about me. I'm not sick, but as you can see, I, umm, did hurt my hand. You happen to have anything on you for pain?" He lifted said bandaged mitt. "I left home without my meds. Just need a couple aspirin to get by, that's all. Nothing serious and I don't want any narcotics. I'm no addict, just an idiot who left his Lortab behind." *Or whatever that prescription was I'm supposed to get filled.*

Why doctors sent written prescriptions home with critically ill patients, who, by the way, couldn't get to the Walgreens on the corner because they were sick, made no sense. But Beau wished he'd made that stop now.

"I have just the thing." The accommodating fellow flipped his visor down and produced one of those seven-day pillboxes older people used.

Shit. Now Beau felt guilty on top of stupid. Stealing from the poor or elderly was not how he rolled. Even on the street, they were the ones he looked out for, at least as much as a homeless kid looked out for anyone. "Never mind, I can't take that from—"

"Yes, please, sure you can. I give to you. For your hand. You are my friend, and friends help each other, yes?"

Beau looked closer as his 'friend' leaned over the back of the seat and dumped seven tiny little pills into his palm. "What are they?"

"Eighty-milligram aspirin. Cherry flavored." The cabbie said proudly as he thumped his chest. "I have a bad heart, but these little pills keep it ticking. Ha! I am like a Timex. I take a licking and keep on ticking. Get it?"

No, I don't get it. You're giving me baby aspirin, when I could use a handful of Vicodin? Beau chucked all seven into his mouth, tossed his head back, and swallowed. Low-dose aspirin was not what he'd had in mind, but hey. *Beggars can't be choosers.*

Climbing out of the cab, he stretched. Carefully. His leather jacket creaked in the midnight silence. Every movement radiated up his arm and into the throbbing stump under his well-wrapped left hand. *She cut off my finger. The bitch!*

"Hey, sir, before you leave…" The cabbie leaned out his window. "I just want to say…"

Now what? "Yes?" Beau asked respectfully.

This guy right here and the millions like him were the reasons Beau had enlisted. He'd done it for honest folks. Hard working folks. The silent American majority. Jesus, he loved them. It hadn't hurt that he'd been down on his luck when he'd run into an Army recruiter in Las Vegas. But from that point on, his best days had been spent knowing he'd served and defended people who were just like him. Not assholes who lived in cry-me-a-river, I'm-moving-to-Canada-because-I-didn't-get-my-way, wah-wah-wah Hollywood. Not Uncle Sam, either. Just. Regular. People.

The cabbie's eyes gleamed in the golden glow of the streetlights. "You're on a quest. I can tell. Once I searched for something, too. I hope you find it like I did. I just hope you're happy when you get what you think you want so bad that you came all this way in the middle of the night." *Whatever that meant.* "Be well, sir. Do not take any wooden nickels."

"Goodnight," Beau replied to get this talkative guy to leave. He had work to do, not enough strength to get it done, and he doubted the cabbie knew what that old timer's saying meant.

Turning his back on the cab, Beau walked a few steps, waiting to hear tires on the street as it rolled away. But it didn't. Forced to take action he wasn't quite up to, Beau stuck his chin to his chest and jogged the stretch of wall beside him. That was one problem he hadn't foreseen. Cabbies weren't supposed to care.

At the end of the wall, he came to an industrial-sized electrical box hidden in the shrubs strategically planted at the corner. *That'll work.*

Glancing back at the cab still parked at the curb with its headlights still on, he hoped the cabbie had dozed off. As handily as he could, Beau scaled the box, hoisted his aching body over the wall, and was finally inside.

Now, to backtrack to where he'd last seen Alex's evil neighbor.

Chapter Fourteen

Glad to be home, McKenna lounged for hours in her tub with a good book and a bottle of *Soft Huckleberry* from Idaho's lovely *Ste. Chapelle* Winery. She'd come here to relax, so of course she'd ignored the urgent pounding at her front door hours earlier. She knew who it was.

Had to be Maverick, which was why she'd sunk further into her tub until water settled over her ears and muffled the noise. The man was handsome as sin, but he didn't bend to logical arguments why she needed to work. What would he have said if she'd let him in? Yeah, not going there. She would've been dragged out the door to somewhere he deemed safe. Somewhere he could keep an eye on her. Or he would've camped out in her secluded little apartment and followed her to work every day.

That simply wasn't going to happen. She didn't want to hear his high-pressure pitch or face his wrath. So she'd stayed in her tub and took an extra-long swallow of wine to steady her nerves and reinforce her decision. She had a life to get back to and patients who needed her. In a couple days. As soon as everything calmed down. After Maverick caught that crazy, finger-stealing woman.

After the banging finally stopped, and her heart resumed a semi-normal rhythm, McKenna experienced a tiny bit of guilt for running out on Maverick and Gabe like she had. For being ungrateful. Alex and his men meant well, but the whole concept of protective custody reminded her of all those times she'd been locked inside dark closets for hours on end. Okay, so the two had nothing in common. Protective custody was a good thing, while closets and small dark places were definite triggers, but still. She just couldn't do it.

"I'll call Alex as soon as I get out of this tub," she reasoned out loud. "He's a professional. He'll understand."

That actually sounded good, like something Alex would agree to. But after her fingertips were sufficiently pruned, the last swallow of wine gone, and the last of her hot water used—*because how long can a woman stay in the tub?*—McKenna knew better. Alex would be just as stubborn and unyielding as Maverick and Gabe.

Instead of placing that well-intentioned call, she dallied in her seldom-used kitchen and prepared a pan of her dad's favorite Chicken Alfredo. Craving a carb overload after her exciting day, she toasted two slices of garlic bread in her oven. Besides, she needed something to absorb all the wine. Then, with a glass of sparkling water, she settled down in a pair of flannel pajamas in front of her television to watch the late-night news while she feasted. After all, why wake the man now, right? Apologies could wait until morning. After he'd had a good night's sleep. When she felt braver.

But as the news proved to be less information and more celebrity drama than she cared to know, McKenna rethought her previous plan. She should at least let Alex know where she was and that she was safe. That was only fair. But the hour *was* late, and by then, she was seriously embarrassed for the way she'd acted.

Instead of texting Kelsey and begging forgiveness for over-reacting—another good idea—McKenna clicked off the television and shuffled back to her kitchen. She washed her dinner dishes in the sink instead of stuffing them in the dishwasher. Then she proceeded into her home office, intent on burying her guilt by transcribing her own notes for transfer to Margo's inbox come morning. Wouldn't she be surprised?

For hours, procrastination and diversion kept McKenna's mind busy, her hands occupied, and her conscience quiet. But around one thirty in the morning, the house phone rang. Interesting. "Dad?" she asked, concerned. "What's—?"

"Doctor Fitzgerald?" a woman interrupted, her voice uncommonly brittle and certainly not one McKenna recognized.

"Yes, what can I do for you?" She knew everyone at the center. Who was this person? "Is this about my father?" *Please say no.*

"It's not what you can do for me. It's what I can do for you."

That sounded ominous. "Who is this and what do you want? Are you selling something?" Man, the world was full of telephone scammers these days. The nerve of some people!

"I'm a friend. In fact, I can be your very good friend if you let me. You father is Sanders Fitzgerald, is that right?"

Panic climbed up McKenna's throat. This was no courtesy or spam call. "What's going on?"

"Why don't you come to your door and find out?"

Afraid for her dad, McKenna flew to her door and undid the lock. "Who are you?" she asked again as she opened her door and scanned the white painted railing behind the woman standing there. "And where's my father?"

"How would I know? You're a physician. You work at the family practice clinic on Rosewood Drive."

"So?" McKenna blinked at those odd info-bytes. Was this about her dad or did this woman need a doctor? "If you've been spying on me, you know I help lots of people. That's what doctors do. Is that why you're here?"

"You take care of men who lost, say… a finger?" The stranger cocked her head in an oddly coy way, revealing a long slender neck inked with tattoos, as well as a thick, black braid coiled over one shoulder like a snake. Long black skirt. Silvery bracelets jangled at her wrist.

This can't be her. Just. No.

But only Catalina Montego would know about Beau's missing finger. Because she'd taken it. Which was why she now stood on McKenna's very private front porch. She'd somehow seen and then tracked the physician who'd assisted Beau. Well after midnight. On the same day McKenna had foolishly ditched the protection she should've enjoyed. Relished. Appreciated!

Montego's skirt rustled as she aimed a gun at McKenna's chest. "Let me in, child."

McKenna's heart jumped up into her throat. *Oh, crap.*

Chapter Fifteen

Beau landed hard on his feet in someone's backyard. But not in a bramble of thorns this time, which would've been his luck. No motion sensor lights flashed on. No alarms sounded. Both good signs that not everyone in this neighborhood was as compulsively paranoid as Alex. But damn, his wounded hand throbbed like it was on fire. That was the thing about injuries. The wicked pain from surgery now radiated up his arm, stormed over his shoulder like a cat-o-nine-tails on steroids, and stretched its nerve racking claws up his neck. A migraine threatened. He'd have to rest soon. After. Not now. But damned soon.

Swallowing hard, Beau headed east toward Stewarts', cradling his injured hand against his chest to manage the pain as well as his nerves. There was no need to jog. The neighborhood was quiet, locked down for the night, and he had time. But he worried he'd undone what Dr. Decker had painstakingly accomplished. For a small thing, that baby finger certainly lit up every last nerve ending in his body.

It was too bad some things couldn't wait, but finding that maniacal woman before she got her hooks into anyone else was definitely one of them. Beau endured his misery because his gut kept talking. It wasn't telling him it needed food, though a hot dinner would've been nice. No, this annoying pain registered deep, low, and annoying. It wasn't so much heartburn and nausea, as the same hollow feeling that hounded him since he'd hit the streets as a kid. The gnawing sensation that something was drastically wrong with the universe.

It hadn't taken long for a kid gone feral to develop the basest survival instincts. Honed razor-sharp after a few years in the Army, those instincts were all that kept a guy in the line of fire alive. And Beau had been in the line of fire since he could walk.

"Yeah, life's a bitch and then you die," he grumbled to himself. "Get over it, asshole."

But those finely tuned, keep-me-alive instincts were screaming now. Telling him to be more careful than he'd ever been on any night patrol. By the time he arrived at the home with the desert landscape job gone horribly wrong, he was edgy. The police tape strung along and over the fence meant nothing to a guy who'd lived outside the law for most of his first fifteen years. Lifting the long, yellow tape between him and the front walk, he ducked into the yard he'd narrowly escaped from days earlier.

Icy fingers tiptoed up the back of his bare neck as he approached the front door. No motion detecting lights flashed to life. No alarm sounded. Not like that meant anything. Silent alarms could be just as deadly. He glanced over his shoulder, sure someone was watching. But nothing in the shadows moved, so he continued as planned.

More tape blocked the massive double entryway with a great big X, as if flimsy plastic could keep anyone out. He twisted the knob, but the way was locked. No big surprise there. Looking over his shoulder one last time, Beau still detected nothing behind him but the middle of a long dark night and plenty of dead air.

Let's do this then but be smart. Break and enter through the side door.

Rounding the front corner of the home on his way to said smart entry, he came upon a bizarre sight. One tall and butt-ugly saguaro cactus stood in his way. He hadn't noticed it on his run for freedom. The poor prickly thing looked out of place, and it was dying, its limbs emaciated and twisted from too much moisture. Yet there it stood, holding a pair of shears hooked over one arm some maniacal gardener had left behind like an unwilling but valiant helper. *What the fuck?*

Intent on following correct protocol while breaking the law, Beau pulled one of the surgical gloves he'd lifted from his hospital room out of his jacket pocket. All evidence from the front doorknob had already been compromised, but not this. After he pulled the cuff of the glove over his wrist with his teeth, he reached one-handed up into the saguaro and tugged the tool free of its lofty perch. Carefully, he avoided the cactus spines that would stick to him like burrs on a dog's ass if he were dumb enough to bump them.

Interesting. The shears were a hefty, scissor-type implement, its blades sharp and clean, with a divot machined into one of them. Intended for heavy pruning, the divot provided a tight stop where branches—or fingers—could be trapped before being lopped off. Just looking at the finely-honed blade made his reattached pinkie hurt even more. So why were the shears left behind, and who'd left them? Were the police blind that they'd missed them?

Beau glanced over his shoulder to the front entry where most of the police action would've taken place. He could see how this lack of discovery might've gone down. The way the shears had been stuck open, its blades extended in an X, and its handles over the arm of the saguaro, it could've looked like a branch to a detective in a hurry. Possibly. The cactus *was* butt-ugly. Its arms were more like sticks. Who would've given it a second glance? Not anyone in this neighborhood, where each home truly was built as an island unto itself.

So yeah. A harried detective or officer on the run, possibly one who'd been shaken at the gruesomeness of what he'd seen inside Ringer's, could've missed the shears. But wasn't Montego clever to have hidden a piece of evidence in plain sight? She'd made them look normal. Damn, she was good.

Unlike tract housing built in sprawling moderate-income suburbs, each of these lavish homes had been designed by different architects for pretentious millionaires. Each was unique, and all were mansions. Some stone. Some cedar. Some impressive brick sculptures to their owners' wealth and success. All the yards were wide and deep, some wider than others.

Stewarts' home two doors east of Congressman Ringer's sat dead center, just like a bulls-eye, in an extra-wide double lot. No doubt Alex planned the house and the yard himself. While the two-foot thick granite wall fenced the immediate yard and protected the house, an impenetrable forest Beau knew for a fact held enough security cameras, traps, and triggers to rival Fort Knox, stretched beyond and behind the house just outside that fence. Which was why Beau had been able to vault over the side fence when he'd escaped Montego. Alex hadn't planted any trees there. They would've ruined a clear shot.

His backyard was something different. On a bad day, Whisper and Smoke made it an intruder's worst nightmare. On a good day or when the dogs were inside, the wide expanse held a butt-load more cameras. And every last one of those lenses, when activated, pinged an alarm to the app on Alex's phone, as well as to the matching apps at Mother's desk and at local police dispatch. Alex didn't mess with security companies to contact the police for him, not since his business put most of them to shame.

Beau had heard the scuttlebutt how Gabe killed a man inside Stewarts' former home in Alexandria. Gabe had nearly died that night. Kelsey hadn't been there at the time, but Alex wasn't a man who took chances, which was why they'd moved out here. Like any husband who adored his wife, he'd forbidden her to set foot back in their first home ever again. Then he'd built this stone monument to her, and he made sure no one could get close to his family without him knowing it. If Beau recalled correctly, another agent, Jake Weylin and his wife had recently purchased Stewarts' old place when it hit the market as a fixer-upper. Talk about one freaky coincidence.

Not that the rest of these homes hadn't also been built for maximum privacy. No two entries or driveways faced each other. Between each dwelling, either a berm or some type of natural privacy shield blocked most owners' views of each other.

These people never had to look at each other at the butt crack of dawn on their way out the door like common residential dwellers. Beau doubted these folks even knew their neighbors. Hell, most of them probably didn't work as much as they *managed* their wealth. Their stock portfolios.

Investments. Assets. Things Beau was just learning about since he'd started working for Alex.

"Where are you, you evil bitch?" Beau hissed as he scanned Ringer's side yard, the lopping shears still in his hand. Equally sized maples lined this portion of the lawn, starting at the front fence line. Wasn't that an odd landscape design, a badly managed desert scene in the front yard, but hardwood trees all in a row on the side? Dumb. Who was the senator trying to impress?

Sticking to the shadows, Beau located Ringer's side door between two expansive bay windows. Approaching cautiously, he licked his lips, edgier than when he'd searched Syrian homes for insurgents. This time was different. He'd left something behind and he wanted it back. His nerve.

Tucking the shears under his bad arm, he released the holster's snap over the pistol stored there. Disgust quirked the corner of his mouth. Out of habit, he'd strapped on his twin holster before leaving home, and because he was a dumbass, he carried two loaded pistols, one under each arm. Like he needed two weapons? This one-handed business was going to take some getting used to. He just hoped his rash decision to throw caution to the wind today hadn't made it permanent.

Ringer's place was now dark and quiet. Once inside, Beau flipped the wall light switch that brightened the dining room. Carefully, he set the shears on the counter between that room and the adjoining kitchen. It was obvious the police had come and gone. Placards and tags where forensic photos had been taken were scattered everywhere. Discarded booties and gloves lay on the floor and counters. Drawers, closets, and cupboards had been left open. Crap like that.

Beau froze at sight of the wooden table where he'd been restrained like meat to be sliced and diced. It was a surprising piece of furniture for a house as fine as this one. Whereas most wealthy people would've had a pricy, pretty carved wooden piece of art on display, this was nothing but a coarse workbench, a rough construct of recently purchased lumber, not even sanded.

Grabbing the nearest corner, he gave it a shake. Hell, the legs weren't balanced. Dried blood where his left wrist had been cuffed told a gruesome story. So did the bloody smears he'd left behind in his panic to get away.

It wasn't a chopping block, yet it might have become one. Stapled price tags still adorned the ends of the four-by-fours. Why would Montego have gone to the trouble of building her own table? What was she—? Erase that thought. He knew precisely what she was—one crazy bitch.

His skin crawled to see this instrument of torture up close again. To remember. He'd come damned close to not escaping that psychotic she-devil. If not for the sheer terror at what she would've done had she caught him...

Panic raced through him as he recalled the moment she'd opened the side door and caught him in the act of escaping. Gut-wrenching terror had pretty much scrambled his instincts then. He'd been so close. Seconds. His being alive today had come down to the mere seconds it had taken him to jerk his ankle out of that last cuff. He'd damned near taken his foot off in the process. Honestly. He had no idea how he'd gotten away. Jesus must've been looking out for him. That was the only explanation Beau could come up with. He surely hadn't saved himself.

But damn her to Hell. She'd emasculated him, first by taking his finger, then by taking his courage. Making him run when he should've manned up and knocked her on her ass. When he should've ended her. That troubled him most. He'd damned near shit his pants like a scared little kid on that table. *Freakin' bitch!*

Beau took a deliberate step back from Montego's wretched *workbench*. Things didn't add up. How had she, a mere woman, abducted a grown man from a bar in the District? How had she then driven him to this particular neighborhood, only to wrangle him out of a car, drag him in through Ringer's house, and cuff him to that table? Then she returned to Crystal City to leave Alex a threat? Seemed like a helluva a lot for one woman to manage alone and in one night.

For that matter, where were the Ringers? He'd lost part of a finger. What had they lost? Their lives? During recovery, he'd overheard Maverick and Gabe chatting about the multiple plastic containers of bloody DNA evidence the police recovered from Ringer's freezer. Was that where they'd ended up?

Everywhere he looked, he now saw instruments of torture. The meat grinder was gone but the black puddles on the floor remained. Shit, what a nightmare.

He knew how the date-rape drug worked. That crap was easy to drop into an unsuspecting guy's glass in the middle of a busy bar, but it was what had happened after he'd been drugged that made no sense. He was no tiny, little thing. For certain, Catalina Montego hadn't acted alone, but if she'd truly intended to torment Alex, the prevailing theory between Gabe and Maverick, why hadn't she waited until Beau came to, and then filmed him being brutalized for Alex's viewing pleasure? That seemed a more sensational way for a sadist to get a former Marine's attention. Film it. Broadcast it. Put it on YouTube for the rest of the world to watch, while Alex sweated bullets because he couldn't make it stop.

It turned Beau's stomach to think how close he'd come to dying. Taking another step back, he swallowed the bile pooling at the back of his throat. If he hadn't been drugged, he would've screamed his guts out when she'd lopped his pinkie off. But if she'd really wanted to send Alex a disturbing message, filming the diabolical stunt would've done so much more psychological damage. *Torture. Slice off body part after body part. Laugh while her victim screamed. You know, the grisly crap ISIS is so good at filming and exploiting.*

Alex would've come unglued. Surely listening to his agent scream for mercy would've wrecked him more than just finding that agent passed out and bleeding in his kitchen. But Beau hadn't been gagged, and he would've made plenty—PLENTY—of noise. Was that why the evil bitch hadn't taken more extreme tactics? Was she afraid of that noise? Or was she afraid of Alex?

Weary of the puzzle and the threatening migraine, Beau slanted his weary eyes, needing to see what he was missing. After standing there for another few minutes, he wasn't any wiser. There was no more evidence. He would call local dispatch and tell them what he had found stuck in the cactus the first chance he got. He'd tell them who he was and admit to the B and E. After that, he'd hunt Montego down and make her pay.

His left arm had grown oddly numb, a disconcerting development for which he didn't want to imagine the ramifications, permanent nerve damage or worse—being a one-handed guy for the rest of his life. Time to go.

Unnerved, Beau backed to the side door and turned the light off. The place looked downright creepy in the dark, as if Montego's evil spirit lingered. As if she could reach out and touch him. Cut him. Make him bleed. Hurt him again. Like his old man had.

The Montego siblings were renowned in the law enforcement community for their level of extreme brutality. Sadists got off on torturing their victims. How well Beau knew. So where was Catalina now? Who was she torturing? Who wasn't safely stowed behind the stone walls that Alex built?

Only one face sprang to mind. *Doc Fitzgerald. McKenna. That's who.*

Chapter Sixteen

"Why are you doing this to me?" McKenna whimpered, not her usual style. But this bitch was crazy with a capital K. Dressed in a slinky, black, short-sleeved shirt over an equally black broomstick skirt, Catalina was a vision of unholy terror. A truly evil witch. Since she'd possessed the only weapon in the place, she'd had no problem forcing McKenna into her bedroom, then to undress down to her underwear and onto her back on the bed.

But what Catalina did now was just plain sick. She'd stretched McKenna's arms between the top posts of her four-poster bed, then snapped a spring-loaded clamp onto each of her palms, effectively pinning McKenna like a frog about to be dissected in junior high biology class. The clamps themselves were connected to chains nailed to the top posts of the four-poster bed. There was no way to escape.

Which frightened the hell out of McKenna. Someone had been inside her apartment, possibly since she'd come home, setting this in motion. Maybe while she'd been dallying in her tub, playing like a spoiled, privileged brat who thought she knew better than her trained bodyguards. Her stomach pitched acid up her throat at the terrifying thought.

With every tug, the clamps dug into the thin bones and tender flesh of McKenna's hands. To make matters worse, metal teeth lined the clamps. With every tiny move, those teeth chewed deeper, inciting the nerve-endings throughout the rest of her body.

But when Catalina stretched wires across McKenna's hips, then under her breasts, McKenna could no longer control herself. She bucked and screamed, certain that death was minutes away. Only when Catalina jerked the wires until they were tight and cutting, then attached the ends, somehow, to the sides of the bed frame for maximum agony, did McKenna cease thrashing.

Finally, Catalina looped another wire around McKenna's neck, which only frightened her more. When Montego tugged at what resembled a fishing reel now clamped to the foot of the bed, the wire beneath McKenna's jaw jerked her chin up. Her heart faltered. *This can't be happening to me!*

But it was. With every small move McKenna made, the wires rubbed across her skin. Eventually, they'd saw through the tougher epidermis and dermis layers and into the blood-rich subcutaneous tissue where nerves ran like electrical networks. Where veins pulsed with oxygen-rich, red blood. Slicing deeper, the wires finally rendered her helpless at Montego's mercy. Her throat was bleeding. McKenna could smell it. A warm pool gathered in the hollow of her neck. *Get me out of here!*

But help would not be coming. She'd made sure of that, when she'd thought she was clever and eluded Maverick and Gabe. Here she would die, dressed only in her underwear, erotically and disgustingly displayed for the investigating officers—when they showed—in all her gruesome, but dead, glory. *God, please don't let Beau be with them.*

Why her brain sought him out of her short list of would-be rescuers, McKenna didn't know, other than he seemed like her. Lost. Wondering where he fit in. If he belonged...

As Catalina went around the bed tightening the screws that reduced the slack in those wires, McKenna fought her panic and tears. No one would know what happened here tonight until it was too late. Quivering from pain and the shock of being tortured, she had no choice but to bear it. This was her fault, every last bit of it. Maverick, Gabe, and Alex had tried to warn her.

Grinding her teeth at her stiff-necked stupidity, she focused on the ceiling overhead. Her father's perpetually cheerful smile came to mind. She'd been so lucky to have him in her life. He'd never let her down, and this would hurt him terribly once her body was discovered. The fear that he might be the one to find her, that he'd come looking for her when she didn't call tomorrow, pained McKenna to her soul.

I love you, Dad. I'm sorry. If I don't live through this, please stay strong. This isn't your fault, it's mine. I'm the truly stupid one, not you. Never give up, okay? And oh yeah, tell Stu he plays a lousy game of chess. The unexpected optimism that thought brought to her heart, nearly made her smile. Any other time, insulting Stu would've been funny. Not tonight.

There was nothing she could do, so McKenna forced herself to think like Sanders. *But hey, how about all the children I serve every day? Every last one of them has enriched my life in ways they'll never know.* She'd loved them both selfishly and selflessly. They'd been her substitutes for the children she'd never planned to have.

Instead of marching into motherhood as so many of her generation had, instead of shacking-up or marrying the first guy who asked, she'd chosen the safer path. She'd gone to college, studied hard, then marched onto medical school with the high and mighty goal of working miracles to save children's lives and to help their mothers. To serve and protect every last one of them.

So what if she'd only doctored and nursed other people's kids? She'd never experienced a deep-seated biological need to have her own. Why should she? Even the best mothers had bad days and made horrible mistakes. They got impatient, overworked, and overtired. When they did, sometimes they lashed out, and occasionally, they hurt the ones they loved most—their children. Not McKenna. She'd never do that because she'd set herself apart and never planned to be a mother. That way she ensured she'd cause no harm to any child or mother. Ever. It was safer that way.

"You're much too quiet, my little dumpling," Catalina murmured, her voice a slick, evil whisper that crept over McKenna's skin in the dark like the belly of a cold-blooded snake.

Tug. Tug. The wire forced McKenna's chin a notch higher. Stretched her neck tighter. By then she could only stare at the wall above her headboard. She didn't dare try to look at the wicked woman at the foot of her bed. Hell, she could barely see the ceiling. Her peripheral vision was that compromised with her neck forced up like it was. If she so much as arched her back, the wires laced across her body responded with sharp, stinging bites.

But now, the air smelled of smoke and incense. Catalina kept humming something low and rumbling, almost chanting. What was that about?

"What do you want?" McKenna whispered. "Why are you doing this? I've never hurt you."

The wire noose at her neck relaxed a tiny bit as the swish of the broomstick skirt told McKenna that Catalina was now at her right side. "Oh, but you have," she crooned as she ran her fingertips over McKenna's brow. "But that's not why we're here, is it?"

"Then why" —McKenna gulped— "why are we here? What do you want from me?"

"I want what you took from me, Dr. Fitzgerald, and since I can't get that back, I've decided you'll do. In exchange for your life, I need information. Ready to talk?"

Montego had tortured Beau for information? That didn't make sense. From what he'd told Alex, he woke already cuffed to a table and missing his finger. Where was the information gathering in torturing an unconscious man? McKenna blinked to keep her panic at bay. "What do you want to know?"

The woman leaned too close to McKenna's ear for comfort. "Tell me about Alex Stewart's wife. Kelsey, isn't it? You like her, don't you? Is she a good mother? She's really quite lovely, isn't she? What does she like to eat? What restaurants does she frequent when her husband's out of town? Where does she shop? When? Every day, or does she prefer evenings? Does she always take that precocious little girl with her when she leaves her monstrosity of a house? Is that daughter ever alone? Does she sleep in her own room?"

This was about hurting Kelsey. No way. McKenna would rather die than betray Alex or his sweet wife. Never Lexie. Those three were a genuine love story in motion. They deserved to live more than McKenna did. Thinking fast, she focused on Beau to keep the spotlight off them. "You mean Beau Jennings? You replaced him with me? He's why I'm here? B-because he eluded you, and I helped him?"

She received another motherly swipe over her forehead for that, and along with it came the sickening anise scent of black licorice. "I have no idea what you're talking about but do keep talking. You'll get there."

McKenna licked her lips, her mind pinging at the dire situation. This wasn't about Beau? Then what? "I… I really don't know anything about him. He was just a one-time patient, not even mine once the ambulance took him away. The only reason I was at Stewarts was because I was on call for my clinic's acute care patients. I'm just a pediatrician." Surely Catalina knew Beau required specialized orthopedic surgery after what she'd done to him, not a sucker from McKenna's candy drawer. "I take care of babies. Mothers."

"I like babies," Catalina whispered encouragingly, rubbing her chin over McKenna's cheek, her breath heavy with the scent of licorice. "Then start taking care of this little girl" —she tapped her fingernail to the center of McKenna's forehead— "or mommy's going to be upset, and you know what will happen. Tell me about Kelsey Stewart, child. Tell me about her little girl. Lexie, right? Does she talk yet? Does she cry? Tell me everything you know."

Damn! I'm back in the closet, only this woman's crazier than Mom.

Chapter Seventeen

It was a good thing the cabbie ended up being a stubborn old fart. He was right where Beau left him, the engine running, and his head tilted out his window in that quiet, I-know-better-than-you way that Beau was beginning to recognize. And respect.

"Need a ride?" the kindly gentleman asked.

"I do," Beau admitted easily. He didn't often make friends, but this guy had gotten under his skin just by being nice.

"Hand still hurt?"

Beau nodded. Hurt, nothing. The sensation in it had gone from a tingling numbness to hot-out-of-the-furnace throbbing. Maybe even glowing under all that gauze.

He'd stored his pistol once he'd left the crime scene, but that last leap over the wall hadn't done his injury any good. Despite his leather jacket, he shivered. Yeah, he knew he was feverish, and stupid for being out here. But cradling his arm and damaged hand no longer staved off the pain. He knew now why wolves chewed their paws off when they stepped in those vicious steel-toothed traps. Missing a limb couldn't hurt any worse.

Oh, wait. Scratch that. A missing finger was what started all this.

After Beau dropped his tired ass onto the back seat of the cab, he met his benefactor's questioning gaze in the rearview. It was time to get personal. "What's your name?"

The guy stretched one arm over the seat to shake hands as he grinned a truly face-splitting smile. "It's Ethiopian, and quite long. Most Americans find it too hard to pronounce. You may call me Marcus."

Beau clamped onto the cabbie's long-fingered grip. "I know a Mark. Good name. Good guy. Thanks for sticking around, Marcus. I'm Beau Jennings."

"You are a soldier," he said quietly, his gaze lowered as if he had something to fear.

"Was. Not anymore," Beau assured him. "Former Army. How'd you know?"

"By way you walk and how you hold your head up, Mr. Jennings. You are suffering, yet you still walk with purpose. You are a good man."

It's funny how people see what they want. But Beau knew better. If anything, he walked alone, and he never let his guard down.

"It *is* very late," Marcus said.

Beau shook his head at the implied question. "Got one more stop. I'll go home then." *Maybe.*

"But you don't look so good, son."

Son. Another word Beau craved but hadn't heard much during his twenty-some years. Not unless *son-of-a-bitch* counted. He was no one's son, just the bastard offspring of a two-bit pimp who ran his girls into the dirt, then demanded they clean up and be ready to debase themselves again the next morning, afternoon, whenever. Nothing to be proud of there.

Instead of answering, he huffed out a weary breath, lowered his head, and pulled his cell from his jacket pocket to search online for Dr. Fitzgerald. *Fitz. Interesting name for a pretty woman.*

A profile picture from a nearby family practice clinic popped up in his browser. Searching further, he located her home address and passed it over the seat. "This is where I need to go."

Marcus nodded, and the cab moved forward. It didn't take more than five, six minutes to get to Fitzgerald's street address. She lived in one of three apartments carved out of a rambling colonial hidden behind a cluster of birch trees, their barks gleaming white amidst the shadows.

But Beau was beat, and he was stupid out of his mind for thinking he could find Montego all by himself. Or that she'd even come here.

His hand throbbed all the way up his aching neck to the top of his pounding head. By now, there wasn't a part of his body that didn't cry for relief from this marathon day. He'd worked through plenty ops when he'd been sick or injured, but never in this much pain.

The Army's killer/hunter teams operated by twos. Always one shooter. Always one spotter. He'd worked with more than one team at a time, but he couldn't recall once that he'd been singled out to go after a target alone. So, yeah. Stupid out of his mind, that was what he was.

"I will wait for you," the cabbie stated.

Damn, the meter wasn't running. This guy was working for free. That made Beau's decision easier. "No need. I'm calling the game. Let's head home."

"As you should," Marcus agreed with a single nod. "It will be my privilege to bring you back to this very place tomorrow, if you would like to continue your quest."

Yeah, that's me all right, a fuckin' knight of the round table on a quest for the unholy grail and the witch who stole it along with my finger.

"Nah." Sighing, Beau stopped being a hero. He was wrong. Doc Fitz was right. She won. Fine by him. She'd kept arguing against Alex's protection order, and really. How would Catalina Montego have known McKenna's name, where she worked or where she lived? Montego wasn't one of those clairvoyant killers in horror flicks out of Hollywood. Weary to his soul, Beau pointed toward the windshield and said, "Home."

"Very good," Marcus murmured. "I will wake you when we arrive at your apartment building. Rest easy, my friend."

As if Beau could. Glancing into the night, he wondered what the hell he'd been thinking coming here. Doc Fitzgerald didn't need protection. She was one of those lucky, pretty folks, the ones karma smiled on without them having to do a damned thing but rise and shine every morning. Yeah. She didn't need rescuing.

He'd almost convinced himself when a gallon of acid unleashed in his gut. "Wait," blurted out of his mouth before he knew he'd spoken. There were no lights on the property. Not. A. One.

Marcus eyed him in the rearview. "You are going," was all he said.

"Won't be long," Beau replied, his hand on the door handle.

"Is no problem," Marcus said as he turned the engine off. "I wait. I will be here."

Beau clapped the old guy's shoulder before he bailed. "Thanks, man. I'll make it worth your while when I get back. But lock your doors okay? Be safe."

The older gentleman smiled. "Trust me, I will do that. For you."

On his feet again, Beau adjusted to the searing pain enveloping the left side of his body. If motion was lotion, sitting on his ass was atrophy. From hipbone to the top of his hard head, every last muscle felt like unholy shit stacked steaming hot in his work boots. But this was what Rangers did. They bucked up and they got the ugly jobs done, no matter the personal cost. Gritting his teeth, he ventured forth.

Except for the single gas lamp on at the curb, no lights glimmered from any windows in the house ahead. The first apartment he came to wasn't Fitzgerald's number, though. He kept going. Skirting the shrubbery lining the walkway that led to the rear of the building and parking lot, he palmed his pistol once more, the barrel down, the weapon hidden against his black jeans.

The next apartment wasn't hers, either. No, Doc Fitz had to live all the way around back. Not smart as dark and quiet as it was. A place like this should've been lit with industrial outdoor security lights. Motion detectors. Something. But just like the Ringers, Doc Fitz had probably put her faith in what? Another hollow-core door that wouldn't keep shit out?

Grumbling to himself for no reason other than this day sucked, Beau kept going. He didn't care what people did these days, or if they took sufficient precautions to protect themselves. Their safety was none of his business, and it wouldn't matter if it was. Most people thought they knew everything. There was no sense talking to them, much less educating them. The first words out of their big mouths were always, "I know." Like hell they did.

His boot had no more than settled on the stairs leading to McKenna's door, when Beau's gut twisted up a storm. It hit him then. The lights on this entire property were all off for a reason. He approached with extreme caution, his pistol up, his head canted, and his senses flared to detect what the hell was happening inside the house. Palming McKenna's front door, it opened inward. The damned thing had been left unlocked.

A rush of adrenaline flooded Beau as he ducked inside, then closed the door quietly behind him. The place was dark, but he wasn't alone. A lone female voice spoke from the hallway at his right, heavy with—something. Drugs, maybe. Alcohol? The voice was odd and sing-songy, the pitch uncommonly low. Guttural. Chanting about revenge, revenge, revenge. Then about love and sisters and family. About blood being thicker than life. Weird shit like that. Had to be Catalina Montego.

Stealthily, with his senses strung tight, Beau advanced down the hall. Now was the moment he'd planned for. He could end her. Finish her reign of terror. There was nothing to stop him, and he was just that good. She needed to die and more than anything, he wanted to kill her. Until McKenna whimpered, "S-stop it. Please, stop."

What the fuck?

"Please! No more!"

And enough! Kicking the door in, Beau bellowed, "Freeze, bitch!" into the dark. He could barely make out

McKenna stretched out on the bed, her arms splayed wide, when a club came out of nowhere and pulverized his injured arm. That couldn't have hurt worse if lightning had struck, yet he didn't let loose of his pistol. Instead he fired one shot into the dark behind the door where that blow came from.

"I'm here to kill you!" he growled as the Ranger inside him stepped up to the plate to finish the job.

"Then try!" Montego cackled like some ghoul with a death wish.

Consider it granted. It was hard to track her in the black-as-sin room, though. Montego attacked again, ramming her head into his gut. Not smart. That put her close and personal, and—

SMACK! He pistol-whipped the bitch, but did that slow her down? Not so much. Growling, she launched again, but caught the heel of his palm with her nose instead. *Crunch. Squish!*

Beau curled his bandaged fingers and punched her full in the face with his bad hand, then backhanded her with his other hand, while angling to protect his now throbbing injury, the one he shouldn't have led with. Damned thing was buzzing like a son-of-a-bitchin' hornet nest. Maybe hitting her with that hand wasn't such a good idea. Of course, Montego knew his weakness, damn her, but she wasn't getting a second chance at it.

She dropped to the floor, but he'd expected that. Old dogs and old tricks. Instead of sweeping him with that lame roundhouse kick, he stomped her thigh.

An oddly masculine "Oomph!" rewarded his effort, but at that point, Beau's only plan was to kill her. Aiming his pistol, he took another shot at where he thought Montego crouched at floor level, when—

Shit!

She had one thing he didn't though. An LED flashlight. With one click, he was blind and running on pure Ranger instinct. She thought that chicken shit move gave her the upper hand? *Guess again, bitch.* He'd had years of experience in the dark tunnels and storm sewers beneath Las Vegas. Beau Jennings knew dark. She was *not* getting away.

He fired at the first rustle to his right. When she growled again like a psycho, the noise came low at his left. He dived after it, and oh, yeah, the bitch had hair. Grabbing a handful of the braid with his free hand, while still holding his pistol, he jerked her forward, then banged his forehead into her face.

When she grabbed for his left forearm, Beau knew what she intended. *No way. Not my injured hand again.*

Head-banging her, he jerked her braid back, meaning to tear that sucker out by the roots. She let loose a bloodcurdling roar instead of the girly scream he'd expected. This bitch put up one helluva fight, clawing his face, growling like a beast in that low, guttural voice. Angular and wiry, the woman was every bit as strong as a man. Except for her hair, there was nothing feminine about her. What the hell was she, a demon from Hell? Sure sounded like it.

Jerking her head back, he caught a knee to his groin. Should've seen that feminine trick coming. Damn, it hurt. Yeah, the bitch was vicious and cunning.

McKenna cried out. The outright terror in her voice distracted Beau. He let go of the braid. But instead of seizing the moment and killing him, Montego bit his bandaged hand again. Like the miserable spawn of Satan she was, that bite felt as if a mouthful of serrated teeth landed on his reattached finger. He dropped to his knees. The pain. The agony. *The bitch!*

By the time he could draw a breath mere seconds later, the bedroom door was wide open. Beau jumped to his feet, dizzy but gunning for blood. She would *not* get away this easy. Not this time. "I'll kill you!" he roared at her, blinded by rage.

A sudden draft came back to him, and he knew damned well a door or window had been opened. He followed, cursing and flipping wall switches as he went, but not lighting shit. Of course not. She'd cut the main power lines. Damned, evil woman.

Smart enough to know the wall switch for McKenna's gas fireplace wouldn't work, Beau didn't waste time trying. Instead, he cranked the valve on the wall beside the fireplace hearth, hit the pilot switch, and poof. Just like the Good Book said, God created light.

But by then, there was nothing to see. Canting his head, he listened for heavy breathing, but only heard McKenna's soft sobs from the back room. Jesus! Montego had gotten away.

Frustrated, Beau retraced his steps and slammed the bedroom door he'd burst through just minutes earlier. With his back to that door, he breathed hard, filled with enough piss and vinegar to extinguish the whole mother-fuckin'—

"B-Beau?" McKenna asked plaintively. "Is... is that really you?"

He took one step forward, when he stepped on something round and damned near fell on his ass. The witch left her flashlight behind. Beau flicked it on and—

Holy Jesus. The sight spread on the bed before him left him speechless. So much blood. Still armed, he flew to McKenna's side. "What the fuck did she do to you?"

"H-help me," McKenna cried, her eyes bright with fear even as she kept her chin up like she didn't want to look at him. He didn't blame her. He got that a lot.

But as she stared at the wall above her headboard… Shit. He saw it then. Them. The thinnest wires, more like fishing lines than wires, held McKenna fast to the mattress. One ran across her hips, another just under her breasts, and yet another looped around her neck. She wasn't afraid of him. She plain couldn't move. What the fuck, indeed.

Unsheathing the knife from his boot, Beau made quick work of the wires. Then—son-of-a-bitch! Very gently, he released the cruel clamps crushing McKenna's tiny hands and holding her arms in place. Montego was one sick piece of work.

"Ow, ow, ow," McKenna cried, her tone rapping higher as she lowered her arms and rubbed her palms even while blood trickled from the thin slice on her neck. "That h-h-hurts. It st-stings."

He bent over her, his thumbs pressing into her palms to get her circulation flowing again. "It's just the blood rushing back into your muscles and veins where it belongs. I promise. The pain will fade. You're a doctor. You know that."

"I do, b-b-but…" Shivers racked her slender body, sending her long legs bouncing on the mattress. "Hurts, Beau. Everything hurts."

"Don't move," he told her, needing to pack her wounds before she bled to death.

But did she listen? Uh-uh. Trembling and in obvious shock, she curled her quivering body into his. Into him. Him. The biggest loser in the universe. The wannabe. The forever castaway and the never good enough. And then she... oh Jesus, she cried. In his arms. Like a scared little girl. She pushed her nose into the wrinkles of his sweaty shirt and she wept.

What a powerful sensation to be so—trusted. Beau honestly didn't know what to do. He had no experience dealing with women as elegant or as smart as this lady. As dainty. He'd never dared. Street trash slummed with other street trash, never anyone better. They didn't social climb, and if they wanted to live, they stayed clear of decent folks. They weren't worthy or smart enough to know how to move from point A in the invisible castes of American society, up on the ladder of success to point B. Yet his arms seemed to know instinctively what to do. His injured hand rose above its pain, that same forearm pressing her into him, pulling her close to where she seemed determined to go. Against his chest. Against his heart.

His shoulders hunched over her like a gargoyle shielding a precious jewel from the evil world. His heart physically hurt as the tiniest tendrils of warmth trickled within it, as if the stone creature that he was could suddenly grow veins and chambers and—all the cardiac stuff.

"I've got you, baby," he murmured hoarsely, because that was what he'd said in the past, and he had no idea what else to say to a trembling, falling apart woman. Yet even as he still gripped his pistol in his free hand, his all-male body reacted to the feminine body it encased. Caging McKenna inside its tough, protective sinews and larger male bones. Shielding her from danger within its callused layers of skin and muscle. Its scars. This he knew how to do. Protect and serve. Rescue. Save.

Inexplicably, the tip of his nose dipped into the sweaty curls at the crown of her trembling head. His eardrums zeroed in on the rapid panting from her lips, and the throbbing beat of her pulse. Her panic felt like a flock of hummingbirds against his chest. His lips moved as his tongue uttered words he'd said before. "I've got you, baby. You're safe with me."

"I... I know," McKenna whimpered as she flattened her nose into his shirt, bleeding all over him. Drenching him. Blessing him.

You know? Honored beyond all earthly reason, Beau set his pistol on the mattress beside her rump, where he could reach it quickly. Digging into his jeans pocket, he palmed the burner phone he'd bought solely to avoid his employer. It was time to come clean.

Guess Marcus would be driving home alone tonight.

The number Beau dialed rang once. Beau didn't wait for his employer to speak before he told Alex Stewart, "I need your help."

Then, because he'd left Marcus unprotected, Beau tucked McKenna into her pillows. "There's something I've got to do. Don't move. I'll be right back."

"But—"

To calm her fear, he did something crazy. Beau kissed McKenna's sweaty forehead as if she were a little girl. "Trust me," he told her quietly. "You're safe now, Dr. Fitz, but I have to make sure my cabbie's safe, too."

"Oh," was all she whispered.

Beau had never run so hard or so fast in all his life. Out to the front of the building he hurried, where Marcus—thank you, Jesus—sat patiently waiting. It took seconds to make good on his promise to over-compensate his friend, but Beau needed the man gone and safely on his way home. Then, as if Satan were breathing down his neck, Beau ran back into the house. To McKenna. Murmuring all the way, "Hurry, Alex. Damn you, hurry!"

Chapter Eighteen

Alex couldn't have been more surprised when his cell rang. For the first time since Beau Jennings had joined The TEAM, he'd reached out. But instead of running to his wayward agent's rescue, Alex sent the pissed off agent who lived nearest McKenna's apartment, the one who'd spent all afternoon scouring the county looking for her and blaming himself for losing her.

But by the time Maverick arrived back with two belligerents who lacked the sense the good Lord gave them, both Kelsey and Libby Houston were up, and Alex was beyond pissed. His pig-headed junior agent had a butt-reaming coming. Beau would've gotten it the moment he'd staggered through the door, if not for the bloody woman curled inside his arms. And the fact that Kelsey and Libby took over before Alex could growl.

As fast as they could, the two anxious women ushered Beau and the sad lady in his arms into the ground level guestroom already prepared for them. Kelsey had the nerve to close the door in Alex's face. Not like that would've stopped him. But Maverick did.

"Boss, stop. He can't take it right now. Trust me. Beau's on his last legs. Did you get a good look at him?"

"I don't give a shit what he looks like. He's fired!"

"You don't mean that. You're just mad."

"Want to bet?" Alex barked. "What I don't need is someone who's too stubborn to listen, working for me. That's not how my TEAM works, damn it!"

Maverick nodded. "Understood, but Beau did exactly what we would've done. He tracked Montego. He would've had her if not for McKenna's injuries. I can't believe I'm defending him, but it's obvious he's injured, and he's just been in the fight of his life. Whoever he tangled with beat the shit out of him. You got a beer?"

Alex shot Maverick a death glare at that obvious segue. But he also rolled the tweak out of his neck, backed off, and let this come-to-Jesus meeting slide. For now.

"So talk," he ordered as he opened his bar, handed Maverick a frosty Sam Adams Lager from the fridge, and poured himself a Jameson. He needed fire in his gut. To hell with the ice. He knocked that shot back, then poured another, still breathing fire and brimstone, and pissed at his stiff-necked junior agent who had more balls than brains.

Maverick quenched his thirst before he sank into the leather couch in Alex's expansive front room, set the dripping long neck on his knee, and blew out an exasperated sigh. "To tell you the truth, I wanted to kick his ass too, only…" His cowboy hat hit the end table. He'd already removed it the moment he'd seen the women. That was Maverick to a T. Politely reserved. Usually quiet. Prone to let others take the lead. *Just don't piss him off.*

Alex drained the second shot and poured another before he took the matching leather chair across from Maverick. "Only what?"

"He's hurting, Boss, and not just from that missing pinkie. Gabe noticed it at the hospital. We talked while Beau slept, and I have to agree. Something's eating him, and it's not just what Montego took. What do we really know about Beau? Why the hell's he ready to fight us all the time? Hell, we should be the family he relies on. He's got nobody else. What do you know that we don't?"

"He fights because he's Army and the rest of us are mostly Marines," Alex bit out, though he knew interdepartmental competition had nothing to do with Beau's nasty level of disdain. It wasn't just the guys and gals, the former sailors and jarheads on The TEAM he hated. Since the moment Alex had met Beau and hired him, he'd seemed pissed off at the entire world.

"Yeah, well…" Maverick's gaze stayed on his bottle. "That's not what Gabe thinks."

"Then what? PTSD? Drugs?" Alex snapped. "What's got his ass wound so tight around the axle that he can't be civil for one son-of-a-bitchin' day of his life?" Alex glared at the Jameson across the room, wishing he'd brought the bottle with him.

Both Maverick's shoulders lifted. "I was hoping you could tell me. But Gabe says Beau reminds him of, umm, me," he said, more to his bottle than to his boss.

Well, son-of-a-bitch. That knocked Alex down a peg. Maverick was another one of those guilty survivors. Sorry that they'd lived. Wishing at some deep, dark level, they hadn't. But surviving and coping with what they'd lost— make that who they'd lost—every day. Just like Alex. Just like Kelsey and Mark and Zack and most every other man and woman he'd ever hired. That was The TEAM for you, a weary bunch of guilty survivors who couldn't go back in time to change one damned thing.

Alex drew in a long, slow breath. Let it fill his lungs. Let it clear his head. Then let his temper go with one deliberate exhalation. He was tired of fighting the same demons. But he also knew there was a good man beneath the rancor Beau so quickly displayed. A lost man, maybe. One possibly headed in the wrong direction. But good. Else Alex would've told him to pound sand instead of signing him.

Guys and gals like Beau often came from tough beginnings. After serving, often in combat, they came to Alex as scarred, edgy warriors. Women and men who'd seen too much, and some who'd lost too much. Like Maverick.

There was a time he'd walked away from The TEAM. He'd just stood up at his desk one morning and quit without any more notice than, "I've had enough." He'd ended up in Wyoming before he'd gotten his head straight. That was what proud men who lost their baby brother in war did sometimes. They struggled back the only way they knew how. Footstep by footstep. Mile by mile. If it took the soles off a hundred pairs of boots, so be it.

Okay, then.

Alex blew out another sigh. "I only know what Beau divulged on his personnel record. It wasn't much, and I don't share personal information." *But I do read it.*

"I know, and I'm not asking you to," Maverick agreed. "I'm just tired of knocking heads with him every time we work together. He's got a burr under his saddle I can't seem to reach. He's like a stallion that can't stand the rope, not even a halter. China noticed it at the last picnic. He was new to The TEAM, but he sat on the lawn with his beer, away from every one of us. Like a leper. When she tried to talk to him, he up and walked away without so much as a *'Go to hell, leave me alone.'*"

"He'll come around. Give him time," said the man who'd just threatened to fire Beau.

"I don't know that, Boss, and neither do you." Maverick upended the lager and finished it off before he said, "Have you seen how he treats Izza? If Connor doesn't rip his head off one of these days, I will."

"What about Izza?"

Agent Isabella Ramos, Izza for short, aka Mrs. Connor Maher, as in Agent Connor Maher's wife. An affable former Marine who adored his wife and lived to tease her, Connor was by far the most lethal man on The TEAM, especially when it came to protecting his wife and family. He cold-bloodedly annihilated the men who'd hurt her a couple years back. Beau had better not rattle that beehive because Connor would end him.

"He can't look at her without biting her head off. And he's downright demeaning when he talks to her. Treats her like she's stupid. I don't know, Boss. Some guys come back from war, but they don't really, know what I mean?"

"Like you," Alex stated flatly. "You had a damned rough time settling back into civilian life."

Maverick kept his gaze on the empty bottle at his knee. "That's what's got me worried. I'll tell you something I'm not proud of. But you have no idea how close I came to offing myself after Darrell died like he did."

Maverick stuck one long, lean leg out, and Alex knew he'd rather be kicking the shit out of something instead of sitting in his living room chatting. So he said what Kelsey always told him. Because it was true. Painful to hear, and most days, impossible to do. But still true. "The hardest person to forgive is always ourself."

By then, Alex couldn't look Maverick in the eye, either. Too many memories flooded back. His pretty first wife, Sara. Abby, the firstborn daughter he'd always adore. The dearest lives he'd lost, and the ones he hadn't been there to protect when they'd needed him most. The struggle he still wrestled with. There were moments he truly hated himself for not being behind the wheel when *it* happened. Sara would still be alive, if he'd been driving. Maybe Abby, too. He'd be that name on the headstone in his family plot. Not them. Instead…

Jumping to his feet, he set his empty glass on the edge of the bar, not drinking himself into a stupor like he did back then. He had Kelsey now, and things were different. She loved him more than he deserved, and he damned well knew it. Maybe he was still the same jackass he ever was, but life was a blessing. Most days.

"That's the problem." Maverick looked at Alex then. "I'm not sure Beau thinks he's got that kind of time. I think he's got a death wish, Boss. Else. why did he go back to Congressman Ringer's all by himself? Today when he'd just left the hospital? Why didn't he wait until he had backup? Why'd he track McKenna down after he found nothing at Ringer's but police tape and misery? That's what he's been doing all night. He told me. Jesus, if he hadn't had his pistols with him, we could've lost him and McKenna."

Alex cocked his head. "But we didn't. She's alive because Beau took a chance and—"

"And he could have gotten them both killed!"

"True, but…"

"No buts, Boss!" Maverick slammed his empty bottle on the coffee table. "He's not a team player. He's going to get someone killed. Himself! Beau needs help, an intervention, or… or… something."

"Like you?" Alex asked thoughtfully. "You beat the shit out of, who was it, Landon? Right in the office?"

Now it was Maverick's turn to growl. "That was different. What a lying sack of—"

"It's not different. In fact…" Alex leaned forward, his elbows to his knees, seeing what he should've seen all along. Just like Beau, Maverick was still hurting. Something must've stirred up all those painful memories. "How long's it been?" he asked, though he damned well knew.

Maverick took his time answering, his belly expanding, then deflating with one long, miserable breath. "Four years," he said quietly. "Darrell died exactly four years ago on the day I flew home from Indonesia. The flight took us over India and Afghanistan. I wasn't expecting that. Not then. Not… that."

Alex cleared his throat, stiffened his spine, and he did what he did best. "How about you let me take care of what's going on between Beau and Izza. For now, keep Beau and his doctor friend at your place. Make sure he stays put long enough that he doesn't lose that finger, got it?"

If looks could kill…

"Me?" Maverick spat, his nose wrinkled in disgust. "You want *me* to ride herd on that ass?"

"Why not? You train horses, don't you?"

Chapter Nineteen

Beau sucked in his gut instead of snapping at Kelsey, acutely aware that he was so damned out of his element. The second he'd cleared the door to this elegant guest bedroom, he knew he was in the wrong place, the wrong man for the job. Obediently, he'd settled McKenna onto the queen-sized bed as Libby Houston requested. But when he'd headed for the door and the fast way out, Kelsey had stopped him with a gentle hand in the middle of his chest. He'd come to a dead halt because, well, this was Kelsey, and she was touching him, and—yeah. That slender clean hand of hers could stop a hurricane.

"Sit," she'd told him, then pushed until his legs hit the edge of the other queen-sized bed in the room.

He had no choice, so he sat. What else could he do? He liked Kelsey. The problem was him, not her. Never her.

"Let me look at that poor face," she said as she dipped a clean white cloth into the basin on the nightstand between the beds. "Oh, my. You're running a fever, Beau. You should be in bed."

"No, ma'am. I'm fine." He didn't flinch when she ran the rag over his forehead and dabbed at the claw marks across his nose and down one cheek. She applied something that stung, then instantly turned cold to his bloodied brow.

"Put your chin up," she told him when, with two gentle fingers under his chin, she positioned his face into the light. "You're not fine. You're tired and you're sick. I can see it in your eyes."

He'd never felt more awkward. More vulnerable. He wasn't sick, and she shouldn't be doctoring him. She was Alex's wife for Hell's sake, a queen, not some servant. Yet on and on she went, giving him no say. Soothing his ragged nerves with just the motherly touch of her hand. Being nice, everything he didn't deserve.

Beau focused on the room around him while Kelsey fussed. Apparently, Alex provided luxury hotel accommodations to his guests, like that was a surprise. Everything in this spare room was big. The TV screen on the wall. The window covered by room-darkening, floor-to-ceiling drapes. Even the lavish ensuite head he'd glimpsed on his way in, looked more than adequate for a family of five to shower in—at the same time. This single room made his apartment look cheap and old. Not that he wanted to live here, but once again, he was where he didn't belong. The tender care had to stop.

"I'll be okay, ma'am," he assured Kelsey.

"No, you're most certainly not okay," she came back at him. "Now lean back and let me take care of you for a change."

This was so not happening. "No, ma'am," he said as he returned his ass to a stern upright position, needing to be gone, and going to be, real damned soon. When he'd first released McKenna, he'd unbuckled his holster and set his weaponry on the nightstand. He'd wanted it handy, just in case. Now he just wanted it back and to be gone.

"If she said sit, you'd better do what you're told," Libby Houston piped up from where she leaned over McKenna. "We might need your help."

Yeah, like he believed they needed him for anything. "Doing what?"

"Holding McKenna while I bath and bandage her wounds. She's hurt pretty bad. She might need a few stitches, and what I have to do will hurt. She might fight and—"

"I can do that." His gaze shifted from Libby to the brave woman in bed staring at the ceiling and fighting her tears. "McKenna," he said to get her attention. "How you doing, sweetheart?"

He didn't mean to let slip that tender endearment, honest. Had in fact never said it before, not to an adult woman anyway. It just blurted out, and once he heard it out loud, it sounded right.

She turned her head and the saddest eyes locked onto his. "I'm g-good."

The liar. Her lower lip quivered like she was cold, giving her away. The professional doctor-voice she'd used on him at the hospital was gone. A frightened little girl had answered him instead.

"That's my line," Beau teased as he brushed past Kelsey to get closer to McKenna. "I'm here," he said as he tugged the light blanket Libby had draped over McKenna back under her chin to cover what Libby had exposed. "There now, I didn't hurt you when I did that, did I?"

"No," she murmured even as her shoulders stiffened.

"I'm sure sorry if I did," he said, meaning it with all his heart. Hurting for her, he tucked her tiny hands into his one good hand, while Libby worked around him. He only did that because McKenna seemed to need something to hold onto, and he knew what being alone felt like when you were battered and hurt. When you'd been humiliated and abused. When you had no one to turn to. There was no reason she had to deal with this crappy night by herself. He was here, and he meant to stay.

But the very second his much larger, more callused fingers came into contact with her much smaller, more delicate fingers, tears ran like tiny rivers out of those pretty eyes. *Aw, shit.* Beau had no resistance to a woman's tears. He sank to his knees beside her. "Hey there, don't cry, Doc. Everything's going to be okay."

Until then, he hadn't noticed what a gorgeous color her eyes were. Green, but not dark. More emerald with tiny flecks of gold radiating from the center like tiny bicycle spokes. But so sad.

"Th-thanks for c-coming after me," she cried, trembling so hard he had a notion to pick her up and hold her on his lap, while Libby did whatever she had to do. To comfort McKenna until she knew she'd always be safe with him. How weird was that?

"I thought I was going to die," McKenna squeaked. "She would've killed me, Beau. How'd you know where I lived or that she was there?"

Jesus, he loved the sound of his name on her lips. "Just a hunch," he said as he leaned in, his nose to her nose, filling her line of sight, and forcing her to focus on his ugly face. To hear and see only him. "But she didn't kill you, McKenna, and you're safe now. Kelsey and Libby are going to fix you up, and honest, I'd never lie to a girl as pretty as you. You can trust me."

"I know," she whispered, a ragged catch in her voice. "I do trust you."

Their eyes locked, and the second they did, Beau lost his breath, what was left of his soul, and quite possibly the last of his common sense. Women, for all their wisdom and intelligence, for all their willingness to pitch in when times got tough, whether in the office, in factories building warplanes or in combat, were still, and would always be, the fairer sex. They would always be tinier than most men, made more delicately and for things different than fighting and killing. For better things.

"Not that I lie to ugly girls," he teased, needing McKenna to keep looking at him.

Lifting to his feet, he settled on the bed at her knee, so Libby could do her thing. Kelsey had joined Libby, and together they eased the blanket covering McKenna aside to wash and treat her wounds.

"It's not as bad as I thought," Libby murmured even as McKenna cringed from being handled.

"No, but it's bad enough," Kelsey replied. "You poor thing. We'll take good care of you, McKenna. Just breathe, hon."

It seemed they'd had practice treating patients before, so Beau minded his business. Portion by portion, the women removed the packing that he and Maverick had hastily applied before they'd bundled McKenna into her bed sheet and raced her to safety. And portion-by-portion, the ice around his heart began to thaw.

Helping McKenna was a new experience. Yes, he'd assisted plenty when guys got shot or injured in the field, but never had he been there when a woman went down. They were so much—smaller. Their bones thinner. Their skin lighter. Their pain so much harder for him to take. He couldn't imagine losing a female soldier in combat. Talk about feeling like a failure.

Methodically, Libby and Kelsey washed her wounds, repacked, and re-bandaged. Finally, the only one that remained was hidden below her breasts. But when McKenna arched back into her pillow and hissed, Beau warned Libby, "Take it easy. You're hurting her."

Libby nodded that she'd heard but kept up the pressure under McKenna's bare breast. Beau jerked his eyes off that intimate female body part he hadn't meant to look at. But now that he had, he spared another quick glance. The tip was a lovely pink and flat, nothing like hookers' tits in Vegas. McKenna's breast was real. More innocent. Soft. Pure.

"Can you please hold this packing in place while I give her something for pain?" Libby asked him. Him, the guy with just one good hand. "Press hard. That one's going to need stitches."

"I can," Beau murmured, not sure he was worthy of the honor, but damned sure not going to let McKenna down again. "I didn't know you could prescribe pain meds," he said to Libby. As far as he knew, Mark Houston's wife was just a nurse. But there she was, taking charge like she meant business.

"She can since she graduated medical school," Kelsey murmured as she tugged the sheet out of Libby's way. "You're talking to Dr. Houston, didn't you know?"

"Huh," was all Beau could come up with. Of course he didn't know. He'd have to really belong to The TEAM to know Mark's wife was now a capable doctor, wouldn't he? "Guess I should've called you Dr. Houston before then."

"Please don't. You're family, Beau, and…"

He lost track of Libby's answer when she took hold of his good hand and shoved his open palm under McKenna's breast. The sweet thing jiggled at his touch, but when McKenna closed her eyes and hissed, he knew he'd hurt her. Closing his thumb over the plush, warm mound, he told her, "I'm sorry."

"'S okay," she murmured as Libby came back to the side of the bed with a small hypo. It was a good thing she was a physician now. Seemed like Alex needed one on staff.

"I hate to dope you up, but this wound is deeper. Stitching might take a while. Small sting," Libby told McKenna before she pulled back the cover and administered the shot.

"What is it?" McKenna asked.

"Something to help you sleep while we finish up. I have a little quilting to do, and there's no reason you have to suffer through it. You've had enough for one day. By the time you wake up, you'll be wrapped, and all these cuts will be closed and medicated."

"But I want to call Dad. He'll be worried."

"Take it easy. You can call him once we're finished unless you'd rather one of us call him now. But we don't want to scare him, do we?"

Beau studied the calm, professional tone to Libby's question. Mark Houston was a lucky man.

"No, I'd rather he hears the news from me. Where… where's Beau?" McKenna asked, a tiny note of hysteria in her voice. "Did he… did he leave me—?"

Quick as he could, Beau peered around Libby. He wasn't an easy guy to miss, still supporting her breast like he was, but she'd panicked when Libby stepped in front of him, and he needed to put her mind at ease.

"I'm not going anywhere. In fact, there's a bed with my name on it right next to yours if it's okay with you. Isn't there, ladies?" He hoped he hadn't spoken out of turn. "You don't mind if I sleep in here tonight, do you? Just tonight?"

Libby eased his palm out from under McKenna's breast while she readied the site for suturing.

"I hoped you would," Kelsey answered without a single hint of sarcasm or annoyance. "All my patients stay in this room, not like I get that many. There's a phone on the nightstand between the beds, and feel free to use the TV if you can't sleep or want to watch a movie. The kitchens' down the hall if you're hungry." She shot him a quick smile. "Guess you already know where that is, though, don't you? Anyway, eat whatever you like. That's why I bought it. Anything else I can do before I tend to that hand of yours?"

She looked straight into Beau's eyes when she asked, and he honestly didn't know what to say. He just stared. Wishing he were a better man for the likes of her and McKenna.

Without asking, Kelsey's fingers went to his face again, tracing the bloody bruises and scrapes Catalina had left behind. Kelsey had already cleaned each injury and dosed them with either ointment or butterfly bandages, but this was different. She wasn't looking at his physical, beat-up self as much as looking for the real him. The weak little kid who hadn't been strong enough to stop—that.

"She got you good, huh?" That was Kelsey. She had room in her heart for oddballs and losers like him. She was the reason Beau knew Alex was smarter than he was. He had her, didn't he?

All Beau could manage was to nod like some high school jock out with the homecoming queen. Kelsey had that effect on him. Gracious to a fault, she never said an unkind word to anyone, least of all to him. Not once had she made him feel unwelcome, unwanted, or hurried. If anything, the one time he'd visited her house during that office picnic, she'd catered to him and made him feel special. Like he was somebody.

"Thank you, ma'am, but I'm okay," he murmured humbly. "I'm just staying here for McKenna. In case, you know, she needs anything. Not like she needs me. I just... I'm staying." And that was him, tongue-tied and unsure of himself when a pretty woman, make that a real woman, got past his radar.

Kelsey cocked her head and smiled, her brown eyes soft and forgiving. "She's one of my best friends, and I think she likes you."

He shook his head. McKenna didn't like him. He'd just been the one who'd saved her. That was all, and he knew damned well there was an ocean of difference between gratitude and actually liking a man like him. But when he made the mistake of glancing down at the sleepy lady holding onto his one good hand like she'd never let it go, his fingers tightened automatically around hers. A sneaky truth whispered over his shoulder. *You like her, too.*

Already masked, Libby sat on a stool, leaning over McKenna, her chest now covered in light blue surgical draping. A plastic covered tray of instruments rested on McKenna's stomach. A goose-necked floor lamp stood at the bedside.

McKenna was definitely smiling up at him, albeit in a drowsy way. He felt the impact of that tender gaze all the way to his gut and into his worthless, unsalvageable soul. How could anyone torture an innocent like McKenna? Against a woman who'd done nothing wrong in her life? One who'd taken a vow to help *all* others? Even him.

He didn't understand what made people cruel, while others remained true and good and—holy. For that was what McKenna was, a holy angel from heaven sent down to earth. Not for him, though, he got that. No one like him deserved something as rare as this woman smiling dreamily up at him. Okay, so she was drugged, but still. She was worth a thousand of him.

"Goodnight," he told her quietly, confused why she affected him like she did. "I'll be here when you wake up."

"P-promise you'll... you'll s-stay?" she asked, her eyelids heavier by the second.

"Promise," he whispered, filled with a sudden urge to hold her. To protect her. To make every last razor-sharp slice marking her skin better and every future scar invisible. That was all men like him were good for, to stand between the bitches roaming this land and the angels blessing it.

"G'night," she mumbled.

Beau would've leaned over and dropped a tiny, chaste kiss to the middle of her forehead if Libby and Kelsey hadn't been there. Every nerve and muscle in his ruggedized body certainly wanted to. Instead, he accepted the chair Kelsey had just pushed across the room to him.

"Sit," she told him kindly.

So he sat. But while she double-checked the blood-soaked bandage on his hand, then changed it out with clean dressing, while she *'Hmmm'ed'* over his bloody nose and the scratches on his face, while she ran to the kitchen for a sandwich and a bottle of water, so his stomach could handle the Percocet Libby told him to take—Beau never took his eyes off McKenna. Not once. She needed a hard man standing watch while she slept, and for this one night, he was that man. And—*thank you, Jesus*—that made him lucky enough.

Chapter Twenty

Beau waited until the women were done cleaning up and stowing their medical supplies, before he unlaced his boots and slid them under the bed. Not the one McKenna slept in, though. That seemed proprietary, like he was staking a claim, which he'd never do. Not with her. She deserved better than a rough man like him. Another doctor, maybe. Someone she had things in common with. Or a lawyer who could provide like she was accustomed to. Anyone but him.

At last Kelsey and Libby gathered their things and closed the door behind them when they left. Beau almost relaxed. Until two minutes later. The door opened to Maverick and Alex, and why not? Beau had expected they'd have something to say. Might as well get it over with. He blew out a gut full of resignation.

Guess I won't be keeping that promise to McKenna after all.

He stayed where he was, perched on the edge of the empty bed, his forearms on his knees, and his eyes on the floor while he waited for the reprisal sure to come. A fuckin' great day this turned out to be. *Save the day. Save the girl. Still not good enough.*

"When do you want me to leave?" he asked quietly, but resolutely. Might as well rip it off like one of those extra-sticky Band-Aids and get it over with. "Now? In the middle of the night? Or can I at least grab a nap before I go?"

"Look at me when you talk to me," Alex growled, just as quietly.

Lifting his head, Beau met his employer's eyes. The man could drill through solid granite with those hard, blue diamonds.

"We're moving you to Maverick's ranch," Alex bit out. "The sooner the better."

Beau swallowed hard. That figured. Why would Alex allow someone like him to stay in his house? He wasn't part of the almighty inner circle within The TEAM. He wasn't tight with the senior agents, Harley, Mark, or David, either. He wasn't even sure he wanted to work for Alex. The man was unbearably abrupt, incredibly arrogant, and a pain in the ass perfectionist. Beau hadn't done one thing right since he'd hired on, and Alex had let him know every single time.

What was the use of arguing?

"We need to move now, though," Maverick said. "While Montego's licking her wounds. Before she's wise to what we've done and where you are."

"Agreed. We're not certain how she's tracking us, but she seems to have a hard-on for anyone who's working with or for me," Alex admitted, his tone grim. "Maverick's got an arsenal, hired hands, and a bigger spread. You'll be just as safe there until this blows over."

"And my wife's a dead-eye. Montego's about to meet her match if she sets foot on the Wild Wolf East. China'd as soon send her to Hell as let her get near Kyrie or the horses."

Weary to the dirt floor of his wicked, dismal soul, Beau dropped his gaze again and shook that idiotic notion off. "I don't need anyone keeping me safe. I'll just leave. Then you guys won't have to—"

"No, but McKenna does," Maverick snapped.

That brought Beau's head back up. "She's coming with me, I mean, us?"

Something glowered behind Maverick's stern USMC stare. Once a Marine, always a Marine, they never lost that *'I can rip your fuckin' heart out, feed it to you, and you will enjoy it'*, toughest-dog-on-the-heap stare. "This is about keeping both of you alive and out of harm's way. Libby thinks it's best to move McKenna while she's medicated. Get your boots on. Alex and I'll wrap her in a blanket, and in the meantime—"

"No! I'll do it. *I'll* wrap her," Beau declared, on his feet now and ready to go. Who needed boots when there was a lady to protect?

That got both men's attention. Maverick cocked his head like he was seeing something for the first time. Alex blinked. Just once. Then ordered, "Then do it. We leave in five. Through the garage. Kelsey and Libby will help."

Beau worked his throat muscles extra hard just to swallow before he said, "We'll be ready."

With one curt nod, Alex left the way he came, in a huff, but Maverick stayed. "You saved her life," he said, his tone flat. "I hope you understand the kind of bravery it took to walk into her house after what you lived through at Montego's hands. God, you should've been home in bed. You'd just left the hospital."

"Yeah. So?"

"So if we've got time over the next few days, I'll tell you about the time I saved China. Boots, man. Don't forget your gear." And he was gone.

Beau stared at the door, wondering what the hell just happened. Maverick was a hard man to read, one minute friendly enough, the next ruder than shit and all-out hostile. Not that Beau cared to understand the guy. Mostly he stayed clear of everyone he worked with unless absolutely necessary. Lesson's learned the hard way and all that bullshit.

It took sixty seconds to be steady on his feet. He set his gear and his leather jacket on the other bed. But he stalled out when he leaned over McKenna. Damn, she was a beautiful woman, lying there asleep like she was. Her facial features were relaxed now, her chest heaving with deep, slow breaths. She looked innocent. Peaceful. He didn't want to disturb her.

Kelsey and Libby had changed her into a soft cotton gown. A tiny satin ribbon nestled between the swell of her breasts, breasts he hadn't been moved by until now. But Beau could stand watch over her forever, and this stolen moment would be the only reward he'd need. To breathe in sync with her. To take up the same space if only for a few more minutes. Just knowing she was finally safe. Talk about unrequited love. Gah, he was made for that job, too. There would never come a day when he deserved a woman like her. There was no sense dreaming it could ever be. But for now, he just stood there and counted himself the luckiest man alive.

Beau didn't need help getting McKenna ready to travel. This privilege belonged to him and him alone. For once, his left hand didn't ache as he gently lifted her into his arms. Whatever Libby had deadened it with had worked miracles.

But honestly, even if he were to lose his finger or his hand because he'd rescued McKenna? It'd be a small price to pay.

Beau had her wrapped like a baby before the women returned.

"It looks like you don't need our help," Kelsey murmured as she cleared the doorway with Libby behind her.

"Of course not. Haven't you heard? Beau's fast," Libby teased, winking.

"And smooth," Kelsey said, waggling her brows.

"Just doing whatever it takes to keep Dr. Fitzgerald safe," he told them sincerely.

Libby hip-checked Kelsey. "So now she's *Doctor* Fitzgerald. Wasn't she McKenna just a few minutes ago?"

"Ah-huh, I see how it is." Kelsey grinned, her warm gaze drifting over Beau standing there with the lady in question in his arms. "She looks plenty safe to me."

Women. If he lived to be one hundred, he'd never understand them. Why were they teasing him? What'd these two want? Him to admit he cared more than he should for their lady friend? Not happening. The less a guy said, the less people could say behind his back.

He'd just been in the right place at the right time tonight. That was all. McKenna would never be safer than right now, but he knew his place. This moment with her was just a temporary reprieve. She belonged to the stars, and he was Army cannon fodder, a grunt with a Ranger tab on his shirt that hadn't helped him sleep any better at night.

"There," Kelsey whispered as she added another light blanket over McKenna, while Libby waited at the open door. "I'll follow along with your gear and your holster. Alex won't allow us to visit you kids until this is over, Beau, so Gabe and

Shelby will stay at Maverick and China's with you. Shelby's a nurse. She'll know what to do. Take good care of McKenna. I'm counting on you."

Beau nodded, her humble servant to the end. For whatever reason, Harley and Kelsey were the two who'd inspired him to stay with The TEAM. Harley for the job offer, Kelsey for the unconditional light in her eyes. Not Alex.

"I will ma'am. Trust me."

"I do trust you, Beau. I trust you more than you know. Do what's best for McKenna. Now let's hurry. Alex is waiting."

Before long, Beau stood in Maverick's massive garage with Alex and McKenna. It took a minute to lift up and out of the back seat of Carson's Yukon with her in his arms, but he managed. By then, the long day and night had caught up with him. He needed to sit. Lay down. Anything. Just to stop moving would be good enough.

China met them at the garage door that led through a spacious mudroom/laundry room combination into a lighted hallway. "Second door on your right," she whispered as she held the hallway door open for him. "Hi, Cowboy. I waited up for you."

"I see that," Maverick said gruffly as he pressed a kiss to her mouth, then asked, "Kyrie too?"

"No, I sent her to bed hours ago. Gabe called. Said he should be here first thing in the morning but to let him know if we need anything sooner."

Beau only half-listened to the intimate husband and wife exchange as he angled McKenna through the door, down the hall, and into the extra-large bedroom with the light on and the door open. The affection between Maverick and China surprised him. How could she stand to live with the moody ass? Guess opposites really did attract. Like the Stewarts. Kelsey was a saint to put up with Alex.

A small lamp glowed on the nightstand between the two queen-sized beds. Once China joined him, she drifted the brown and green-checkered bedcovers back, and Beau set his precious cargo on the clean sheets. Together they unwrapped McKenna. Once she was out of those extra blankets, Beau tucked the bedcovers around his sleeping beauty once more.

The second his thumb bumped her chin, a certain calm crept over him at the intimate duty he'd so carefully performed. A soldier was never more faithful than when standing guard over someone he cared for, and for sure, there was no fiercer warrior in the universe than a man protecting his woman and his home. But why those emotions surged through Beau's body like a heated tsunami, he had no idea. He meant nothing to McKenna. Never would. Never could.

He was first and foremost—just and only—that hard man alone in the darkest night, holding the thin line against his homeland's enemies, destroyers, and invaders. That was all. He was a Viking. One of King Leonidas' suicidal Spartans. A man created to be forever alone and forever on guard.

Like so many soldiers before him, he was and would never be more special than that. War was what he'd been made for, and what he did best. He killed America's enemies, and sometimes, he made them suffer for the innocent lives they'd taken before he let them die. They never died courageously. He wasn't made that way.

Beau wasn't proud of what he did as an expertly trained sniper and a cunning survivor, but neither was he ashamed. Someone had to protect the sheep of the world, the lambs, and the innocents like McKenna. The pundits, talking heads, and know-it-alls in the world sure as hell couldn't, not as much as they fought a decent, law-abiding man's right to bear arms. No. Only hard men like him would stand against the Montegos of the world.

He'd long ago accepted his place in society. Not even on his best day would he be worthy of a woman as smart, as classy, and as uniquely feminine as McKenna. She saved people. He managed that supreme act of courage once in a rare while if he were lucky. Like he had been tonight. Mostly, he just killed who he was told to and moved on. That was his vocation in life. It might not be pretty, but it was a job worth doing. Like cleaning rats out of sewers and picking up trash, it kept the world safe and clean.

With a gentle swipe over McKenna's swollen bottom lip, he knew it to his soul. She was the one who belonged inside the protection of The TEAM. Not him. People liked her, and why shouldn't they? She was sunshine, light, and saving grace. He was the unrepentant and the unforgiven sinner in the dark. And there he would forever stay.

Beau shook his head at the pensive thoughts bubbling to the surface inside his hard head tonight. Had to be the drugs.

"You look like you've had a tough day," China whispered, her head inclined toward his, the dim bedroom light sparkling in her eyes. "Maverick's bringing your gear inside. Can I get you something to drink before I leave you two alone? A beer? Water? Anything?"

Alex and Maverick hadn't offered to help care for McKenna. That, at least, was a relief. But China was the complete opposite of Kelsey. Not that she was cruel. Just— different. More... *Hell, I don't know.*

Beau cleared his throat, not accepting any more than the basics from his cantankerous teammate's wife. "Water'll be fine. Thank you, ma'am."

"If Gabe and Shelby get in early, I'll ask them to hold off checking McKenna until morning. I imagine you're exhausted. Go ahead and sleep late if you can. You look like you're ready to collapse. Do you need any aspirin before I go?"

It was funny she'd said Shelby would check McKenna. Like his wounds were invisible? Like he didn't deserve Gabe's wife's attention or care? But why should that surprise him? Truth was, it didn't.

"I'll be fine. Libby fixed me up with a few painkillers." *Leave me the fuck alone already.*

"I'm glad you told me. I'll be right back." China nodded toward the ensuite head. "I left a new set of pajamas on the counter for you. Use whatever toiletries you can find. I try to keep this room stocked for company. We never know who's going to show."

Beau wasn't about to sit while a lady was present, but the room spun, and he went down on the edge of the bed with a graceless thump.

China flew to his side. "Damn it, you're not well. What can I do? What do you need? Tell me."

He was sweating by then, but he wasn't about to accept more than absolutely necessary from anyone related to Maverick. "Nothing, ma'am. Just need to sleep. I'll be fine in the morning." *Then I'll be gone.*

"Sorry, it just frightened me when you fell. If you're sure you're okay, I'll get out of your hair."

"I'm sure." He didn't want to be rude, but it'd sure be nice if she'd go.

The minute China closed the door behind her, he stumbled into the head, partially closed the door in case McKenna stirred or cried out, and he undressed. The pajamas China had left were flannel. But the package of boxers was something else. One hundred percent cotton. One pair was all he needed, and he meant to send Maverick a check to cover his expenses.

After a quick shower, during which Beau managed to keep his left hand mostly dry, he brushed his teeth, and called the day good enough for government work.

A surprise met him as he re-entered the bedroom, still running a towel over his head, so he didn't get the pillow wet. His gear bag and holster were hung over a couple of sturdy hooks on the wall behind the door. Some nice person had also left a tray of cheese, crackers, sliced smoked sausage, and a condiment cup of hot mustard on the nightstand. Along with four bottled waters. That was thoughtful of China.

Mental note to self: *Don't forget to thank her come morning. But mail a check to pay for this stuff first chance I get. Don't need Maverick holding anything over my head. Not ever.*

Sitting at the edge of the bed opposite McKenna, he cradled his injured limb in his lap while he ate what his stomach could handle, then took the last dose of the painkiller Libby had given him. Like Kelsey, he trusted her.

Beau turned off the lamp on the nightstand between the beds. Enough ambient light from the halogen yard lights between Maverick's big house and his ostentations barn filtered through the window blinds. But when it came time to throw back the blankets and climb into the other bed? Beau couldn't do it. He might sleep too soundly. What if McKenna needed him during the night? What if she had a nightmare? What if Montego came back and broke in? That worried him most. She might already know he and McKenna had hid out at Stewart's. She might not wait until morning to attack.

So, slowly...

Carefully...

Silently…

Beau lifted McKenna's blanket, settled his weight onto her bed without disturbing her, and slid his much bigger body alongside hers. Only for this one night. He just needed to be sure.

His body spiked, instantly hard with a need he'd denied for years. Maybe forever. But not for sex. Not that an intimate moment with McKenna wouldn't have been heaven. But because Beau was the kind of man who needed more than a quick *'slam, bam, thank-you, ma'am.'* Whatever that elusive *more* was, he'd been looking for it all his life. Just hadn't found it yet, and he didn't intend to settle for less.

A sigh escaped as he eased his good arm around McKenna's shoulder and pulled her against him. Lifting his wounded hand over his head, he rested it on his pillow. This, right here. Just lying next to McKenna. This was reward enough.

Closing his eyes, he imagined a world where little boys all had loving mothers and fathers and enough food to come home to. Where they didn't scurry like cockroaches in dark underground tunnels to avoid the bigger, meaner castoffs of society. Where someone like McKenna waited at the end of the day. To ask them what they did during the day. Were they happy? Tired? Had they played hard? Did they get hurt? Were they good boys?

He could see her tucking a tow-headed little guy into bed at night. Reading him his favorite bedtime story. Kissing him goodnight. Stupid, impossible stuff like that. All those seemingly trivial things most kids in America took for granted. Because they could. Because men like him made sure they could.

Old memories and ugly taunts always roared back during peaceful moments like this. *Worthless punk. Cocksucker. Dead weight.* And those were the kinder ones. Not since he'd fled the rundown house he'd called home had Beau ever looked back. There was no need to. He might have left that shithole far behind, but the ghosts of it hadn't left him.

Already a mature seven-and-a-half when it happened, he'd grown up fast and wary, staying low to avoid cops and other do-gooders. Dumpster diving to quell the stomach cramps. All the littler kids did it—once. But when that innocent need to survive came up against the brutal reinforcement of whichever gang owned that part of the hood and the Dumpsters in it, he'd resorted to begging. Stealing. Back then, he would've lied to his own mother if it meant a full stomach. Not that she'd come looking for him once he'd run. That was another nightmare altogether.

People talked about Vegas like it was a world-class destination, full of glamorous vices, and allowable sin. And it was—for movie stars and celebrities, whales and sharks. But for the homeless and throwaways, the runaways and kids on the street, Vegas was a damned brutal place to wake up to every morning. Hot as hell in the summer, prone to flash floods in the tunnels, and below zero temps when you least expected them in winter. Yeah, no. Vegas wasn't home. It was just another speck of dirt in the shit storm called life. *Suck it up and keep on moving.*

For once his bad hand didn't throb. The pain pills were working, and he wanted to spend his last waking seconds looking at McKenna. He eased the tip of the index finger of his good hand along the curve of her jaw, ending at her chin.

Beau almost laughed out loud. Good hand. Bad hand. He had no *good* hand, not considering the things he'd done with them.

"Sleep tight," he whispered as he ended the one illicit contact with McKenna he'd ever allow. She was safe, and that was all that mattered. For him, this was only a one-night reprieve. Tomorrow, he had a bitch to hunt. When the sun came up, and McKenna opened her pretty eyes to her brand-new day, he'd already be gone. It was a good plan, one he meant to implement after a couple hours rest.

Until McKenna mumbled in her sleep.

Until she whimpered.

Until she turned and pressed her face into his neck, burrowing her shoulder under his arm. Her head settled under his chin. Against his pounding heart. Jesus, she was a soft, warm armful. A man could live like this forever.

Beau bowed his nose into the silky tendrils of her lush hair, unable to think straight and nearly unable to breathe. He'd learned one prayer in his life, that from a multidenominational Army chaplain who handed out comfort on hard days like this one.

Beau didn't often pray. He had no idea what waited for him at the end of his life, and he wasn't sure he cared to find out. All he'd been destined for was grief and pain. It seemed a useless wish to hope for anything better. So he didn't.

But there was one story the Army chaplain told that Beau related to. One sermon that spoke to him while the others about kindness and charity, about looking out for your brother because all men were your brothers—yeah, right—did not. It was the one about that guy who'd been scourged, betrayed, and left to die. Yeah, that guy.

Beau could relate to Him. Better yet, the one time he'd whispered one of the prayers the chaplain used to say, he'd felt something. A connection with Him. Scared the shit out of Beau at the time. But the more he'd said that simple prayer, the more he'd felt that same connecting sensation. He didn't know what it was. Might've just been heartburn. But it was just possible the chaplain was right. Of all the liquor, smokes, and other shit Beau had put into his worthless body over the years, that one prayer to the Man Upstairs never failed to make Beau feel better. Maybe even—

Nah. Not salvageable. Not saved or redeemed or any of that other bullshit, either. Not him. Beau wasn't stupid enough to believe every word the chaplain had spewed. He was and would always be gutter trash, thrown away by his real mother, whoever she was. Abused and discarded by the bastard whose last name he'd had the utter misfortune to share.

Nonetheless, that one true prayer whispered off Beau's lips now. "Thank you, Jesus."

Chapter Twenty-One

She didn't remember falling asleep. Only waking up to the earthy scent of the clean, masculine body under her nose. As in literally, right under her flaring nostrils. Drawing in another deep breath of pure nirvana, McKenna couldn't recall ever enjoying the simple act of breathing in and out as much as she did this time.

Ruggedly masculine, this scent called to her. It soothed her. At the most primitive level of her soul, it told her she was safer than she'd ever been. It told her to stay. So she took another breath and held it, like the last bite of the chocolate chip cookies her dad used to bake. The last warm, gooey, melted treat on her tongue. How she'd savored every bite, but the last was always the best.

With a tentative yawn, she let that yummy scent escape as she stretched, then froze when the tape stretched over various parts of her body reminded her that everything had changed. She wasn't the unsuspecting woman she'd been yesterday. A desperate urge to hide under the bed like she'd done in years past when her mother had one of her bad days, stormed over her.

Her carefully constructed reality shattered. She was back to being that frightened little girl locked in a closet. McKenna didn't dare close her eyes, afraid of the flashbacks her brain was adept at throwing at her. Her confidence really was gone.

"But I *am* a good person," she told herself as sternly as she could, striving to rise above the darkness. "I'm a dedicated pediatrician. I do good work in this town, and people respect me. They should. I might be my mother's daughter, but I am *not* my mother. I *am* a survivor. I *am* strong. I *am* smart." *But I'm still afraid.*

Fighting panic now and struggling to clear her brain from the muck and webs of childhood abuse, McKenna forced a deep breath and focused on her strange surroundings. She'd never been here before, and she wasn't exactly certain where *here* was. It wasn't Kelsey's place. She remembered being treated by Libby and Kelsey, had in fact taught Kelsey first-aid tactics. Those two friends of hers couldn't be too far away. Alex and Maverick, also. They'd been in her apartment last night. They'd helped her. She was almost sure of it.

But Beau... He'd been there, too. She definitely remembered him. The feral look that washed over his face right before he'd fought Montego. McKenna had risked the cutting wire at her throat to catch that one glimpse of him. He'd killed Montego, hadn't he? *Oh, please, please, let that cruel heartless excuse for a human being be cold and dead, on her back in some morgue.*

Trembling, McKenna forced a slow inhalation instead of the quick hard breaths pounding at her. Expanding her belly with the masculine scent she never wanted to be without, she held her breath as long as she could. Then, oh, so slowly, she let it hiss out of her nostrils, even as tears brimmed her eyes, and her fingertips dug into the solid muscles beneath her hands. For years, she'd fought to NOT be afraid of shadows, but with one brutal, chance encounter, Catalina Montego had stripped all sense of security away.

Except for the steady breathing from the man whose side she found herself tucked neatly into, the room was quiet. All by itself that sure masculine contact calmed her ragged nerves. She wasn't alone, and Montego couldn't get her. If anyone could keep her from that heartless woman's grasp, it was this man right here, the one so sure of himself that he slept like a rock. Her rock.

Okay. I can do this. I can be strong. Now. Before he sees me. I can get a grip and gather my wits and not fall apart like some hysterical bimbo on television. I'm smarter than that. I'm stronger. I can be who I was yesterday. I can. I know I can. I will!

Maybe…

Still breathing hard, she focused on Beau. He was the strong one. He didn't need to wake up because of her panic attack. Man. He was beautiful in slumber. Peaceful. Oblivious to the wreck he held in his arm. Laying on his back, his magnificent chest was laid bare, the sheet pooled at his hips barely covered his waist. Talk about mouth-watering washboard abs. Everything about him declared his rugged masculinity.

His skin was darker than hers and rough where hers was smooth. Dark curly hairs dusted his pecs, then narrowed to a trail from his belly button to below the sheet. Distracted by the friendly beast she found herself snuggled up to, and calmer now, McKenna continued her very astute examination of the massive body beside her. In the same bed. Like he belonged here.

He'd lifted his poor left arm, the wrist over his eyes, and his hand was still bandaged. With his wavy, black hair swept back, the need to run her fingers through it persisted. It looked thick and soft. Luscious. Her nostrils flared at the scent of whatever shampoo or body wash he'd used.

He'd survived the fight with Montego, but it gave McKenna pause. She'd never seen a woman fight before, not that she'd seen much of this fight either, not with her head and neck restrained by that wire under her chin. But she'd listened intently, and it had sounded like Montego hadn't hesitated for a second. Like she'd been prepared. Attack, attack, attack. That seemed her only agenda, and she'd thrown herself at Beau the second he'd opened the bedroom door. Almost as if she'd known he'd show up, as if she'd set a trap for him.

Shuddering at the possibility that Montego was just that cunning and evil, McKenna rubbed her cheek against his pec, basking in the musky, male scent of his skin, and so damned thankful for this courageous man. He'd not only shown up in the nick of time, but he'd come alone, and he'd fought like the devil for her. Beau was one of those brave first responders, the guys who ran into burning buildings when everyone else ran out.

A sob sneaked up on McKenna, catching in her throat. If not for this man right here, she would've been sliced to ribbons and in a morgue by now. He'd come for her. He was her hero.

Tears sprang to her eyes, but she couldn't help but cry. She licked her lips again at the wealth of muscles encasing his taut body. His arms alone were massive, constructed of bulges over more bulges. He must work out a lot considering the large dark veins tracking up his forearms and biceps like roadmaps.

For sure, this guy was a solid chunk of eye candy. The white bed sheets enhanced his olive skin. His ebony eyelashes were so thick, they looked more like brushes. His lips were lush, and his mouth barely open. Again, his thick dark hair tempted McKenna to run her hand over his head. To cup the back of his head. To hold him still and kiss him senseless.

Heat pooled at her core. What woman wouldn't want to wake up to find this drool-worthy, albeit scruffy and somewhat banged up alley cat beside her? Even in his sleep, Beau seemed determined to hold her. She was more than okay with his right palm splayed at the middle of her back like he'd never let her go.

Fluttering her fingertips over the crisp hairs on his chest, she purposely inhaled his distinct male scent again. Not to wake him, but to remind herself that she was safe. He was precisely what McKenna needed, the man who could take Montego down.

But just as fast as she breathed a sigh of relief, the nightmare she'd lived through last night rolled over her like a crackling thunderstorm, each lightning strike full of night terrors and a reminder of how close she'd come to not just dying, but to being murdered. The cruel wires. The frightening noose. The slimy rasp of Montego's chin against her cheek when Montego warned, *"...or mommy's going to be very upset, and you know what will happen then."*

Argh! How had she known about Aurora? Or did she? Was Montego simply a witch who'd gotten lucky when she'd conjured the worst nightmare of McKenna's life? Or had Montego known precisely how to scare the hell out of her? Was she a mind reader?

"Never! I'm not your child," McKenna hissed at the vicious ghost still playing evil tricks with her mind. Outright disgust shivered up her spine. But when she jerked away, Beau's palm moved reflexively. His fingers splayed wider, crushing her against his ribs as if he knew precisely how much she needed his brand of assurance. His breathing became stronger. His breaths came faster. Harsher.

"Thank you, Beau," she whispered in case he was awake, the knot in her throat so hard to swallow. "You didn't have to, but you came to my rescue, and you saved my life. I'll never forget you."

"Ah-huh," he murmured, his eyes still closed, but his hand exactly where she needed it.

That was enough for McKenna. She sagged against him and at last, her eyelids grew heavy. The last thing she felt was the brush of his whiskers and the gentlest kiss against her forehead when he muttered a sleepy, "Thank you, Jesus."

Chapter Twenty-Two

"I want to know where she is now, and how she got to Dr. Fitzgerald as quickly as she did," Alex growled over the phone.

He'd been doing a lot of growling since he'd awakened. Truth was he'd hardly closed his eyes last night after Maverick drove him home. That was what happened when some moron threatened his team. This power struggle with Catalina Montego, the woman Kelsey had met as *Athena*, was all out warfare. Just the idea that his sweet wife had been close enough to the murderess, that she could've joined Beau on that gruesome workbench inside Ringer's, galled Alex to his soul. Montego had to be located quickly and put down like the rabid dog she was.

She had to have an accomplice as easily as she'd gotten inside Fitzgerald's quaint colonial. His reasoning? Sheriff Howie Prince's men had found Montego's fingerprints all over McKenna's apartment, as well as on the outdoor main electrical panel. Dr. Fitz wasn't going back into that death trap if Alex had anything to say about it.

Not only had Montego cut the electrical lines to the entire building, she'd also rigged quite the contraption beneath McKenna's bed. That had to have taken time. A regular trap and pulley system, once fully engaged, it was intended not only to cut McKenna's throat, but to slice her into sections by the time Montego finished.

Beau hadn't known when he'd interrupted the psychotic bitch, but she'd set up a video cam to film that particular gruesome work. Howie Prince had that evidence, too. Which meant Montego or someone else had been inside McKenna's before she'd fled protective custody. Not a smart move, but Alex understood why she'd done it. Civilians assumed they were safe once they locked their front doors and turned off their lights at night.

Guess again, people. Anyone—ANYONE—who seriously wanted to kill you, could and would unless you were smart enough to accept responsibility for your own defense. Why was that such a hard concept for the American public to grasp?

But Montego's obsession with The TEAM had escalated overnight. Who'd be next?

Catalina Montego, that's who.

"I've got nothing, Boss," Mother said again, her tone unusually somber.

A techno-genius like no other, she'd only recently revealed to Alex and The TEAM that she'd given birth to a seriously handicapped daughter when she was younger. As in years younger. Dempsey was eighteen now and dealing with Downs Syndrome, complicated by a rare genetic lung disorder.

Imagine that unsettling surprise inside a close-knit team where men and women's lives hung in a delicate balance from one day to the next. To say they'd been shocked put it mildly. Most agents understood, at least they'd said they did. But Mother's lack of faith in the people she worked with had deeply shaken the bedrock of The TEAM that Alex had nurtured for years.

Dempsey hadn't died as young as Mother's physicians had predicted she would, though. Thanks to recent medical advances, Dempsey's health was better today than it had ever been. Mother now held hope that her only child would live past the age of twenty. But her deceit, although Mother termed it being an overly protective single parent, had come at a high price. One Alex was still leveraging.

Revealing the secret of Dempsey had been shocking enough, but when Mother had also revealed she was, oh, by the way, one of the wealthiest women in the United States? That she in fact owned patents galore on hundreds of video games and spy-tech inventions? That she only worked because she needed something productive to do with her overactive brain?

Yeah. Not good. Unintentionally, she'd rocked The TEAM's confidence in her to the point they no longer trusted her. They found ways to work around her. Without her. Which in turn, hurt Mother deeply. Even Ember Dennison, Mother's savvy comspec assistant, had distanced herself from her one-time BFF. As obnoxiously nosey as Mother could be, The TEAM was her family. And she missed them.

Trouble on the home front was never a good thing. Alex had to find a way to fix it before he lost Sasha Kennedy, the woman he'd nicknamed Mother on her first day at work, and not because she was Suzy Homemaker material in any way, shape, or form.

"I don't believe that," he challenged her. "She's got to have someone working with her."

"If she does, that person's just as invisible as she is. I'm beginning to think you're dealing with a real ghost this time."

"There are no such things," Alex grumbled at that notion. "Anything on Aaron Pope yet?"

"Only this," Mother murmured, no doubt because, as usual, she was half-listening while she worked. "The FBI found his thumbprint on a murder case last year. It was only a partial, but I checked. It matches his military records."

"Impossible. He's been dead for years."

"You don't know that for sure. People disappear all the time when they want to. Maybe Aaron did, too. Did you ever think of that?"

"No," Alex stated unequivocally. "He wouldn't have done something so heinous to his family as walk away and never look back. I worked with him, damn it. He wrote home every week, twice on Sundays. I know him."

"Do you also know how many good friends and neighbors say that about serial killers?"

She had a point there.

"Tell me about the murder he supposedly attended."

"Air Force cadet on TDY orders at Andrews Air Force Base. Nineteen-year-old Phillip Stansky. His body was found in a nursery's compost pile. But get this. All his fingers were missing." TDY orders were temporary travel orders authorizing travel for military members or Department of Defense civilians.

The body had to have been in a state of rapid decomp by then. "How'd the police get Aaron's fingerprint off a body?"

"They didn't. The print was on a challenge coin they found in Stansky's shirt pocket."

"How long had he been missing?"

"Two years."

"Shit," Alex hissed, rolling the rigid cramp out of his neck. Wishing, just once, he didn't wake up with a son-of-a-bitchin' migraine already nagging him. "Where'd it come from?"

"LeJeune."

A USMC challenge coin? Wasn't that odd? Alex had a few of those coins left. It could mean nothing. Testosterone driven males one-upped each other all the time. But God? Was it possible? But nah. It couldn't be. Alex refused to believe Aaron Pope was still alive, but what a coincidence.

"I've got to go," Mother said quietly

Alex changed the subject. "How's Dempsey?"

Another sigh. "Remember that boy I told you about, the one at the medical facility with her? The one who continually disobeyed all the rules?"

Alex winced. "Yes, Scott." *Don't say it.*

"David and his wife took her to Scott's funeral today. I couldn't bear to go, and David was kind and asked, so—"

Damn. It was no wonder Mother was off her game. "I'm sorry," Alex said quickly. David Tao, one of Alex's three senior agents, and his wife Nancy were good people. "That was kind of them. I know it's hard."

"Dempsey doesn't understand why he had to die, and I'm tired. I'm just… tired."

"Then come stay with Kelsey and Lexie until this nightmare is over. You and Dempsey will be plenty safe. Zack and Jake are already here with their families. Harley, Judy, and the boys, too. You'll be in good company, and you know Lexie adores Dempsey. It'll be good for both of you."

"No, I've got work to—"

"I'm not asking, Sasha. I need you here with me. Today. I'll contact Lee and Adam to escort you. Stay at the office until they arrive."

"I can't..." Mother choked, a sure sign she was emotional. "There's something else. Her latest test results... They're not good."

Son-of-a-bitch. "How bad?" Alex knew this day would come. The holistic approach to modern medicine that had saved Dempsey the last time she'd nearly died couldn't hold back the inevitable forever. The poor girl had been living on borrowed time for years. Like so many friends Alex had known, she'd rallied. But time was not on her side.

It took a full minute before Mother replied. "I have to be here when she gets back. I can't—" Her voice broke.

"David will bring her to my place, Sasha. Come. Be with us instead of alone. Bring Justice, too." Alex waited, his impatience in check while she struggled to speak.

Justice Sandler, a stately African American gentleman from the Old South, had once served as chief of security in the hotel Mother owned. During Dempsey's last struggle, he'd come forward as her trusted confidant and faithful friend. Damned straight, she needed him in her corner, and she'd better not turn stubborn like Alex knew she could.

At last, she whispered, "I'll bring my laptop. That'll give me something to do until David delivers Dempsey. I'll find Montego for you."

"I know you will. Now get packed. The guys will be there soon." He hung up the phone and tagged Agents Lee Hart and Adam Torrey to escort Mother and Dempsey to his place. One mission accomplished. One tender one about to unfold whether he wanted it to or not. One hellacious one to go. And the sun wasn't up yet.

Chapter Twenty-Three

Beau's first thought of the day? *'If this is a dream, I don't ever want to wake up.'* It was immediately followed by, *'Let this be real, Jesus. Please let this be real.'* A man like him didn't wake up with his nose in such a lovely bouquet every morning. Certainly not with his hand all over the soft-as-sin ass of his former physician. It almost made the nagging ache of his injury worth it.

Cocking his head, Beau peered down at the angelic countenance of the sleeping lady snuggled up against him. Now that was a sight worth waking up to. Better than coffee any day. His blood overheated, and his heart started pumping like caffeine had never made it pump before. With an urgency to take McKenna. Hold her. Kiss her. Fold her up in his arms and never let her go. Yeah, he was stupid like that, and waking up with her so soft and pliable in his arms made him a total idiot.

Wondering how she happened to be there with her head on his chest, he licked his lips in manly satisfaction. The cinnamon sugar freckles sprinkled across her nose were tempting, and he was hungry enough to risk running just the tip of his tongue over them. Would they taste as sweet as they looked? He ached to know the answer.

What a perfect armful this valiant Joan of Arc was. His nostrils flared at her feminine scent mingled with some kind of medical antiseptic odor. Yes, she was a little banged up, but he still detected a hint of cream and sugar drifting off her skin. Sugar cookies. That's what the delicious aroma was, vanilla sugar cookies, the kind in the baker's window he'd drooled over back in the day. That scent probably explained why he wanted to eat her up. Beginning with those lush, juicy lips pressed together in an adorable, sleepy pout.

Her nose crinkled. She sniffed, and something unusual happened. He couldn't help it. He smiled. Could anything have touched that cold spot in his heart as quickly? He didn't think so.

They weren't made of the same things. McKenna was sugar and spice and sunshine. He was all things that lurked in shadow. By the sheer force of Mother Nature, they were destined to live apart like polar opposites. She was the tropical equator, where every living species, be it plant, animal, or human, thrived in abundance. He was the North Pole, the barren end of the world, where frigid death ruled, and life could not. Never the twain shall meet, and all that crap.

It was time to leave before she rose like the morning sun and cast that beautiful light of hers across the land. Beau wasn't sure what he'd do then, but it'd probably be stupid, and he simply couldn't take the chance.

Reluctantly, he eased his body out from beneath the luscious warmth of hers. Then he looked twice. There McKenna lay, so warm and soft, her head in a cloud of raspberry blonde. She was the epitome of why he did what he did. Why he was willing to leave that bed and march into battle. Again. Women like McKenna deserved to live long lives full of peace and prosperity. He meant to ensure that she did. Yet even as he stood there debating how badly he needed to leave, he couldn't remember sleeping as well or as deeply as he had last night. What the fuck was that about?

Dressing quietly in the clothes he'd worn yesterday, Beau worked his feet into his boots with one hand. Lacing them and tying them took time, but he managed with just a few whispered cuss words. Donning his holster was just as difficult, but finally, he eased his bandaged hand into his jacket sleeve, promising this was the last time. By the time the sun set today, Montego would be cold and dead. He didn't know exactly how that would go down, but it would. McKenna needed to be safe, and that was enough incentive. End of story.

Stealthily, he made his way to the door, and was soon seated on the bench inside Maverick's front door, retying a boot lace that had come undone, because, hell. He needed two hands and all ten fingers for even the simplest tasks, and tying a lace was no longer easy. The house was quiet, and Beau had work to do. It was better this way.

"Leaving so soon?"

Beau stiffened, his hand barely on the knob that would've gotten him gone. "What's it look like?"

As quiet as the house was this morning, Beau hadn't realized anyone was up until Maverick spoke, but Jesus. His sarcasm could kill a horse as big as one of the gigantic Clydesdales prancing out back in his pasture.

"Looks like you're running away again. Doesn't that ever get old?" Pushing up from the leather couch, Maverick rolled his neck like he thought he was a prizefighter before the first round.

Beau curled his one good hand into a fist. *Guess again, jerk-off. I don't run.*

China strolled out of the kitchen in a bathrobe draped over long navy-blue pajama bottoms, and a top that said, **Ride 'Em, Cowboy**, in big, bold script across her chest. Two mugs steamed in her hand. Like the strong-willed, over-confident, annoying woman he'd always found her to be, China walked straight up to him and handed one mug over. "Thought you'd be gone by now, but I'm glad you're not. Here. I made this for you. You like it black, right?"

He couldn't help it. His nostrils flared at the tempting aroma. His stomach growled. "Yes, ma'am. Thanks," he said as he accepted the delay tactic. One cup wouldn't hurt.

"How'd you like the meat and cheese tray?" she asked, a saucy gleam in her eye. "I wasn't sure what you preferred, so I gave you a sample of the best we had. I would've brought beer, but drugs and booze don't sit well on a guy's stomach. Was the bottled water cold enough?"

"It was fine," he answered, dipping his head in deference to the lady. "Everything you've done for me is very much appreciated."

"You'll accomplish more after a hearty breakfast, you know," she said, staring him down. Taunting him. Making him wish he'd gotten up ten minutes earlier and left sooner. "If you leave now, you'll miss the fun."

"I don't do fun," he growled even as he took a sip of the aromatic beverage in his hand.

Maverick rolled his eyes. "No, really? Tell me something I don't know."

"But you do care for McKenna," China insisted, her deep blue eyes glimmering with truth Beau couldn't deny. "And while she's here, I intend for her to rest and be happy. Don't you want that for her, too?"

His reasons for leaving were slipping away. "She's a client, that's all."

"Uh-huh. That's not what I hear. Kelsey told me how panicked McKenna was when you got her to safety last night. How she clung to you. You might not know it right now, but that woman needs you. She's not strong like you are, and she's falling apart. Maybe she needs you more than you need her. I don't really care, but you will not desert her in her hour of need."

He cocked his head at the nerve of the woman Maverick married. "If I recall correctly, ma'am, I was the only one there for her in her *hour of need*," Beau reminded her with a sarcastic twist.

Maverick nodded from the couch. "You're right, and that makes you responsible. I don't know what she sees in you, but when she wakes and finds you gone, what do you think she'll do? I'll tell you what. She's going to freak. She'll think you deserted her. You're her life line right now. You leave, she sinks. Might not be what you want to hear, but that woman in there" —he tipped his head toward the bedroom Beau had just snuck out of— "is hanging on by a thread. For Hell's sake, stay until she's ready to let you go."

Beau gave Maverick his chin. "You make me sound like a cane. A walker. Isn't that your job?"

China had the nerve to giggle. "I never thought of it that way, but that's exactly what you are, Beau, and precisely what McKenna needs. Someone to keep her from falling off the deep end. We're not asking you to marry her. Just hang around until she catches her balance. That's all. She's a strong woman, but she's traumatized. It won't take long. You'll see."

They made it sound easy, but Beau knew better. He wasn't good enough for McKenna, even as a walker. She needed someone better than a broken-down sniper, who hadn't yet caught his own balance after all life had thrown at him. Yeah, Kelsey and China seemed okay with the rugged men they'd married, but Alex and Maverick were made of different stuff. They were still assholes, but not broken assholes. They were that indefinable *'good enough'* he would never be.

It was time to go. He had a bitch to hunt. Until the door he'd closed only a few moments earlier reopened, and McKenna caught him standing there. Leaving her.

Her soft green eyes glimmered as if she'd woken up alone, confused, and afraid. As if she'd been crying. Her nose was red. Her eyelids were puffy. The simple cotton shift clung to her body, revealing her shape in ways she probably didn't realize. But he did. The tender peaks of her taut nipples pointed at him like twin lasers. Accusing him of betrayal. Of promises broken. The bandage covering the razor-thin line at her neck mocked his righteous intentions and outright called him, *'Liar.'*

"You're leaving?" she said, the squeak of a tremor in her voice and her fluttering fingers unsteady on the doorjamb. That was what got to him. He couldn't make himself look away, her devastated countenance daring him to keep lying. To keep leaving.

"It's what I do, ma'am," he replied evenly to keep this farewell brief. "You wouldn't be here to begin with if not for me doing my job last night. That's all this is, a job."

"Oh," she whispered, blinking like a deer about to bolt for cover.

His head canted with the first inkling of indecision. His heart stuttered. This was a first. Nobody had ever looked so forlorn at his leaving before. Hell, no one had missed him, not once in his life. The feeling unsettled the steel in his spine.

"Okay then, b-b-but, umm… are you leaving?" she asked again, like she hadn't heard his answer the first time. What she really meant was, *'Do you have to go? Why can't you stay? How can you do this to me?'*

Because you don't need someone like me in your life. Trust me. You don't.

China and Maverick were watching out there somewhere, but Beau had lost track of them. "Doctor Fitzgerald. I..." *Damn, I don't know what to say. Or do. I can't hurt you again, but I have to.*

"B-b-but I... I..." McKenna leaned into the doorframe, her eyes glistening and on the verge of tears. She was making this hard. It had to end.

"Ma'am," he said sternly. Purposefully. Using the same voice he'd used on others he'd rescued over the years. "I save people for a living. It's what I do. Go back to bed. Trust me, you're just one of many." *Only you're not, and I'm only leaving because I can't risk anything happening to you.*

Someone stifled a growl behind him. Sounded like a wolf. Could've been Maverick. But it might've been his wife.

"Oh-okay, then. B-bye," McKenna said softly, her voice breaking as she backed away and shut herself inside the guest bedroom once more.

"That was cold, you ass," China snapped. "You really don't have any social skills, do you, Jennings?"

"That what your hubby told you?" Beau bit out.

Maverick waved him off. "Leave him be, China. It's better this way. McKenna doesn't need the grief. Go, Jennings. Do your thing. Leave. Be a fuckin' hero. Don't know why the boss wastes time on you."

Beau leveled a lethal glare at his alleged teammate. "That makes two of us."

It wasn't hard to leave then. With a rapid about-face, he turned and shut Maverick's front door as quietly as he'd closed McKenna's bedroom door only moments earlier. There was no sense slamming it like a two-year-old and making a ruckus. This was who he was, and hunting predators was what he did. Catalina Montego *would* die today. He'd make sure of it.

He made it halfway down the long gravel driveway when Maverick yelled, "Wait up!"

Beau whirled on the guy, his fist clenched, sick to death of having to defend every last one of his actions. This shit needed to stop. Right. Damned. Now. "What the fuck do you want now, Carson?"

Damn Maverick stopped short and ran a hand through his hair. "Before you go, I, ah, I hate to ask, but I... Shit, I need a hand. It'll just take a couple minutes, I hope. China'd help if she could, but she won't leave McKenna and—"

"And I will, right?" Beau spat. "Fuck, I get it, Carson. I'm an asshole, and the rest of you are fuckin' saints who walk among us inferior little people, gracing us with your divine presence. Well, you can just back the fuck off and let me be. I don't need you or anyone else on this fuckin' mess you call a team!"

Maverick cocked his head as if he didn't understand.

"For Christ's sake, Carson! Do I have to spell it out? What the fuck do you need, one last swing at—?"

Maverick's hands came up, placating. "I'm not here to fight you, man. Settle down before you give yourself another heart attack. Did you just hear yourself? That was the longest string of fucks I've heard since I left the Corps. Why are you pissed all the time? We're only trying to help you and Doc Fitz."

Beau stood there breathing hard, his heart pounding a merciless beat. Too late he remembered that damned thing in his chest had quit on him only a couple days ago. He shouldn't get so spun up that it stopped again. He'd never find Montego then, and McKenna might die because of him this time around.

Not going to happen.

Maverick might be right. Deliberately, Beau inhaled as slowly as he could. Through his nostrils. Then blew it out through his mouth and did it again. But there was no way he'd answer that stupid question. Beau wasn't just pissed. A lifetime of stored self-loathing and misdirected anger put him light years beyond simply being pissed. Try nuclear.

For whatever reason, the same instant Beau exhaled, Maverick also blew out a long, slow breath. What the hell? Did he have heart trouble, too?

He licked his top lip like he was nervous. Like he didn't want to be standing there with Beau any more than Beau wanted to be held up by him. "To be honest, I need your help with one of my mares, and it might take more than a few minutes. She's been in labor all night, but the foal's stuck. She's in trouble. I lost her grandmother in a fire a couple years back. I can't lose her, too."

So not what Beau had expected. His lips curled in a sneer. "You want *me* to help you? *Me?* Do you remember who you're talking to? You sure you don't need Gabe or Taylor? Aren't they your buddies? I hear Cartwright was supposed to be here by now. So, where's your shadow?"

Maverick shook his head, fire flashing in those dark, mean browns again. "Knock it off. It doesn't matter where he is, but you're here now. I've been up all the night, and I can't do this alone. I've got two hired hands, but they're old geezers. I can't risk them getting hurt." The guy sure sounded sincere. What if he was? What if he was really asking for help?

Beau looked at the dark clouds gathering in the western sky beyond Maverick's shoulder, not certain of anything that had to do with the Carsons. For all he knew, Gabe was probably inside the ranch with his wife. Keeping her safe. Being the good husband Beau would never be. Hell, it might rain before he caught a ride to where he still wasn't sure he was going. Too bad Marcus and his cab weren't around.

Jesus Christ, if it'd been anyone but Maverick asking for help...

"Yeah, fine," he finally grumbled. "I'll help, but this better go down quick. McKenna needs to live, damn it, and I intend to make sure she does. Now move it. I've got a bitch to hunt."

Maverick canted his hard head, the shaft of morning sun glinting off the side of his face a sharp contrast to the thunder clouds at his six. "That's why you're leaving? To protect her?"

That pissed Beau off. "What'd you think, asshole? That I'd run out on her when the going gets tough?" He clenched his one good fist into a hammer. Damn these arrogant sons-of-bitches! Everyone on the whole fuckin' TEAM thought they were better than him. Well, they weren't! He saved McKenna, him—only him—while they were out chasing their asses. He'd done it and he'd done it alone. Because alone was what Beau did best. Why couldn't these pricks get that through their fat heads?

"Doesn't matter what I thought," Maverick replied quietly, some of the tension gone from his ugly face. "Come with me. I gave the mare something to help speed things up earlier this morning. This shouldn't take long." He nodded at the barn that took up most of the rest of his property. Might have been a stable. Beau didn't know the difference. There were a few horses browsing the fence line, though.

"Where we going?" he asked before he willingly committed one more step to a path that hadn't felt right to him since he'd signed onto The TEAM.

Maverick tossed over his shoulder, "To do what you do best, Jennings. Save a life."

Chapter Twenty-Four

"You're not my mom anymore," McKenna said out loud as she sat at the edge of the bed, blinking her fears away. "You threw that gift away, when you killed yourself, Aurora. When you hanged yourself with your gown. Remember that day? I do, because I never saw Dad cry before they called and told him what you did. You should've been there with him and me, but you weren't, were you? No, because you were always more important than everyone else. Even him."

Both McKenna's demons sat with her. The one with a long, black braid. The one with shorter-than-short blonde hair, spiked because Aurora hacked it off in a fit one day. Then said she'd done it because *'short hair makes me look so much younger'*. And a lot crazier.

"I'm safe now. You c-c-can't hurt me," McKenna murmured, rocking forward and backward, not willing to look either of them in the eye, yet fully aware how close they both hovered over her shoulder. Watching. Peering down at her. Waiting. Ever ready to push her off the thin tightrope she balanced on. To shove her over the edge to where she'd never be seen again. Into the abyss or a closet. Either way, she'd be out of sight and out of mind.

Demons breathed, bet you didn't know that. But, yeah. Icy breaths skated beneath the cotton shift and drifted down McKenna's spine like nagging frigid fingertips. Tap, tap, tapping her shoulders, threatening her fragile hold on self-control. Reminding her that they knew better. Loosening the threads that bound her to the real world. Eroding the world beneath her feet, until strand by strand and bit by bit, she unraveled. Like sand on a never-ending beach of solitude and sin, McKenna could feel herself sinking. She'd felt the sting of Beau's curt dismissal more than she thought she would. It shouldn't have hurt, but after the gentle way he'd handled her last night and this morning...

After the promise he'd made that he'd stay... she'd thought... she'd thought...

"I'm stupid," she said out loud. That was exactly what she was. Stupid to think the nightmare her mother branded her soul with would ever go away. Stupid to believe lightning didn't strike twice.

'Stupid. Dumb. Insignificant. They're all the same,' the ghost of her mentally-ill mother taunted. *'And all you'll ever be.'*

'Child,' was all the evil spirit of that other crazy woman had to whisper to make McKenna's blood run cold.

"I'm not your child and you're not my mothers," McKenna told her tormentors unequivocally as she shrugged them off, her resolve shaking as much as her shoulders. This wasn't her first panic attack. It wouldn't be her last, but she could overcome this one. She could... if she could only get a grip.

Even on her best days, McKenna hated loud noises and small, crowded places. The tiniest things threw her back in time, back into that dark bedroom closet where her mother stored coats, the vacuum cleaner, winter boots and...

'You.'

McKenna slapped her hands over her ears. "Stop it, Aurora! Just stop!" Swallowing hard, she said what she'd said so many times before. "I am a doctor, a pediatrician. I do good work in this town, and people respect me. They should. I studied, and I worked hard to become who and what I am today. I might be my mother's daughter, but I am *not* my mother. I am a survivor. I am strong. I am smart."

'You can't escape this. Bi-polar disorder is genetic. It's a mental illness, and it's passed from one generation to the next. From mother to daughter. From the weakest to the weakest,' the most insidious spirit at her side whispered, the one who should've always had her back but never did.

"No, no, no!" McKenna shook her head angrily at that untruth, not arguing with ghosts that weren't really there. Just because Aurora had been bi-polar and unstable didn't mean McKenna would be. Mental illness wasn't always passed. That wasn't true.

'But sometimes...'

"You're wrong. No!" McKenna rocked harder. Faster. She closed her eyes and focused on what she knew to be true. "You're not my mother. Not anymore. I am a doctor, a pediatrician. I do good work in this town, and people respect me. They should. I might be my mother's daughter, but I am *not* my mother. I *am* a survivor. I *am* strong. I *am* smart."

'No, you're not. You're just like me...'

Breathing hard now, McKenna jumped to her feet, needing to run, but trapped like always. "You are not my mother," she hissed. "You gave up that right when *you* left *me*. When you beat me, do you hear? When you hanged yourself? You weren't my mom then, and you're not my mom now. Dad's right. Mothers love their babies. I will survive you!"

Chapter Twenty-Five

Turned out Maverick wasn't kidding. The magnificent mare standing in what he'd called the birthing stall was as big as a house, and she growled when he and Beau approached.

"Easy, Gorgeous," Maverick soothed as he climbed over the rails and stepped alongside her, his flat palm on the animal's long, sweaty snout.

"I didn't know horses growled," Beau muttered, because, well. He didn't know anything about horses, and he had other places to be. Setting his gear inside the barn door, he removed his jacket, but left his holster on.

"Only when they're extremely stressed, and this mama's having a hard time, aren't you, girl?" Maverick said, a particularly calm tone in his voice.

What was that, his horse whisperer voice? Beau nearly snorted. Of all The TEAM, Maverick was the most arrogant. Almost as bad as Alex.

The horse tossed her head and gave another low growl, which ended in a groan. Beau had to admit that she was a pretty thing, her creamy white coat slick with sweat. She had the longest, whitest mane and tail. Her black eyes were too big for her face. Standing there in a single shaft of sun from somewhere overhead, she looked like a mythical unicorn straight out of a fairytale.

"So what'd you want me to do?" Beau asked, testy and needing to be gone.

Maverick answered with an extended palm, a definite hand signal to shut the fuck up.

Beau rolled the pain in his neck off, wishing he could shrug Maverick off as easily.

The horse kept shifting, not lifting those massive hooves off the floor as much as shuffling over it. Her nostrils flared as she bared her teeth. Her prehensile horse lips peeled back, displaying a magnificent set of choppers that Beau had no intention of getting close to. Animals in pain bit people, and he'd already been bitten one too many times. Cradling his injured arm to his chest, he stopped on the safe side of the stall, where nothing would kick the shit out of him.

Speaking of shit… Beau thought he'd be stepping in layers of it by now, but clean hay covered the entire floor of that stall, and the rest of the barn was tidy. Clean. Almost immaculate. There was no pungent odor of mold and urine, only the sweet scent of clean hay. Fresh air. Not what he expected. Most barns he'd been in overseas were manure nightmares, more like dirty shacks where people lived alongside their livestock.

"What now?" he asked, his temper in check for the first time since he'd left McKenna behind.

"Now I need you to hold her halter while I wrap her tail. Climb on in." Maverick held out a long plastic bag that he'd pulled from a drawer in the cupboard in the corner of the stall.

Beau shook his head and extended his good hand. "Bring her over here. I can hold her halter from where I am right now."

"Not happening. She needs both of us, now get in here. She won't bite." Maverick shot him a lethal glare. "What are you, US Army Ranger or chicken?"

That did it. Snorting, Beau put one boot to the stall bars and carefully climbed to the top rail, using only his good hand for balance. Now was not the time to fall on his face and prove Maverick right. The asshole would probably tell everyone else, and he'd never live it down.

The horse reared back and whinnied—or something. She made a rumbling sound deep in her chest, her eyeballs rimmed with white as if she dared him to join her. Beau planted his ass on the top rail, not chicken. More like concerned. That was all. Cautious. Yeah. "Damn it, Carson. You trying to get me killed?"

Maverick didn't answer. He'd stuffed the plastic bag in his rear pocket, and there it dangled like a touch football flag, taunting Beau to man up. Too busy running his palms over the mare's big belly, along her ribs, and down her rump, Maverick seemed oblivious to everything but the horse. The damned guy had nerve, as close as he'd gotten to an animal that could stomp him into all that nice clean hay with one massive hoof. Hell, all that mare had to do was squeeze him against the stall bars, and he'd be pulp.

But did he have one lick of common sense? Uh-uh. Moving back to her front quarters, Maverick wrapped one arm around her sweaty neck and pressed his face against her big cheek. Damned if the mare didn't bow that big long head of hers and close her eyes like she and Maverick were communicating. Like they were hugging. What the hell?

But if a dumb-as-shit jarhead could do it...

Beau dropped quietly to the floor inside the stall.

"You're hurting, baby, aren't you?" Maverick murmured in the horse's ear as his hand took long, flat strokes down her neck.

Beau snapped the plastic bag out of Maverick's pocket and eased his injured hand into what really was just a long, plastic sleeve with fingers at one end. Interesting. "I thought horses dropped their, umm, colts in the field?"

"Not mine," Maverick answered, one arm still wrapped around the mare's wide neck and his head up close and personal with hers. My hell, what if she reared back or bucked or decided he was worth stepping on? What if she panicked because of her pain and lost her head? Maverick could get hurt.

Not that Beau cared. But he still approached cautiously, so he didn't disturb the Zen thing going on between Maverick and his horse. "Have you done this a lot before?" *Because it's really weird.*

With a slow, deliberate breath, Maverick stepped away from his *'baby'* and tugged the rope Beau hadn't noticed from around his neck. He clipped it to the mare's halter, then passed the other end to Beau. "Yes, I've done this a few times. Here. Keep her on her feet while I take care of business."

Whatever that meant. Beau stepped into the danger zone. He wrapped the woven rope over the knuckles of his good hand, while he pressed his plastic covered injured arm to his chest to keep it from getting hurt. Thank you, Jesus, that Libby was now a doctor amd could prescribe pain pills.

Surprisingly, the horse still had her head down and her eyes closed. She'd still nicker once in a while, but she didn't seem to mind him holding her halter. He'd gotten close enough now to detect how her withers and her big belly shivered. How she groaned softly. This mother was in obvious pain. She wasn't mean. Reaching his good hand to the end of her velvety nose, he said, "You're not so bad, are you?"

Of course she didn't answer. She was just a horse, and he was no horse whisperer.

"How long's it usually take? For a Clydesdale to, umm, drop a colt I mean?" Beau asked, genuinely interested. As big as this mare was, she appeared docile—for now.

"Gorgeous is a Percheron, not a Clydesdale," Maverick replied from the south end of the horse, where he was busy doing something Beau didn't want to see. "There's a difference."

"If you say so," Beau muttered. The mare was bigger, wider, and taller than him by a good foot. Maybe more. Her sheer size intimidated him—a little—not that he'd admit it out loud. "You call her Gorgeous?"

Maverick grunted. "Long story, but yeah. That's not her registered name, but she looks so much like her grandmother. Seemed the right thing to do at the time."

Beau tossed a glance over his shoulder. One curious and just as big, brown horse hung its head over a stall gate at the opened end of the barn, as if trying to see what Maverick was doing. "That her father, umm, her stud down there?" Beau had no idea how to ask what he meant. He was out of his element. Put a weapon in his hand and he'd sound smarter.

Maverick peered around Gorgeous's tremendous hindquarters to the horse in question. "The bay? Nah, that's no stud, that's Star. He's a gelding and he's just nosey."

"Where are your other horses? Out to pasture?"

"They're either in the stable or behind the barn, yeah." Maverick cocked his head as he came around Gorgeous, his hand smoothing over her quivering ribs and up under her mane. "You've never been around horses before, have you?"

"Isn't that obvious?"

For the first time since Beau joined The TEAM, a genuine light lit Maverick's normally dark, foreboding eyes. "Trust me, you've got nothing to worry about with any of these kids, well, except for Joker. He likes to introduce himself by stepping on your foot and leaning into you until you fall on your ass, so watch out for him. The rest are just good kids. Now let's get this mama comfortable, so I can go back inside and tell China she's a grandma again."

"You talk about this old nag like she's a person," Beau scoffed even as he looked over his shoulder, wondering *'Where's Joker?'*

"Some days I like her better than most people." Maverick fingered a circle in the air. "Walk her around but take it slow. This one's larger than we expected."

Beau took a few steps before he asked, "You mean the colt's bigger?"

Maverick stood there watching Gorgeous, his chin in his fist and his brows narrowed. "Yes, but it's called a foal, Beau. A newborn horse is a foal. If it's a male, it's a colt. A female's a filly. Once a filly throws her first foal, she's a mare. Once a colt's old enough, he's gelded unless China decides she wants another stallion. Right now, three's her limit."

"Where are the stallions?"

"We keep Ebony, Aces Wild, and Hex in a separate paddock away from the geldings and mares. They're high strung and can be volatile. We don't take chances with any of our kids."

Beau grunted. Kids. Maverick kept calling these monsters kids.

"Is she pulling on the lead?" Maverick asked.

"A little." Gorgeous acted more like she wanted to stop moving, so Beau had slowed his pace, just in case, you know, something dropped out of her south end. "Want me to walk her faster?"

"Nah, you're doing fine. Just make sure you keep that injured hand clean. I'm still surprised you're on your feet instead of flat on your back where you should be. That finger operation was no small deal."

Beau shrugged. "I've been hurt worse. This is nothing."

Maverick opened his mouth to speak, but the horse beat him to it. She groaned. Her whole body shuddered. She twisted to the side like she wanted to see what was happening behind her, and—Oomph! The biggest colt, um, foal, um, whatever slid out of her posterior and into home base.

"She did it. Look, it's a baby!" blurted out of Beau's big mouth before he knew what he'd said. But he'd never seen anything so wet and pretty as that foal when it wriggled out of the bag it came in. Beau wasn't sure why, but tears stung his eyes like the sap he wasn't and had never been. He'd learned that lesson early. He. Did. Not. Cry.

But something was happening, and Beau wanted it to stop. His chest felt like someone had just punched him, a direct hit to his solar plexus. The foal lay exhausted in the hay, its sides heaving as if being born was a tough job, and with every breath, something happened inside Beau. It couldn't be another heart attack, though he was pretty sure he hadn't had one before, either. He pressed his plastic-covered hand to his breastbone, needing that funny, awkward pain to stop pinching him, damn it. To stop squeezing the life out of him. This peculiar sensation was by far, the biggest high he'd ever known. Apparently, birth hurt so much better than death. Who would've thought?

Out of nowhere, a firm hand slapped his shoulder, startling him. "You okay, buddy?"

"Hell, yeah," Beau answered quickly, embarrassed for his unexpected PDA, as in public display of emotion, and more than a little shocked at Maverick's word choice. No one had called him *buddy* in a while.

Maverick stood there beside the mare, glowing, the corners of his mouth barely lifted like it hurt his face to smile, too. "I knew you could do it," he said quietly.

Gorgeous tossed her head and whinnied as if she agreed, which made Beau want to smile. But he didn't. He wasn't so sure Maverick had meant him or the mare by that last remark. Damned unsettling the way Maverick was suddenly—someone else. Like Gorgeous. She wasn't mean. She'd just been in pain with something that large working its way out of her body. Beau couldn't imagine what giving birth to a baby as big as a smart car felt like. And those long spindly legs. Ouch! Just the thought! He winced in empathy.

Damned if Maverick wasn't someone else out here in his barn. He'd changed into—a friend? Beau shrugged it off, not ready to believe. But wondering nonetheless what awful thing Maverick's soul wrestled to expel.

"Oh no," he said, suddenly lighthearted, when only moments ago he'd been sure Maverick was out to denigrate him and everything he said. "That *big* baby did not come out of me, wise ass."

A crooked grin twisted Maverick's normally grumpy face. "You can let go of the lead now."

Beau looked down at the rope looped around his good fingers. He looked back at Maverick. "So why'd she need to walk?"

"She didn't. Most horses drop their foals while standing on their feet. Like you said. It's no big deal."

"Then why'd I walk her in circles?"

"Because *you* needed it. You came into this stall like you were stepping into a lion's den. Except for stallions, most horses are the gentlest creatures on the planet. So tell me, are you afraid of her now?"

Beau dropped the lead. "I wasn't afraid," he growled, though his growl didn't hold much bite. "I was cautious."

Liar.

To prove his newfound respect for equines—and that he was no chicken—Beau ran his good hand down the mare's long snout, while Maverick tended to the foal and whatever else was going on back there. With a toss of her head, Gorgeous ditched Beau's attention for the foal in the hay at her feet, nickering as her tongue took a long swipe over its fuzzy face.

The little thing blinked at the face washing. It was cute in the way of all baby animals. Big brown eyes. Exquisitely long eyelashes. But it was the same color as that Star fellow down the way. Brown with black mane and tail. Not pearly white like the mare.

"So what it is? A colt or a filly?"

Maverick looked up at him from where he knelt in the hay, his dark eyes gleaming in a shaft of golden sunlight that came from somewhere overhead. Maybe straight from heaven, he looked that happy. "We got us a filly," he said proudly.

"Is that good?"

"Oh, yeah." Maverick nodded. "I hate cutting the colts, so hell yeah. It's a damn good day when we get a future mare."

Beau crouched beside Maverick and the foal, curious. "Cutting must be…?" He let the question trail away.

"Cutting *them* off," Maverick said. "I know it's the smart thing to do, and it's for their benefit. But it just seems wrong, robbing these perfect little guys of their manhood before they even know what to do with it."

Automatically, Beau's manhood shrunk in his jeans. McKenna would love this new baby horse. With that errant, crazy notion still pinging in his head, guilt came with it. *Oh, damn.* Beau glanced over his shoulder at the barn door. He'd walked out when she'd needed him. Unlike so many others in his life, she hadn't wanted him to go. He'd hurt her when he'd left, then made it worse, when, like a dumbass, he'd told her, *'I save people for a living. Go back to bed. Trust me, you're just one of many.'*

The truth was far different. She was one of damned few. His gaze dropped to the miracle in the straw at his feet. So pure. So fresh. But not the miracle that McKenna was. Not by a long shot. He lifted to his feet. "I gotta go."

"Where?" Maverick barked. Like he cared?

Beau turned on him then. He'd never seen this side of Maverick before. The man flipped so fast, one minute calm, the next ready to fight, Beau couldn't keep up. *Jesus, he's just like me. He's mad, too.* Beau looked for telltale scars on Maverick, but he simply didn't have time for the man or his horses anymore. Beau had a lady to rescue, this time from himself.

All he said was, "McKenna. I gotta go see McKenna."

Chapter Twenty-Six

McKenna had never felt more alone. She didn't dare call her father, not yet. Sanders Fitzgerald deserved to hear from the sane daughter he'd spoken with yesterday, not the rambling, weeping mess she'd turned into since. With her back to the padded headboard, she rocked, lost in the world she'd honestly thought she'd put in her past.

China had been in with coffee and toast after Beau left, but McKenna didn't want anything from China, even as nice as she was. And she didn't want breakfast. No. To purge the ghosts from her life once and for all, McKenna needed one thing, to get back into her apartment. With a gun. That was what she needed, to ensure her one place of safety was clean and clear again, damn it. Not that she'd shoot anyone, but a weapon seemed the only way to confront that vicious Catalina woman. Not that McKenna knew how to shoot, but she could learn.

She'd been to enough psychologists and counselors to know the only way forward was to confront her fears. Again. Her previous escape from the trauma inflicted by her twisted mother hadn't been easy. McKenna would NOT relive any of that. She knew what to do.

Never give in. Never give up. Survive. Survive. Survive, damn it. Even if it took all you had to give. The most important thing a victim could learn was to: *Survive!*

As patiently as if she were speaking to her youngest patient, she told her ghosts one more time. "I am a doctor, a pediatrician. I do good work in this town, and people respect me. They should. I might be my mother's daughter, but I am *not* my mother. I *am* a survivor. I *am* strong. I *am* smart."

But none of her patients were as evil as these, so she started again. "You are not my mother—"

"Thank you, Jesus."

Her head snapped up at the firm, masculine voice. Beau stood there with the door hiding half of his body. Half in the room. Half out. Like a coward. Despite the promises he'd made, he'd left her as easily as her mother did.

McKenna knew one thing. She didn't need another ghost. She straightened in the bed, running her fingers through her hair while waves of dizziness from that simple movement swarmed her. Trying not to look as hysterical or as unbalanced as she felt, she stared him down, not feeling particularly kind or gracious or forgiving.

Big whoop. Beau's back. Who needs him? Not me. He had his chance. What's he want now?

"Did you forget something?" she asked through the glimmer of tears she refused to let fall. She'd never cry in front of this man again. Tears were for people she trusted. To prove it, she got to her feet, crossed her arms over her chest in the universal symbol of defiance, and gave him her chin.

"Yeah. You." He dropped something just inside the door. In two long strides, he crossed the room and was standing in front of her. "I forgot taking care of you was more important than hunting that mongrel bitch, Montego. I forgot you're the most important person in the universe. I forgot my most important job is—you."

McKenna stared up at him. "M-me?" she asked, amazed he had the nerve to come right out and say precisely what she needed to hear. But then her stubbornness took over. "I'm not just a job," she said defiantly. He needed to back off.

If only she hadn't sounded like a lost little girl. But oh! How she wanted to climb inside the leather jacket on that hard, male body and never be seen again. He'd held her last night. Would he do it again? She caught herself leaning into him.

Damn Montego! This was her fault!

It wasn't like McKenna to be timid. So scared or so needy. She *did* do good work in this town. She *was* a respected physician and a good person, and she didn't need anyone else in order to be who she was. She—Dr. McKenna Fitzgerald—was good enough all by herself!

Until Beau said softly, his eyes more black than brown for a change, and full of tenderness, "Yes, you, baby. I came back for you. Only you."

"Me?" She asked again, blinking the burgeoning flood of tears away.

He really did have a beautiful face, his dark hair framing the angles and lines of a masculine sculpture made from the richest caramel marble. So tan. So incredibly perfect. The last time she'd seen him, he'd been clean-shaven. This morning, sexy stubble shadowed his jaw and cheeks, accentuating the slash of his lips.

If not for the bruises and claw marks Montego had inflicted, he'd be solid male-model material. Yet even marked and defiled, he was still the handsomest, most cantankerous, onerous, stubborn man McKenna had ever met. She swallowed the lump in her throat, afraid to believe someone as hard and brave and courageous as Beau had really came back for her. *And he called me baby.*

When he dipped his head to hers and pressed a warm kiss to her forehead, she couldn't help herself. Her nostrils flared to capture his unique scent, a combination of earth, wind, and fire. Of alfalfa, the great outdoors, and a lingering hint of leather and smoke. *My heavens, this man smells like autumn, my favorite time of year.*

"I'm sorry I walked out on you," he muttered, his tone a silky rumble, "but I'm not real smart. I'm a hard man who's had to fight every day of his life. I didn't waste time in boarding schools or college, but if you'll let me, I will fight for you. I understand if you want me to leave—"

"No!" she cried as she buried her face in his black shirt and sobbed, her nerves so damned raw and her defenses crumbling at this unexpected apology. "No, no, no," she told him, her fingers knotted in his collar. Burrowing her shoulders between the zippers of his jacket, her words came between choppy, hard hiccups. "D-don't l-l-leave me. I c-can't do this alone."

"Do what alone?" he growled as his one good hand smoothed over her shoulder, pulling her in close until he had her wrapped tight under his chin, encased within the steel bands of his arms like he'd never let her go.

"This," she said as she trembled, content to breathe in the scent she loved best because it was his. "Live without being afraid of sh-shadows."

"Jesus, you're shaking like a leaf."

"I'm sorry," she squeaked, her eyes brimming as tears leaked into his shirt.

"You have nothing to be sorry about, so stop apologizing," he murmured soft and low in her ear. "You want to be afraid, you go ahead and be scared. It'll pass. You're the victim here, not the perpetrator. And I'm the fool. I never should've walked away from you. I won't do it again. Breathe for me, baby. Just breathe. You're having a panic attack like most people who've been attacked and tortured. But I'm here now, and you can let it go. Be afraid for as long as you want, because deep down inside, you're stronger than you think you are. You'll see. These attacks won't get the best of you for long. Not Doctor Fitzgerald, and that's who you are."

"It is," she agreed, "but I hate being the victim. I've worked so hard to rise above what happened before, b-b-but now… but now…" Ashamed of stuttering, she nuzzled deeper into the hollow of his neck, needing his sure strength to keep from falling apart. Needing his scent all over her, like a shield. Like a force field that would surely keep Montego at bay.

"What happened before?" he asked, his lips in her hair.

Haltingly, McKenna opened her heart and told him what she'd never told anyone else before. About her mother's bi-polar highs and lows. Her mental illness. The closet. The beatings. The temper tantrums, the wild accusations, and the screaming. The day her dad discovered the truth about his happy little family. McKenna ended with, "I hate being a victim."

"Trust me, no one likes being victimized. That bitch got a piece of me, too," he told her.

With that reminder of Montego's vicious cruelty, McKenna lost control. Was he whining like a weak little girl? No, but... but...

The torrent she'd been holding back burst like fragile glass against an unmovable rock. Beau held her while she sobbed like a baby. He'd suffered a worse atrocity at Montego's hand than she had, yet here he was, comforting her, when he should've been flat on his back in bed healing.

"There, there," he said, his voice soft and sweet and gravelly low. Soothing. He never let go, not for a second. Just let her take what she desperately needed. His firm touch. His heavenly, masculine scent. The power he commanded.

She'd heard him fight last night. He'd sounded viciously mean battling Catalina, and McKenna needed a powerfully vicious man in her corner. Beau was that man, and somehow, he could put all her broken pieces back together.

She didn't know how many hours she'd spent caught in Montego's wire web. It had seemed like forever, but McKenna knew just how cunningly clever that evil woman was. Not just anyone could defeat Montego. Only someone who truly understood the depravity of her crimes. Only one willing to do what Beau did.

In my house! Oh, my God, that woman was in my house! While I was naked and talking to my dad and being stupid!

Another panic attack rattled over McKenna, but she had something to hang onto this time. Her hands had long since slid under Beau's leather jacket around to his back. Her fingers bumped against the hard leather of his side holsters when she did that, and she was glad for every death-dealing round in the chambers of those pistols. Yes, Beau would keep her safe.

With her face nestled deep inside that jacket, he held her tight, rocking ever so slightly. At last her tears subsided. McKenna drew in a fortifying breath. By then, his shirt was drenched, and she was thoroughly ashamed. *I am not weak!*

"This is all your fault," she told him petulantly. "You left me. Why'd you have to go and do that?" *I was holding it together until then. Honest, I was.*

"Because I'm stupid," he muttered. "But I learned something about myself today. You need someone in your corner right now, McKenna, and I want that person to be me. Not Maverick or China Carson. Not Alex or anyone else, understood? Just me. You got that?"

Despite her independent spirit, she nodded, her fingers tight around his neck, her ear pressed against the taut muscles of his chest while he stroked her hair. Compliance wasn't her normal response, but last night had shaken her feminine paradigms to the foundation. There were predators in the world, sometimes where you least expected them.

She didn't doubt she'd be strong enough to—one day— lift her head up high. But never again would she fight a protection order. Never would she think she knew better than experts like Alex. And never, ever would she leave herself as exposed as she had with Montego. *I let that witch into my house!*

A shiver lanced her heart. That was wrong. Montego had already been inside her apartment. In her bedroom. *Maybe even while I was naked and sipping wine in my bathtub like a Hollywood starlet who runs into the basement, when she already knows there's a killer with an ax in the house. How stupid am I?*

A shudder roared over McKenna, shaking her like a dog with a rug, at how ugly last night could have gone and how lucky she'd been. Instantly Beau squeezed until she could barely breathe. And that was okay with McKenna. She needed this man with his crude words and his big muscular arms and every last one of his f-bombs. He could swear all he wanted. She needed him, just him.

But she could do bossy, too. "You really should elevate that hand more," the doctor within her told him even as she settled down to listen to the strong, male heartbeat under her ear. Was there any better sound in the world? If there was, she didn't know it. "I want to learn how to defend myself. I want you to teach me gun safety, and I want a gun just like yours, Beau. Maybe a bigger one."

He had the nerve to chuckle. The vibration of that deep baritone radiated all the way to her nearly defeated soul. "A really big gun?" he asked, a definite tease in his voice.

She could tell he was laughing at her. She nodded, the top of her head bumping his chin. "Yes. A really, really big gun. Maybe like the one *Dirty Harry* used."

"Sorry for poking fun at you, ma'am. I don't mean to, but the first thing they told us in the Army is that our pistols and rifles are weapons, not guns."

That doesn't make sense. A gun is a gun.

"It's all semantics, but..." He smoothed his right hand down her arm until he reached her clenched left hand, and then he settled it between their bodies on his—*oh, my*—cock. "This is a gun. So if you want a really big one, I can certainly oblige."

He probably thought he'd embarrassed her by that crude gesture, but McKenna left her hand right where he'd put it.

The size of that steel spike in his pants and the way his breath hitched at her touch told her exactly what she needed to know. He was all man, and for the moment, all hers.

"You're hired," she said. He could figure out for what job she meant later.

"Say it with me," he said, his tone filled with the same rumbly gentleness she only vaguely remembered from last night when he'd first picked her up and held her. "I might be my mother's daughter, but I am not my mother. I am a survivor. I am strong. I am smart, and I am beautiful. I have a heart of gold, and I will survive, because I'm like a gingerbread man. I'm not done baking yet. I have a glorious future ahead of me, so stick that up your pipe and smoke it."

She repeated her revised mantra, word for word. Well, until she got to the part about her being a gingerbread man. A smile nearly curled the corners of McKenna's lips. Her, a cookie?

A tiny chuckle gurgled at the back of her throat. Which was precisely what she needed, a silly distraction to end the vicious loop powered by her demons, the one still spinning inside her brain.

Funny. Once Beau had shown up, both Aurora and Catalina had vanished like the evil spirits they were. She could breathe again. So she did, filling her lungs with a sense of self-worth, positivity, and his rich, masculine scent while she caressed the big boy in his pants. How'd she get so lucky?

"Don't you mean *'so stick that* in *your pipe and smoke it?'*" she asked as she took another stroke.

His chin brushed over her hair, his whiskers tugging at the strands. "No, ma'am. I meant precisely what I said. Your mother and that bitch, Montego, can stick what me and you think of them straight up their pipes. They can't have you."

She rubbed her nose into the warm skin of his neck, calmed by his fiercely protective declaration. He'd made it sound like she belonged to him. Which was okay with her. "Thank you for coming back, Beau," she whispered. "I missed you."

"And again, McKenna," he prompted, his voice gruff and tender at the same time, like a big, bad, cuddly grizzly bear that didn't know how to accept gratitude or heartfelt feelings.

To make him happy, she repeated the mantra word for word while she stroked him. "I might be my mother's daughter, but I am not my mother. I am a survivor. I am strong. I am smart, and I am beautiful. I have a heart of gold and I will survive, because I'm a gingerbread man. I'm not done baking yet. I have a glorious future ahead of me, so stick that up your pipe and smoke it."

And let me keep fondling you, because I want this. Soon, she promised herself as she calmed her fingers and stopped petting the tiger in her bed. Now wasn't the time to jump into anything crazy like romance. But soon...

Chapter Twenty-Seven

Damned if that confounded mantra didn't creep into Beau's soul with every reiteration despite McKenna's gentle fingers strumming his cock. Every gentle stroke of her hand made it hard—yeah, hard—to focus. It was like one of those songs that got stuck in your head, only his soul had translated her words into: *'I might be my father's son, but I am not him. I am a survivor. Look at me, damn you. I am stronger, and I am smarter than you, you bastard. I'm a better man, too.'"*

The more he repeated McKenna's feel-good formula, the better his heart heard the version of the message meant for him. It helped when she stopped cupping him, not that he wanted her to stop, but neither of them needed to go down on the other, not yet. He let the distraction win—this time— while the message rolled on. *'I am not my fuckin' father. He was dead-assed wrong to treat me like he did. I was just a kid. None of what happened to me or mom or AJ was my fault. He's the sinner, but I survived. Because I am strong. I am smart. I am not your punching bag, you son-of-a-bitch!'*

When McKenna turned soft and mellow in his arms, Beau relaxed. He was still weaker than he'd ever admit, but he had one more job to do before he let his guard down.

"Wait right here," he said as he hurried to the head and retrieved a cool, damp washcloth. Scrambling back, he wiped the tears and sweat from her pretty face. "Better?"

"Yes, thank you. C-come to bed with me? S-stay?"

Jesus, he hated that quiver in her voice. That was on him. He'd put it there. But that accompanying note of trust swept his better sense away. He tossed the cloth into the head. "You bet. Move over."

Carefully, he slipped his good hand out of his jacket, then slid the sleeve down his injured arm to avoid putting pressure on it. After the kind of night he'd lived through, Beau knew he was probably going to lose that finger, but saving McKenna made the loss of a digit worth it.

After he hung his jacket on a hook behind the door and secured his gear, he slid out of his boots, jeans, and shirt, then climbed alongside McKenna in just his boxers. For the first time in a long time, he didn't bring a pistol to bed with him.

Instead of obeying like the docile lamb she wasn't, McKenna had watched intently, her eyes all over him. Mostly on his back. "What happened to you?"

Shit. He'd forgotten his number one rule: *Keep your shirt on, dumbass*. It was out in the open now. He was as exposed as he'd never been. Revealed was more like it.

But instead of lashing her with a belligerent, 'Fuck off!' like he usually did when caught shirtless, Beau let her see a glimpse of his miserable life. They weren't exactly best friends. Might never be more than what they were at this moment, but considering what she'd revealed about her mother, he figured she had a right to know what made him tick. Another survivor might understand.

"My father was a mean old bastard. Used to take a strap to me." *All the damned time.*

"My God, Beau, why?"

"Because he could." His gaze drifted to her slender fingers clutching the white sheet like a last line of defense. Her hands were clean. Not even a broken nail. No calluses either. Just the way a lady's hands should be. Untouched by the dirt of the world. So unlike his.

"Talk to me," she said as she let the sheet go and reached for him.

That single response meant the world to Beau. Her guard was down. He would've pulled back. Should have. No one as pure as McKenna should ever hear what he'd lived through. But he was weary of holding onto the evil of his past. It was time to let someone in. Might as well be someone who cared. Might as well be now.

Carefully, he accepted that tender hand. But that was as far as Beau could make himself go. She didn't need more ugliness in her life, not after last night. Swallowing hard, he changed his mind. "Forget about it. I've moved on."

She cocked her head, her pretty green eyes still puffy and red, but—Jesus, he couldn't name the emotion glimmering there. It wasn't love, that was for damned sure. But whatever it was, it was just as scary.

"You don't have to tell me anything you don't want to," she said evenly, not a hint of pressure in her tone as she intertwined her fingers with his.

He cleared his throat. "Nothing to tell."

"Okay then," she said as she settled beside him and tugged him until he joined her.

Turning her onto her right side, mostly because he couldn't handle the soft light in her gaze, he aligned his body with hers, her back to his chest, then pinched his thumb to his bandaged fingers to grip the sheet and tug it up over them both. He draped his left arm over her, making sure to keep his bandaged mitt high on her shoulder. That ought to be elevated enough.

If he hadn't been injured, Beau would've taken the chance and cupped her breast. But now wasn't the time, and he plain wasn't capable of cupping anything at the moment. Hell, between all the gauze wrapping Kelsey had so carefully reapplied, and the pain meds Libby had shot him up with, he couldn't have felt McKenna's breast in his hand anyway, a true tragedy. If that moment ever came, he wanted every last tactile sensation that a soft and sweet miracle like that had to offer.

Begrudgingly, he now understood he had to let his reattached finger heal or he'd lose it. He also understood that Maverick was a decent guy after all. He was plenty capable of holding the line. It was okay to rest easy. It might even be time for Beau to change his thinking.

Besides, McKenna didn't need some guy groping her. Lying in bed with her like this was about him finally wising up and holding onto the one good thing in his life. It was about him admitting he was as fucked up as they came, but that he could change. That he would. That he needed McKenna as much, maybe more, than she needed him. He might even tell her. Later.

Because, Maverick was right. Beau was chicken, and he knew it. The ire he'd harbored all his life had made him plenty tough and mean. The violence and fury he'd carried like a flaming shield into combat, gave others second thoughts about starting anything with him. Which was what he'd always wanted, that invisible demarcation that dared anyone to step too close or think he was their friend. He wasn't. He'd meant every 'Fuck off!' he'd ever roared.

But that carefully honed anger had also made him weak. It kept him safe, and it had surely earned him one helluva badass rep. But it left him isolated. Shut off from the rough and tumble camaraderie he'd witnessed between other special operators.

Because of the resentment he'd lived with during his childhood, his first course of action was always to lash out. Push back. Make damned sure that no one came too close. He hit first every damned time, and he hit hard. One look at the perpetual sneer on his ugly face, and most people tended to give him a wide berth. And they should.

Until that moment in the barn… Until that big, little filly entered his world like a long-legged gift fresh from heaven. Breathtaking, that was what it was. Jesus, he'd almost cried. That little horse was so pure. So perfect and clean. Like AJ.

Since he'd lost his little sister, Beau thought of himself first, every time. He'd had to. That was how he'd survived all these years. Wasn't anyone on this whole mother-effin' planet looking out for him. But now he knew. He wasn't the important one. Neither was Montego. She might think she was, and for a while, Beau had believed the lie.

But Catalina-Fuckin'-Montego was nothing more than an ugly speed bump on the road of life. Soon he'd mow her down, and she'd be roadkill, and years from now, no one would care how she'd died—which she most certainly would. But every child and baby that McKenna treated, every mother and father whose fears she'd calmed in the dark nights when their babies were sick, would surely remember Dr. Fitzgerald.

Because she was the important one in this nightmare, and by hell, she *would* live the rest of her life in peace. Beau would make sure of that, too.

Chapter Twenty-Eight

She closed her eyes, so thankful for the warm wall of manly muscle at her back. For the heavy arm around her. When Beau's nose ended up in her hair, she didn't care that her locks needed to be shampooed and brushed. Nothing mattered but being safe inside the circle of his arms.

"You think I'm a gingerbread cookie?" she asked, needing to ease the tension that had grown between them when she'd called him on his scars. She shouldn't have drawn attention to them, but the obvious stripes on his shoulders and back were shocking. There were so many, and some were thick, as if his skin had been laid open and never stitched closed. As if he'd been whipped and left untreated. She knew scars and those were not from combat.

The blanket moved as he shrugged. "It was the first thing that came to my mind. Stupid, huh?"

"Not stupid at all. In fact, it was sweet. But why gingerbread?" McKenna had no intention of letting this go. Even as tired as she was, her heart called out to help him. She just needed a different angle. Beau wasn't a man to confront head-on. He'd never accept a handout, so she wouldn't give him one. But a hand up was something else.

He answered with another shrug. "Gino's bakery was only a block away from where I, umm, lived. Used to wait outside the window every morning, waiting while he and his wife loaded the displays. At Christmas, they always had rows of little gingerbread men decorated in red and green frosting."

"Ah, so you're a gingerbread connoisseur," she said, loving the feel of his strong arm on her shoulder.

"Nah. Never tasted one."

That was unexpected. "Why not? That was what you waited for, wasn't it?"

He let out a big puff of air that sent a strand of her hair over her forehead. "That didn't mean I ever got one. Gino didn't like us kids hanging around his place. Said we scared off paying customers and made him look bad."

"Aw, so he shooed you off?" How could an adult do that to little kids? What would it hurt to give away a few cookies?

"I wish. More like he shot us with rock salt. Peppered our asses the few times he hit us."

"He didn't!"

Beau's chin bumped the side of her head when he nodded. "Oh, yeah. I didn't exactly grow up in a high-class neighborhood like you did."

"Where's home?"

"Las Vegas, northeast of the strip in what they call the *Cultural Corridor* because the mayor won't let them put *Shithole* on the map."

McKenna squirmed around while Beau lifted his injured hand until she faced him. "You were in a gang?" she asked as she combed her fingers over his ear through his thick, lush hair, thrilled at the softness of it.

He closed his eyes at her touch, reminding her of a big jungle cat, one who very much needed to be petted. "The kids I ran around with weren't gang material. We were young. Too much trouble."

Her brows crinkled. "How young were you?"

He gave her what she now recognized as his go-to for anything he didn't want to answer. A noncommittal shrug. "I don't know. Young. What's it matter?"

McKenna cupped the back of his head and pulled it to her forehead. "Because I care about you, Beau. You might not know that, but it's true. How old?"

He shrugged again but a soft light softened those hard as flint windows to his soul. "Seven and a half," he admitted begrudgingly.

That couldn't be right. Little kids didn't run wild on city streets, did they? "Seven and a half?"

His chin lifted like he needed to defend himself. "Yeah. So?"

"Where was your mom? Your dad?" *Don't tell me you were alone at that age.*

The shades went down, and the bars came up. He shrugged. Which meant he wasn't ready to share. She'd suspected someone in his past life had broken him, leaving him guarded and scarred. But she'd imagined he'd come from humble beginnings, maybe a single parent home, not that he'd had no family at all. And never in her wildest imaginations could she see a child of seven alone on the streets. Her heart hurt. But okay then. Now that she was calm, thanks to her reluctant hero, it was his turn. McKenna began to assess what she really knew about Beau.

Former Army Ranger. Hispanic descent. Good-looking was the greatest understatement of them all. Deep tawny skin as if his tan had a tan. Thick chested. Built like an ox. Light on his feet. Well over six feet tall. Wide. Stubborn as all get out. She assigned those traits positive marks.

Into the negative column went: Hostile. Defensive. Hot-tempered. Insubordinate. Non-compliant. Argumentative. Possibly scarred for life, both inside and out. Yet none of those seemingly negative traits screamed that he was cruel. Beau wasn't the type to deliberately go out of his way to hurt anyone. He just demanded that the world get out of his way and give him his space.

When she'd first met him in Kelsey's kitchen, he'd been injured and weak by the time she'd arrived. Yet he'd tried valiantly to give Alex what details he could remember. Yes, the tough guy had barked a lot, especially when she'd administered the numbing shots to what was left of his poor finger. But beneath that badass veneer and his prolific f-bombs, she'd detected a hard man coming undone. He'd been disoriented and scared, which made sense. Most military members thought themselves invincible until they were shot, knifed, or—someone hacked off their finger.

Mortality's bitter wake-up call tended to shock guys who thought they were Superman. That was when the real person, the frightened little kid behind the adult male mask, appeared. Beau was no different. Tougher than most, maybe. Edgy and ready to fight the world, definitely. But also hiding a world of hurt behind that macho mask.

Those scars he carried were frightening evidence of past brutality. Not only was he hiding behind them, but he wielded them like a shield in his fight against the world. He used the energy from all that latent anger like an electrically charged force field to keep everyone out of his way.

She'd seen this specific type of survival mechanism before in adopted children from other countries. Not all nations treated their castoffs well. Some only warehoused their unwanted babies in state-run facilities that could never in a million years pass U.S. health codes. But she'd also seen the same survival skills displayed by children who'd endured child abuse. It was a clear case of dissociation, the defensive reflex of a child who'd never known affection or a parent's gentle touch. How sad.

Yes, she'd had her own childhood monster to deal with, but she'd also had her dad. Who did Beau have? Anyone?

She traced a finger from his chin to his earlobe, needing to calm that frightened little boy who'd grown into one frightening mass of lean muscle and temperamental attitude. "Have you ever blacked out?" Blackouts were another indicator of dissociation. The mind could only compensate for so much abuse before it gave up and turned off.

He scrunched his shoulder, which impacted his injured hand, a hand she wanted kept as elevated and as immobile as possible. He should be in the hospital, but that was a battle she wouldn't attempt. Not now. Not yet. She had to tame this surly beast first. Yet he had effectively deflected another question, a definite admission that he had blacked out in the past. Okay then. She'd asked enough for now. "Have you ever been to Belize?"

He huffed through his nostrils. "Been in the jungle west of there, why?"

"Just wondering if you've ever relaxed enough to take a real vacation."

A gruff grunt answered. "You want to? Go there, I mean?"

"I do, but I'm not confident enough to travel by myself, especially to foreign countries. And I'm directionally challenged. I'd probably get lost the first day I arrived and never be seen again."

"I'd go with you. You know. For company. If you wanted to."

There it was, yet another defense mechanism. An offer of companionship with an escape clause.

"But would you take me dancing?" she asked, pushing his limits. "On the beach? Under the stars?"

"I don't dance." Exactly what she thought he would say. "But I'd try. For you."

That was unexpected. McKenna met his gaze then. Her heart stalled at the feral intensity gleaming down at her. This was a man hovering on the verge of yet another scary new world. Intimacy. Truly opening up. How she wanted him to kiss her. Not just kiss her but...

He just had surgery.

Still…

In a raw, feral way, he was so pretty to look at, it hurt. Fire pooled hot and low in her belly, where it had no business pooling after what she'd barely survived. But she wanted Beau Jennings like she'd wanted no man before. His mouth. His body. His heart.

"We should get some sleep," he growled.

"Okay," she whispered, breathing hard, another way of telling him she was his for the taking if he'd only take that first step. If he'd only let her in.

Their hearts pounded a fierce jungle beat of desire in the chasm of uncertainty between them. Until he pressed his mouth to her forehead and said, "Just you wait." Right before he cupped her head and pulled her back under his chin. Nothing more.

Shivering at what could've happened, McKenna swallowed her silly expectations even as she eased one hand around his waist and let her fingertips rub circles on that poor back.

Just you wait.

Chapter Twenty-Nine

"Where is he? Which room?" Alex had no patience for agents who committed sins of omission.

"He's asleep," Maverick growled. "Let him be."

Not what Alex expected. He cocked an irritated, get-the-hell-out-of-my-way glare over his shoulder at the guy who only the day before hadn't wanted Junior Agent Beau Jennings in his house. Why the hell was Maverick defending him now? "Excuse me?"

"He just got back to bed. He's running on empty. Let him rest, damn it."

Alex backtracked up the hall from Maverick's guest room. "What'd he do now?"

"Nothing, Boss. He helped me with Gorgeous. Damned foal wouldn't drop all night, but then Beau…" Maverick scraped one hand over his head. "I gave her some medicine and I made him stay and help me until she foaled, all right? That's all."

But it wasn't all. Alex could tell. "What?" he snapped.

"He means to end Montego, Boss. I thought he was just being a selfish prick, leaving McKenna like he nearly did, but he's not. He's the biggest asshole I've ever met, but he's also madder than any guy come back from service I've ever seen. He's pissed at you and me, but…" There went that hand again. "Boss. I don't know how to say it but… it's like he's me all over again."

The taut cords in Maverick's neck belied his raging emotions. "I was him not long ago. Right before I quit The TEAM, I was wound as tight as Beau is today. You don't know this, but I meant to end myself when I walked out on you. I had nothing left to live for. Least I didn't think I did then. Trust me. I wasn't headed for Wyoming. This" —he gestured at the rustically styled home around him— "just happened."

Suicide? Really? Maverick couldn't have shocked Alex more.

Yet he stood there glaring, his lips thin and his eyes as dark as Hell warmed over. "China saved my life. China and her horses. Kyrie. X and Z." His Adam's apple bobbed like he had something caught in his throat. "Beau doesn't know it, but I think he needs us more than he realizes. You. Me. Hell, he might just need our wives and our kids, too. He needs The TEAM. I don't know what happened to him or when everything in his life turned to shit, but if you know, tell me."

Alex drew in a steadying breath. If he'd suspected for one second how low Maverick had been that day… That he'd quit with the intention of killing himself... *I never should've let him out of my sight.*

Chastened, Alex jerked his chin at the couch. Now was not the time for belligerence. "Sit," he ordered quietly.

Maverick took the far end but settled at the edge of it like he was ready to run.

"All I know is what I've just uncovered from his military records and what Mother's found from the state of Nevada. It's public knowledge, so I can tell you. Beau's got enough

U.S. Army commendations to wallpaper my office. But he's got a few disciplinary actions against him, too, one in particular that will land him in federal prison. He should've had the guts to tell me he was one of the six Rangers who went into Nangarhar Province, Afghanistan, after the Syrian terrorist, Abdul Salim. Beau was the only one who lived to talk about it. That should've been in his personnel records, damn it."

"So? He's not the only one to survive a firefight." Maverick ought to know. "Christ, take a number."

"This one was different. The infil into Nangarhar Province morphed into a nightmare shortly after they fast-roped in. The Army's kept everything under wraps until they finish their investigation."

Maverick's brows narrowed. "They're investigating Beau? For what? Murder?"

"Precisely." Alex nodded at Maverick's disbelief. "That's right. He hasn't been formally charged, but he's suspected in the deaths of the five men who were with him. He's engaged an attorney, but the only evidence he's got is his word, and you know how far that'll fly in a military court of law. The problem is Beau's big mouth and his record. He was seen brawling with all those same men the night before the op. He threatened to kill them. Plenty of witnesses are ready to testify he's said that more than once, and that he did, in fact, murder those men. Those witnesses are screaming for his blood on a rock."

"They all Rangers?" Maverick asked, as sarcastic as ever. "Let me guess. Sure they are. Want to bet those guys threatened to kill him, too? Hell, Boss, that's nothing. I'd like to kill Beau myself most days, but that doesn't mean I will.

Guys say that crap all the time over there, you know that. Doesn't mean they'd actually follow through and do it. They were blowing off steam, same as him. Instead of hearsay, what physical proof does the Army have that he killed them? Anything other than a bunch of hotheads shooting their mouths off? Did anyone see him do it? What kind of air support did they have that day? Drones? Any damned thing?"

Alex shook his head. He'd known a few hotheaded spec ops guys in his life. Hell, he'd been one. "There are no eye-witnesses, and the Army hasn't been back into Nangarhar Province since. But here's the kicker. Beau radioed for an assist out of there, then dragged Captain Dornigan Trenton back with him."

Maverick nodded as if, *'There, problem solved.'*

"Unfortunately, Trenton died on the operating table before he could report his version."

"So what? Beau rescued one of his men. That's a good thing. He didn't just walk away and leave them like others have done. He did what he could. He deserves the MOH for that, not a court-martial." Maverick's angst rapped higher with every declaration.

Which Alex found interesting. It seemed he and Maverick were caught in a loop, one defending Beau at every altercation, one ready to tear him apart. And vice versa. But he couldn't encourage hope that a Medal of Honor was anywhere in Beau's future. Neither could he lie. "Not when the slug that killed Trenton came from Beau's pistol."

Maverick's face fell. "Friendly fire? How'd Beau explain that?"

"Said it was chaos. That one of the terrorists who ambushed them got hold of his pistol when he went down.

Told the MPs he'd lost track of it when he was hit, that all he had at the end was his rifle, which is true. The MPs confiscated that when the rescue chopper brought him and Trenton back."

Maverick huffed his disgust. "He got shot, too?"

"That's right. According to his after action report, a dozen or so Afghans ambushed his team within yards of the LZ, minutes after the Black Hawk dropped them. Four of his men went down instantly. Beau went down next, but the shot only winged him. Knocked him on his ass and took out his radio. When Trenton got hit, Beau maintained suppressive fire until he killed the last terrorist."

Maverick's fingers clenched into white-knuckled fists. "Are you telling me Beau fought off an ambush, was himself injured, yet still brought one of his men back alive? Without back up? Sure as hell doesn't sound like a murderer to me."

Alex nodded. "No, and Beau used Trenton's radio to call for help. Trenton was alive when the PJs got to them." PJs were US Air Force Operations Command and Air Combat Command pararescue team, the spec ops guys tasked with medical treatment and extraction of military personnel in combat zones.

"Then how's the Army certain that was Beau's slug inside Trenton?"

Alex huffed a long-suffering sigh. "Because Beau used that exact pistol the day before during drills. All they had to do was retrieve any one of the rounds he fired then, and they had the matching evidence they needed. You know how it works. All weapons go through the base armory, no exceptions. All the Army needs is a single positive match. That isn't the worst of it. Beau claimed it was a green on blue attack. Friendlies ambushed his team. He named names, and not once has he changed his original story."

Green on blue occurred when a supposed *'friendlies'* opened fire on American or Coalition forces. It wasn't unusual for those forces to employ and train local merchants, interpreters, or drivers.

Maverick's brows narrowed. "Which means the Afghan government's involved now—"

"And covering their asses. But Beau knew the bastards who fired on his team by sight. He turned names over to the Army Judge Advocate."

"Let me guess," Maverick bit out. "The US Army doesn't want to make waves with the new Afghan administration. They'd rather play politics. Which means, no matter what evidence Beau provided, no matter how credible, the brass won't waste time chasing those leads. They don't want trouble, so to make things go away, he's fucked ten ways to Sunday."

Alex nodded, more to himself than at Maverick. The Islamic Republic of Afghanistan had recently elected a semi-democratic president. It was in the United States' interest to play nice. But not at Beau's expense, which was why Alex had already contacted the SECDEF, Secretary of Defense Arthur Turner. Men and women who served America were not political pawns, damn it.

There was a time Alex had gone out a limb to help Maverick save China Wolf and her niece, Kyrie, now her adopted daughter, from certain death. He'd do it again in a heartbeat for Beau if he only knew how to reach him. But Beau continually bit the hand that fed him, and Alex had frankly had enough. He couldn't save someone who wouldn't let him, someone who fought the world for no good reason other than he was mad as hell. Alex ought to know.

Maverick growled, his elbows on his knees and his eyes on the floor. "Sounds just like Beau, doesn't it? Always pissed. Can't say anything nice. Can't even be decent most days, and I know damned well he's holding a grudge against Izza. I've never seen a guy more hell-bent on being his own worst enemy. The only one he seems to connect with is your wife. You ever notice how he's always polite to Kelsey when he can't seem to stand the rest of us?"

"Which made me wonder why," Alex said quietly. "So I asked Mother to do a little digging while she's holed up at my place."

"Great. I was wondering if she'd join us. Are Justice and Dempsey with her?" Maverick asked. "Hope so. Kyrie's dying to see Dempsey again."

Alex shook his head at Maverick's unfortunate choice of words. "Dempsey's sick again."

"No."

"It doesn't look good," Alex said quietly.

"Damn. How's Mother taking it?"

Yeah, damn. "She's holding her own. You know how she is." Alex had no good news to share. He wouldn't elaborate further on Dempsey's condition. That was for Mother to tell. But the more she'd uncovered about Beau Jennings, the more Alex worried. He might not be able to save this one.

"Before he joined the Army, he'd been in and out of the Las Vegas juvenile system since he was ten. But authorities suspected he'd been on the streets long before that, possibly since his mother died of a drug overdose."

"Great. Drug addict mother. He got a father in this story?"

Alex pursed his lips, wondering how Beau had even survived long enough to join the Army. "He's got an asshole for an old man, that's what Beau's got. Bass Jennings is a two-bit pimp. He's incarcerated at the Nevada High Desert State Prison, convicted of murdering three women who'd *'worked'* for him, one night in a drug-induced rage."

On one hand, Beau's military record was exactly what Alex expected from a juvenile delinquent. Most of his disciplinary actions had begun with bar fights and brawls, but nearly all of them occurred when other military departments mingled with Army personnel. He seemed to hold a particular grudge against Marines, as according to MP reports, seven out of the eight actions involved Beau's fist landing in some loud-mouthed jarhead's face. Which wasn't entirely unexpected in combat zones where tempers, ego, and testosterone ran high. Rangers and Devil Dogs were warriors, and sometimes those warriors blew off steam the only way they knew how. With their big mouths, nasty tempers, and fists.

Yet every commendation in Beau's record had screamed potential. He'd excelled at every level, was promoted early, and sailed through enough correspondence courses to have earned a business degree before he'd been discharged pending the current Army investigation. Which meant when he hadn't been off-base on assignment, he'd had his nose stuck in a computer screen working to better himself. That behavior was not typical for a man headed to prison. Alex knew how hard taking college courses while on deployment was. He also knew how poorly Rangers and Marines mixed.

You didn't take two lead dogs and ask them *'can't we all just get along?'*

The answer to that stupid question was always an unequivocal *'Hell, no.'*

Scout snipers, Rangers, and SEALS weren't trained to *'get along.'* They were trained to bust ass and get the hard jobs done under the worst conditions. The hardest job during deployment was not wasting free time and always working on Y.O.U.

"Boss? You zoned out on me. What's got you so tight you can't talk about it?"

That brought Alex back to ground zero. He ran a hand up the back of his neck. "It's not that I can't talk. Las Vegas authorities claim they couldn't track Beau for years. So where was he all that time?"

Maverick let out a slow hiss through pursed lips. "Jesus. It's no wonder he's mad at the world."

It also explained why Beau gravitated toward Kelsey. Without even trying, she seemed to attract the homeless and motherless. By then Alex was sick at heart. How had that little boy survived living on the streets of a crime-ridden city like Las Vegas? There had to be a way to help Beau, but Alex was damned if he knew what it was. "I need to talk to him. Wake him up."

"Doctor Fitzgerald thinks the world of him."

Alex nodded at that oddly timed insight. Maverick seemed to have stepped up as big brother to Beau, an unlikely alliance. "Still need to hear his side of the story."

Maverick didn't balk this time, just pushed to his feet, and headed down the hall.

Doc Fitz and Beau, huh? Yeah. Not happening. She's too good for him, and he knows it.

Chapter Thirty

"And I said it's none of your fuckin' business." Beau sneered at Alex Stewart. It seemed safer than knocking his employer on his pompous ass. How dare he bring this shit up? Why now?

He'd been summoned out of a sound sleep to Maverick's front room like a criminal to his parole hearing. At the moment, McKenna sat at his side on the loveseat in Maverick's front room, which sat perpendicular to the couch. That put Maverick at his right and Alex directly across from him.

Beau found McKenna's choice to sit with him, when she could've distanced herself like most folks would have, particularly generous of her. But he also knew she still suffered from her ordeal. Maverick and China were right. McKenna was clingy this afternoon, not that he minded. But he wasn't an idiot. She'd soon come to her senses and shove away like every other woman in his pitiful fucked up life had. But for now, a man could dream.

Dressed in jeans like everyone else, she wore a lavender pullover with a pocket over her belly. Guess the girls called it a hoody, not that Beau cared. He just knew the color didn't make her look washed-out like the white bed sheets had. She'd taken a sponge bath since she couldn't get into the shower with all those bandages, and that had partially restored her sunny disposition. Plus, China had helped her wash her hair. McKenna liked that. Beau could tell by the way she ran her fingers through the silky tangles, the way he wanted to.

He still wore his same clothes, though China had washed and dried them while he'd slept. The woman was kind. Not how he'd expected to be treated in Maverick's house.

"Beau," Maverick said quietly, his brows furrowed, but the snarky reprimand missing from his tone. "Kyrie's in the kitchen with Suzette. She's only ten and Suzette's three. Could you please do China and me a favor and not drop so many f-bombs? Those little girls don't need to cuss like drill sergeants."

That was different, Maverick asking a favor instead of barking orders.

"None would be better," China added, her brows raised along with her shoulders. "Please?"

"Sure, yeah," Beau replied begrudgingly. Suzette, the mahogany-haired little imp with big green eyes belonged to Gabe and Shelby Cartwright, who had apparently dropped their daughter off, then took off to who-knew-where to do who-knew-what. Probably to shop.

Maverick sat on the couch with China at his side. After coming in from the barn, he'd changed into a clean pair of jeans, a simple white t-shirt, and gray athletic shoes. The guy wasn't as bad as Beau had thought.

As usual, his wife dressed in jeans, cowboy boots, and a red, western-style blouse complete with shiny silver snaps instead of buttons. She'd tied her thick, dark hair back in a ponytail, the perky kind that bobbed when her head moved. The red ribbon dangling from the ponytail matched her shirt.

Then there was Alex, perched like the Grand Inquisitor on the edge of the recliner, directly across from Beau and McKenna, ready to torture the truth out of Beau. Dressed in casual jeans and a gray sweatshirt that proudly announced USMC, his bony fingers were interlocked between his spread knees like he ruled the fuckin' world. *Oops.* Beau shot Maverick a look. He hadn't intended to even think that word inside the ranch house.

Alex stared at Beau. Beau stared back, not going to blink, damn it. That was all this was, a power struggle, one alpha pitted against another. Well, guess again—

Alex blinked.

Shit. What the hell's going on?

"This is what I believe happened. You ran away from home when your mother died of an overdose. But the man you thought was your father—"

"Stop! Bass Jennings means nothing to me!" Beau spat, his hackles lifted, and his heart shredded all over again. He knew exactly what happened that day. The gloves were off. *I was there, damn you! Shut the fuck up!*

Alex nodded. For some reason, the man seemed extra patient. Extra steady. But twice the asshole. How dare he?

"Copy that. I wouldn't have wanted Bass Jennings for a dad, either. But he can't get to you anymore. He's incarcerated at—"

"Don't know, don't care!" Beau turned his head to the wall, but stuck out his palm, all five fingers splayed to deflect Alex's attack. *So stop asking and quit telling.*

McKenna's warm palm suddenly cupped his kneecap, her thumb rubbing circles on his knee. "You don't have to listen if you don't want to. We can leave here and go somewhere else."

"I'm fine," he told her, his words bitter and abrupt. But fine was the last thing Beau was. Pissed off at being outed was more like it. He cocked his head at Alex, daring him to keep opening that big mouth of his. "What do you want from me? My resignation because I'm the worthless spawn of a whore and her pimp? You got it! Consider me gone."

"Resignation not accepted, Junior Agent." Alex shook his head, the patience in those icy blues never wavering and his voice as calm as the Strip at sunrise. "I don't let good men walk away just because they throw a temper tantrum. Even if you quit The TEAM, I'll still keep the light on."

Beau snorted at that outright lie. Like he'd ever felt at home in that pretentious brick building in Alexandria, with its red, white, and blue *'Never Forget'* bullshit splashed over the whole damned lobby wall and with its high-tech armory. Who needed it? He'd been looking for a job when he'd found this one.

Liar.

Beau rolled his shoulder, glad he hadn't blurted out that last snarky info-byte. He hadn't been *looking* for this job, and he hadn't *found* it. Not really. The damned thing fell in his lap two days after he'd come home from the sandbox. He'd been told not to leave the country, that the Army'd come looking for him. That he'd better get his affairs in order. That kind of stuff before a man went to prison.

But then some guy he'd never met before approached him at a local pub, Boxster's in fact, stuck a welcome home hand in his face, and told Beau he needed a few good men. That he needed Beau in particular. That not just any guy was a good fit with The TEAM. Senior Agent Harley Mortimer was the one who'd believed in Beau from the beginning. Not Alex. Harley, damn it. Guess he was wrong.

"Alex never gives up on a guy, Beau. I would know," Maverick added. "Trust me."

Beau glared at his teammate. *Trust you?* It was interesting how close Maverick sat to his wife. You'd have thought they couldn't get enough of each other the way his hand rested on her knee, and it bugged Beau. Hell, everything about The TEAM bugged him. They were all living the American dream, and he was just some ghost caught at the peripheral, half-in and half-out of the thing he craved most, but never had. *Shit. What's a guy supposed to do?*

"Then what do you want?" he challenged Alex. "What the f—?"

Beau lowered his head. *Cough. Cough. Choke. Choke.* "What the heck" —*Jesus, that was a hard, bland word to spit out*— "do you want from me? And what difference does my past have to do with locating Catalina Montego today? Is anyone even looking for that b...b..." —*self-control wasn't getting easier*— "witch or is everyone sitting around with their thumbs up their—!"

I can't do this! With a roll of his very tense neck, Beau gave up trying to talk in this house with too many damned rules. He didn't want to offend those little girls playing in the kitchen, but Jesus! Translating profanity into baby talk was out of his fuckin' league!

A tiny smirk graced the corner of Alex's mouth before one shoulder lifted. "I'm not worried about catching Montego as much as keeping you alive."

"You're what? Worried about me? A Ranger?" *Oh, give me a break.* "You honestly expect me to believe that BS?" Beau couldn't sit still one more second. He jumped to his feet, instantly knocking McKenna aside and jolting his aching hand in the process.

Of course, brain-piercing pain shot up his arm to his neck and shuddered into his skull like a lightning bolt with its never-ending power to hurt him. And he couldn't swear! Where the bloody hell were the Cartwrights? It was way past time for a pill. Or a hypo. Make it a double!

Alex crossed his arms over his chest, still as smug and in control as ever.

What Beau wouldn't give to knock the arrogance off his face.

"I need you here protecting Doctor Fitzgerald more than I need you out hunting Montego," he said calmly. "Maverick and China have a ranch to run. They can't handle that and protective custody, too, so your duty station is here until further notice. I've got other agents just as capable as you of tracking Montego. Cassidy Dancer for one. She provided indisputable evidence of how psychotic Montego and her brother were, remember? Besides, I'm sure Doc Fitz would rather you stay."

Ambushed by that insight, Beau aimed an accusing glare at McKenna. She had the grace to blush, which instantly denied his suspicion that she was in on this ambush. That helped.

A knock at the front door interrupted before Beau could tell Alex where to stuff his concern. Without waiting for admission, Gabe stomped inside the house with his pretty wife protectively under his arm. "Hey, Boss, I miss anything?" he asked as he secured the heavy wooden door behind him and pocketed the key he'd used.

Did all TEAM agents have copies of each other's house keys? *Everyone but me? Figures.*

"Yeah. Hurry. Double-time, Gabe," Maverick said, then turned to Shelby before Beau could get a word out. "Beau needs something before he kills one of us."

What the fuck was that supposed to mean? "I never killed those guys," Beau blurted, his good hand instantly fisted, his weight shifted, and ready to fight. "I never killed anyone who didn't deserve it!" *Certainly not—her.*

Easing back into the couch, Maverick had the nerve to grin. "Relax, I'm just kidding. Can't you take a joke?"

"No!" rumbled out of Beau before he could restrain himself. He'd never kid about—that.

Out of breath and feeling trapped, he ran his tongue over his dry lips. He shot a covert glance at Alex. Did he and Maverick know all about his childhood? Was that what this was about? It'd sure explain things. They were psych-profiling him. *Figure out the parents. Explain the child. Bullshit!*

"I'm so sorry," Shelby said as she rushed straightaway to Beau's side, her honey-blonde hair glistening in the light. "But we had to run over to Kelsey's to get the meds from Libby first. She's the physician. I'm just a home health care nurse, and we got to talking, and… I'm really sorry."

"It's okay." He didn't want to like her, but the woman was a good foot shorter, and she had the loveliest eyes. Only today they were more like frightened violets behind her square, horn-rimmed glasses, and she was out of breath. Her fingers trembled when they landed on his wrist.

Gabe's eyes had narrowed the moment his wife stepped up to Beau. Yeah. Something was definitely going on between these two. Beau's worry heightened when Shelby's fingertips skimmed up his forearm.

"You're shaking?" he told her quietly, in case she didn't want anyone, like her big tough husband, to know. Was Gabe bullying her?

"I am," she replied evenly, blinking like she might break down and cry.

Whoa. Just whoa! He stepped back from her in case he was the problem. In case she was afraid of him. What the fuck had Gabe been telling her behind his back?

Stabbing her glasses higher on her nose, she grabbed onto Beau's wrist, unintentionally tugging him back to her. And holy Jesus! A lightning bolt shot up his arm at her less than gentle touch. He couldn't help the belligerent "Fuck!" that hissed out of him.

That brought Gabe across the room in two floor-eating strides and a threatening, "Goddammit, Jennings!"

She lifted her palm to his face. "No. I'm okay, honey. I'm fine, really. I need to do this. And I'm sure sorry, Beau. I didn't mean to hurt you."

Gabe froze in his tracks, but her voice had quavered too much for her to be fine, and his fists were still clenched like he needed to hit someone.

"You're not okay," Beau murmured, keeping a sharp eye on her volatile husband, daring Gabe to take one more step. "But if you don't want to treat a guy like me—"

"God, will you shut up?" Gabe growled. "Stop feeling sorry for yourself. Everything is not about you."

Then what's wrong with Shelby?

At last she lifted her chin and looked him in the eye. "I'm sorry if I've ever given you that impression. But really, it's not you." She swallowed hard, her head bobbing. "It's me. Honest. I almost lost a patient one time, and I'm sorry if I offended you, but giving shots is still hard for me to do. I'm afraid I'll hurt you, too."

Jesus, as hard as she was shaking, she just might. "I'm not that easy to kill," Beau told her kindly, anything to calm her down. "Would you rather I give myself the hypo? I can do that, you know."

Shelby shook her head and bit her bottom lip. "No, Agent Jennings. I mean, Beau. Please," she said as she ran a fingertip under one side of her glasses. "Let me do this. It's my job. Just like everyone else, I have to face my fears, and the only way to do that is to run through them, right?"

He got it then. As tiny as she was, she meant to be as strong as that Devil Dog husband of hers. That explained Gabe's protective stance, too. He was worried. For her—not what Beau might do to her. Only Gabe couldn't protect her from everything, could he? How well Beau knew.

Her candor took the wind out of his sails, though. "I'd have said 'run them through'," he teased as he let Shelby do her thing. She did real good, and the second she stowed the empty hypo back into its plastic case, he told her so. "Thank you, ma'am. That didn't even sting."

Those pretty violets beamed up at him. "Really? You're not just saying that to be nice?"

"No, ma'am, I didn't feel a thing." Beau glanced at Gabe. "Thanks for running her over to get my meds. I could've done without them, but—"

"Like hell," Alex growled. "He's been a pain in the ass since he woke up. Give him a double."

Damned if Maverick didn't add, "Not that he wasn't already an ass."

Even China grunted like she agreed.

Did everyone need to pile on?

"I won't be late again, Alex," Shelby promised.

"You're fine," Alex assured her. "Take a seat."

Beau turned back to Alex, the painkiller taking almost immediate effect. *Thank you, Jesus.*

"Now, where were we?" he asked as he settled alongside McKenna for more *'enlightenment'* from a man who knew virtually nothing about him.

Leaning back in his chair, Alex stretched his long legs out in front of him. "This team has your back, Beau. You don't have to like it; you just have to know it. And I've got—"

Brrrrrrring!

"Stewart," Alex answered his cell. "Is that so? Good. I knew you could do it. Hold on, Mother, I'm putting you on speaker." With that, he set his phone face-up on the side table. "I want you all to hear what she has to say."

"Hey, Beau? Are you there?"

He nodded though Mother couldn't see him, then said, "Yeah. I'm here," because, well, she couldn't see him. Maybe Alex was right. That lifesaving hypo had already shifted Beau's temper into the manageable zone. So what if everyone knew what his mother and father were? They didn't matter.

"I've been researching my archives, looking over the satellite images from a few years back in Nangarhar Province. You know the place and time I mean, right?"

Beau's mouth went dry. Shit. Alex knew.

"Listen, do you remember the name of that interpreter you had along with you that day? I sure hope so, because…"

No. Just no.

Beau lost track of the world while Mother droned on. Alex and McKenna were out there somewhere. Maybe it was the painkiller. Maybe it was the memories. It was hard to know with the images from *that day* flooding his head. His men dying. The fuckin' meat grinder they'd been dropped into. The lying Afghan bastards he'd once called friends.

"I don't want to talk about it," was all he could say without swearing up a storm.

Because talking about it before had only gotten him arrested on suspicion of murdering his guys. Like he honestly would've done something so heinous? Murder the five Rangers who'd had his back? Yeah, he'd argued and tussled with them plenty. They were assholes just like him.

But fighting was what hard men did. Those guys weren't his drinking buddies, but they'd been every bit the professional he was. They got the hard jobs done, and they would've done the same that day. They would've brought that bastard Abdul Salim in to answer for his crimes.

If they'd lived.

All at once Beau couldn't breathe. Instinctively his gaze flitted from Maverick at his right over to where Gabe had settled with Shelby on the couch beside China. Then across the room to Alex. Jesus, did they all know? Did they suspect him of committing coldblooded murder? Was this one of those damned interventions that people sprang on guys before MPs burst through the door and dragged him away?

Jesus H. Christ, I need to go. I never should've agreed to stay. I don't belong here, either.

"Beau," McKenna murmured, her fingers tapping his kneecap to get his attention. "It's okay. You're okay. I'm here, and I'm not going anywhere without you."

She said it so quietly that he turned and fastened his gaze on the only safe place in the room. There was no doubt in her soft, warm eyes. Only the emerald glow of that indefinable something he craved like his mother had once craved her drugs.

Just as quickly, suspicion lifted its ugly head. Would McKenna kick him out, too? Would she turn away like everyone else, now that she knew what he'd been accused of? What others who hadn't been there that day but claimed to know everything, had accused him of? *Is she in on this, too?*

It was so hard to know who to trust.

The purest green eyes continued to stare back at him. She winked. One corner of her mouth twitched. Her shoulders lifted like she knew what he was thinking. "I'm right here, big guy," she said simply, her fingers so small and warm on his knee.

"Beau? Beau? Are you still on the line?" Mother called out, tapping at her headpiece with those extra-long fingernails of hers like she did in the office. "Come on, talk to me. I don't have all day."

"Here," he replied woodenly, his gaze still fixed on his one true north. McKenna's slender hand had moved from his kneecap to his left forearm. Not holding on tightly. Not holding him back. Just grounding him. Lending emotional support like a lightning rod in a shit storm he couldn't seem to escape.

Mother rattled on. "Anyway, I think I've got enough evidence to support what you told the MPs and the Judge

Advocate. I invented a device that sharpens satellite imagery until even the tiniest details…" *Blah, blah, blah.*

"Wait a minute," Beau growled. "Say again?"

"What part? Did you hear anything I just told you?"

Honestly, no. Not after his panic attack set in. But like everything else in his life, Beau would never admit it. "Sorry. I had some interference on my end. Please repeat."

Mother tsked. "Which part? All of it?"

"Just where you wanted my interpreter's name until the part where you said you've got evidence. Evidence on what?"

"Okay, sure," she grumbled, "but listen up. I don't like to repeat myself. I have hard evidence that your interpreter sold you and your team out. He worked for Abdul Salim, least he did until that A-10 Warthog took Salim and most of his men out. But that interpreter is the reason you were attacked as soon as your chopper left the scene. You want me to text a portion of the video proof I downloaded? It's no trouble. I've already highlighted precisely what the Judge Advocate needs to focus on. Even circled the face of the guy that shot you, and the man who shot Captain Trenton with your pistol. Did you hear that? I have concrete proof you didn't shoot Trenton. It's no trouble to send it. I do that with Alex all the time."

Beau honestly had no idea what to say. No one had ever—ever—gone out of their way to help Bass Jennings' worthless guttersnipe of a son. Not one day in Beau's entire life had things come easy. If anything, every minute of his life had been one nightmare after another since he'd watched the light fade from his little sister's beautiful blue eyes. Since his despicable excuse of a father had damned near beaten him to death for—get this—living.

Now Alex knew everything.

Chapter Thirty-One

By the time Beau dared look his employer in the eye, Mother had stopped talking. Alex's phone wasn't on the side table anymore. The room had gone scary silent, like those few deadly seconds before a bullet pierces your heart. The one a guy never heard. The round with his name on it. Somehow, Dorn's sweaty face lifted up from the murk of that desperate day. His last words were, "Tell my wife I died loving her."

Like a faithful dog who'd needed one more kick in the ass, Beau had delivered that message at Dorn's funeral. After the honor guard had handed the flag to his widow, and most of the crowd had dispersed, Beau had cautiously approached Dorn's wife and told her everything that happened, but especially Dorn's last words. His wife had cried, and Beau had fought not to cry with her. She'd told him to keep in touch. He'd lied and said he would.

The years of meaningless abuse ambushed him now. Lifting his clenched fist to his lips, Beau tried to clear his dry throat. Didn't work. Didn't matter. There was no way to rationalize what he now knew to be nothing more than a lifetime of child neglect and abuse.

Alex was right. Beau's need to fight the world and everyone in it began the day his mom died. He should hate her for what she'd done but try telling that to his heart. Her name was Fidget, a stupid name for a nervous drug addict whore who'd obsessively twitched until she'd scored. But she was still his mom, and she'd given just as bizarre a name to her only daughter, AJ. Ha. Named after a candy bar. Almond Joy.

And I loved them.

And they both left.

Just like McKenna will.

Shit. Beau sucked in one last breath before he'd have to face the truth and let her go. Damned if she didn't squeeze his wrist just enough to get his attention again. Turning his head, he looked down into her trusting face. There was so much he wanted to say to her. He lifted one finger to the tangle spiraling over her forehead and tucked it behind her ear, never more certain than now that all this ugly information was news to her. That she wasn't complicit in yet another ambush. With that gentle confidence in him, it was time to leave before he ruined everything for her, too.

"Did you hear anything Mother just said?" Alex asked.

Beau nodded, the fight finally stomped out of him as he turned from McKenna to face another hard man. "Yeah, I heard. What do you want me to say?"

"Just thought you'd be a little more excited. Relieved maybe."

Holding onto the last of his shredded pride, Beau shrugged. "I lied on my job app. So sue me."

Alex cocked his head, his brows narrowed as if he didn't understand.

"Will you knock it off?" Maverick snapped, gesturing at Alex. "What the boss is trying to tell you, dumbass, is he can clear you of the military charges you're facing. Mother's spent all morning tracking down solid proof to support what you told the Army Judge Advocate."

"Yeah, Beau. Stop with the perpetual pity party," Gabe added, though he said it with less venom. "You're not the only one who's had a shitty life. Look at what Izza's been through."

See that right there, that whole *'them versus us'* mentality? That was the real problem with this sanctimonious TEAM. Just because Izza Maher was obviously Hispanic did not make her family. So was the brutal gang that had ruled Beau's neighborhood back then. They were all Latino. A violent combination of mean teenage guys and meaner girls, they'd made sure he ran for his life that first bloody day when he could barely stand on his feet. They were the ones who'd hunted him like a rat through the tunnels and byways of Las Vegas, not the police. Bass Jennings had paid that gang to kill his son. They just never ran fast enough.

"What's Izza to you, Beau?" Alex asked, his elbow on the armrest now, and his index finger over one brow. Tapping at his forehead like he was trying to figure things out. "Do you even know why you can't be civil to her?"

"She means nothing," Beau said. *And neither do you.* But that wasn't precisely true, and Beau knew it. Alex had done him a favor. He might deserve hearing the truth. Beau cleared his throat as best he could. A bottle of water sure would've been nice.

Damned if Shelby didn't jump to her feet, run into the kitchen, and return with just that. She handed it over like it was no big deal, when it was so damned kind. Maverick and Gabe wouldn't have thought to do that. Hell, Beau wouldn't have, either. He didn't know what made women the way they were, but most of them were so much more perceptive than guys.

He blinked at the unwanted moisture clouding his vision. When it wouldn't leave, he uncapped the bottle and took a long, cool swallow, struggling to get his inner Ranger back in control. But as he lowered his head to meet Alex's stare, it struck him hard. Beau Jennings had never—not once in his whole fucked up life—been in control.

Judgment day had finally arrived.

"His name was Farzaad Hannan. He was our interpreter and he was vetted. We took him everywhere. He accompanied us when we visited tribes or villages." Every damned time.

Alex leaned forward, his elbows on his knees. "I've read the after action report. I know their names."

That figured. Beau swallowed hard. "Then what do you want from me?"

"The same commitment you gave your men the day they died," Alex said quietly. "Honesty. Loyalty. That's all."

Beau nodded, the fight stomped out of him. "I can do that."

Alex settled back into his chair. "I know."

"So, what, umm…" He cleared his throat. "What's Izza been through?"

"You'll have to ask her."

"I don't dislike her. Hell, I don't even know her. She's just a reminder of… shit… Every time I see her… shit…" He swallowed hard. "I get so mad I want to fight the whole f… umm, shit" —not cursing was impossible— "the whole damned world. Do any of you even know how it feels to wake up every day and never once have a single thing to smile about?"

Of all the people in the room, Shelby raised her hand like a little kid in school. "I do," she said, blinking fast and trembling again. "I struggle every day, Beau. If you ever want to come with me to my PTSD meetings, you'd be welcomed there with open arms. I'll go with you. Everyone there's been through worse things than me, but they care. They listen, and they don't judge."

Beau couldn't miss the mellow glimmer of pride in Gabe's eyes. He swiped the back of his hand over his face. His own eyes kept clouding up, damn it. "Thank you, ma'am" —he struggled saying that— "but I'm good." *And I'm real good at lying.*

"No, you're not good, Beau," McKenna murmured as her strong but gentle palm settled in the center of his back.

Damn, he was surrounded, but for the first time in his miserable life, Beau didn't feel like he had to come up swinging. Guess McKenna was pretty perceptive, too.

"We're not your enemies, brother," Maverick said, his voice uncommonly ragged. "Trust me. I know just what you're going through."

Brother. Beau turned his head to truly look at Maverick. But for that one word, he would've said some uncomplimentary things right then. Maybe chucked the water bottle at the guy's fat head. Called him a few choice names. But he'd seen a different side of Maverick out there in the barn.

Still, he had to ask, "What can you possibly know about being accused of murdering your men? Enlighten me." Okay that came out more bitter than Beau intended, but still. By the looks of the Wild Wolf Ranch, Maverick and China had it all.

"For one thing, I know what it's like to want to blow your brains out, smartass. Don't think you own all the sorrow in the world. After I lost my brother... After I... Shit." The story ground to an abrupt stop. Maverick's fierce gaze dropped to his feet. His jaw turned to granite that could've cracked walnuts, not just cracked them, but pulverized them to dust.

China's hand settled over his shoulder, much like McKenna's hand still rested on Beau's back. Beau saw it then. *Shit. He lost his brother. I lost my sister. I'm Maverick and Maverick's me. How fuckin' weird.*

"How old?" he asked gently because he had no idea what to say.

"Twenty. Twenty and ten times dumber than you," Maverick ground out. His eyes stayed on the floor, his face ashen, and the cords in his neck taut. "The stupid shit was just like you. He always knew more than anyone else. Always had to be first out of the gate. Never listened to a thing I told him. Stupid ass." Maverick spat each word at Beau like a killer bee.

"What was his name?"

Lifting his head, Maverick shot Beau what only that morning he would've interpreted as a hateful, disgusting glare. But things had changed since then, and Beau could finally see what he hadn't seen before. Maverick looked angry and sad. Not so much pissed as lost. Beau could relate.

"His name *is* Darrell," Maverick corrected as his gaze shifted to the large framed portrait on the fireplace mantel of a grinning kid in USMC dress blues who could've passed for Maverick's twin. Dark-haired and downright cocky, he had one arm around a pretty woman, the other on the baby boy on his lap.

China kept rubbing Maverick's shoulders. McKenna kept holding onto Beau. Jesus, he and Maverick were mirror images of each other, both two broken down sons-of-bitches being comforted by women they didn't deserve.

"I am sorry for your loss," he told Maverick sincerely. "Honest. I didn't know."

"There's a lot you don't know," McKenna said quietly. "Every single one of the men and women you work with has lost more than you may ever know. Babies, brothers, sisters, and a few beloved animals. They might not know all you've suffered, and they don't need to. That isn't what makes your team a family, Alex."

She directed that at the man across the room, the one sitting back stern and silent, his elbows on his knees again and his steepled fingers under his chin. "It's this right here, what's going on in this room right now, that allows your team to do what most others can't. It's Shelby reaching out when she's scared. It's Maverick opening his home when he didn't want to. It's you and Mother working behind the scenes to help a man who'd rather spit in your eye than ever admit he needed your help."

Ouch. Beau winced at that very astute description of him.

"They're all good men and women," Alex growled. "I didn't start out to make a son-of-a-bitchin' family. I was like Beau. I started out pissed at the world and everyone in it. So stow your sad stories, Beau. We've all got our share of memories, and trust me, yours aren't any heavier than anyone else's."

Beau leaned back into the loveseat, taking McKenna with him, needing the warm, lush feel of her body in his arms. What a day. He wrapped his bad arm around her shoulder and pulled her into his side. Funny how that hand didn't hurt as much when he held her.

"I'll talk to Izza," he said. "I'll make it right with her. It's not about her. Never was."

"See that you do," Gabe muttered. "Cuz I'm here to tell you, Connor's going to whip your ass if you bark at her one more time."

Beau gave Gabe his chin. "He tell you that?"

Gabe leaned forward, his elbows to his knees. "That's another thing. You act like you're so damned important that everyone's talking behind your back. Get the hell over yourself. I've got news for you, Jennings. You're not that interesting."

"Jesus, do I do anything right?" he had to ask, because right then, he was feeling a little ambushed.

"Yes, asshole," Maverick bit out. "You're the *stubbornest* jerk I've ever met, and that's why Doc Fitz is alive today. You saved her, dipshit. Keep it up."

That almost sounded like a compliment.

Just then, a giggling whirlwind blew in from the kitchen. While shy Kyrie headed straight for her mom and dad and snuggled up against Maverick, Suzette ran at Beau. He barely caught her before she crashed into his knees and slapped a ragged cloth book in the middle of his chest. "Look, Unco Bo Bo! Kitties!" she squealed as she climbed onto his lap. "Kyrie been telling me 'bout kitties. Wanna read a kitty stowy?"

Jesus, she was cute. But since when had he turned into Unco Bo Bo? From the other end of the couch, Shelby lifted both shoulders, her eyes bright with amusement. "Looks like you're family, Beau."

As if it were no big deal, the back of Suzette's fuzzy little head thudded against his chest while she settled in under his chin and wrapped his good arm around her like—shit. Just like AJ used to do when she was sick and worn out from crying.

Beau blinked at the damnedest sensation flooding his heart.

"Hurry," Suzette urged. "I wike the tiger ones, and Kyrie does, too, and there's some in here!"

Beau could barely make out the cartoon pictures in the book, much less the words under the pictures through the moisture in his eyes. He did as commanded, but he'd never been an uncle before, and that thing in his chest felt tight and uncomfortably warm. For the first time in years, he licked his thumb and settled down to tell a tiny little girl a *stowy* about kitties. A *stowy* AJ would've loved. *Jesus, I miss her.*

He cleared his throat and began with, "Once upon a time—"

"Oh, wook!" Suzette stabbed her perfect little finger at the first kitten she saw. "This one's hungwy, and he wants his widdle sister! Turn da page. Turn da page! I show you his widdle baby sister!"

Beau could relate to the sad looking cartoon boy-kitten. Of course he wanted his little sister. Big brothers were like that. He dipped his nose into the riot of curls at the crown of Suzette's tender head, his heart breaking for the sublime innocence he'd lost so long ago. For the baby girl he'd never see again. Jesus, he didn't even have a picture of AJ. What he wouldn't give for one more day with her.

At last he shot his employer a piercing look over Suzette's head. This was all Alex's fault.

As usual, Alex stared right back. Ever defiant. Ever the know-it-all.

Swallowing the bitter rage and the pain of too many years, Beau nodded just once.

Alex nodded back. Message received. He had no idea what'd he'd just done by forcing this confrontation. Or maybe he did.

Chapter Thirty-Two

McKenna pressed against Beau's ribs, careful not to bump the wounded hand draped over her shoulder. Considering all he'd been through in the last few days, the man was shockingly resilient. She doubted most guys would've been on their feet after the intense surgery he'd had, much less tackling their jobs. Yet here he was, hard at work and determined to be the one who brought Catalina Montego to justice. Better yet, he was finally surrounded by a rag-tag company of snipers who understood him, yet who weren't afraid to hold his feet to the fire when he screwed up.

If she didn't know better, she'd think Beau loved her, but didn't know how to say it. Yes, it was way too soon for premature declarations. Those were what led to babies born out of wedlock and most divorces. But if she were to fall for any man, it was this one right here. This rough-around-the-edges guy reading a story about kittens, of all things, to a fairy princess, who even now stared adoringly up at him from beneath the longest lashes McKenna had ever seen on a child. Suzette, the sweet, innocent little thing, was in love, too.

Alex had excused himself and vanished into the kitchen. Maverick and Gabe passed puzzled glances at each other, as if they couldn't believe what they were witnessing. But China and Shelby seemed smug, as if they knew something McKenna and the men did not.

By the time the short story ended, little Suzette had her butt firmly wedged in the corner of Beau's muscular arm. It did resemble a sturdy tree branch where a kid would be sheltered and safe. Nothing looked dearer than that little girl snuggled into a man as big and rugged as Beau. Talk about *"Beauty and the Beast."*

McKenna ran a dry finger under her eye to catch the tear welling up at the tender bass notes in Beau's masculine voice. He sounded like a lion that had finally been tamed.

"The end," Beau said softly to the fairy princess on his lap.

"I yike you," Suzette told him solemnly, her eyes big and round, and those curved lashes fluttering like butterfly wings about to take flight. "You is my favowit unco."

He seemed to have a hard time swallowing, so McKenna passed the water bottle. Resting the book on Suzette's lap, he growled as he unscrewed the already loosened cap and asked his new girlfriend, "You thirsty? You want some?"

Suzette pursed her lips and shook her head. "Uh-uh. Mommy says kids should never dwink outta someone else's stuff. I could get germs."

"Your mommy's smart," Beau told her as he took a swallow.

"Hey, Suzy-Q," Gabe interjected with a lazy grin. "Kyrie's got a new baby horse. If you're done reading with Uncle Bo Bo, want to go see it?"

She slid off Beau's knee to the floor, her *'favowit unco'* quickly forgotten. "Oh, goody! Wet's go, Daddy. Whatcha waitin' for?"

"Do all kids talk like that?" Beau asked as he leaned into McKenna. "Are they all that cute?"

"I like to think so," she answered.

From the couch, Shelby beamed up at Gabe as he swung Suzette onto his shoulders.

"Bring your old man, Kyrie," he said as he jerked his thumb for Maverick to join him. "I want to see that litter of kittens you found, too. How many babies did that mean mama cat have this time?"

Kyrie tugged at Maverick with, "Come on, Dad. Move your keister, mister."

He resisted until she planted her feet, grabbed his hand, and tried to tug him to his feet. That didn't work. In a second, he had her giggling in his arms, tickling her until she squealed. McKenna could've watched those two play all day. He was so gentle with Kyrie. Her pretty face, so much like China's, split with a happy smile.

Maverick ended their wrestling match with a hug and a kiss to her cheek. "Jumping Jiminy, what have you been eating? Did you leave any oats for the horses?"

"No, Dad," she drawled as she bounced to her feet, her dark tangles bouncing along with her. "I ate the giant chocolate chip pancakes you made for breakfast, don't you remember? Or are you as forgetful as Z?"

One dark brow lifted on his forehead into a devilish spike. "You calling me old?"

McKenna couldn't believe the playful side of the brooding man she'd sat with in the hospital. Was this adorable guy the same person?

Kyrie backed away from him her eyes alight with mischief. "You do kinda look like X and Z now that I think about it. And you talk like Z, too. *Jumping Jiminy?* Really, old fella?"

"That's it." He lifted to his feet. "No more pancakes for you. From now on, celery. Broccoli. Okra!"

Still grinning and teasing, Kyrie scurried to her Uncle Gabe, putting him and Suzette between her and her dad. "Betcha can't catch me," she taunted.

And just like that the game was over. Maverick sat back on the couch and waved for her to come sit with him. "No, Kyrie. Don't run from me. Not today. You know what Mom and I talked about this morning. We can play games inside, but once outside, you need to stay between Uncle Gabe and me. He won't have Suzette on his shoulders then, either. This is serious, kiddo. And we're only going out to check on the new foal and feed the cats. You two can't run off and play like you usually do. Understand, sweetheart?"

Aww, he melted McKenna's heart the way he'd reached out for Kyrie, and the way she came back to him and snuggled between his knees to sit on his lap. "I know, Dad. I'm not a little girl anymore. I'll be extra careful, and I'll watch over Suzette, too. You've got your pistol, right?"

"You know I do." He pulled her into a one-armed hug and ended with another kiss to her cheek. "Good, then get off my knee, tubby. You're breaking my leg."

Her mouth dropped open. "Only cuz it's so skinny and bony!" she shot back at him as she stood and grabbed his hand. "Come on, old guy. Let's get our chores done."

While the men and girls headed out through the kitchen to the barn, Beau sagged back into the loveseat. "I'm too old for this shit."

"It has been quite the morning. You really do need to rest," Shelby told him. "You too, McKenna. With Alex, Maverick, and Gabe here, you'll be fine."

McKenna couldn't have agreed more. "Just what the doctor ordered," she said as she lifted to her feet, then turned to Beau and asked, "You need a hand up, old guy?"

He shook his head, stubborn to the bitter end. "I'm going to check in with Alex."

"Of course you are," she muttered to herself as he headed for the kitchen. "You don't need post-operative care. I forgot. You're Superman."

"Men, huh?" Shelby said as she grinned. "Gabe was the same way when he got shot."

"He didn't go to the hospital?"

"Oh, yes, he did. By ambulance because he was unconscious and had no choice. But he had visitors as soon as he was out of recovery. Next thing I knew, we were both at TEAM headquarters, because he wasn't about to miss the showdown between Mark Houston and Alex. You should've been there."

"Showdown?" McKenna joined Shelby on the couch. She couldn't imagine anyone taking on Alex.

"That was a day to remember," Shelby said, her eyes bright.

McKenna settled in for some girl talk. When Beau had first stepped away from her, she'd almost gone to the kitchen to stay near him. It was either that or fight off another panic attack. But then Shelby reached out to her and made her feel at home. That was all it took. Beau wasn't the only one being sucked into this fascinating family of snipers.

Chapter Thirty-Three

Alex stared out the kitchen window at all Maverick and China had accomplished since she'd moved east to be with him. The barn. Those horses. *Wild Wolf East*, the name of their ranch, had prospered. Between China's talent with her magnificent Percherons, Maverick's success with his charity, *Everyone's a Cowboy,* and *Cat Haven*, Kyrie's homeless shelter for stray and unwanted cats, it was easy to see why Beau thought the Carsons had everything. In a way, they did.

But what he couldn't see was the wreck Maverick had been when he'd first joined The TEAM. How he'd sat for days staring at his computer screen. Not friendly. Barely approachable. Not talking unless spoken to. If it hadn't been for Gabe Cartwright and Taylor Armstrong flying cover for him, Alex now knew Maverick might've gone off in a dark corner and offed himself during those first weeks. That would've been tragic. Maverick had so much to give, even back then. But he couldn't see the forest through the trees at that dark time in his life, and Alex knew how he'd felt.

"Hey, Boss? Got a minute?"

Speak of the devil. Alex turned his back on the window to face the junior agent who had for the first time called him Boss. "Yes?"

"I don't think Catalina's a woman."

That was unexpected. "How do you figure?"

Naturally, Beau couldn't just answer the question. "Tell me how you know her."

"Who says I do?"

"I overheard Maverick and Gabe while I was laid up in the hospital. They said you ran into her years ago. That you suspect she killed a friend of yours."

Alex crossed his arms over his chest. "Sounds like you know what I know."

Beau shook his head. "Tell me what she looked like then. What's wrong with her?"

Maybe there was hope for this junior agent after all. Alex came clean. "There's nothing wrong with her. I've never actually spoken with Montego, but I saw her in a bar in Norfolk years ago the night before I first deployed. I was there with my buddies, Aaron Pope, Vic Irvinson, and Rodney Barr. Her hair was blonde. She weighed around one-ten. Stood five feet tall and came into the place with her brights on high-beam. Never noticed her hanging around before then, but she doubled down on Aaron the second she saw him. Her face lit up like she knew he'd be there. Like she'd been waiting for him. They left the bar together. Never saw Aaron again."

Beau cocked his head. "Then we're talking two different women. The one I fought was my height, and she packed more muscle than tits. She fought like a man. Long, stringy hair in a braid, and her breath smelled like black licorice, or some kind of chewing tobacco maybe."

"Not so. Mother's got a copy of the surveillance at Dulles. I've seen it. Catalina Montego *was* at the airport and at the hotel. I've seen those security cameras, too. She's still five feet nothing and blonde. She's the one who left your finger in her room."

Beau shook his head. "You're wrong. No five-foot chick could've gotten me out of Boxster's on her own, much less wrangled me onto that stinking worktable at Ringers. Did you even think to check their security cameras? Most congressmen have them."

Who does this ass think he is? Alex nodded, his patience wearing thin. With Beau it was always two steps forward and ten back. "I had Mother check them after the EMTs took you away the day you escaped. She also checked every available cam within a two-block radius of Boxster's, and I had Lee and Adam retrieve your bike from curbside parking before Metro PD had it towed. Is that good enough for you?"

Of course, Beau ignored the part about Lee and Adam rescuing his motorcycle. "So what'd you find on the cameras? Anything? Or haven't you looked at them yet?"

"I looked at them," Alex bit out, sick and tired of this agent's bullshit attitude. "Nothing conclusive, unless you being stuffed into a cab by two of Boxster's bouncers counts as incontrovertible evidence, which it does not."

"Wait. Was I conscious?"

Alex shook his head. "You were drunk and barely standing on your feet. But that's the only sign of you being at Boxster's that we've located."

"Which doesn't mean fuck." Beau staggered to the nearest kitchen chair and all but fell into it. About time, too.

Alex hadn't noticed how pale he was or how sunken and black his eyes were until then. Yet he wasn't one to baby his men. If Beau thought he could walk on water, let him.

"Shit. She drugged me. I didn't come to until after she cut my finger off. If she's out to hurt you, why not film the bloody amputation? Why not wait until I was lucid and screaming? How's she getting a thrill out of this" —he held up his bandaged hand "—without making sure you see it?"

"Because there are worse kinds of torture," Alex growled, for the first time a note of true menace in his voice.

"Oh, yeah? Like what?" There went that damned hand again, like Alex needed to be reminded he'd failed his friend.

He leaned into his junior agent's taunt, as tight as he'd been since he'd lost his first wife and daughter. "Think, for once, damn it. What's worse than knowing, than watching exactly what you went through? What's worse than watching torture? What's every parent's worst nightmare, when they send their sons and daughters off to war? Hell, when they send their kids to their first day of school!"

Beau's eyes glazed over. He had no clue.

"Death is quantifiable," Alex hissed. "It comes to us all, but when you know what happened... When you read the police report, and you finally know the name of the bastard who got the DUI for running the red light that killed your family... When you read the attending physician's findings in the emergency room... When you know without a doubt that your little girl is never coming back..." He swallowed hard. "Then you *know*, don't you?"

Beau nodded like he knew, but he still didn't have a clue what Alex was talking about.

Weary to the deepest part of his soul for the misery Aaron's parents were still going through, Alex breathed a tortured sigh. "Not knowing, Beau. Not knowing what happened to the people you care about hurts worse than knowing. It never stops hurting and it never gets better. I wake up every day thinking about Aaron. I think about his mom and dad. His sister. What they're going through. At Christmas. On his birthday. On any damned day of the week. They're out there, and they're hurting, and they're still waiting for him to come home. They're still praying. They haven't given up yet." *And neither have I.*

Understanding flickered deep in Beau's eyes. His chin tipped up like a wave on the ocean with a quiet swell of, *'Oh, I get it now.'*

Alex ended with, "Knowing and seeing what really happened brings closure, but not knowing is the worst torture, the kind you get to live with every day and night, every second for the rest of your life."

"So if all you'd ever found of me was my little finger…" Beau let his words trail away. Yeah. Now it was sinking into that hard Army head. "You would've kept worrying? About me? Really?"

The way this asshole asked that simple question gutted Alex. Why'd Beau find it so hard to believe that people cared? How could anyone go through life not knowing what it felt like to be worried over?

"Every day for the rest of my life," he finished, switching gears before he lost hold of his emotions. "I asked Detective Oberg to send a forensic artist. I want to know precisely who you *think* you saw." Emphasis on *think*. Considering Beau's condition when times he'd seen Montego, Alex doubted he really knew what he'd seen.

"When will he be here?"

Man, this guy never let up. "First thing tomorrow morning. Is that soon enough?" Heavy on the sarcasm.

Beau had the damned nerve to nod like Alex needed his concurrence, which he did not. He would've come back at Beau for being such an ass, but sweat beaded at the guy's temples, and Alex knew how much energy it took to maintain that badass persona.

Swallowing his pride, he walked the distance from the window to the kitchen table and told his smart-assed agent, "You're confined to quarters until further notice. I'll have…" He was going to say he'd have dinner delivered but stopped short. "You haven't eaten yet today, have you?"

Beau—being Beau—waved his good hand at the notion he might actually need sustenance. "I'm good."

Said every stupid man ever.

Good, my ass. "Stay. Sit," Alex snapped. "You take it black?"

That brought Beau's head up. "What?" he asked, his lip curled like he thought Alex was the stupider of the two of them. His dark brown eyes looked like two pee-holes in a bank of cream-colored snow, he was that pale.

"Your coffee. You like it black or is that too strong for a pussy Ranger?"

"You trying to piss me off?"

"No, dumbass. I'm fixing you coffee and an omelet, so shut up."

She stood in the dark shadows cast by the covered patio at Golden Horizons Assisted Living Home. Which was very much to her liking. The late afternoon sun had created perfect, long shadows that draped like ghouls over the comfortable pink and mint green chaise lounges. She'd never seen so many wicker peacock chairs in her life, which told her what she needed to know about the rich old people living here. Not that she cared about them. She only wanted one. The prissy daughter might've gotten away, but Sanders Fitzgerald would not.

The lying bastard.

Chapter Thirty-Four

"Are you sure?" Beau asked McKenna one last time as he eyed the other bed, the one she hadn't yet slept in. Sleeping with her while she was unconscious was different. Hell, this whole damned day had been different, and he had no idea where he stood anymore. Not with McKenna or Alex or—shit. Not even with himself. How could one man get so fucked in the head in less than twelve hours?

"No, I'm not sure," she said, biting her bottom lip like a frightened little girl again. "All I know is I don't want to be alone when it gets dark."

And that was the problem. He didn't want anyone else comforting her or her seeking out anyone else, not the way she trembled when she said *'dark.'* Not since he'd awakened with her in his arms this morning had he felt so... so... something.

Hell, he wasn't in touch with his feminine side. He just didn't want McKenna in anyone else's arms, okay? The thought drove him crazy in a scary way he'd never known before. As per usual, he needed to hit something. That was his go-to when things got intense. Physical pain. Sometimes, it helped.

But he couldn't act like that with McKenna. She was so soft. Malleable. Vulnerable. She fit inside his callused body like a pearl in an ugly oyster. Pure and clean. Precious. He was the throwaway shell, good for nothing but the trash.

Lifting his good arm, Beau scraped his fingers over his head, unsure for the first time in forever. He didn't want to screw up the delicate thing happening between McKenna and him. It'd only take one wrong word out of his big mouth to crush it, and he was the king of destruction.

In no way did he deserve her, and for sure she was still coping with what she'd lived through. But damn. She had no business wanting him in her bed. Admitting him into her life just didn't seem right. As much as he hungered for what Alex had with Kelsey, what Maverick and Gabe had with their wives, Beau had never been half of a couple. Any couple. He did alone, and he was damned good at it. But alone was never enough, and she was here, and so was he, and...

Shit. At least she'd dressed in two-piece pajamas instead of that flimsy shift. Still… Most nights he slept in boxers, and those pajama bottoms of hers with that thin elastic band were removable. Easily.

Swallowing hard, he nodded. "Then climb in. Face the other way. I'll join you."

From behind. Not like that meant her ass would be any safer from his all-male, starved-for-a-woman's-body than her front, but it was the best he could do. He would keep her safe, even from himself. Putting her in a separate bedroom like China suggested earlier—which McKenna had shot down the second she brought it up—was a risk Beau couldn't take.

Meekly, she pulled the blanket back and slid beneath the covers, her back to him. Lifting her head up from the pillow, she gathered her raspberry blonde hair into a lovely ponytail that draped over her shoulder like a fragrant temptation he wanted to get lost in.

She tugged the blanket up to her neck. Like that helped. No red-blooded man on earth could ignore the gentle tuck and swell of her hip under the cover. Or the way her long legs stretched. The way she sighed as if she were finally comfortable. Ready. In his bed.

He was so hard he could pound nails. Made undressing, umm, harder. It was a good thing she didn't see the spike in his boxers, when he doused the lamp and climbed in behind her. Careful so he didn't bump her, Beau maneuvered his bad arm, bending it above her head so his bandaged hand rested on her shoulder like he'd done before.

But what to do with that good arm and those itchy fingers at the end of it? The ones that wanted to slide beneath those pajama bottoms of hers and explore every last one of her secret places.

Holding that arm to his chest would trap it between McKenna and him. It'd be uncomfortable. Stretching it down between their bodies would put his fingers within range of the delectably soft rump that already rested too close to his erection. He cocked his arm tight, thinking to use it for a pillow until—

"Oh, for Pete's sake," McKenna grumbled as she lifted her head again and tugged his elbow over her pillow until she rested her head on his bicep. "Don't make this harder than it has to be."

He squeezed both eyes shut. *Why'd she have to use that word?* If he was hard before, he was a steel spike now. And the damned thing kept growing.

Beau stiffened, every ounce of his blood rushing to complete the one mission he'd give his left nut for, but would never, ever be good enough for. Swallowing *hard,* because that was the one thing he could do, Beau forced his horny mind to the simple mechanics of cleaning his gear, of field stripping his rifle.

Now there's a word for you. Field stripping. Visions of stripping McKenna bare, of tasting her luscious body from her soft lips to her toes and over every succulent pleasure spot in between…

A groan escaped before he could call it back.

"Is this as hard for you as it is for me?" she asked, still being a good girl and facing the other way.

That word was going to be the death of him! "No problem," he lied.

"Then lift your arm, so I don't hurt your finger," she told him, which he did since she'd already commenced wiggling around to face him. That put her knees within his danger zone. He winced, expecting a sharp jab to his groin, which would hurt like a mother.

But it also put her head on his shoulder, and he didn't mind looking down into her pretty face. There was a strength inside McKenna. Maybe because she was a medical professional and trained, but she seemed to have recovered from her night of trauma better than he'd expected. To be honest, she seemed steadier than him at the moment.

Tracing his jaw with just one fingertip, she said, "I wish I'd known you when you were a little boy."

"That would've been nice," he told her, because, well, that was what she expected him to say. In reality, a friend back then—any friend—would've been a godsend. But gutter trash didn't make friends. They stabbed each other in the back because survival was more important than friendship, and it didn't pay to trust others. No good deed ever went unpunished and all that. Kids on the street learned fast.

"You don't believe me," she whispered, her eyes wide and so damned innocent.

He shrugged. Believing wasn't the problem. Remembering was. When a kid's own parents didn't think enough of him to protect him... When they were the ones who'd thrown him out like a piece of trash... What difference did anyone else make?

Leaning into him, she pressed her fingers to his chest and her lips to his mouth.

Beau closed his eyes, instantly inhaling the sugary cookie scent of the woman in his arms.

This.

She canted her head, pushing into him for fuller access, and Beau held on, his bandaged hand and arm pressing her to keep going. Her tongue teased his lips, and he had no problem opening for her, not as good as she tasted.

Yeah. This.

She growled and nipped his bottom lip, then kissed it, her tongue stroking and tangling with his, tasting the inside of his mouth until he was lost in heaven. Bumping teeth. Angling her head for more and more access until...

He pulled back, breaking the connection. "Are you sure," he breathed, his heart about to explode, the blood in his veins running hot and ready to set this night on fire. Burn it up. Light the fuse that already throbbed with its one sure mission in life. Make love to this woman.

She nodded, her lips wet and swollen and...

Jesus. What a sight. He blinked, the raging fire in his heart a new and different meteor of epic proportions. One that after it touched down—if it ever did—he'd never be the same.

"I want you," she murmured, her eyes big and wide and glimmering with a feral intensity that looked good on her.

Okay then. Beau took possession of the night. He pressed his bandaged hand to the back of her head and kissed McKenna with every last beat of his heart.

Chapter Thirty-Five

"More," McKenna murmured, never more certain that this was the time and Beau Jennings was the right man. Breathing through her nose brought the musky, masculine scent of his skin to her, but kissing his mouth flooded her with a heady dose of feral lust for the first time in her life. The molten burn in her veins consumed her. She needed him, wanted him inside her body, now.

Yet he seemed determined to take his time, savoring her lips and tongue as if she were a rare delicacy and he hadn't eaten in years. Carefully, he'd taken her wrists in his one good hand and straddled her, stretching her arms over her head while he rested his injured hand alongside her and made a meal of her mouth. Nipping at her bottom lip and suckling it like she was a decadent dessert. Groaning, his deep masculine voice vibrated against her mouth.

He breathed her in and his breath became her only air. She drew it inside for all she was worth. With each inhalation, he became her world. Without missing a beat, Beau trailed warm, wet kisses down her chin to her neck. Yet he was careful with her bandaged wounds. Pausing at the hollow of her neck with his nose flat against her skin, he inhaled deeply. What a funny, pleasant sensation.

She shivered. "Are you smelling me?"

"Yes," he admitted, his voice ragged as he rubbed his nose back and forth. "I love how you smell and taste. You're incredibly delicious." His tongue made a swipe up her throat where he nipped her chin. "Like a cookie. Hmm, I could eat you up."

Her body exploded with a surge of wet anticipation. "Then do it," she cried, throbbing for him to stop kissing and get down to business.

"No, baby, this is about you tonight, not me," he said as he worshiped her mouth again.

And she was lost in the tumultuous sensation of whiskers scraping her chin and cheeks. The heat of his all-male body surrounding her. The luscious masculine scent that whispered to her psyche of smoke, earth, and wind. His moist kisses on her lips and forehead, her eyelids, and the tip of her nose. The slick anointing of his tongue sliding against her lips and tongue, tasting her. For an angry, solitary man, Beau certainly knew how to make soft, sweet love to her mouth.

Not to be outdone, she wiggled her hands free and clutched his head. McKenna loved her fingers in his hair, her fingertips on his scalp. She loved the obstinate angles and planes to his rugged, scruffy face. But mostly, she wanted that perpetual frown turned into smiles. She wanted to hear him laugh for once.

Sighing, she smoothed her fingers down his muscled back to his ass. What a fine ass it was, every inch of him taut and firm. Not a jiggle. She stuck all ten fingers under those cotton boxers and grabbed two hands full of pay dirt, then slid one around front to prove she meant business.

Easing to his knees, he looked down at her tenacious grip, his chest heaving and his forearms caging her. When his head came back up, his heavy-lidded stare told her all she needed to know. This man was on fire for her as much as she was for him. They were burning together.

Her body reacted automatically at that erotic picture of them consumed by flames of animal lust and human love. Was there anything better? Her hips arched off the bed, begging him to take her, to grind into her. The instant she saw the question in his eye, she moaned, "Yes, I'm sure. Don't make me tell you again. I want you and I need you."

"But do you want me enough to keep me... after?"

Her raging hormones screamed, *'Yes! Yes! Yes!'* But her heart broke at the plaintive question only a little boy could have asked.

McKenna pulled him into her body then, cradling his head against her chest. Her breasts flattened as he pressed heavily into her. Tears filled her eyes at the injustice of the world, at all the stupid, ignorant people in his life who'd thrown him away. She threaded her fingers up his neck into his thick hair to the back of what she knew was a very hard head. Only action could erase the damage done by others, and she intended to prove every last word she'd said.

If there were one lesson she'd learned well from her father, it was that once you gave your heart away, it was no longer yours to command. You couldn't take it back, and if you were smart, you didn't want to. It was the gift of a lifetime. Which was why Sanders Fitzgerald had never divorced Aurora. Instead, he'd spent the days of his life living between the daughter he adored and the damaged woman he'd vowed to love and honor the rest of his life.

McKenna had asked him once why he hadn't divorced Aurora. It made sense from her childish view. His reply came back at her in the guise of a truthful reprimand. "Because she's my wife, McKenna, and I promised I'd love her through sickness and in health, 'til death do we part. That hasn't changed."

The humility of that statement in a world overrun with pornography for pornography's sake had awed McKenna then and still did today. She was proud to be the daughter of Sanders Fitzgerald.

Fast forward to now. She'd given her heart to Beau the first time she'd seen him making sappy eyes at Kelsey. Of all the times to fall in love, that was when it happened. Before he even knew McKenna's name. Back when he respected the one woman he could never have, Beau had proven himself to be a better man in so many ways. Because as much as he adored Kelsey—and who didn't?—he respected her marriage vows. There were few men left in the world who honored such things, but Beau Jennings was one of them.

"Yes, Beau Jennings," she told him honestly, her eyes squeezed tight at the very big step she meant to take. Still holding his magnificent all-male body in her arms. "You're most definitely a keeper."

He shifted his hips just enough to let his hand slide between them. In seconds, he eliminated the cloth barriers. Resting on both forearms, he stared at her as, inch by inch, he slipped inside of her body.

Ah, the sweet, slick burn. The warm wet intrusion. Her muscles hugged him as only those muscles could. Pulsing. Clenching. Drawing him inside. Wanting every last inch. Why, oh why, had she waited to have sex? This was incredible. This fullness. This heat.

Yet how could she not? This was a first. It was her gift to him. Lifting her ass up from the mattress, she thrust into him as he set a rhythm, his hips matching hers. His eyes never breaking contact until…

"Ah, damn. Wow," she cried out, on the verge of—something.

"Come for me," he growled, setting her ablaze. "Come for me, McKenna. Do it now."

Enough! Her body exploded into warm, vibrant, burning hues. It fragmented into a kaleidoscope of him and of her. Of fire and time and space and—

Ah! So, so good! Wanting every last inch of his handsome body, his honorable heart, and his obstinate soul, she thrust upward, craving the connection, her fingernails digging into his ass to hold him where she needed him to stay. *Yeah. Right. There.*

Growling like a bear, he buried his face in her neck and joined her in his release. Despite worrying about the precautions she should've taken, McKenna spread her legs wide to receive his gift. For that was what this was, Beau finally giving a part of himself away. And she wanted every last drop.

Holding onto him and the tremendous high that came with their joining, her heart filled to the brim. Now was the time to talk, to tell him this was her first time. To tell him she was glad she'd waited. That he'd exceeded every hero in every romantic movie and romance novel she'd ever watched or read. That he had rocked her world and she'd never be the same.

But sleep deprived and sexually sated, her body turned deliciously languid. When he didn't seem inclined to chat, she nuzzled his ear and whispered a breathy, "Goodnight, Beau."

It was hard to hear his muffled reply with his face in her hair. But before she let her exhaustion win, McKenna was fairly certain he whispered, "Thank you, Jesus."

Chapter Thirty-Six

A light knock woke Beau just before dawn. He made certain McKenna's bare body was covered before he scrambled into his jeans, cracked the door, and answered. Maverick stood in the dark hallway. "Get dressed. Now."

"Copy that." Beau nodded, his heart pounding. Silently, he finished dressing, strapped on his holster, eased into his leather jacket, and filled his pockets with his assorted weaponry and loaded magazines. "What's up?" he asked once he'd stealthily left McKenna snoring softly behind him.

Maverick waited with Alex and Gabe in his front room, each of them dressed in jeans and wearing light jackets, no doubt to conceal their pistols, knives, and other armament. "Mother's been following reports of missing persons within the area. The latest just arrived ten minutes ago."

Beau nodded, ready to charge into Hell as needed. "Who's missing and when do we leave?"

"Sanders Fitzgerald disappeared from Golden Horizons late last night," Alex replied grimly. "Hasn't been seen since. Given what happened to his daughter—"

"Montego's got him," Beau spat, his hackles up at what this news would do to McKenna. "What are we waiting for?"

"You're staying here."

Beau's brain forwarded a flashing neon *'Does not compute'* to his frontal lobe. "Say what?"

"You heard me," Alex growled. "We can't all leave. As it is, you're unfit for active duty—"

"I am not."

"And I've called Lee and Adam to join—"

"I'm going."

"They'll be here shortly. Until then—"

"Bullshit!"

"Son-of-a-bitch. Stand down!" Alex hissed. "Someone needs to stay with the women, and that someone is you, *Junior Agent*." He cocked his head like he wanted to knock *someone* on his ass. Beau knew the feeling. "The forensic artist will be here soon. Work with him, Beau. Protect the women and kids until Lee and Adam show. By then, we may actually know where Sanders is."

Because you sure as hell don't know anything now.

"Ringer's place is vacant," Beau shot at Alex. "You ever think of looking for her there? If she's doing this just to get at you, wouldn't that make sense? It's familiar, and it'd be just like her."

"Good thinking," Maverick said calmly.

"Or she may break into another vacant home in the vicinity," Gabe added. "I've been checking around. Not all these houses are lived in. Some are vacation homes. Some are under construction. Boss, we need to alert the local—"

"Already did," Alex replied in that *'do you all think I'm stupid?'* tone of his. "Chief Prince has extra patrols canvassing the neighborhoods, checking with each homeowner to make sure everyone's accounted for."

"Then where are Ringers?" Beau spat. "Does anyone know? Do you?" *You arrogant son-of-a-bitch.*

Alex took the snarky hit without batting an eye. "Still unaccounted for like you nearly were."

Bulls-eye. Damn. Beau stepped back from the first man he'd backed down from in a long time. Alex was right. He wasn't a hundred percent, and these men needed a full-up battle ready operator on their six, not some one-handed wannabe packing two pistols when he could only fire one. "Fine. I'll stay back. This time."

Alex rolled his shoulder like he thought he was still the supreme alpha. *My ass.*

"Lee and Adam will call when they're close, but…" Maverick stepped into Beau's comfort zone. "Check this out." He directed Beau down the hall. "I've got a little system here that'll help you keep track of things while I'm gone."

When Maverick opened what looked like just another closet door, he revealed a security system to rival Alex's. Little, nothing. A panel of monitors watched over the barn from inside as well as out, the expansive yard between and around the house and all outbuildings, as well as the pastures. "Paranoid much?"

"Always," Maverick admitted. "An arsonist burned China's barn a couple years back. She lost two horses. It won't happen again."

"This'll make my job easier. Don't worry. I'll take care of the women and children while you're gone."

"I know you will. China and Shelby are here, and they both know how to shoot. Kyrie too. Don't think you can't rely on them in case—"

"Go," Beau said. "Find that bitch. Nothing will happen here. You can count on me."

With that uneasy truce, Alex, Maverick, and Gabe shouldered their gear bags and left through the garage, headed for the assisted living home. Aggravated at being the odd man out, Beau prowled the house and checked all points of egress. Back at the security closet, he studied which cameras did what, until he knew the lay of the land. All looked quiet on the home front. But damn. Montego now had Sanders Fitzgerald. McKenna would come unglued at this development.

Not wanting to tell her until he absolutely had to, Beau set up post in Maverick's living room. He didn't like that Alex had taken two agents with him. He knew something he wasn't sharing.

In less than an hour, Lee Hart and Adam Torrey arrived. Beau met them at the garage door off the mudroom. Lee was another damned cowboy, the taller of the two, green-eyed and big in the way of weightlifters. A regular doorstopper, that one.

Beau had heard the stories. Lee did hard time in one of Afghanistan's brutal prisons while in the Corps. That he'd survived testified to his sheer endurance and willpower. But as a direct result of those near-death experiences, he now religiously ascribed to the rigorous bodybuilding routine of one powerhouse of a man, Zack Lennox, another muscled agent. Lessons learned and all that.

Adam Torrey was one of two former Navy SEALs on The TEAM. With his hair nearly bleached white from the sun of some Mideastern country, he came into the house with that same easy lope of a predator. He'd had the extreme good fortune to marry Shannon Reagan, the one-time heir to Reagan Industries, a multi-million-dollar defense corporation.

Word on the street was she'd killed her egomaniac father in self-defense, then signed nearly all of Reagan Industries over to Jed McCormack, another defense contractor who'd made it big. Now she and Adam lived like regular people with their son, Jimmy Malone. She still ran the publishing business she'd started, and he worked for Alex. Talk about a small world.

"Hey," Adam grunted as he angled past Beau, his arms full of more surveillance hardware. "Heard anything?"

"No, have you?"

"Only that Alex and the guys are combing through Golden Horizons as we speak."

"They find anything?"

"Not yet."

"No police involved?"

Ky shook his head and kept going.

"Police haven't responded yet," Lee replied as he entered, tossing his head to keep his thick, mahogany hair from flopping into his eyes. "Golden Horizons only reported Sanders Fitzgerald as a critically missing adult. How's the finger?"

"Still attached." *I hope.*

"Boss said you're to rest until he gets back. He wants that arm elevated like—"

"Alex sure wants a lot, doesn't he?" Beau countered, shutting and locking the garage door behind Lee, making certain no one entered behind them. "So what're the rules on critically missing adults?"

Until recently, the written code of Virginia was silent on missing persons between twenty-one to sixty years of age. There were no Amber Alert systems like for missing children, and Search and Rescue units weren't authorized to commence searching until specific criteria were met. The critically missing adult had to be over sixty years of age and suffering from cognitive impairment. Sanders didn't fit either criteria. But laws were different now.

"Means no waiting period for one, but it still takes time for law enforcement to engage, and SAR's another story." Volunteers comprised Virginia's Search and Rescue. They could be mobilized as quickly as local law enforcement resources. Sometimes faster. "Have you told her yet?"

"Told me what?" A sleepy McKenna stood where the hall divided into the front room one way, the kitchen the other. She wore the same cotton shift as before, but had covered that with a fuzzy robe, the sash tied tight. Her fingers were stuck in her hair, combing it up over her head, and Beau wanted to flash-freeze that moment in time. She seemed to have moved beyond her fears. He didn't want to shatter her all over again, not just for her sake. But for selfish reasons.

They'd just shared an intimacy he'd never known before. He'd felt something rare and impossibly warm in her arms. Once he gave her this awful news, she'd never want to hold him again. She'd shove back, and he wasn't sure he could take that kind of rejection from her. From everyone else, yeah. They didn't matter, but McKenna had sneaked inside his perimeter and done something to his heart.

He swallowed hard, his jaw locked.

She cocked her head, her sleepy eyes now sharp and alert enough to cut glass. Her chest heaved. "Is it my dad?"

He nodded. "Everyone's out looking for him. Mother was right on it. Alex, Maverick, and Gabe left an hour ago." Like any of those details mattered now?

"Montego," she breathed.

And there it was. Beau had failed to protect the one person McKenna held most dear. "Yes," he confessed. "I'm afraid so."

"But... but..."

"But I'm sorry," he told her from the deepest part of his worthless heart. "I should've—"

"No!" she cried, one second standing across the room from him, the next she'd crashed past Lee and was inside Beau's arms, one arm around his head, and her face buried in his neck. "You didn't do this. Montego did. But you have to help him, Beau. He's all I've got left."

"I will. I will," he promised, unsure what had just happened. She still wanted him?

He dared tug her in close. McKenna did that burrowing thing, pressing and wriggling into his body like she wanted inside his skin. He'd been so busy scouting the premises that he still had his jacket on, only now her hands and arms were beneath the leather. Along with her pretty face, buried in his chest.

He dipped his nose to the crown of her head and held on. "I've got you, McKenna."

And I'm never letting you go.

Chapter Thirty-Seven

McKenna sat with Beau in China's very lovely solarium off the back of her house. With walls and ceiling of glass, the light was better here. She'd changed into jeans and the buttery soft button-up blouse that China let her borrow. Maverick's wife had certainly opened her home and her closet, but that seemed the way of these former military men and their wives. They took care of each other.

The police forensic artist had arrived, Officer Taige Crenshaw. Blonde, perky, and distinctly professional, she'd gotten right down to business. Maverick and Gabe had left earlier with Alex. Lee and Adam were in the barn with China, Kyrie, and Suzette tending to the horses and Kyrie's barn cats. Shelby was busy in the kitchen. She seemed obsessed with keeping things orderly and clean. McKenna was always looking for capable help. Shelby would make a good addition at the clinic.

The early summer sun cast an almost golden light on everything, but it couldn't reach McKenna's heart. It had frozen at the news of her father's disappearance. Her nerves were stretched tight. If Montego had him... *Oh God, oh God, oh God!*

Beau squeezed her hand, drawing her to the surface again where she could breathe. "We will find him," he assured her, emphasis on 'will'.

But he wasn't out looking for Sanders, was he? Neither were Lee or Ky. No, they were all safe, while her dad was... *I can't sit here and do nothing! My Dad!*

But where to run and what to do?

"McKenna," Beau said quietly, his fingers wrapped warm and tight around her entire hand now. Like he thought he could keep her from running? Yet even if she could, where would she go? Still, the compulsion to do something—anything—screamed, "Run!"

If not for Beau's hold on her...

If not for his stalwart strength beside her...

She forced her focus back to the picture Officer Crenshaw had adeptly sketched. Little by little, Montego's image evolved from the charcoals and smudges at the artist's talented fingertips. As Beau defined and described, Montego came to life. Long rectangular face. Thin lips. Black eyes, the lids lined by thick kohl that flared outward, reaching sideways to her temples. Her eyelashes were obviously fake, they were that long. Her nose flared, making her look haughty and proud. But Crenshaw hadn't captured the essence of evil that Montego evoked that night in McKenna's bedroom. This was just charcoal on paper.

What was Montego doing to Sanders? Right now? This very minute? *Oh, God, oh, God, oh God! While he suffers, I sit here safe and do nothing!*

"Breathe baby, just breathe," Beau murmured as he drew her into his side.

"I can't," she admitted as she collapsed into him, her hand on his chest. He had the patience of a saint, the way he seemed to know the precise moment she fell apart. "I should be doing something. Anything."

"I know it's hard to wait, but my boss will find your father."

"You believe that?"

She had him there. Beau hesitated. That he and Alex didn't mix well together was obvious, yet he finally said, "Yes, McKenna. I believe that. Like Maverick says, Alex doesn't know how to give up."

Officer Crenshaw's pencil tap on the tabletop drew McKenna's attention back to the drawing. "Dr. Fitzgerald, do you agree with Agent Jennings version? Is this the same woman who broke into your home and held you captive?" she asked, one pert eyebrow arched.

McKenna nodded without seeing the portrait displayed on a simple wooden easel from Crenshaw's artist toolbox.

"Please, ma'am. I know this is hard," the officer said, her neck crooked forward as she peered intently at McKenna. "But I need you to study this portrait for a couple minutes. Really look at Montego. Take your time. Think about that night, from the first moment you laid eyes on her on your front porch to your bedroom. Did she ever smile? Did she cough? Sneeze? Mumble? Was she cold and cruel, or did she act like she knew you? If I've missed anything, a wart, or a mole, a tattoo, or a scar, tell me. Even if it seems insignificant, I want to know."

McKenna nodded and finally, looked Montego in the face again. Beau had given an accurate description. She truly was a witch. All she needed was a black cat and a broom to go with that broomstick skirt—

"A snake. On her neck. Or at least…" McKenna gulped down the bile that kept climbing up her throat at facing her tormentor again. "Or at least a pattern like snakeskin. Here."

She ran her fingers up the right side of her throat to her ear. "Black. It was black and creepy."

Beau tightened his hold. "Good catch. It was dark. I missed that."

Officer Crenshaw returned the paper to the table and added a mottled pattern of small shapes to Montego's neck. "Like this? Just on one side or both? Bigger scales? Smaller?"

McKenna nodded, her brain still pinging between how to save her dad and what Montego looked like. "No, that's right. I can't remember the exact pattern, but y-y-yes."

"Did it extend into her hair or did it end at her earlobe?"

"All the way up, I think, but I couldn't exactly see where it ended, because I was… I was…" Gulp. *Trying to stay alive while she strangled me.*

"No head or eyes? No fangs or anything like that? Just snakeskin?"

"Yes, just… that."

"Every little detail helps, you two. Thanks," the officer said. "Take your time, McKenna. If you think of anything else, tell me, and please call me Taige from now on. I'm a woman, and trust me, I know how hard this is for you."

Did she really? McKenna stared into Taige's crystal blue eyes and saw a shadow hidden there she dared not explore. But knowing this female officer might somehow understand the humiliation of nearly being murdered, of being so out of control that she wanted to tear her hair out just thinking of that night—helped. "I will. Thank you."

"Ah, honey." Taige reached out and patted McKenna's other hand. "Like your boyfriend said, just breathe. If there's any detail you forgot, it will come back to you once you relax."

My boyfriend? McKenna cast a shy glance and caught Beau staring down at her. One brow lifted as if that descriptor caught him by surprise, too. McKenna would've smiled if her heart hadn't been breaking.

Chapter Thirty-Eight

"Now let's think back to your first run-in with Catalina Montego, the night you were abducted," Taige said as she turned her attention on Beau.

He shook his head. "No need to, ma'am. It's the same woman. I'm sure."

"But are you?" she asked as she opened her sketchpad and settled her right wrist to the paper, her pencil between her fingers, and her chin tilted expectantly. "Tell me what you remember from Boxster's Pub. That's where this all started, right?"

His mouth twisted in a sneer. Alex. Damn him. Couldn't keep his big mouth shut, could he? "Like I said—"

"Agent Jennings," she interrupted sternly, the top of her pencil tapping the tablet like a metronome. "This is a police investigation, and I need you to cooperate. Fully. Now think back to the night you were abducted like I asked. You were sitting at the bar in Boxster's. I know the place, and I know that exact bar. It's a carved monstrosity brought over from Ireland, but it's gorgeous in its way, isn't it? All that polished dark oak? There's a mirror in that cabinet that runs the length of the room, but you can barely see it with all the liquor bottles on the front shelf and counter. Yet Mac always polishes that glass until it shines. That's got to be a pain in the ass job, to move all those bottles just to Windex a mirror most people can't see, don't you think?"

Beau nodded. The mirror was always spotless. If Mac didn't polish it, someone certainly did. Which was why Beau always sat where he did, at the far end of the bar. He could see most of the room in that mirror. From there he kept an eye on everything, anyone who arrived through the front door, and anyone sneaking up behind him. Others might not have noticed that mirror, but he had the first time he'd walked into Boxster's.

One Hennessey, neat. His usual. That was all he had to drink before everything went fuzzy. Which meant Montego had been close, like right at his elbow close, to have slipped something into his glass.

"Which stool were you sitting on?"

"Last one, far end." *Where I always sit. Far away from foot traffic and the hostess station at the front door. Far enough to never be caught by surprise.*

"You know Mac, don't you?" Taige asked, an odd tone to her question. "Mac McPherson, the owner?"

"Yeah, sure." Everyone knew Mac. "But he wasn't barkeep that night. The place was busy. The TV was blaring. Too loud. Too much noise." *I remember now...* "Some woman was working behind the bar."

"He's missing."

Beau stared at the officer. "Montego's got McPherson?"

Both of her shoulders lifted. "Right now, we only know he's missing. It's an open investigation, so let's get your facts straight, Agent Jennings. His life might depend on you."

That heartless bitch!

He blinked, recalling the hubbub as a noisy group of businessmen from the District flooded Boxster's. Damn, they were rowdy and brash, bumping him and standing behind him. Squeezing in between him and the guy beside him to order their beers and mixed drinks. He'd just been served when some jerk slammed his elbow. Almost spilled his drink.

It came to him in a flash. "Blonde. The barkeep was blonde." *Could Alex be right?*

"How tall?" Taige pressed, her pencil poised over the sketchpad.

"Nothing like Mac. She was…" *Gulp.* "…short. Maybe five nothing." *Just like Alex said.*

"Color of eyes? Were you close enough to notice? Was the light dim or bright enough to notice details? Long hair? Short hair? Shape of her face? Heart-shaped? Round? Rectangular or—?"

"Square," Beau said as the night came back to him. "Blonde. Short hair but long bangs hanging in her face, in her eyes. She kept blowing them out of her way. Smiled a lot. Heavy Spanish accent. Definitely first-generation immigrant. Brown eyes." *Pretty. Friendly. Attractive. Smart. Shit, I never saw her coming.*

Taige's fingers flew over her tablet, drawing with sure, adept strokes and smudging with the edge of her pinkie finger as she went. She sketched so quickly, it seemed she already knew what Catalina Montego looked like.

Beau glanced at McKenna, wondering how she'd take this abrupt change in direction. Wondering what she'd think of him for not recalling crucial evidence a helluva lot sooner, like he should have. How could she have faith in a man who couldn't remember shit?

But she sat staring into space.

"You okay?" he asked as he tugged at her fingers to draw her out of the spell she seemed to be under.

Her head bobbed, but in a distracted way as if her mind wasn't in the room. The last few days had been tough, and there seemed no end to the stress. Alex, Gabe, and Maverick had better return with good news.

"Agent Jennings?" Taige asked as she turned her tablet toward him and McKenna. "Is this the woman bartending the night you were physically removed from Boxster's?"

That was a nice way of telling him he'd let his guard down and got himself shanghaied. He nodded, shocked he'd forgotten the coy, good-looking blonde staring back at him now. Even in charcoal, her eyes sparkled with a sly glint.

He remembered. Damn it, she'd asked if he wanted to try something different with that Hennessey. He'd said no, he was fine. She'd shrugged, and the easy way she'd handled rejection got to him. He'd relented because she was—cute— in a sultry, mysterious way. For that, he was rewarded with a splash of coconut cream that sank to the bottom of his glass.

"It was in the coconut cream," he told McKenna.

She stared back at him, disconnected from the work at hand.

"At Boxster's. The only thing I didn't watch the bartender add to my drink was the coconut cream she talked me into. That was when she slipped me the roofie, or whatever it was." *And like a dumbass I said, 'Sure. Why not? Step right up and take a finger while you're at it. I've got plenty to spare.'*

"I'm sorry, what?" McKenna asked, blinking.

He jerked his chin at the latest sketch, wishing McKenna would re-engage as he asked Taige, "You've sketched this face before, right?"

She nodded. "Yes, for Alex Stewart a couple days ago."

"Is she—?"

"Catalina Montego? Age twenty-seven, five feet tall, one-hundred ten pounds? Yes, the same one Alex has on airport security footage. She's also on the FBI's most wanted list for human trafficking, murder, desecration of more than one body, drug running, and a few other distasteful things."

Beau put his elbow to the table and cupped his chin. Stroking the beginning of what would grow into a thick beard in less than a week, he had nothing to say. If blondie was Catalina Montego, who the hell was the bitch with the braid?

Taking a deep breath, Taige flipped her sketchpad to a clean sheet. "And now, you are going to tell me exactly what the woman you saw in Congressman Ringer's home looked like."

His head bobbed, even as his mind skittered over what he'd been so positive he'd known before Taige arrived. He'd been wrong, damn it, and Alex was right. Talk about a blow to a guy's ego. "I'll do my best," Beau said meekly.

Taige leaned into him. "This happens all the time, Agent Jennings, so stop beating yourself up. Even trained professionals lose track of significant details under stress."

"Yes, but…" *I'm a Ranger. A sniper. I'm different. Least, I was.*

"Trust me. I've interviewed dozens of SWAT officers, detectives, and others who weren't able to remember specifics until they sat with me while I sketched what they thought they remembered. There's something about recreating the scene that stirs more distinct memories than what we initially recall. It's a survival reflex, Beau. Terror alters how our brains work, and trust me, after I read the police report on you, you were under extreme stress both times you encountered Miss Montego. I could tell you what goes on with our neural networks and how radically we shift from logical, problem-solving professionals to emotional creatures who just want to survive, but I think you already know that."

"I froze," he said simply. *Like a fuckin' new guy.*

She shook her head. "You, sir, did not freeze. You reacted, and the primal instinct to survive hard-wired in all human brains, overrode your capacity for higher thinking to make certain that you did live. That is your brain's primary function, and trust me, it did a damned good job that morning. You're still here, aren't you?"

He nodded. *But I was so sure...*

"And that makes you the winner, Agent Jennings. You, not Catalina Montego. You escaped insurmountable odds. While you were bleeding to death. While you were cuffed and ready to be—who knows what—on that table?" She cocked her head like he had better listen up and shut up. "You lived, and with your help, let's make certain Catalina Montego and this other woman, whoever she is, don't get away with their crimes. Now, let's all take a deep breath..." She inhaled like she needed to teach him how to breathe.

Which she kind of did. At the moment, Beau couldn't get past the awful fact that—damn—Alex was right. He inhaled slowly, his traitorous mind reliving what happened the morning he'd come to inside Ringer's house. The dim lights.

The shadows. His own loss of blood and the accompanying panic that had damned near choked him.

"So…" Taige paused, the pencil in her fingers poised and ready to work its charcoal magic. "Tell me what you think you recall, and we'll go from there."

An icy chill shivered up the back of Beau's neck. What truly had happened that morning? Aside from the utter terror of the atrocity committed against him? Aside from the shadow standing at the door screaming at him? Aside from the stark black silhouette of—shit—a diminutive Spanish woman spitting nails like she wanted to kill him?

Beau took another deep breath and told Taige Crenshaw what he honestly remembered. Not much...

Chapter Thirty-Nine

McKenna couldn't take her eyes off the first sketch, the one of the woman who wasn't Montego.

"She screamed when she opened Ringer's side door." Beau meant the real Catalina, the one who'd severed his finger, not this strange, other woman with so much hate in her eyes.

"Do you recall her exact words?"

"Yes. She said, 'Where do you think you're going, Benjamin Jennings?' Heavy on the Spanish accent."

The woman at Ringer's and Boxster's was the same.

"Excellent," Officer Crenshaw purred. "Did the woman at McKenna's apartment speak with any kind of inflection? An accent?"

Beau took an extra-long minute thinking before he grumbled, "Umm, no. Not that I recall. Did she, McKenna?"

He seemed to be asking for help more and more as Taige led him through the details of his abduction and his fight with the woman with the heavy black braid Beau and McKenna had thought was Montego. Officer Crenshaw had yet to put pencil to paper, but she knew how to reach inside Beau and help him separate fact from fiction. She was very good at her job.

"No. She sounded American," McKenna whispered. Every ugly word she'd murmured had been American English. No accent. No compassion, either.

His brows furrowed into a deep V. "Jingling. I heard jingling when she opened the door. Not like bells. More like bangles and bracelets."

Officer Crenshaw nodded. "Good. How about the woman in the bar? Did she wear any jewelry?"

"Not that I remember." Beau snorted and scratched his head. "Not that what I thought I saw was right, but yeah. I'm pretty sure that woman" —he pointed to the blonde Montego— "didn't jingle."

But there was something extremely unsettling about the woman with the braid. The shape of her nose. The harsh curve of her brows. Even the unrealistic length of her eyelashes and the distant look in those charcoal eyes felt familiar in a creepy way. McKenna couldn't concentrate long enough to figure it out, not with her dad missing.

Taige's description of what terror did to a brain was spot-on. McKenna could no more solve a simple addition problem at the moment, than think straight, not with her emotions running as high as they were. She kept going back to her last conversation with Sanders. She'd planned to meet him for dinner, but so much had happened since. She should've called him to explain, so he wouldn't worry, but she hadn't. Why not?

He'd distinctly said, *'I'm penciling you in.'* Like the faithful father he'd always been, he was still waiting to hear from her, but she hadn't called. Yet his last words to her were, *'Love you, Princess.'*

"Love you, too," she whispered, choking on repentance for being a less than faithful daughter. *Wherever you are...*

Beau's good arm tightened around her. "Hey, McKenna. Where'd you go?"

She shook her head, forcing her attention back to yet another drawing beneath Officer Crenshaw's skilled fingers. Once again, she'd drawn the same blonde woman as her second sketch instead of the monster McKenna remembered so vividly. Okay, so the blonde abducted Beau from the bar and severed his finger at Congressman Ringer's home.

"Two," she whispered. "We're looking at two different women."

Her world tilted at the thought that they might be working together. One was bad enough, but two explained how Beau had ended up inside Congressman Ringer's. The blonde couldn't have handled a guy as heavy as Beau all by herself. It also explained how the dark-haired woman had strung that contraption under McKenna's bed. She'd had help. But what did these two strangers have in common? How did they know each other?

A random memory intruded. "She called me little dumpling."

Beau cocked his head in disbelief. "Seriously? That doesn't sound very Spanish. Chica maybe, but dumpling?"

"What else did she say?" Officer Crenshaw asked.

"She… she said I took something from her, and she couldn't get it back. I thought she meant you." McKenna looked up at Beau's grim face. "But then she wanted information in exchange for my life. She asked about Kelsey. What she liked to eat. Where she shopped."

"Which sounds like something that Catalina" —Beau jerked his chin at the sketch of the blonde woman— "would ask to get back at Alex. She'd want to hurt Kelsey. What else?"

McKenna blinked as random info-bytes came to her. "She tapped my forehead. Told me to take care of this little girl first, meaning me" —a shiver sneaked up her spine— "or, these are her words, *'mommy's going to be very upset, and you know what'll happen then.'* It was like she knew me." McKenna scrubbed her biceps with hard up and down strokes, needing the sensation of that woman—whoever she was—off her skin and out of her head. "I can't get these goosebumps to stop."

"Anything else?" Beau asked as he tugged her under his arm.

"She called me *'child'*, but not in a motherly way. She said, *'tell me about Kelsey Stewart, child.'* Isn't that creepy?" McKenna shivered again, and once more Beau responded, scrubbing his good hand up her bicep and down again.

"Sounds like she knew what happened when you were…" Beau let his voice fade.

McKenna nodded. "Exactly. She knew how to rattle me. She knew what happened when I was a kid."

Taige canted her head. "What happened?"

McKenna looked at Beau. Before she could speak, he pointed to the fierce Amazon with the braid and snakeskin tattoo and asked, "Do you have any idea who this one is, McKenna? Could she be the mother or grandmother of a patient you've treated? I mean, Alex is certain that this one" —he pointed to the short blonde— "is Catalina Montego, and that she's after him and his team. He thinks that's why she came after me. But this other one… Is it possible she's after you for malpractice or mistreatment or" —Beau shrugged— "something that has nothing to do with Alex or The TEAM?"

McKenna shook her head. "I guess, but I haven't had any malpractice suits filed against me. The clinic had one, but it didn't include me, and it was settled months ago. I guess it's possible one of my parents is upset with me, but if they are, I don't know it yet. My patients like me, Beau. I know they do. There is something familiar about her, though, but I don't recall seeing her at the office or in the hospital. I can't place her." She canted her head, looking at the sketch from a different angle. "Sorry. Wish I could help, but no, I don't know her."

But yes... The more she stared into those cruel black eyes, the more McKenna recognized—something. She lifted two fingers to her lips and brushed down on them like she used to do when—

"What are you doing?" Beau asked.

"Nothing. I'm just—"

He turned his body toward her then, his shoulders wide and powerful but the look in his eyes piercingly kind. "Baby, you're crying."

"No, I'm not." But lifting those same fingertips to her eyes, they came away wet. *Why yes, I am. How odd?* A distant memory hovered at the edge of forgetfulness, like a fluttering moth McKenna couldn't catch no matter how hard she tried. Elusive. Evasive. Painful...

"Now that you jogged my memory…" Beau swallowed noisily. "McKenna, what was Montego's evil twin chanting that night? When I first breached your door, I heard her say something about revenge and weird shit like blood and sisters. Thought I smelled incense, too." He lifted the back of his injured hand to his forehead. "What was that about?"

McKenna shrugged, hating that she felt like a helpless female instead of the capable physician she'd been only days ago. How could he still be so confident, when she and her world were falling apart? "I have no idea," she bit out, suddenly frustrated. "What do you expect me to say? My dad's missing, and one of these women has him. Not good odds, is it?"

"That's not what I—"

"Damn it! My dad's in trouble, but you're not doing anything to help him." She jumped to her feet. "Is that so hard to understand? He's not hard and cold like you. He's a gentle man, and he's kind, and funny, and he's probably hurt and bleeding, and he's—" A stupid hiccup jerked out of her, making her look even more out of control.

Suddenly, Beau was on his feet, and she was back in his arms, her cheek pressed against his hard chest. "I got you," he murmured, his arms locked tightly around her, his one good hand trapping her against him, and his heart pounding.

"But you don't *got* my dad, do you?" It was no use. She couldn't break loose, and Beau gave no quarter, just drew her under his chin while she fumed and cussed and turned into a weepy, blubbering mess.

"No, but I will find him," Beau told her, his voice so kind despite what she'd said.

"I'm sorry," came easily to her lips. "You're not hard or cold, I'm just... I'm so—"

"Scared, I know. Trust me, baby, I know. But you're not fighting these bitches by yourself. Officer Crenshaw here is—"

"Is at this moment transmitting three very good likenesses of our two suspects to my captain at the precinct," Taige finished. "In seconds, every police officer and FBI agent in a five-state radius will know who we're looking for. You both did excellent work here today."

McKenna turned her head to argue, but Taige was good for her word. She'd sketched the pictures by hand, but one of her drawings now lay face down on what looked like a portable fax machine.

Taige inclined her head to McKenna. "I've had the good luck to work with Alex Stewart before. His men are above reproach, and I've never known guys who worked harder. You should trust Agent Jennings. I can't promise, but with The TEAM on your side, your father's chance of survival just went up a notch."

A notch, really? One whole notch? Like that's supposed to make me feel better?

Damn, but talk was cheap. McKenna had heard promises before, from her mother. After Aurora let McKenna out of the closet, always just in time for her to get washed and her hair brushed before her father came home. Just in time to look normal, when she was far from it. Just as soon as...

The oddest tremor of déjà vu rippled up McKenna's spine. She was a child again. Crying. Aching. Breathless with—

Brrrrrrrring! The old-fashioned ring tone from Taige's cell jolted McKenna from her childhood reverie.

"Excuse me. I have to take this. Officer Crenshaw. Yes. Put it through." Taige laid the phone to the table and said, "This pre-recorded call just came into my precinct."

"McKenna, listen to me," a man said, *his voice laced with terror. "There's a lot you don't know, princess. Whatever you do, don't come looking for me. Please! Stay safe. Stay—!"*

The call disconnected.

"That's my dad," McKenna cried out. "He's in trouble."

Beau was already thumbing his cell phone. "Boss?"

Taige was barking into her phone, asking if her people had traced the call.

McKenna just wanted to scream.

Chapter Forty

"I didn't press her harder because that night she was injured, and I doubt—"

"You should have!" Beau spat. "We would've known we were dealing with Montego and Bitch Two sooner. Fuck, Stewart! What were you thinking?"

So now I'm Stewart again. You son-of-a-bitch…

"Why didn't *you* question her if you're so damned smart? You're sleeping with her!" he bellowed, wishing he hadn't accepted this hands-free call from the pain in the ass agent he'd mistakenly hired. Alex hated driving when his temper was up. He tended toward aggression on good days, but the way Beau continually talked back, pushed him toward full-blown road rage.

On the highway headed back to Maverick's ranch, Alex would rather have been going home to his wife where another emergency was unfolding. In the middle of investigating not only Golden Horizons facility, staff, and the few leads that surfaced, Mother called. Dempsey had taken a turn for the worse. Mother already contacted her private medical team to transport her daughter back to her private hospital. And Beau had the nerve to call him out?

As usual the hothead didn't answer Alex's question. "What'd you find at the assisted living home, huh? Anything?"

The snark in that terse question was enough to choke a camel—or get someone killed. Alex stabbed the end call button on his steering wheel before he punched his dash and broke it. Son-of-a-bitch, he was pissed. He'd no more than clenched the wheel, wishing it were Beau's thick neck, when an incoming buzzed.

"Stewart!" he growled. *So help me, Jennings—*

"Alex?" Kelsey asked, a tremor in her voice.

"Yes?" he asked though he already knew what was coming.

"They didn't make it. Dempsey's gone. The chopper's going on into the hospital, so her doctor can declare time of death. Mother needs me. I have to go."

Son-of-a-bitch! "No. I'm almost home. Wait for me and we'll fly into the city together."

Silence. And Alex knew Kelsey's heart was breaking all over again, that survivor's guilt was riding her hard.

"Please, sweetheart," he begged. "I'm almost home."

"I will," Kelsey murmured, her voice so incredibly sad. "I... I can't do this without you."

She always thought she was the weaker one, but he knew better. He'd be nothing without her. "I'll be there in ten. Bring Lexie with you."

"Copy that," she whispered as the line disconnected.

Alex shook his head at the pain twisting his gut. Beau had to go. That was all there was to it. After Montego and the woman who'd assaulted McKenna were apprehended, after this mess was done, Beau Jennings could go to hell. Alex didn't have the patience to kiss that bastard's ass every time he turned around. That was no way to run a business. The TEAM was not only successful, but Americans needed it.

What they didn't need was Beau Jennings. No. Damned. More.

Alex made it home in six minutes and parked his car inside his security gate in seven. Maverick and Gabe were still back at the assisted living home, working with the local police and investigating the unknown fingerprints found on the outside door at one of the rear exits. At least *they* followed orders.

Running for Kelsey, needing her in his arms, Alex left his car in the driveway, barking instructions for Lee to ensure that everyone at the Wild Wolf Ranch stayed secure. The last thing he needed was Mother's loss to distract his team. Montego was still out there gunning for him. Someone else could get hurt.

Lee came back with a steady, "No problem, Boss. Officer Crenshaw just left. I take it you know the police received a call from McKenna's father."

"Heard it from Beau," Alex growled as he hit his front porch and pressed his palm to the scanner. "Do we know anything else? Were they able to trace the call?"

"No, they weren't. How's Mother?"

"I'm on my way to see her now," Alex said as he stepped inside his home, the one place no murderer would ever—EVER—enter. "Justice is with her. I never should've—"

"Don't go there. We didn't have a lot of choices with Montego on the loose. It's just life, Boss. Sometimes it rains; sometimes it pours."

"Copy that." Alex disconnected as he met Kelsey's tearful stare from the hallway, an overnight bag in her hand. But no Lexie. "Where is everyone?"

Kelsey nodded behind her. "Zack, Harley, Eric, and Jake are with the kids. They're talking to them about Dempsey and... you know."

As it should be, the men explaining death to their little ones. "Where's Lexie?"

"I don't want to take her. She's too young. She'll be safe here." Kelsey ran a hand through her hair, and Alex wished those were his fingers caught in her tangles. "What are you up to, Alex? David called. He's bringing Nancy and the kids over, but he's not staying. He said we've got enough firepower here, that you need him elsewhere."

Alex nodded. "David, Rory, Taylor, and Cassidy are working with Detective Oberg hunting the real Catalina Montego. Connor and Izza are on another lead. But this other woman… The one who hurt McKenna…" He shook his head. "Her prints aren't in any known database. Hell, we don't even know what to call her." *Aside from Bitch Two, Beau's name for her. At least, he got that right.* "There's no paper trail. No way to pin her down. When we get back, I've got to talk with McKenna and find out what else she remembers."

"Talk with her now," Kelsey urged. "We need to catch her assailant as much as Montego."

He shook his head. "No. Mother needs us more. You ready?"

It seemed as if Kelsey deflated where she stood. She nodded. Her eyes brimmed, and Alex went to her and folded her inside his arms. "I know, sweetheart, I know," he whispered as she burrowed under his chin and clung to him as if he were her life. God knew she was his. "It's never easy. Let's go be strong for Mother."

"You're right."

Alex glanced over his shoulder at his home while he led Kelsey to the door. He needed a head count of agents and all family members soon. He'd have time do that once he and Kelsey were in the air. For the first time in months, most of his team was home instead of on missions. Only Mark Houston and Hunter Christian were OUTCONUS, out of the country.

The feeling that something truly evil was bearing down on him lingered. *Well, bring it on,* he thought. *You think I can't whip your ass, Montego? You too, Bitch Two? Try me. Fuckin' try me! I'll end the both of you before you hurt one more person!*

Pissed that the expletive reminded Alex of his headstrong agent and another problem he didn't need, Alex shielded Kelsey from street traffic while he escorted her quickly to their car. He'd no more than opened the door when he saw it. Jerking her back into his arms, he pressed her face into his chest before she could see what lay on the back seat. His pistol sprang automatically from his underarm holster to his hand.

Son-of-a-bitch, had that been behind the driver's seat all along? Since he'd left Golden Horizons? *Which meant Montego's been inside my car.*

"Alex? What's—"

"In the house. Now," he ordered, his sharp eyes measuring shadows and every minuscule movement as adrenaline coursed through him.

Kelsey promptly did as she was told, while he backed with her to the front door, his arm around her and his weapon ready to kill. In seconds, they were safely inside. *She's been in my driveway!* "I want Zack, Harley and Jake in here now. Please get them."

"You bet," she murmured as she hurried to obey.

The agents he trusted soon swarmed the living room, all armed and all prepared—like Kelsey—to follow his lead. Bronzed as a Tahitian god with three times the testosterone, Zack arrived first. "What's up?"

A lanky survivor of one too many combat tours, Harley followed on his six. "Don't tell me, Montego's dumb enough to come after you here?"

"Not sure," Alex bit out. "It's either her or Bitch Two."

Jake Weylin, another survivor and a former Marine who'd proven to be a damned good infiltrator, cocked his head. "Bitch Two? There something you need to tell us, Boss?"

"Yes, but first, Harley and Jake, check the perimeter. Hurry." Alex didn't have to look to know his men had instantly followed orders, that they were already scouring the house and grounds for intruders. Which Alex doubted they'd find, since his dogs hadn't raised an alarm.

Zack approached Alex with his pistol drawn, the barrel raised. "So what's going on? Is Montego really here?"

"Someone sure as hell was. There's a severed finger on the back seat of my car, and now we've got two suspects."

"Montego's got help?"

Alex closed his steel entry door, slapped the deadbolt, and activated the alarm. "Not sure, but while Beau and McKenna were sitting with the forensic artist, they both remembered different things from their attacks." Alex ran a hand up his stiff and aching neck, wishing he'd listened to Beau instead of discounting his version of who he'd sincerely thought he'd seen. A man? No damned way. But a different woman altogether? That made sense.

"From what Beau recalled, we're dealing with two psychotic women who may or may not be working together. I've got to get over to Maverick's to question him and Doc Fitz."

"Then go," Zack replied quickly. "Jake, Harley, and I can take care of things here."

"No, I need to visit Mother first." *And I need to wait for Howie, and, son-of-a-bitch! Is it asking too much for Karma to stop dogpiling on my TEAM!*

"But what's the biggest rock?" Zack asked.

"What are you talking about?"

"The biggest problem. You can't push them all up hill at the same time. Pick one and let us handle the rest. Now choose."

Alex wiped his hand over his face. If it were only that easy. Delegation in the line of fire or on the front line didn't come easy. He didn't shirk responsibility or ask his men and women to step up to chores he himself wouldn't do. Ever! He led, not pushed from the rear where things were safe, orderly, and clean. Combat was ugly, and it was dirty, but a real man stepped up and fought alongside his troops. If Grandpa Stewart, who'd fought at Iwo Jima, had taught Alex anything, it was how to be that real man.

Yet, something had to give. And his people came first. Like he'd told Kelsey, "I'm going into the city," Alex said as the first kink in his neck let loose its tight grip on his jugular, not that his migraine felt any better. "Maverick and Gabe can sort Beau and McKenna once they get back to the ranch. I won't be gone long. In the meantime, keep my daughter safe."

Zack inclined his head to Alex. "She's my daughter, too."

And there it was, the miracle seed Alex had never intended to plant. His TEAM had matured into a family like no other.

"Thanks, Zack," he said humbly as he took his leave. "Tell Howie I'll talk to him when I return, or he can visit me at Maverick's. For the record, I'd only been out of the car maybe ten minutes at most. Montego or Bitch Two has to be close by to have placed that finger between when I parked the car and when I returned to it with Kelsey. I don't want you looking for her, though. That's what she wants, to get one of us alone, and we're not playing into her hands."

Zack nodded, his weapon now holstered, and his arms folded across his big chest. "Understood. Protect home base. We can do that."

Alex fast-tracked to his expansive in-home theater, where Kelsey now sat somberly with The TEAM wives: Mei Lennox, Libby Houston, Judy Mortimer, Shea Reynolds, Ember Dennison, Gracie Armstrong, Meredith Christian, Lacey Whelan, Devereaux McCray, Shannon Reagan Torrey, as well as Tess Hart, Lee's wife. The children hung close to their mothers. David Tao would arrive soon with Nancy and their children. Cassidy's husband, Jude sat on the floor with their daughter Judith.

Alex's heart stuttered as he realized he was now charged with protecting all he held dear. He'd die for each one of these people, his incredible wife, his miracle-baby daughter, and his second-to-none family. But he was not a man given to hiding.

Surreptitiously, he sent a wink to Kelsey and received a silent air kiss in return. She was stronger than people gave her credit for, himself included. Resilient and a damned good shot, it was true. She wasn't the battered, defenseless waif he'd found on his cabin porch all those years ago. She was extra-smart and extra-careful, and she was also right. The wives were every bit as strong as their men. They didn't work for him, but at one time or another, he'd worked with every last one of them. Like their husbands, they also served. It was high time he admitted it.

"Listen up," he told them, his stubborn heart still in his throat at what he was about to do. "I have to leave, but Zack will stay here to coordinate your defense strategy." That earned him a crooked smile and a nod from the big guy. "He knows what to do, and so do you. All of you know how to defend yourselves. I've seen you with your husbands and some of your kids at the range." He glanced at Mei and Libby when he said that. Their oldest daughters were well acquainted with firearms. "You're all capable. And some of you are smarter than me."

Kelsey shot him a tender smile that told him she was proud. And he was so damned proud of her. He couldn't hover over her forever. She didn't need him like that. Kelsey also had wings. It was time to let her loose, so she could fly. The wives—not just him and not just the men and women of his TEAM—had work to do.

"I'll keep in touch," he told them before his emotions got the best of him and he reneged on every brave word he'd just uttered. Son-of-a-bitch! This was the hardest thing Alex had ever done. But as if he were their commander-in-chief, as if they all knew what to do—because they did—he turned his back on them and the assignments just given.

He swallowed hard, but he did it. He walked away and let them do what they did best. Protect their men.

Chapter Forty-One

McKenna's wrong. She doesn't think I'm cold and hard, but that's all I am. My staying here's a mistake. It's time to let her go. She needs to get on with her life. She's scared now, but she'll be okay.

Beau stood at the same kitchen window where he'd accosted Alex only the day before. Word from Stewarts wasn't good. Besides Mother's tragedy, Montego had left another finger for Alex, and she'd done it right under his nose. Didn't it figure? Catalina had been here all along, just waiting to pop in and prove she could get at Alex any time she wanted. And he thought he was so smart.

Alex was lucky Montego hadn't gotten past the rest of his fancy security and taken one of the kids. Or Kelsey, if all those questions Montego had asked McKenna meant anything. Anymore Beau wasn't sure what these two evil women were up to. He had a feeling he and McKenna had both been pawns, used by two different, but crazy females with a death wish he very much wanted to grant. He just had to find them.

The police hadn't yet identified the hapless owner of the latest severed offering, but Beau didn't intend to wait for their forensic report. It was time to strike back. The best defense was a good offense—and Beau meant to be damned offensive.

As soon as he could get away without attracting attention. For now, Shelby and McKenna chatted quietly in China's front room with Suzette and Kyrie. Lee was walking the perimeter, which meant he'd be gone the better part of an hour. Adam was somewhere in the house, hopefully not scrutinizing the security monitors in the hall closet.

Beau found it interesting that Ky's and Lee's wives and children were staying at Alex's house instead of here with them at Maverick's. What was that about? In the end it didn't really matter. Beau had a job to do before Montego or Bitch Two struck again.

Stealthily, he slid his injured hand into the sleeve of his leather jacket, only wincing when he bent his elbow. Ducking his other arm into the leather, he zipped it shut to conceal his hardware and flipped the collar up. Lifting his gear bag from the floor, where he'd left it when Officer Crenshaw arrived, he cast one quick backward glance toward the quiet chatter in the front room.

He could see McKenna's profile from where he stood. Seated in the corner of the couch with her arm on the armrest, her other hand lay filled with tissues on her lap. She was the picture of a woman in distress, which was why he had to leave. McKenna would be safe here. He meant to make sure of that.

Easing the glass door to the solarium open, he stepped swiftly onto the paved walkway that led to the driveway. Walking fast, Beau kept to the hedge between the barn and the house until he cleared the front property. From there, he was still a good ten miles to Alex's place.

But that wasn't where he planned to go. A fox with a pack of hounds on its scent was a dangerous animal, but Beau didn't need that pack of hounds following him, either. He needed space and time to do what he did best. While he was fairly certain Alex had everyone else scouring his gated-community to locate Montego, Beau began his search for her evil twin.

Whoever Bitch Two was, he'd make sure she never hurt McKenna again.

Alex sat with Mother in one of the small consolation rooms at Fowler's Memorial funeral parlor, where families made final arrangements. Wearing her usual crisply ironed blouse and light blue, tailored skirt, and matching jacket, she clenched a tissue in one hand, an electronic device in the other. He hadn't bothered to change and still wore the black TEAM polo over the jeans he'd started the day with. A light jacket covered his holsters. People didn't need to know he carried. Even holstered firearms tended to freak certain civilians.

Mother had planned for this day a thousand times over, yet he wouldn't let her handle the last-minute details alone. Even with Justice Sandler, her steadfast companion, at her side, she was still very much alone. But that was life for you. It came and it went, and there you stood at the grave when it was done with you. Forever bereft and all by yourself.

"I need to talk to you," she told him quietly, her voice subdued, and her heart broken. "It's about Beau."

Alex shook his head. "Not now. Beau can wait until hell freezes over for all I care."

"No, he can't. This is important," she said as she lifted the tissue to her reddened nose and sniffed. "I've never seen a man as volatile as he is, not even you back in the day." She stretched her hand out to Alex.

He took hold of her fingers. Damn, they were cold. A glimmer of tears sprang to his eyes at what she was going through. No mother should have to bury her child. *No father either...*

"I was a bastard when we first met," he admitted easily as they sat there, hand in hand, the awful commonality of grief between them. "I am sorry."

Mother nodded. "Yes, you were, but don't apologize. You were hurting, and all of us understood. We're not ourselves when our hearts are broken, are we?"

"True," he replied, meeting her tender gaze. There were days he had fought Mother's nosey, inquisitive, gossiping ways. She'd always known precisely how to rile him, but all he saw now were the same icy blue eyes as his, staring back at him. If not for her perfectly coifed, silvery white hair, she could pass for his twin. Which made her talent for riling him even more interesting. That was what sisters did. They knew their brother well enough to also know his triggers. Not that Alex had any brothers or sisters, but he'd heard stories. And he definitely had triggers.

"So what's up with Beau now?" he finally asked, keeping his sarcasm to a minimum.

"This," Mother said as she handed over the electronic device, the kind Alex hated.

He rolled his shoulder, instantly combating the cramp in his sphincter that modern technology brought with it. The IT world changed so quickly and so often. Of the two of them, she was the IT genius. Not him. Why couldn't she just tell him what she wanted him to know? Why'd he have to figure out another computer?

Reluctantly, he set the tablet on his knee. "Whatever you found, it can wait."

She shook her head. "No, Boss, it can't. You asked me to look into Beau's childhood, and I did. We both know he's not just upset because of those trumped-up Army charges. Something else is driving him like the devil. Read what my Las Vegas point of contact found, and then talk to me about it, okay? Right now..." She dabbed at the corner of her eye, careful not to smudge her make-up. "I've got other things I need to do."

"Understood." Alex nodded and took his leave. She did have Justice after all.

But he didn't go far. Just out to the lobby to fiddle with this damned modern invention. He tapped the screen like Mother had shown him so many times before, and, what do you know? A collage of framed boxes sprang to view. Retrieving the reading glasses from his inner suit jacket, he did what she'd requested. What the hell...

Mother had located not only a transcript of Beau's military record, which Alex already knew, but a detailed report from her Las Vegas informant, along with vivid photos of his childhood home. Shit. Alex found himself staring at interviews the informant had with Beau's neighbor and teachers. A baker named Gino. A social worker. His mother's probation officer. Several LVPD officers.

Skimming the ugly revelations, Alex brushed his fingers over the screen until he came to the informant's summary laid out bullet by bullet.

•SUBJECT: Benjamin Beauregard Jennings.

•Former US Army Ranger.

•Current employer, Alex Stewart, Owner and CEO, The TEAM, Alexandria, Virginia.

•Father: Bass Jennings, drug dealer, pimp, convicted of murdering three females in a drug-induced rage, currently incarcerated at Nevada High Desert State Prison

•Mother: Fidget Jennings, alias and/or maiden name unknown at this time, possible runaway from Kansas. Deceased. Investigation continues.

•Sister: Almond Joy, aka AJ. Deceased. Two-years-old at TOD.

•Subject resided at aforementioned residence on East Washington Avenue in North Las Vegas, Nevada, from age two until age seven-and-a-half, at which point he vanished. I have located no sign of him in any public records from then until age ten.

•Any residence subject lived in prior to East Washington Avenue is unknown at this time. Investigation continues.

•I found no record subject attended pre-school, kindergarten, or was enrolled in any childcare or daycare. He attended two years elementary prior to his disappearance. Attendance spotty at best. Records are attached.

•To my knowledge, subject received no healthcare until he joined the Army on his eighteenth birthday. Copies of ARMY dental and medical records are attached.

•I located no state health department vaccination records. Neither have I located subject's birth certificate. Investigation continues.

•On September 22 of said year, subject's mother died at home of a self-induced heroin overdose. See attached morgue photo.

•On same day, subject's two-year-old sister, Almond Joy, also died, also from a heroin overdose, possibly at the same time as her mother. See attached morgue photo. Interestingly, I had no problem locating Almond Joy's birth certificate.

•See attached video of local news report and interview with subject's father.

Alex swallowed hard as, on and on, the investigator presented a dire picture of a childhood no one should have endured. The most incriminating evidence against Bass Jennings that Alex found was not that he'd killed three women, but what he'd screamed at the news reporter during the video clip. "That bastard killed her! He killed 'em both! He was always jealous of my baby girl, so yeah, I beat that little shit, and then I kicked his ass out. Don't want no baby killer living in my house! Hell, no! If I ever see his fuckin' face again...!"

The reporter had the good grace to cease filming at that point, but that interview was shot the same day Beau disappeared. The investigator hadn't found any record of Beau again until the day an LVPD officer apprehended him inside a local grocery store for shoplifting. By then he was ten years old. Where had he been during all of that lost time?

Once in custody, the LV juvenile courts dropped Beau into foster care, which he promptly ditched. Seven months later, LVPD apprehended him again, once again for shoplifting, and back Beau went into the system and yet another foster home. For whatever reason, he stayed in that one until he enlisted.

Not that getting into the Army was easy. Mother's investigator had done his due diligence. Somehow, he'd acquired transcripts of Beau's night school classes and his subsequent GED scores. Holy shit. That Army recruiter had helped a young man who'd desperately wanted to join the Army. Alex had no more thought the question, when he found name and rank of one now retired Sergeant Emery Pickett of Henderson, Nevada.

Alex brushed his fingertips over the tablet's screen and sure enough. Mother's guy had also spoken with Pickett, who'd remembered Beau and admitted to taking him under his wing. Said the kid had shown promise and was a hard worker. That Beau never gave him a minute of trouble. That he'd studied hard and he'd learned quickly. That he was trustworthy. That in Pickett's opinion, all Beau needed was a hand up and a place to stay while he caught up on his schooling.

Are we talking about the same person?

Alex stared at the bitter findings now displayed at his fingertips. The photos Mother's guy provided of Beau's childhood home were scary enough. It was nothing but a rat-infested, filthy nightmare, and neighbors said it had been for years.

But the video of Bass screaming at the reporter and bragging that he'd beat a seven-year-old child, then kicked him into the streets, rankled deep in the catacombs of Alex's warrior's soul. He'd seen a lot of shit in his life, but a father accusing his son of murder, then proudly admitting to child abuse? Of a seven-year-old, for God's sake! *Flaming asshole.*

No way had that kid killed his mother and sister. Bass could have, though. Alex wouldn't put it past a loser like that.

He'd done it before. Hell, Fidget might've accidentally killed that little girl for all anyone knew. But how had blonde-haired Bass ended up with an intelligent Hispanic son, but had no birth certificate for him?

Alex's fingers drummed the screen. *What to do... What to do...*

Since the investigator seemed to think Fidget came from the heartland, Alex suspected she'd been Caucasian as well. Yet Beau was definitely Hispanic, his skin a rich, caramel tan, his eyes dark brown, and his hair as black as coal. Not one feature linked him genetically to Bass' ugly redneck face or pasty-white Fidget's morgue shot. Both were definitely Caucasian. Both were some degree of dishwater blond. There was no resemblance between Beau and poor little AJ's morgue photo, either. Not that two blondes couldn't produce a dark-haired child. It wasn't unheard of, but for a lean, sniveling man like Bass to have fathered a son with completely different musculature and definite Hispanic markers of Beau? An innate sense of honor? Damned improbable.

Alex tapped his fingers to his knee, his mind wandering to thoughts he had no business thinking and challenges he didn't have time for. He was in the middle of an active investigation that had already turned ugly. The TEAM was a livelihood, not a charity and yet...

Alex's gut told him true. Bass wasn't Beau's father. Which meant what?

Mother's investigator included his contact information at the end of his findings. He'd done a stand-up job and he'd commented that his investigation continued several times. He wasn't yet finished with Beau.

Neither am I.

One call...

It'd take just one call...

Damn it, no. I've got enough on my plate. The puzzle of Beau Jennings was best left for another time when resources weren't spread so thin. Yet even as he pushed the mega-challenge of Beau Jennings out of his mind—once and for all—Alex stared at the floor between his feet.

Thinking...

Always thinking…

Could Mother's Las Vegas contact get his hands on a copy of Fidget's autopsy report? He'd provided her morgue photo. The guy obviously had a solid network he trusted, maybe his version of confidential informants. Could he track down her parents in Kansas or wherever she came from? Maybe she'd kept in touch with them. A friend. A sister.

But what rankled Alex most was wondering what that little boy had eaten all those missing days and years. Where had Beau slept? How had he kept warm in winter, and what'd he do when he was sick? A kid with no inoculations would've caught every germ that came along. Who took care of him then? Or when he had a toothache or came down with an earache? When his belly ached? When he was sick with fever, too racked with pain and chills to move? Anyone?

The misery that kid had lived through stuck in Alex's gut like a dead weight. The years of abuse. The neglect. All he could see was Lexie, dirty, skinny, and lost in the dark. Hungry. Frightened. Alone in some cold, underground sewer and crying for her mommy. For Kelsey.

Son-of-a-bitch. When Beau should've been safe inside a loving home and family, he'd had no one. How did a man—any man—turn a blind-eye to that?

Alex ran a hand over his head, pissed at men like Bass Jennings. What kind of sick bastard denied his son and did it so viciously, on the same day that kid had lost his mom and baby sister? Hell, Beau had probably watched one or both of them die. No wonder he bucked every order and fought every TEAM protocol. He'd grown up fast, mean, and hard. Also explained why he was a stubborn ass and an insufferable prick. He'd had to be all that and more to survive in Las Vegas on his own. As a seven-year-old.

Alex tapped the power down button at the top right corner of Mother's clever device. It was time to face the truth. He had two women to catch. The entire TEAM was going to war. And whether he liked it or not, Beau Jennings was going with them.

Chapter Forty-Two

Breaking and entering was as easy as brushing aside the police tape and pressing his shoulder to her locked door. Silently, Beau entered McKenna's apartment and closed the front door behind him. He locked it this time, just in case he encountered a shrew with a snakeskin tat on her skinny neck who thought she could escape. Not happening. He'd failed McKenna once. He wouldn't do it again.

Just like he remembered. Kitchen on his right. Living room on his left. Beau aimed for the bedrooms down the hall straight ahead. Palming the first door he came to open, he encountered a moderately sized head, complete with shower stall and tub. One small window over the tub. Nothing a peeping tom could utilize, though. Good enough.

He stood there a minute longer than he needed to when his nostrils flared at the lovely scent hanging in the air. Vanilla and something else he couldn't identify. Not a flowery fragrance, but just as feminine. McKenna. He remembered the scent of her skin and her hair. The way she turned coy before she came all over him. It didn't take much to picture her naked and willing in that tub with mountains of foaming bubbles around her. A smile on her pretty face. Her toes pink and wrinkled from playing in the water too long. Maybe from playing with him. After he'd sucked them and a few of her other body parts, too.

Shaking off the dream that could never be, Beau closed that door and locked his heart. Dreams were for others, not him. He was a hunter. Nothing more. Nothing less. And hunters did not dream of things they couldn't have and didn't deserve. They kept their eyes on target, and they made the world safe. End of story. The sooner he set his mind to that bitter reality, the better.

The next room in that hallway revealed an office and a simple, uncluttered wooden desk with an office chair tucked into it. Computer. Printer. A dusty silk plant stuffed in the far corner. McKenna had no use for frivolous bullshit in her life, another thing they had in common. Duly noted.

The framed photo on her desk caught Beau's attention. Had to be Sanders Fitzgerald with that wide-open smile. He'd written *Love you, Princess* in gold ink across the lower right corner.

"So where are you, Sanders?" Beau asked the photo.

Rifling the desk drawers, he came across his first clue, another framed picture, much smaller but face down in the far back corner of McKenna's pencil drawer. That was odd. He flipped it over and blinked at the family photo. The happy, green-eyed little girl on Sanders' lap he knew. That could only be McKenna, the way she had both arms linked around her father's neck like she'd never let him go.

But the grouping was odd. Most family portraits linked the husband and wife, the children between or around them. In this one, Sanders sat with his shoulders turned into McKenna, while the woman who had to be McKenna's mother, sat nearly at his back. Instead of her hand resting comfortably on his shoulder—or anywhere on him—hers were curled on her lap. While Sanders and McKenna smiled, this woman looked like a cold fish. Damn near bug-eyed. Straight at the camera. If that wasn't odd enough—holy shit! Beau recognized the face.

Palming his burner phone, he thumb-dialed Alex. "I know who's got Sanders Fitzgerald," he said before Alex could answer.

"Who?"

"Don't have a name yet, but—"

"Then where is he?"

"Don't know that either, but—"

"What the hell do you know?" Alex snarled.

"I know Bitch Two looks exactly like McKenna's mother!" *You flaming ass hat!*

That shut Alex up. For a second. "Where are you, Junior Agent?"

"At McKenna's." *Duh.* "Where else should I be?"

A long-suffering sigh hissed over the phone. "Stay put. I'll be right there."

"Where are you?"

"On my way."

You pompous ass, Beau thought. *You don't have to tell me where you are because you know better than me and more than me every damned time, right?* He'd no more than stuffed his phone into his jeans pocket when a car door slammed outside. What do you know? Alex must've already been in the vicinity.

Retreating to the front room, Beau peered out the window as his employer climbed out of his vehicle. But he wasn't alone. A pale-yellow sedan rolled between Dan Alex and the steps to the apartment building, blocking his way. Alex's hand instantly went to the pistol under his left arm, but the woman exiting the sedan didn't seem to notice his alert stance or his firearm.

Beau could only see her from the back. Dressed in a pencil skirt that hugged her hips, and comfortable heels, she rounded the front of her vehicle and approached Alex, her head bobbing. She was one of those types who used their hands when they talked, and her fingers were flying.

He guessed her age between forty to fifty, her weight at maybe one hundred twenty. She walked with long, sure, confident strides, almost aggressive, like a real estate agent or a used car saleswoman. *Or a psychotic bitch.*

Beau opened McKenna's front door, so Alex would know he was there. Just as he did, the woman flicked her fingernails dismissively at Alex and turned her shoulders. Fuck! The hairstyle was different, but the face was the same. It was her. Well, not exactly her, but so damned close—

"Get down!" Beau bellowed as he drew his pistol and assumed firing position, his poor throbbing left hand instantly cradling the weapon in his right.

Alex drew on the woman as well. But whoever she was, she slapped her palms to her hips like she couldn't believe that they didn't trust little old her. Interesting reaction for a female civilian with two weapons pointed at her head.

"Keep your hands where I can see them," Alex bellowed. "Now!"

She didn't obey. Didn't even act like she'd heard him. Instead, her shoulders lifted like this was all a big misunderstanding instead of a damned scary situation. "Oh, come on, guys. I'm just here with a message for Doc Fitz," she said breezily.

"I said hands up. Do it now," Alex ordered.

Still no compliance.

Beau angled down the steps to cover his employer's back. At least Alex maintained his cool. It was also smart he hadn't opened his big mouth and questioned Beau's judgment for a change.

"You guys have this all wrong." The woman shook her head as she brushed the side of her index finger to her nose—like a signal to someone else. "I'm not the one you need to worry about, it's—"

"Oh, look! It's us! You should worry about us, guys!" a cocky female voice with a bite of Spanish sarcasm sounded from the other side of McKenna's porch.

Beau shot Izza Maher a nod of relief when she and her husband Connor approached, both with their weapons drawn on yet another version of McKenna's mother. Taller and more muscular than the one with Alex, she looked like a man.

It's her. Bitch Two. The one who tortured McKenna. I was right, damn it!

Same wrinkly skirt. Same long, black braid and snakeskin tat. Better yet, her eyes were black and blue, and her nose sported a strip of flesh-toned tape where he'd head-butted her ugly face the night she'd nearly killed McKenna. She strutted ahead of the Mahers with her elbows forward, her hands cuffed behind her head like she was proud of herself.

Jesus H Christ, how many What's-Her-Name clones are there?

"Halt. That's close enough," Izza told her. "One more step and I'll end you, I promise."

"Told you not to get close to her," Connor teased.

Like she'd done with Beau in the office, Izza tossed her head and snorted even as she brushed the back of her hand over several bright red scratches on her cheek. "Yeah, well I'm not afraid of a little bitch-on-bitch contact. You on the other hand—"

"Know when to let my woman do what she does best." Connor leaned close enough to hip-check Izza. "You're the kickboxer in the family, babe, not me."

"Damned straight," she muttered, a definite twinkle in her eye. "Bitch is cuffed, isn't she?"

"That she is." Connor jerked his head at the house. "Too bad she got a piece of you, though."

Bitch Two's upper lip lifted as she came to a full stop. Beau switched targets, needing to end this evil woman for what she'd done to McKenna. "Told you I'd kill you."

"You can't touch me," she hissed, extending that long neck like a snake about to strike.

"Wrong again. I'm the one with the pistol."

Her brows lifted, and her eyes widened until the whites showed. "Go ahead and shoot. It'll go right through me. You'll see. I'm untouchable," she crowed.

"Then why are you cuffed and not me?"

Connor's face split into a grin. "See what I mean? She's bona fide cra-zee, that's for sure. And you want to talk strange" —his eyes shifted toward the upper level— "we found plenty of other strange in the apartment over Doc Fitz's. Chicken heads and feathers. A dead goat that's still fresh, laid out on its back in the middle of some weird painting on the floor. Black cats. Jars of blood. Candles and incense burners. Sheesh. It's a regular *Carnival* up there."

"Zombie lady here thinks she's a mystical, magical voodoo *priestesssssssss*," Izza hissed, twisting that last word, her pistol still directed at the woman Beau wanted to end.

"You notify Chief Prince?" Alex asked, still covering the other woman.

"You bet. He's on his way," Connor confirmed. "Who's your friend?"

By then, Miss Pencil Skirt cocked a nasty glare at Bitch Two, her hands still on her hips and her head swaying like a prizefighter's in a grudge match. "I told you to stop sacrificing people's pets! It ain't funny!"

Bitch Two stuck her chin out at the accusation. "And I told you to find me a baby!"

Whoa, what? A baby? This day had just turned from weird to just plain sick.

"Name," Alex barked at Pencil Skirt.

Her lips parted revealing white clenched teeth. She cocked her head as if she too had a pain in her neck. "Minnie Lynch, Mr. Stewart. So how are Kelsey and Lexie? How's that guy Doc Fitz treated last week? The one with the missing finger." She cranked her neck sideways to Beau, glaring at him. "Would that be you?"

'She knows who we are,' Beau thought.

"And you are…?" Connor asked Bitch Two.

"Dai-sy," she replied, only she broke her name into two long breathy syllables and made it sound like *Dai-zee*. Marilyn Monroe, she was not.

Beau cocked his head. Okay, so his skull was a little on the hard side, but why did those names sound familiar? "Aurora? Minnie? Daisy?"

Connor waggled his brows. "Yeah, Beau. You don't have any little girls, so you may not know all the Disney characters like Izza and I do. Not that these two have anything to do with the real heroines, but—"

"Yeah." Izza let loose another snort. "The Lynch sisters are more like evil queens. That'd make a good movie, Disney presents the Evil Bitches."

Connor beamed. "Yeah, Beau. You could play yourself and—"

"And you two can be Tweedle Dee and Tweedle Dum," he bit out before the smartass could finish.

Izza choked, her eyes wide. "Oh, my hell, did you just crack a funny, Junior Agent? Seriously? You know how to joke?"

"Guys," Alex interrupted. "The real Catalina Montego is still out there."

"You knew it was one of McKenna's aunts who tried to kill her?" Beau asked his boss as he finally lowered his weapon. Between Alex and the Maher's, these two women weren't going anywhere.

"Just suspected. After Sanders was taken, David ran a profile on McKenna's mother, which is why I sent Connor and Izza here. Also why I told you to stay put. Figured Daisy Lynch would return to admire her handiwork. She's a narcissist, and she'd put too much effort into that contraption under McKenna's bed to walk away from it. Just didn't realize she lived upstairs or that Minnie was in on it with her."

"Yeah, Jennings. You're not the only agent on The TEAM, you know," Connor drawled as the distant whine of a police cruiser sounded. "While you're supposed to be recovering, David discovered that McKenna's mother, Aurora, was mentally ill, like her mother, and her mother before her and—"

"She was not!" Daisy shrieked. "Don't you dare say that! She was cured! I know she was. She was just like me!"

Connor waggled his brows again. "See what I mean?"

"This is all your fault!" Daisy sneered at Minnie. "I told you to keep away from me."

Slightly shorter, Minnie sneered right back, nodding at Beau. "What was I supposed to do after you let him get away? I couldn't just sit around and do nothing."

Izza grunted. "Got news for you two. Sanders Fitzgerald didn't *get away*. We rescued him while you were arguing about blowing this place up with him in it."

"I didn't mean him!" Minnie shrieked, pointing at Beau. "I meant him! He saw you! He knew what you looked like, you imbecile!"

Well, not technically... Beau grunted at how things turned out. McKenna was the one who had described Daisy down to her silly tattoo. Not that he was going to tell these two women that their niece could conceivably put them in prison. Turned out Beau Jennings hadn't really seen what he'd thought he'd seen at Ringer's or at McKenna's after all.

"Why'd you hurt McKenna? She's your niece." He rolled one shoulder as he approached Daisy.

"Oh, her," she answered in that masculine breathy way. "It was never about her. That's why the camera. I just planned to film the night and show Sanders what it's like to watch the person you love suffer and—"

"Shut up!" Minnie hissed as Alex cuffed her hands behind her back.

Daisy stuck her nose in the air. "Why? So you can steal the limelight like you always do? Not this time, Minnie Mouse!" She rolled those impressively dark eyes, made even more sinister by the black liner that flared from her eyelids into her temples.

"Don't call me Minnie Mouse! Mama told you never to do that, you imbecile."

"Stop calling me an imbecile! I'm smarter than you."

"You're as sharp as a tack that's been mashed by a hammer!"

"All I needed was a baby to sacrifice, but *you* never delivered, did you? And you and Bambi had plenty of opportunities where—"

"This was never about sacrificing babies or cats or dogs or chickens!" Minnie screamed. "This was supposed to be about paying Sanders back for what he did to our sister! But you—!"

Chapter Forty-Three

Sniffing, McKenna steeled her nerve. Beau, damn him, was gone again and why that should surprise her, she didn't know. As good as she knew he was, the man had lied every time he'd said he'd stay. Maybe he couldn't help himself, but enough was enough. It was time to move on without him. Who needed a jerk in her life? Not McKenna Fitzgerald.

Besides, she had other things to worry about. The exercise with Officer Crenshaw played like a video that she couldn't shut off at the back of her mind. Over and over again. Around and around. She knew the woman Beau had dubbed Bitch Two from somewhere. She was sure of it, she just couldn't place where. Restless and unable to sit still, she paced the hallway to her room, then circled back through the family room and into the kitchen, her mind working the puzzle.

Despite the fact that China's home was an older colonial, she'd decorated it with a distinct western theme. Decorated wasn't the right word, though. Utilized was better. Yes, China hadn't filled her home with showy knick-knacks as much as she'd utilized every space for the important things in hers and Maverick's life. The rack of fishing poles and the creel baskets hanging from the horseshoe hooks on the wall beside the fireplace looked worn and used. So did the assortment of dusty boots in the boot tray at the other side of the door.

Framed pictures and portraits of family competed for space on the mantle, and an entire glass enclosed bookshelf housed a plethora of magnificent trophies, most of them from China's horses. Only one photo commanded center stage of that bookcase, that of a beautiful white horse with a charming, silvery-white colt at its side. While the colt's mane was fuzzy and its tail stumpy, the mare's gossamer mane draped like a veil off one side of her neck. It fell nearly to the ground, it was so long and elegant. Her sleek tail was as stunning, and if McKenna didn't know better, that mother horse looked happy. Why shouldn't she? China and Maverick owned some beautiful animals.

An exquisitely tooled leather saddle rested on a wooden stand in the corner by the fireplace. Another bookshelf lined the opposite wall. An impressive gun rack. An enormous gun safe. Everywhere McKenna looked, she saw the efforts of a working ranch, and a loving couple who were totally committed to each other. Even sweet Kyrie, whom McKenna knew China and Maverick had adopted after China's sister had killed herself, belonged in this genuine home.

And I do not.

McKenna stopped at the wide kitchen window, not seeing the expansive green lawn and carefully trimmed rows of shrubbery that bordered the yard. It was time to leave the protective shelter of this fantastic universe that Maverick and China had created for Kyrie and themselves. Not for her.

Filled with an unexplainable need to return to her apartment, McKenna walked through the mudroom and into the garage. Sheesh, even that was a place of pure practicality. Wooden bins lined the wall nearest the door. Garbage bins.

Several recycling bins. Stacks of newspapers and flattened cardboard. This family took everything they did seriously.

A kitten mewed from somewhere. That couldn't be good. McKenna ventured into the dark garage. One of Kyrie's babies must've gotten lost. Following the pitiful mewls, she dropped to her knees between a rugged GMC pickup and the sleek, black Infinity Maverick had whisked her into that first day.

"Here kitty, kitty," McKenna coaxed. Her hair tumbled over her shoulder when she bent to peer under the truck. Something moved in the shadows. Extending her fingers, she blinked, wishing she'd turned on the garage lights so she could see better.

But when the kitten mewed again, a cold shiver of dread skated down her back. Someone else was in the garage. She could feel it. McKenna tipped back on her haunches, her spine stiff and her head cocked as she strained to listen for the sound she'd thought she'd heard. *'I'm not afraid,'* she told herself even as her fingertips nervously stroked the handiwork Montego had left on her throat.

A single kitten crawled out from the shadows on its belly, an orange ball of fluff between four shaky legs. But so tiny. Too young to be away from its mother. Scooping it up from the cold concrete floor, McKenna clutched it under her chin. The poor thing's eyes weren't yet opened. How had it gotten in here by itself? As quickly as that thought materialized, another arrived on its heels. *Someone's watching me.*

Shaken at how foolish she'd been yet again to be out here alone, McKenna dared not breathe unless she gave herself away. Once again, no one knew where she was. *'I'm as bad as Beau. Not smart enough to know when I'm well off. I've got to get out of here!'*

The garage light snapped on overhead. "Bobby?" an older man called out from the mudroom door. "You in here, darn ya?"

McKenna jumped to her feet. Instead of one of Alex Stewart's athletic agents, she found herself staring over the roof of the vehicle at an older gentleman in Carhartt bib overalls. "Who are you?" she asked, instantly embarrassed at the way she screeched at him.

"Who in tarnation are you?" he shot back at her. "And whatcha doin' out here in the dark?'

"I found a kitten," she answered nonsensically, even as she edged toward the safe doorway this fellow was blocking. Surely, he was a friend of the Carsons since he was inside their home. Right?

"You ain't seen a bobtailed minx with two clipped ears out here, have ya?"

McKenna shook her head. "N-no, just th-this." Cupping the tiny furry body in both shaking hands, she held it out for him to see.

His bushy, gray brows furrowed. "Darn that mama cat. Wanna bet she's still in here?"

"Oh…oh… kay," McKenna breathed, her heart still climbing up her throat.

China peered around the guy's shoulders. "You found her, Z?"

"China!" McKenna called out, so damned thankful this wasn't the ambush she'd thought it was. "I'm here!" *Thank God you're there!*

"What are you doing in the garage?" China angled past the man she'd called Z. How weird a name was that?

Trembling, McKenna breathed a shuddering breath of total relief as China took hold of her bicep. "I… I heard something…" she muttered, covering up her plan to leave the security of Maverick's home with a tiny white lie as she vowed never to be so dumb again. "Look. I found a kitten."

China cocked a quizzical look over her shoulder at Z. "Looks like Kyrie's got a new baby to feed. Darn. That Bobby's never going to be a good mama."

Flustered but relieved, McKenna all but ran back into the security of China's home. If only her heart would stop pounding. By then, the kitten purred like a tiny train engine under her chin. China followed, as back through the mudroom they went. Back into the kitchen. McKenna took the first chair she came to before her knees gave out.

"Are you okay?" Z asked as he ran a hand over his thinning hair. "You darned near scared the life outta me when you popped up like you did."

"I heard this baby crying, and I... and I..." Words failed as what she'd lived through at Bitch Two's hand resurfaced with a bitter vengeance. *I made a mistake. Another mistake.*

"Coffee," China blurted as she hurried to the coffeemaker and poured three cups. "The best thing for worry and panic is a good cup of coffee," she said as she returned with the steaming beverages on a simple wooden tray. "Cream or sugar?"

McKenna's head bobbed as she accepted one cup and the kitten settled in to stay. "Both. Where's Beau?" she asked, hating that she sounded so pitifully weak again. Damn it, post-traumatic stress was kicking her butt.

"I imagine he's out looking for that woman," Z replied as he took the chair at her elbow and grabbed another cup. "Don'tcha think, Miss China?"

China's head bobbed even as she growled. "Who knows? Last I heard there's more than one woman out there. Can I get you some cookies, McKenna? I don't think Maverick ate all the chocolate chip ones yet."

"Wh-what?" McKenna asked as she clutched the hot mug tightly in her one free hand to keep her fingers from trembling. "Are you saying Beau's gone? Where's Lee and Ky? What? Are we alone?"

China outright glared as if she thought those were ridiculous questions. "Hell, no, McKenna. We're not alone. Yes, the guys had to leave, but X, Z, and Shelby are here. So am I, Kyrie, and Suzette."

Like that was supposed to make her feel better?

"But who'll protect mmmmmm… us? Why'd Beau leave? Wh-what's going on?" Hysteria pushed its way forward with every stuttered word. "What about my dad?"

China pulled out a chair and angled it sideways, so her knees bumped against McKenna's chair. "Honey, your dad is why the guys all left. Alex needs them to locate him, then to nail these bitches who think they're above the law. And trust me, I took care of myself and my ranch long before Maverick ever showed up in my life. You see that rifle over there?"

McKenna glanced at the firearm in the corner behind the door to the mudroom. Scuffed and by no means new, it looked so small. By then her head was shaking and she wanted to run for cover. "So? Whose is it?"

China's brows furrowed in amusement. "It's mine, and I know how to use it, too. Don't think for one minute that only men can take care of themselves."

"Yer dang right," Z agreed, his head bobbing and his eyes bright with pride. "Ain't no varmint, not even the biggest two-legged kind, stands a chance once miss China draws a bead on it. No worries. You're safe, Miss McKenna. China and me'll take care of ya."

"And X," China added. "He's around here somewhere."

"And me," Shelby declared from the front room doorway, Suzette's tiny hand in hers, and a rifle in the other. "Today'd be a good day to ride horses, don't you think, China? We could all use some fresh air."

"N-now?" McKenna asked, even as Suzette clapped her hands and giggled, "Oh goodie! Spot! I wanna ride Spot."

Shelby smiled at her daughter. "Spot's a miniature donkey, sweetheart. His legs are too short. He might not be able to keep up with the other kids. And yes, now McKenna. We need a break."

China raked her fingers through her thick dark tresses, tossing a handful over her shoulder. "Trust me, Suzy Q. Spot'll keep up just fine. How about you, McKenna? Feel like getting out of the house for a picnic?"

Not really... But finally able to breathe without hyperventilating, McKenna nodded because China and Shelby seemed sure of themselves. "Okay, but..." She stalled, not sure China was the right person to ask. "Who are X and Z? Are those their real names?"

The tiny worry creases between China's brows faded. "I'm sorry, I should've introduced you. X is Xavier Albright and Z is Zeke Knudsen, my hired hands. They like X and Z for short. Where is X anyway?" she asked Z.

Now that McKenna had her wits about her once more, she studied the gentleman China had treated more like family than staff. Z for Zeke—she did that to help remember—sat comfortably at the table, like having coffee with and being served by his boss was no big deal. The poor guy had to be pushing seventy. His poor fingers wrapped around that coffee mug were knotted with arthritic bumps, but his eyes were clear and alert.

"Aw, he's been working on another rock, you know how he is. Says it's for a special friend, and it's got to be jes right." Z chuckled. "Sure be nice if jes once he spelled it right."

"Spell what right?" McKenna asked as she blew softly over her coffee.

"Xavier's our resident artist," China explained. "He's quite a metal sculptor, and his artwork has earned him a name around here, but if he really likes you, he gives you a Friend Rock. I've got one, Maverick has two, maybe more by now, and—"

"He gave me and Gabe each one, too," Shelby said. "X is so sweet, he always spells it the same. F.R.E.N.D. There's no greater honor than getting one of his gifts."

"Kitty!" Kyrie exclaimed as she scampered into the kitchen around Shelby. "You found Bobby's missing kitten! Where was she?"

"She's out in the garage. Bobby's a sweet, but lousy, mama," China explained. "This is her third litter, and she's nervous, so she moves her kittens every day—"

"Every once in a while, she loses one of her babies," Kyrie said.

"And she ends up deserting the others," Shelby ended, shaking her head. "Not all mothers are good mothers."

Wasn't that the truth?

"Poor kitty needs a good mommy," Suzette murmured, her lips pinched in a sad pout that tore at McKenna's heart.

She looked down at the sleeping baby on her lap. "Can I keep this little one?"

Kyrie's brows lifted like two darker versions of the *golden arches*. "Really?"

McKenna nodded. There was just something about cradling this tiny innocent that called to her. This perfect little creature needed someone to take care of it. "I'd love to."

"And?" China hinted, her deep indigo eyes sparkling.

Damn, she was perceptive. "And would you please teach me how to shoot a gun? I mean, a weapon?" McKenna breathed, blushing at Beau's definition of his gun. "I'm so tired of being a defenseless, silly woman."

"Yes, yes, and yes. The kitten is yours. I'd love to teach you all I know, but you are not defenseless. And yes, Beau is the dumbest shit on the planet for not seeing the amazing woman you are."

McKenna nearly laughed out loud.

Shelby grunted from the doorway. "Sometimes good men don't know they're good," she said quietly. Her head canted to the kitten. "Sometimes they get lost. Like that little guy."

Or thrown away. Beaten. And who knew what else Beau had survived.

"You've got to trust Alex and his men, McKenna," Shelby continued, her pretty violet eyes pensive and remote. "Even the grouchy, hostile ones. I learned the hard way. These guys really know what they're doing."

"But so do we," China added. "Now let's saddle up, ladies. I'll pack a quick picnic—"

"And I'll guard the ranch while you're gone, Miss China," Z added solemnly. "Me and X and Mr. Hart and Mr. Torrey. Don't you ladies worry none. Ain't no one gittin' past all the security gizmos Mr. Maverick done jazzed this place up with anyway. Y'all know that."

"Will you babysit my kitten?" McKenna asked, not sure if she should leave her baby behind.

Kyrie scooped the tiny fluff ball up into her arms and cradled it like the sleeping baby it was. "I've got a special nursery for the tiny ones. I'll feed it before we leave, then teach you how to take care of it when we get back. It's so little it'll need a baby bottle for a couple days. Okay?"

"Sounds good. But will we have phones with us? In case my dad calls?"

"You bet," Shelby replied. "I've got mine and—"

"Kyrie and I will have ours," China said. "Come on, McKenna. It'll be good for you. Let's ride."

Blowing out a deep sigh, McKenna nodded as she let go of the angst she'd stored up since Officer Crenshaw left. A day spent riding in the sun might be just what the doctor ordered.

Chapter Forty-Four

"You *what*?" Beau hissed, his pistol back on target, ready to blow this woman back to Hell where she belonged. "That's why you asked McKenna about Kelsey and Lexie? You were going to kill that sweet little girl? For what? One of your voodoo rituals?"

Daisy did her dramatic eye roll thing again. Stupid, stupid move. In less than the time it took her to bat those false lashes, she found herself face down with Izza's knee between her shoulder blades and a pistol snug in the back of her thick skull. "You bitch! You ever kill a baby?"

"Not yet," Daisy huffed as Izza ground her face into the dirt—precisely what Beau wanted to do.

Alex, who now held Minnie's cuffed hands high enough behind her she had to stand on her toes and lean forward to avoid the pressure in her shoulders, said evenly, "I ought to introduce you two to my wife."

"Really?" Daisy asked, the whites of her eyeballs showing again as she struggled to meet Alex's icy blue eyes. "You'd do that for me? Will that little girl be with her?"

Damn, these two didn't get it.

"You bet," Alex replied calmly. "Anytime you're ready. I'm sure Kelsey'd love to meet you. She wasted the last bitch who threatened her family. Gut shot her. Still interested?"

So not what Beau expected. "Kelsey? She did what?"

Minnie stamped her foot at Daisy, still prone on the ground. "Will you shut up?"

Alex spiked a brow. "What the hell did Sanders do to deserve you two?"

Like the unbalanced woman she was, Minnie shot him a vicious glare over her shoulder. "He put our sister in an institution. Can you believe that? He locked Aurora up like a criminal, when all she wanted was to take care of her little girl. He killed her, and he never visited her, not once the whole time she was there. She just wanted to take care of her baby, but—"

"She abused McKenna," Beau hissed, "for years!"

"She did not!" Daisy spat indignantly, pulling against Izza's firm hold on her cuffed wrists. "You're a liar. Just like Sanders! Aurora never hurt that precious child."

"Like you? Like what you did with those wires around her neck was, what? Playtime?"

The bitch had the nerve to giggle. "That was different. I needed a blood sacrifice. I had to make do with what I had since" —she stretched her neck at her sister— "someone couldn't find me a ba-by!"

There was no sense asking more questions. These two were certifiable, and Sheriff Prince had just rolled on scene with two cruisers on his tail. He could have them.

"I thought you said you'd located one?" Howie asked Alex as his men led the Lynch sisters away.

Alex nodded. "Her evil twin showed up in the meantime. You mind if I file my report later? I'm still on a job."

"You bet. Anyone I know?"

"Catalina Montego, the woman who abducted my man" —Alex jerked his chin at Beau— "and left that mess inside

Ringers home. Have you heard anything on their whereabouts yet?"

"About that." Chief Prince grumbled. "Turns out they surfaced at a couples-only retreat in Nashville, Tennessee. The rules prohibited any electronic devices, so they've been incommunicado since they left. Didn't know we were looking for them and hadn't seen the news."

"Thank God," Alex said. "Kelsey's been worried. What about the DNA evidence in their freezer?"

Chief Prince's countenance darkened. "That's another thing altogether. It belongs to three missing Marines, all who disappeared from Quantico, one from the same bar you mentioned in your last report."

Alex's eyes narrowed. "Aaron Pope?"

Chief Prince shook his head. "No, but there's no way he's still alive, Alex. That evidence came in three distinct layers. It was like frozen leftover soups, each layer a different male subject."

Beau swallowed the bile creeping up his throat. "Leftovers? She's... eating them?"

"I have no idea, son," Chief Prince replied grimly. "Just telling you what we know at this point. Please keep it to yourself."

"The Montegos were known for their extreme sadism," Alex said. "I wouldn't put cannibalism past them."

Beau nodded, suddenly lightheaded at what he remembered when he'd come to in Ringer's dining room. The bloody meat grinder on the counter. The fact that he'd been spread out and restrained like a fatted calf on a workbench that could've easily been converted into a dining table. The bloody stump from his severed finger. What was that, an appetizer?

He knew better. His finger had been a warning to Alex. What was it Montego said in that note? *'I know where you live and work, Alex Stewart. Give me what I want, and you can have the rest of him.'* Did 'the rest of him' mean she'd planned to send chunks and pieces of Beau Jennings to Alex until...

Holy Jesus. He could've been reduced to just another gooey layer in those containers.

Before he fell down, Beau backtracked to the steps and sat with a hard thump, breathing hard and struggling to control his roiling gut. Not only was he queasy, but it dawned on him that the man he'd argued with every step of the way, until this very minute, was the same person who'd sprang into action to protect him and McKenna. Not once had Alex hesitated to respond to Beau's call for assistance. He'd showed up. Every. Damned. Time.

Lifting his chin from his chest, Beau looked at his employer with new eyes.

Alex glared back at him. "Let me guess. You walked here? Son-of-a-bitch, are you trying to make sure you lose that finger?"

"I couldn't sit at Maverick's and do nothing," Beau ground out, focused now on not losing his breakfast or his man card. Okay, he was feeling a little ambushed again, and a whole lot of stupid. But mostly, like he needed to hurl because he'd been so idiotically paranoid—for no good reason—that he'd missed what was going on right under his nose. Alex was here. Okay, so he was still an ass, and he growled one helluva lot, but Jesus H. Christ. Alex *was* here. He'd always been here. Every. Damned. Time.

Just then, Maverick and Gabe rounded the other side of the house, both with sniper rifles slung over their shoulders. "What are you guys doing?" Beau asked, hating the uncertainty in his tone. But Jesus. The only reason any of these guys had been activated was because of one little finger. Okay, so the demented witch who'd hacked it off figured into the picture too, but they were doing this because they'd all come to his aid. *My aid.*

The very guys he'd badgered and berated all had his six. Every single one of them. All this time. Beau bowed his very hard head, wondering how he'd gotten so—lucky. And been so blind.

Gabe squawked, "McKenna is so pissed at you, Jennings. China says she's spitting nails. You got some 'splaining to do, tough guy."

"How hard is that damned Ranger head of yours, anyway?" Maverick growled.

You have no idea…

"How many times you going to run out on her?"

"I'd never do that to Izza," Connor muttered.

"Cuz she'd kick your ass," Maverick added.

And McKenna should kick mine…

"Damned straight, or she'd suddenly have a migraine for the rest of your life, and you'd be sleeping on the couch," Gabe chuckled.

"Already got a migraine." Izza glared at Beau, her head canted and a funny light in her eyes. "He stands about six-foot-five and weighs around two-ten, when he's not looking so puny and green. Isn't that right, dumbass?"

Was she teasing him? After he'd dissed her in the office? "Umm, yeah," Beau said, totally flummoxed at the banter flying back and forth. For lethal professionals, these guys and this gal were amazingly cool under pressure. "Who's guarding McKenna? Just Lee and Adam?"

Alex interrupted before Maverick could answer. "Nope. Just China and Shelby. Oh, yeah. Kyrie's there, too. I activated the wives. Everyone but Zack is out tracking Montego."

"You left McKenna unguarded?" *Un-fuckin'-believable!*

Izza's dark brown eyes narrowed. Her upper lip twitched like she wished she had Beau's balls in her gloved hands. "You think women aren't as good as you? You got an issue with us?"

Funny. He hadn't thought of Izza as female before, not with that tough girl swagger and the way she handled firearms and knives like a man. Make that like a former Marine.

"No," he told her honestly. "Not with you, but with the wives, yeah. They shouldn't have to hunt and" —he swallowed extra hard, still fighting a jumpy stomach— "kill. I don't want McKenna to ever have to do that."

Izza's nose twitched. "What *that?* You mean defend herself? You think we like that our husbands have to do— *that?* Get a clue, Jennings. Life's bitchin' hard and—"

"And then you'll die if you keep pissing my wife off," Connor finished quietly. He canted his head at Beau with his usual casual smile, but Beau caught the threat. "It's a new world, buddy, and I'm here to tell you, women are every bit as good in the field as most men I've worked with."

There it was again, that tender something zinging between Connor and Izza that Beau craved in his own life. With his own woman. "I'm sorry, Izza," he told the woman he should've respected from the get-go. "I've been an ass and—"

"You sure as hell are." Her head bobbed and her ponytail with it.

"And you're right," he admitted, licking his dry lips as he kept on keeping on. "I am, but I'm trying to change. Women are every bit as good as men. Maybe better than most."

"Holy shit. Did hell just freeze over?" Maverick plunked his butt on the steps alongside Beau and clapped a hand to his back. "You sure you're okay? I haven't heard you drop not one f-bomb yet."

Beau wasn't sure of anything. He turned to Alex. "I thought you suspected Montego was in your neighborhood." *I certainly did.* "I mean, after you found the second finger in your car..."

"Gut reaction at the time, Junior Agent," Alex replied smoothly. "But we now believe Montego planted it earlier in the day. I made two stops after Golden Horizons, one at Sanders prior residence, the other at my office. Montego doesn't have any interest in McKenna or her father, so she hasn't been seen near Adams Morgan, which means she planted the last finger when I stopped in Alexandria."

"She's been watching TEAM headquarters," Gabe said as he leaned one hip into McKenna's stair railing, his gaze zeroed on Beau. "You sure you're feeling okay? You are pretty green."

Beau nodded. He was sick—damned sick—at heart. For so many years, he'd lived by one set of rules: *Don't trust people. They all lie, and every last one will stab you in the back. Hit first and hit hard. Leave first—before they leave you—because they damned sure will.*

Nothing more than survival instincts learned the hard way, those rules had kept him alive. He'd only made one exception, when he'd wanted to join the Army. The posters back then made it look easy. But when he failed the mock ASVAB, the Armed Services Vocational Aptitude Battery test, that Army recruiter Sergeant Emery Pickett just happened to have on hand, reality had set in cold and hard. Uncle Sam didn't want him, either.

But Pickett must've seen something in Beau that afternoon. He'd cocked that big square head of his, and he'd challenged Beau to come live with him and his wife for a year if he was serious about joining.

At first, Beau shrugged the invite away, just like he'd shrugged any other perv's advances off. But then Pickett said he could turn Beau into something called an Army Ranger. He hadn't known what that term meant at the time, but it sounded honorable, as if he really could be better and smarter than anyone else, two things Beau had desperately wanted back then. In the end he'd decided, why not? What difference was one more wasted year to a life already deemed useless?

Turned out that year made a helluva difference. During that time, not only had Beau qualified for any number of MOSs, military occupations, he learned to read, how to handle the arsenal of weapons in Pickett's private collection, and he discovered he had a head for math and science. He'd made two lasting friends, Emery and his wife, Coretta.

Pickett also made certain Beau had the necessary documentation to enlist. When they couldn't locate a birth certificate, Pickett wrangled a green card out of someone who'd *'owed him a favor'*. And he'd done it all to help some dumb kid on the street whom he didn't know and shouldn't have cared a lick about. That tough sergeant's version of generosity had amazed Beau then, and still did today. He finally understood how a loner might need men like Pickett, Maverick, and Gabe at his back. Women like Izza in his corner. McKenna in his life. Hell, he might even need Alex.

Beau looked his boss in the eye. "I'm not any good at this. I don't know how to be" —he shook his head, searching for the right words— "second best." *Or human. Or approachable. Or a team player. Or whatever it is you want from me.*

Alex stared back at him, ever the leader. Ever the vicious attack trained killer, and the one that—if you were smart— you never riled. "It's not about being second best, Junior Agent. It's knowing that no matter which world war you're headed into, this TEAM's in the fight with you."

Yeah, that. Coughing, Beau cleared his throat as it hit home. He was so damned tired of being an army of one. For the first time in his pitiful excuse of a life, he wanted to crawl back into bed and let someone else fight the good fight for a change. Because these guys and gals would do just that. They'd fight for him, and once he'd rested and healed, they'd welcome him back into the fray with a brotherly—or sisterly—insult. He didn't have to go it alone. Not any more...

"Then what are we waiting for?" he asked meekly.

There was that mean as hell, shit-eating Devil Dog stare again. Alex drew in a slow breath, and then exhaled just as slowly. "'Bout damned time. Let's roll."

Chapter Forty-Five

The horseback ride into the wooded hills surrounding the Wild Wolf Ranch East calmed McKenna's jagged nerves. Listening to the slow, methodical footfall of China's 'kids,' went a long way toward regaining a healthier perspective.

McKenna eased out of her saddle under the stately oaks, and slowly slid to the ground, while China and Shelby tied the horses' reins to a low branch. Kyrie hovered over Suzette like a big sister as they chattered and spread a blanket in the shade not too far from the enormous draft horses. They'd ridden Spot, a miniature Mediterranean donkey, which necessitated the slow pace of the much larger Percherons.

The horse China had ridden was a sleek black stallion named Ebony. He tossed his head and pawed the ground, while the other horses were more sedate. Shelby rode a bay, Joker, while China had selected another bay, Star, for McKenna, because he was gentle. Even now the two bays bumped butts and shoulders like locker buddies, while Ebony rolled his eyes like he had other places to be.

China smoothed a hand under the veil of his coal black mane. "Easy boy. Settle down. You know everyone here, so stop acting up. Spot's the ass, not you."

As if he knew what she'd said, the big guy stopped his anxious pawing.

"You can tell when it's springtime in the Rockies," Shelby chuckled. "Stallions can scent a mare a hundred miles away."

That McKenna understood. "He's your only stallion?" she asked, her gaze shifting to the other, less anxious horses.

"Not the only one I own, just the only one with us today," China said as she moved from horse to horse, rubbing their noses or patting their necks like a mother might with her kids. "I keep Ebony, Hex, and Deuces Wild separate from the geldings and mares. Safer that way."

McKenna understood that concept. "Star's bigger than the other two."

China sighed. "Yes, I made a mistake gelding him. Wish I hadn't. The babies he could've fathered would've been magnificent. Funny thing is, he's Maverick's buddy. Those two share a soul or something."

"How so?"

"Because the day Maverick met China, he also saved Star's life," Shelby replied. "Star and China got caught in a landslide."

"A small landslide," China added. "Just enough that Star's legs were trapped—"

"And you nearly died," Shelby added. "Don't minimize what happened. You had no cell service, and who knows how bad things could've gone if he hadn't run to your rescue like he did."

China shrugged. "He did kind of drop into my life like a big, dark guardian angel."

That was the best description for Maverick that McKenna had ever heard. Alex too. "Aren't they all?"

Shelby nodded, her violet eyes extra blue in the morning sun. "Not sure about your guys, but Gabe surely is mine. I don't know what I'd do without him, and he's so good with Suzette. You should see them in the kitchen. He's teaching her to make waffles. Can you believe that? Of course, all of their waffles have chocolate chips."

"These guys do seem to show up when you least expect them," China added, a dreamy quality to her voice. Just then her cell rang. "Hey. Sure, here she is." China handed the phone to McKenna with a grimace. "It's Beau."

McKenna put the phone to her ear. "Doctor Fitzgerald."

"Umm, yeah," he replied, a definite note of hesitation in his voice at her professional declaration. What was he expecting? A warm greeting?

"I owe you an—"

"You don't owe me anything. No worries, like you said. I'm just one of many. Now how may I help you today?"

A feral snarl growled over the connection before he bit out, "Knock it off. I already know I'm an idiot. You don't have to rub it in."

She nodded at his astute assessment of himself even as she mustered her courage. "Yes, you certainly are, but I imagine it's because you're just busy. I get it. You've got important work to do, and I'm old news. Stop worrying about me. I'll be fine. Now why'd you call?" She didn't mean the sharpness in her tone to cut like a knife, but then, why not? His continual rejection stung like a razor.

"Like hell you will."

"Will what? Be fine?" Who did he think he was? "Bet me."

Of course, he didn't answer. That was his usual MO. Shut down when things became uncomfortable. Clam up. Shrug. At the lull in the argument, she walked away from the picnic taking place behind her, needing privacy to unload on the arrogant male sounding off in her ear.

"Listen," she said firmly as she turned her back to the group and faced downhill. "You and I got off to a crazy start, and yes, my emotions were all over the place. I'll admit to that. Just like you, I probably said things I didn't mean. It happens, right? Especially when people are under emotional stress like we certainly were. Are. But I'm better today, and I don't need—"

"Will you shut up and look at the photo I texted you over China's damned phone?"

"You know, I'm really not in the mood to argue with you, and I don't appreciate your language, and I've got—"

"Look at it! Do you know either of those women?"

Tired of being bossed by a man who had no intention other than to Do His Job, McKenna huffed even as she obeyed—damn him—and checked China's latest text message. Two photos were displayed, one of the evil woman who'd tortured her, the other of another dark-haired woman in a slimming skirt.

"Look closely, McKenna. Do you see any resemblance between those two women and anyone else you know?"

"Like who?"

"Like your mother," he snapped.

My mother? This bully is getting on my last nerve.

Shaking her head, McKenna reverted back to the pictures for one last look. But just one, and then this conversation was over. Okay, the women looked somewhat alike. So what?

Back to the call from Beau she went, what little she could recall of the mother she'd gone through years of therapy to forget. "No, Mom was blonde, pencil thin, and… and..."

And the world tipped on its axis. McKenna dropped to her knees. Turned out she hadn't forgotten a thing. Change the hair color on both those women. Change their eye color to cornflower blue. Pluck the daylights out of the ungodly unibrow stretched across Bitch Two's forehead, and…

"They're my aunts," she breathed as every molecule of saliva evaporated out of her open mouth. "Aren't they?"

"They're two of your mother's five sisters, McKenna, and right now, we're looking for the others. Do you recall anything about them? Like where they live? Anything?"

"No, Dad—"

"For God's sake, tell her!" Maverick bellowed in the background.

McKenna's throat closed. "Tell me what? Is it my dad?" *Don't say it.*

"He's safe. Connor and Izza are with him now," Beau said. "As soon as the police are finished interviewing him, he's free to go. Connor and Izza will accompany him to Maverick's to stay with you until we get the rest of these women in custody."

China scrambled to her side. "What's wrong?"

McKenna could barely ask, "Beau… Did she h-hurt him like she did m-me?"

"No, baby, he's fine. Just tired and thirsty, worried about you, and ready to kick some Lynch butt."

Lynch. My mom's maiden name. Okay, that's just plain scary.

China sank to the ground beside her. "Is it your dad? Did they find him? Is he okay??"

Nodding, McKenna managed a squeaky, "He's fine, but I need to go back to the ranch and—"

"Where the hell are you?" Beau roared.

"It's okay. Really. We... we took a break, and China packed a lunch, and we're riding horses and—"

"You're not behind closed doors?" he all but screamed over the phone.

"Beau. China brought her rifle, and so did Shelby. Gosh, I think even Kyrie's got a gun." Okay, not the correct word, but that was the best McKenna could do. She peered around China to see if there was a pistol in Kyrie's holster as she tried to calm the raging bull at the other end of the line. "I feel safe. Honest. But if Dad's going to be at the ranch—"

"No, stay with China," Beau ordered in her ear. "Trust me. It's better this way."

"But I need to be there when he arrives—"

"You need to do as you're told! I know better than—"

And enough! "I've had enough, Beau. Either stay or go. You keep telling me to trust you, but you're always leaving me," she yelled back at him. "I'm not your damned yo-yo!"

Dead silence met her bold retort. Then a grumbly male cough. He obviously hadn't seen that coming. Well, neither had she, but really? He thought he could boss her just because he'd saved her life? What'd that make her, his slave? No way.

At last a raspy male ego muttered, "Never said I was smart."

"That's for sure," a surly male voice McKenna didn't recognize hooted from Beau's end of the connection.

"Will you guys back off?" he hissed. "I'm talking here!"

McKenna was pretty sure she heard Alex bark something she couldn't interpret before Beau came back to her with, "I'm trying. Honest. This is hard for me, too."

She had to give him credit for admitting that. Especially since she'd seen the scars on his back and the burn on his hand. Even now, as upset as she was with him, she could still picture the nervous uncertainty in his dark eyes when he'd asked if she'd keep him. Someone had to have been utterly cruel to him to have caused the depth of hesitation she'd seen in this pig-headed, know-it-all, bully male.

"Why are those guys being mean to you?" *What'd you do now?*

"Because they're all f-f-fu—" He stuttered. He coughed again. That in itself melted her heart around the edges. He was trying so hard not to curse. "Because they're all like me. Hey, I've got to go, but expect Connor and Izza with your dad at Maverick's in the next couple of hours."

Beau was one of those diamonds in the rough kinds of guys, the cantankerous, short-tempered ones who had no clue what to do with a good woman.

"Where are you?" She needed to know.

"At your apartment. By the way, the gal with short hair is your aunt, Minnie Lynch, and the bitch who cut you is her sister, Daisy. Neither of them married, and they've been cooking up this scheme for years. We suspect all your mom's sisters are in on it. Chief Prince has his men rounding them up to make sure."

"That explains how Daisy knew what to say to hurt me. My mother must've told her." Aurora had been mentally sick like that.

"Get this, Daisy lived right above your apartment. That's how she knew how to cut the power, get inside your place, and construct that lever system under your bed. Who knows how long she's been working on it."

McKenna cringed that her mother's family had deliberately set out to hurt her. "I never knew mom's side of the family. Not even my maternal grandparents. Dad said they were all sick. That he didn't want them to get their hooks into me."

"You were never curious?"

She shook her head, her throat gone dry. China still sat patiently at her side with one hand on her shoulder. "I barely survived Mom, and I knew Dad loved me, so no. I never met them and, honestly, I haven't thought of them in years. But why now? Why after all this time?"

"To get back at your dad for having your mother committed."

"But he loved her. He visited her until she committed suicide. Even then, he spent hours at the cemetery. He'd take her flowers and sit there and talk to her as if she were alive."

"I'm sorry," Beau murmured gently. "That I didn't know."

McKenna stifled a sob as the wretched memory swamped her once more. "I never wanted her to die. I did love my mom, but she needed serious professional help, Beau."

"It's not your fault, baby. You were just a kid, and you can't help someone who won't help themselves. But you can help me." And suddenly, he was that little boy again, reaching out for her. Uncertain as ever. Antagonistic. Yet still trying to overcome the nightmare he'd survived, to reconnect with the one person he seemed to trust.

"Then stop leaving me," she cried, her heart breaking as much for herself as for him. "You said you'd take me to a desert island."

"Belize," he whispered.

Surprised that he remembered, she said, "Yes. Belize. You promised to take me dancing under the stars."

"Uh-uh. No, I did not," he said most definitely, then added a quiet, "but I will. I'd like to see you under the stars."

McKenna knew it to the deepest roots of her timid soul. The stars and the beach were only a backdrop to the real star she wanted in her life. Him. "Then come back to me. You asked if I needed you enough to keep you, remember? Well, it goes both ways. How can I keep you if you keep running away?"

Silence.

Afraid she'd pushed too far, she held her breath.

He cleared his throat.

Then the line went dead.

With a sigh that let the wind out of all her unmet expectations, McKenna stared at the phone. So that was his answer. Hang up. Run away. The man wouldn't commit because he couldn't. It was time to face the truth. Some guys were like that. They could only take a relationship so far before they turned tail and ran. She was a fool for thinking he'd ever change, and it was breaking her heart. Somehow this guy had gotten past all of her defenses, but she wasn't enough. Yeah. A fool.

"He hung up on you?"

Turning to China, McKenna saw the tender sympathy in her deep blue eyes. She nodded, the ache of yet another brush-off choking her. It wouldn't hurt so much if her heart stopped crying out for Beau despite what he kept doing to her. All she could say was, "Yes. The dumbass."

"Then let him loose like horseshit off shitkickers," China said, her blue eyes gone startlingly stormy. "Don't let him treat you like that, honey. You're too good for him. Maverick told me what a jerk Beau is. Dump him. You don't need a man like that in your life. No woman does."

"Yes, but—"

"But nothing. I see how he looks at you, but then he runs off the first chance he gets. He's playing with you, and I'm tired of his attitude. You should be, too."

McKenna swallowed hard, another *'Yes, but...'* stuck in her throat. China didn't know Beau like McKenna did, and wasn't Maverick just as dark and brooding a male as Beau?

Timidly, Shelby approached with a quiet, "You don't mean that, China. You're just mad."

Tossing her riot of thick, sleek curls over her back, China's head came up, her eyes flashing. "Yes, I do. I watched my sister chase one creep after another for years. If she'd had one lick of sense, she'd still be alive today, and—"

McKenna took hold of China's wrist to stop the rant. "I do have a lick of sense, and I'm nothing like Leezel. I know that man you're upset with, and I appreciate the solidarity. But Beau isn't always a jerk, he's just..." She pursed her lips, trying to come up with the best word.

"He's an iceberg," Shelby whispered. "All anyone sees of Beau is the tiniest peak. He wants everyone to think he's mean, but I don't think he is. You both saw him reading to Suzette. The way he held her. There were tears in his eyes."

China shook her head. "Or he's just another ass who's going to break your heart, McKenna."

"I am mad at him," she admitted, "but I also know what he's like when we're alone. I honestly think he's just trying to protect me when he takes off like this."

Shelby nodded, her tender gaze sliding from McKenna and back to China. "McKenna isn't anything like your sister. Leezel deliberately set out to find the worst kind of men. You know that. She had a death wish since the day she was born, and she never gave back one thing she didn't make someone pay for. Even Kyrie."

"Yeah…" Biting her bottom lip, China stared over Shelby's shoulder to the valley below and the land she and Maverick ranched.

"You're as bad as Beau, honey," McKenna said gently. "You're trying to protect me the only way you know how, too. And you're right. Maybe I should tell him to get lost, but I think I'll hang onto him a little longer."

China shook her head. "You'll be sorry."

"Like you're sorry that you hung onto Maverick when he showed up at your ranch out west?"

"That was different," China hissed, but then she cleared her throat. She swallowed. She sniffed and said, "You might be right. Maverick was just as dark back then as Beau is now. And he did leave. Once. Of course he came right back…"

"It's the war," Shelby offered. Between the three of them, she was the daintiest, the most reserved, and the most feminine. "I don't know how Gabe came through it as well as he did."

China snorted. "He lost his foot somewhere in Afghanistan, darling. Don't think that's *coming through it* too well."

"Yes, but he didn't lose his soul like Maverick," Shelby replied softly, the sunbeams dancing over her straight, honey-blonde hair.

"It's just that time of year," China added somberly. "The anniversary of Darrell's death. You know how he gets."

"I'm sorry," McKenna breathed. The anniversary of her mother's death was just as difficult a day for her.

"The thing is," Shelby continued, "Taylor and Maverick came home broken, but Gabe always seemed better equipped to handle whatever happened over there. I only know part of the story. Gabe won't share many details, but Beau seems just as dark and brooding as Maverick. I think he lost someone very important to him, too. It's as if that memory's chewing at him from the inside, and he doesn't know how to get rid of it."

"Or how to let it go," McKenna said thoughtfully.

"Yes, that's right. Sometimes we hang onto our worst demons because they're what we know best." Shelby took hold of McKenna's wrist. "You may not know this about me, but I used to be a bossy witch when I first met Gabe. Everything he did made me angry, and he snubbed me every chance he got. Of course, I snubbed him too, and I deliberately disobeyed the rules he laid out. Back then, he and Zack were sheltering Kelsey, and I..." She paused, her throat muscles working as she gulped. "I was Kelsey's home care nurse, but I was so dumb."

Her brows furrowed when she said that. "And okay, I was proud. I thought I knew better than her bodyguards until I nearly got Kelsey killed. Zack was so mad. He yelled at me, but all of a sudden, Gabe stood up for me, and well..." Both her shoulders lifted. "The rest is history. Gabe's the one who taught me how to protect myself and" —her brows waggled mischievously— "I taught him a few things, too."

"You? Bossy?" McKenna wasn't buying that.

"I've never seen that side of you," China said pensively.

Shelby nodded. "Yes, it's true. Back then I was hiding as much as Beau might be now. I thought if I controlled every little thing, I could make sure nothing bad ever happened to one of my patients again. Gabe actually taught me how to grow into forgiving myself. It might sound corny, but yeah..." She sighed one of those ultra-feminine breathy sighs. "Gabe's my hero, and I think Beau is yours, McKenna. He's a man, so he doesn't know it, but I think he needs you the same way Maverick needs China. The same way I need Gabe. You're like, his better half. He just doesn't know what to do with the feelings he has for you."

China slanted a thoughtful glance McKenna's way. "I grew up with nothing but a crazy, out of control sister and a corral full of horses. My perspective's either kick its ass or shoe it. See why I need my girlfriends?"

"Aw," Shelby gushed as she hooked her arm through China's. "That's the nicest thing anyone's ever said to me."

"We're still crazy, though, you know that, don't you?" China teased.

A tiny smile twitched at the corners of McKenna's mouth. She knew about Leezel's suicide, and how she'd nearly killed Kyrie in the process. Both China, Kyrie, and Shelby had overcome horrendous challenges to get to where they were today. So had she.

Drawing in a breath, McKenna let her annoyance with Beau go on a sigh similar to Shelby's. Then she told her new best girlfriends about her mother, and how she truly felt about grumpy, bull-headed Beau Jennings. That he was so much like Maverick, he could pass for his twin. She ended her tale of romance and woe with, "I still might kick his ass the next time I see him."

But she thought, *'Or kiss it.'*

Chapter Forty-Six

Still on McKenna's front porch waiting on Alex, Beau stared at his cell, sure he'd just made the biggest mistake of his life. If ever there was one, this was it. Yet he was just as sure he'd hung up on her for the right reasons. McKenna deserved more than a broken-down soldier with an uncertain future. Yes, Alex meant well when he'd pursued the Army to drop its charges, but Beau knew the politics behind those charges. Someone had to go down for the deaths of those men. It was the military way. Generals and admirals the world over were fired for unpopular decisions made under their command, and the Army was well known for scape-goating the lowest rank in the room. That'd be Beau.

He'd also known from the get-go that working for Alex was just a temp job. It might take years, but eventually, the Army's charges would catch up with him, and he'd be just another dirtbag locked away in federal custody. McKenna didn't need to be saddled with that.

He didn't have the kind of money it took to hire a decent lawyer. People like him were throw-aways. They didn't get lucky, and they didn't get the girl. He made up his mind. *Finish this job and move on. Rip it off like a Band-aid. Quick. Yeah, leaving her will hurt like a mother, but walk away. Do it. Never look back. All that crap...*

"You hung up? On McKenna? Again!" Maverick asked, his brows arched in disbelief. "What is wrong with you, man?"

Connor and Izza were already in transit to the local sheriff's department to hook up with Sanders Fitzgerald. Gabe and Alex were upstairs inside Daisy's apartment with Chief Prince, looking for clues. Talking strategy. Police stuff like that.

Yeah, well... "I can't hurt her," Beau muttered. "She's been hurt enough, and I'm" —he swallowed hard and decided to trust this guy— "I'm no good for her. You know that. God, you've told me enough times."

Maverick cleared his throat. He coughed into his fist, then finally said, "I've got to tell you something before Alex gets back. Remember what I said about losing my brother?"

Beau nodded, not sure where this was going. "Darrell. Yeah."

"Okay, so..." Maverick coughed into his fist again. Cleared his throat again, too. "Ah, crap. The thing is... Shit. I came home broken. I mean, not only broken, but... fucked up so bad that I quit Alex and walked all the way to Wyoming."

"Jesus, why?"

"It was either that or kill myself, and I honestly couldn't do that to my mom and dad. Yet I couldn't face them, either. I couldn't just go home and say 'hi'. Not after I told them I'd take care of Darrell, and..." A tic started in Maverick's clenched jaw.

"There's no way to take care of another soldier in combat," Beau told Maverick to set him straight. "War is chaos. A lot of shit goes down."

Maverick's head bobbed even as he blinked like a son-of-a-bitch. "I know," he ground out, "but he was my brother, and" —he swallowed hard— "that's what big brothers are supposed to do. They beat the shit out of their younger brothers, but they watch out for them, too, and Darrell..."

This shit was hard to listen to, so Beau kept quiet. He'd taken care of his baby sister the best he could, too. That hadn't worked out, either.

Maverick's cheeks hollowed as he sucked in a deep breath and said, "When I signed on to work for China back when she lived in Wyoming, I was at the end of my rope. I didn't intend to stay. I was tired of living and tired of trying to understand why nothing I did mattered. Honest to God, back then I planned on walking straight west and into the Pacific Ocean, just didn't know if I'd end up drowning myself in California or Alaska. Not that I cared where I died. Just wanted everything to fuckin' stop—"

"Hurting," Beau supplied quietly. That pain he understood. He carried his own little corner of Hell with him, just kept it tucked deep inside the lowest chamber of his heart, so no one could ever take it away from him. Funny the things a warrior holds dear, but that last image of AJ...

When she'd breathed her last breath...

When she'd squeezed his finger before her little body went rigid, then slack...

Yeah. Utter Hell, yet it was all he had left of her.

"But then..." Maverick's Adam's apple ratcheted up his throat, just once. "God, then I met this incredibly bossy woman on a ranch full of Percherons that stood as big as circus elephants, and she called them her kids. Damnedest thing. There stood this tiny little gal, who looked like a stiff wind could blow her away, inside a corral and babying those giant draft horses like they were poodles instead of stallions and mares and… Shit." His eyes watered. "She ran that ranch pretty much all by herself, but the night the barn burned, she taught me that… she taught me…"

Beau clapped his palm to the middle of Maverick's back to steady the man before he fell apart. "You don't have to talk about it. I know. Life's hard and then—"

"But that's the thing," Maverick growled as he blinked and shook it off to regain his composure. "It doesn't have to be that hard, Beau. You and me… We're the ones who make it harder than it has to be. Yeah, I was a broken piece of shit back then, but all China wanted was someone to truly see her for the woman she was. But I came along like a total jerk, absorbed in my own grief, bitter as hell, and…" He wiped a quick hand over his face. "You know what she did?"

Beau hadn't a clue.

"She gave me cookies and milk. Do you believe that?" Maverick's features contorted into a question mark as yet again, his eyes brimmed, and he struggled to clear his throat. "Me? That night. After I let two of her prized babies die. She gave *me* chocolate chip cookies and milk, and…" There went his hand again. "I don't know how she did it, but that simple act of reaching out to me, after she'd just lost two of her most precious kids, her original Gorgeous and her foal, China Love…" Maverick's clenched fist nailed his chest. "Damn, it hit me right here that she could still care for the stupid wreck I was. But she did. China treated me like just another one of her kids. She took me in. She saved me, Beau. Don't you get it?"

He honestly didn't. "Get what?"

Maverick wiped a long slender finger under his nose. "That we're all broken, brother. Not one of us really came home from the war, least not the way we were before we went into it. We've seen and done things no civilian will ever understand, and all that crap's stuck in our heads and hearts forever. We're all fucked up, but when we find that one woman…" He shook his head. "It's like we're whole again. We're okay. The slate's wiped clean, and God reaches into the storm, and He gives us a second chance. Don't walk out on McKenna. I see the way she looks at you. Don't. Just don't."

"I had a baby sister once," Beau breathed, not sure why his mouth blurted that secret misery. The memory of AJ just seemed to need to… breathe.

"You did?" Maverick asked, concern creasing his brows. Digging the heel of one hand into his eye, he put the other hand on Beau's shoulder—like a brother. "How… how old?"

"Two."

"God, I'm so sorry."

Beau nodded as the day came back to him in vivid flashes of soul-rending grief and mind-jolting pain.

"It's all your fault, you sniveling bastard!" Bass Jennings, the two-bit pimp of East Washington screamed like the demented asshole he was. "You killed my baby girl!"

My. Baby. Girl. Bass's declaration of love for his dead child, instead of one smattering of compassion for the still living, still breathing, still scared to death little boy who'd stood shattered and crying hysterically in front of him. Yet that screamed truth hadn't hurt Beau in the least. By then he was numb to the bitter name-calling and the hate. He just stood there and took it like the daily beatings Bass handed out. Why fight it? Beau always knew he was nobody special.

He grunted, not sure why life kept slapping him down. "Her name was AJ," he told Maverick on a whisper. "AJ for Almond Joy. I think my mom killed her, though I'm sure she didn't mean to. I know she loved AJ, but drug addicts don't make good parents." Talk about an understatement. "Neither do asshole fathers." Another profound truth.

Sucking in a breath, he gave life to the nightmare he'd survived. "It's called the Cultural Corridor. It's a poor neighborhood northeast of the Strip in Vegas, mostly full of illegals and immigrants from Mexico and South America. That's where I grew up. Being called names I didn't understand because I stood out, a brown baby stuck in white trash hell. But the day AJ was born... the day she died..." Beau swallowed hard, not sure he could go on.

Not a day ever went by that he didn't think of his sweet, angel sister. That he didn't blame himself for the way she'd been forced to live, and the awful way she'd died. At the end of it, when the brutal sun had finally set on the worst day of his life, he'd crawled, beaten and bloody, on his hands and knees, into a dark alley between some casino and a parking terrace.

Scared, alone, and in more pain than he ever dreamed imaginable, he'd curled into a ball and cried so hard that he'd made himself sick. He'd thrown up, but after the vicious beating he'd been dealt, he was too exhausted to move away from the mess. Instead, he'd lain there in it for the rest of the night like the pitiful loser he was. What difference would moving have made? He was the same as that vomit. Foul. Rank. Rejected.

But there in that stinking alley, with his bloodied, sweaty cheek pressed to the concrete and the smell of his own puke in his nose, he'd also promised AJ that he'd never be weak again. He'd never cry, and he'd never let anyone hit him, either. Turned out that last promise was a tough son-of-a-bitch to keep.

"It's almost funny," Beau said to no one in particular. Funny in a disgusting, surreal, macabre sort of way. "I've been accused of killing my men, my mother, and my baby sister, but I never did it. What kind of sick joke is that?"

"Alex already knows you didn't kill your men," Maverick hissed as his hand clamped over Beau's shoulder, his thumbnail digging hard into Beau's collarbone. "And there's no way a kid like you would've killed his mother or a little girl. I know you, Beau. You didn't do it!"

You know me? Beau's head came up at that loud declaration. He hadn't realized he'd been studying his boots as closely as he had until then. Ordinarily, being touched by another guy was enough to get Maverick punched in the face. Not today. For some ungodly reason, this time that death grip on Beau's shoulder felt okay. He saw a brother in Maverick instead of an enemy. And he desperately needed a brother, because brothers might fight with each other, but they fought the world for each other, too.

"I loved her," he blurted out what he'd never told anyone before. "Jesus, I miss her. Every day. I do."

Something happened to Maverick's face and lips Beau had only seen in combat when a guy'd been shot and writhed in pain. His features twisted. His lips thinned. He blinked like a son-of-a-bitch. He growled. His eyes brimmed. Then he jerked Beau into a crushing guy hug, his elbow around Beau's stiff neck, and his scruffy cheek against Beau's head like he meant to kill him. "I miss Darrell, too. Every. Fuckin'. Day."

Damn, this was embarrassing as hell. Yet Beau stood there, sucking in every last second of that rugged male contact like a sponge left too long in the desert. It felt so damned good. Maverick was no wimpy guy. He was a great big, grieving brother with a hole in his heart as deep and as black as the hole in Beau's. It honestly felt weird, but Beau gave back what little comfort he could. Even as awkward as it was. Even to a guy he'd honestly thought he'd hated on sight the minute he'd joined The TEAM. Wasn't Karma the ever-loving trickster to turn an asshole like Cowboy into a brother?

But, okay. No. Enough already. Too much!

Beau pushed away, but did it gently, and for a change, without profanity. Maverick didn't feel as stupid as he did. "What a couple of pussies," he grumbled, trying to add a smidgen of levity into this rare, depressing, but kind of wonderful moment—that would sure as hell never happen again. Beau didn't like to be touched. Except by McKenna. That was different.

Maverick stepped back, cleared his throat, and growled, "Sorry."

"I'm sorry for lots of things," Beau admitted as he brushed the back of his hand across his eyes and sniffed at the cruelty of life. "But not for loving AJ."

"We need to go out one night when this is over. Throw back a few beers. Tell a few war stories. Reminisce, you know?"

"Yeah, no." Beau shook his head. All his war stories ended badly. He tried not to think about them.

Maverick stiff-armed him again. "There's all kinds of family, Beau. Some you're born with. Some you pick up along the way."

"Like the gum some asshole spits on the sidewalk, then you come along and step in it?"

"Yeah. Or dog shit. Some friends are just that good," Maverick said as he smirked like a little kid.

Beau did something he hadn't done in—hell, he couldn't remember how long. It felt good to talk with Maverick like he was. The corners of his mouth lifted. Well, one corner lifted. He damned near smiled.

"You don't have to say more, Beau. Tell Doc Fitz instead. She's a good woman," Maverick said evenly. "I know you care for her. Everyone does. She's who you need to share your story with. She'll understand."

Beau grimaced. McKenna was made out of the same stuff as Kelsey Stewart. Kindness. They were both saints as far as he was concerned. But he wasn't so sure McKenna would forgive him after this last stunt he'd pulled. Yeah. He was an idiot.

"Just don't walk away like I did," Maverick added. "Don't give up, not when the best thing in your life might be standing in front of you."

"You really walked all the way to Wyoming?"

"Yeah, but I flew back."

"But how'd you know…?" The question flew out of Beau's mouth before he knew he'd asked it.

"How'd I know what? That you're an asshole?"

Beau damned near smiled again. "No, ah…" How to ask this without making a bigger fool of himself? Dumb question. That cat was already out of the bag. He swallowed hard and pressed on. "How'd you know China was the one? The right one?"

Maverick's big, wide palm flattened over his chest. "You get a good feeling. Right here. Like you can't breathe without her being in the same room with you. Like you don't even want to try."

Oh, that. Shit. Then I've loved her since the second I laid eyes on her.

"Thanks," Beau said quietly. Just. Thanks.

Chapter Forty-Seven

"Damn, you're good," Maverick said.

Beau grunted at that offhanded compliment even as he skillfully breached McKenna's home computer. It was a little difficult with his one hand still swathed in gauze and tape, but it wasn't impossible. Most people used familiar phrases and simple numerics for their passwords, and McKenna's was easy to pop. Sanders123 and within just seconds, Beau was in. Before he got into some serious hacking, though, he saved and closed the files she'd left open. Just in case this breach of ethics didn't pan out like he hoped.

"Why isn't this comspec skill in your personnel file, Junior Agent?" Alex bit out.

"There's a lot of stuff not in my file," Beau answered smoothly as he tapped into the secure—yeah, right— Alexandria, Virginia, traffic cam system. Then, just as easily, he hacked The TEAM's exterior surveillance system, while Alex grunted his disapproval. "One, because I didn't plan on working for you for long. Two, because hacking's illegal, and I didn't want to document anything that could land me behind bars. I didn't know you from Adam, remember?"

"I ought to kick your ass."

Yeah, well, take a number. "Probably," Beau breathed as he easily circumvented the protocols Mother relied on to keep hackers like him out of The TEAM's domain. She assumed she knew everything about the systems she'd built, but that was the fast-paced world of high technology for you. As soon as you thought you knew it all, along comes the younger generation to prove that you sure as hell did not.

Beau relaxed as the skill he'd learned while in the Army brig flowed through his fingertips again. A hunter was only as good as his last intel, and since the debacle in Nangarhar Province, Afghanistan, Beau had learned everything he could about hacking to keep that intel current. Not that he'd ever breached Army records like Mother had, but he knew a few things.

Only the two men hovering over his shoulder like vultures over a fresh kill were enough to drive him crazy. Linking the two devices he'd found lying on McKenna's desktop with the laptop he was using, he handed them off to Maverick and Alex, with a, "Sorry, Gabe. You'll have to buddy up with one of these guys if you want to know what's going on."

Alex frowned at the device in his hand. "Great. Another tablet. What the hell am I looking for?"

"Your screens will either display the view from the video cameras Mother insisted you install outside TEAM headquarters, or Alexandria's traffic cams along King Street. Since I didn't know exactly when you were at the office yesterday, Boss, I estimated an approximate time range, hoping we catch Montego casing the vicinity. Keep your eyes open for the real Catalina."

Alex settled cross-legged to the floor and assumed the position of grunts all over the world. Boredom. Maverick and Gabe did the same, which left Beau seated on McKenna's chair, an oddly elevated position for the guy with the least seniority in the room.

"This is going nowhere fast," Gabe muttered after ten minutes of watching nothing but inconsequential pedestrian and vehicular traffic.

"But it's smart," Alex admitted as he cast a wicked glare at Beau. "Wish I'd known we had another IT genius on my team."

Beau took the hit while he watched the same views of The TEAM's headquarters building as his men. Hmmm. His men. *My men.* He actually liked the sound of that.

After a few more minutes of nothing going on, Maverick ordered four pizzas and a barrel of wings from a local restaurant. Gabe took off on a beer run to go with the food. Once the pizza, wings, and beer disappeared as quickly as it arrived, Alex growled, "Son-of-a-bitch, got her."

"You're right," Beau said. He'd seen Montego at the same time.

"Damn, she's something," Gabe growled as he peered over Maverick's shoulder.

"Something out of a nightmare," Maverick agreed.

They watched as the blonde woman in jeans and a glittery short-sleeved top, approached the glass entry doors at TEAM headquarters on King Street. When she couldn't gain access, she stepped far enough back on the sidewalk, tipped her head back, and looked upward.

Deftly, Beau manipulated The TEAM camera she had no idea had captured her image. Narrowing the shot, he caught an up close and personal view of her.

"Man, that's one nasty looking woman," Maverick muttered.

Beau had to admit, Catalina unleashed was entirely different from the chick he remembered at Boxster's. Gone was the saucy smile. In its place, an evil sneer twisted her features.

"She's talking. Anyone know how to read lips?" Gabe asked.

"She said *'I know you're up there, Stewart,'*" Alex growled. "Damn, I wish I'd known she was down there. I'd have ended her."

"Why's she hate you?" Beau asked.

"Because I sent the man to Cuba who killed her brother."

That didn't make sense. "But from the account I heard, she wasn't there when Roland died. How'd she know Seth McCray was the one who'd actually ended her brother or that he works for you? And if she knew, why'd she come after me and not him?"

"I have no idea," Alex muttered, "but it's the only thing that makes sense. Revenge. She wants to destroy me."

"Possibly," Beau replied as Montego strutted across the sidewalk to the passenger loading zone, removed a palm-sized device that looked very much like a key fob from her front jeans pocket, and—

"Son-of-a-bitch!" Alex hissed as they watched her jerk the rear door to his vehicle open, lean inside, then slam the door and walk away without a backward glance.

"That's when she planted that last finger," Maverick said.

"Do we know who it belongs to yet?" Gabe asked.

"Not me," Beau answered, wiggling the bandaged foursome on his left hand.

Alex shook his head. "Haven't heard back from the FBI yet, but damn. She opened my car like nothing."

"The latest techno gadgets are only good for a short time," Beau told him. "Technology advances at the speed of light these days."

"But she could've planted a bomb instead of a finger," Gabe muttered. "Shit, Boss, she could've taken out the whole block. You too."

"Why didn't she? She knew I'd be back."

"Like you said, it's not about killing, Boss. It's about emotional suffering, and it looks like she wants you to suffer for a long, long time," Beau replied.

"She walked away like she's done this before," Maverick added. "Like she wasn't afraid of being caught."

Alex growled softly. "She thinks she's untouchable."

"Where's she going now?" Gabe asked.

Anticipating that question, Beau had already switched all devices to recorded footage from the traffic cams that ran along King Street from the Metro Station to the Potomac River. "Keep in mind, this is old footage, not live input." To make viewing easier, he highlighted Montego with a blurred circle like the NFL did to players during Super Bowl. Two blocks east of TEAM headquarters, she stepped to the curb with one hand lifted as if hailing a cab.

"I knew it," Alex hissed. "She's got help."

The men were silent as Beau jockeyed from one cam to the next, determined to catch not only the license plate on that late model sedan, but a good shot of the driver as well.

"Who's behind the wheel?" Maverick asked. "Can you—?"

"Yes, I can," Beau replied easily, his right-handed fingers flying over the keyboard, strengthening the pixels on Alexandria's lowest bidder version of traffic cams. Jesus, the criminals that could be brought to justice if only every city and township would invest in top-of-the-line surveillance cameras instead of these budget gizmos. "Is that better?" he asked as he narrowed the view and enhanced the image.

"Fuck!"

Beau turned at his favorite curse word from—Alex? "You know who that is?"

"That's son-of-a-bitchin' Aaron Pope."

"Your friend? Are you sure, Boss?" Gabe asked.

Alex nodded, his eyes glazed, but only for a second. Pushing up from the floor, he rolled his neck like the true predator he was. "Break time's over. Gear up. We're going hunting."

"Whoa," Maverick hissed. "Pan that camera back over that sedan again. Look at Pope's hand, guys."

Beau did as directed, narrowing the city cam's view down to the left-handed grip Pope had on the steering wheel. Closer. Closer. Until...

"He's got no fingers on that hand," Gabe stated the obvious. "Just stumps."

"And a thumb," Maverick added.

"Like me," Beau hissed as sympathy pains tweaked his reattached pinkie finger.

"She tortured him," Alex added, all three men now firmly on Beau's six, watching his screen as Montego slid into the sedan. The car headed east on King Street. At Henry Street, it turned north, then right onto Pendleton a couple blocks north.

"She headed for the GW," Alex murmured, his hand on the back of Beau's chair as he leaned over his right shoulder. The GW, aka the George Washington Memorial Parkway, wound through Crystal City and past Reagan National Airport before it turned northwest to follow the Potomac River.

"She could be anywhere by now," Gabe breathed.

Beau shook his head, still engrossed in jumping from one traffic cam's stored footage to the next, linking Montego's day-old route to yet another app on the laptop as he went. "Statistically speaking, serial killers stick to a specific routine. A certain kind of victim. A set neighborhood."

"Which for Montego extends from Paris Island to the son-of-a-bitchin' Shenandoahs," Alex bit out. "Her only pattern is she goes after young military males, and they're never seen again."

"Possibly," Beau murmured as he craned his neck toward the monitor, watching the pre-recorded video clip as the sedan came to a traffic stop. "I mean, yeah, she seems to prefer young males..." *As far as we know.* "But I think her lair, the place where she does her real dirty work, is stationary. Don't forget, I was the idiot on that table back at Congressman Ringer's. It was a hastily thrown together POS. Whoever built it was no carpenter. Its legs weren't balanced, and price tags were still stapled on the two-by-fours. That isn't her primary lair. You saw it, didn't you?"

"I haven't forgotten, Beau," Alex said as he blew out a long, slow breath. "And yes, I saw the crime scene. You're right. Guess it's hard to pound nails without all five fingers."

"You think Aaron did it?" Gabe asked'

"I think that shrew had help," Alex replied, his tone grim. "But Aaron wasn't one of the guys who dragged Beau out of Boxster's Pub."

"Did you know McPherson's missing?" Beau asked his boss.

"Don't worry about Mac. I've got people looking into that."

For the first time in a long time, Beau didn't argue. If Alex said don't worry, well, that was good enough.

"Let's see where her real lair is," Beau murmured as the sedan continued northward. He checked his mobile app again to be sure it was on target.

Eventually, the sedan stopped at the Slaters Lane intersection to the GW. To the east, Slaters Lane connected with the Mount Vernon Trail along the Potomac River. To the west, it wound through an industrial network of warehouses and shipping businesses. When the sedan turned west, then right at the first corner, the traffic cam lost visual.

"Hold on a sec," Beau breathed as his fingers darted over the keyboard, skillfully changing the view to the mobile app he'd been following. Instantly, a satellite perspective of the same area showed on all devices. One quick glance at Alex's squint told Beau his boss was lost again. "This isn't a live shot," he explained, "but neither were the others. This satellite view will however, tell us what we need to know about the neighborhood where Montego and Aaron stopped."

Maverick discarded his tablet. "What is that place?" he asked as he leaned over Beau's shoulder and stabbed his index finger at the only building on the road, a massive narrow warehouse that ran the length of the entire block.

Beau peered up at the scruffy underside of the chin of the brother he never knew he had until today. "Montego Seafood Storage. Sound familiar?"

Gabe angled around Maverick for a closer view. "No shit?"

"I'll be damned," Alex breathed as he joined the men on Beau's six. "That wasn't here when Aaron disappeared."

"It's here now," Beau stated bluntly even as he searched the web for stats on that specific building. "Okay, here goes. Used to be owned by a boat storage company that went belly-up one and a half years ago. R. Montego took possession. Catalina's brother. Want to guess what he used it for?"

Maverick grunted. "Knowing him, human trafficking. That's got to be where he stored the women and children he abducted before he sneaked them out of the country."

"It's been done before," Gabe said.

"We need to move before she knows we're onto her," Beau declared. "It's early. We could end this today. You guys ready?"

"Damned straight," Alex replied. "Maverick and Gabe, grab your gear. Beau, you're with me."

"Copy that," Beau answered automatically—just like any other agent.

Chapter Forty-Eight

By the time McKenna and her new girlfriends made it back to the stables, she was a mixed bundle of jumpy nerves and boiling frustration because she couldn't wait to see her dad. Since Izza Maher had called China to let McKenna know they were now on the premises, and that Sanders was with them, it was all McKenna could do to not kick Star into a gallop. Talk about a walking, talking meltdown waiting to happen.

Finally on her feet back at the barn, China laughed at how McKenna fumbled Star's halter over his big ears. "Never mind. Go see your dad. I'll handle this goofball."

Star nickered as if he knew he'd been swapped for another male, but McKenna only had ears for her dad. *He'd better be unharmed, or Montego was going down.*

Out the stable door she flew and back toward the house.

"McKenna! Wait for me!" Shelby called out.

But McKenna was through waiting. She made it all the way to the solarium doors when lightning struck. She fell to her knees, dimly aware of the dart in her neck. Beau's favorite word hissed off her lips like a tire with a flat. "Fuuuuuuuuuuck."

The helicopter ride into Alexandria was filled with too much noise, hastily drawn battle plans, and hurried combat strategy. The men sat facing each other, Maverick and Alex across from Beau and Gabe. With blueprints of the warehouse that Beau had *extracted* from the city's tax assessment database in hand, he and his team now studied the internal layout of the structure. All TEAM members had a copy.

There were several exits along both the west and east walls of the two-level building. A single row of windows tucked high under the eaves ran the length of the warehouse on both sides. A sales/receiving office had been carved out of the space near the southwestern corner. According to the blueprints, there was no second level or basement, no maintenance pits or underground storage, just one smooth concrete foundation that led to the loading dock along the western wall. An alley lined with smaller storage sheds, waste receptacles, and parking stalls ran the length of the eastern wall.

The pilot put the chopper down east of the GW in the center of a baseball diamond.

"Wait for us," Alex ordered the pilot.

Fast-tracking across the busy highway at Slaters Lane intersection, Beau was aware that he and his men probably looked like SWAT on patrol, as geared up as they were beneath their jackets. All wore enough weaponry to frighten the locals, though none of those weapons were exposed and no one carried rifles. Only pistols.

Beau would have preferred going into Montego's lair alone, setting up a sniper hide, and biding his time until she showed. But there was a different energy to marching with this particular team of ruggedized warriors, one he couldn't wrap his head around. He only knew he felt proud again.

Originally, he'd joined the Army to protect the powerless people of the world. It mattered to be doing that again. But having been personally sought out for this TEAM, suddenly meant more than Beau expected. Harley could've picked on any number of honorably discharged former Rangers. Good men came home every day from the sandbox and other far off reaches of the world. Yet Harley had zeroed down on a guy with multiple murder charges hanging over his head, and hand-selected—*me!* Out of all those other guys. That odd, one-in-a-million bit of good luck made a guy want to stop and scratch his head, was what it did. Because if there were such a thing as a dream job for Beau, this one was it.

Approaching the warehouse, the four men split into two teams. Maverick and Gabe headed north through the alley, while Beau and Alex rounded the southern end and came to a full stop on the front dock outside the alleged office door. Single entry. Common every day OTC doorknob. Guess Montego didn't believe in solid security, either.

Beau kept an alert watch on the busy street behind him and the way forward. He and Alex wouldn't breach Catalina's lair until Maverick or Gabe reported they were inside and ready.

The plan was simply for each team to ghost diagonally from one end of the warehouse to the opposite, and hopefully end Montego or anyone dumb enough to get in their way in the process. Beau suspected she'd be in the office. At least, he hoped. That was where he meant to go first to end her. Then assist his buddies in tracking down Aaron Pope and any other guys in her employ. That's the only way he could see this operation going down, him killing Montego. Yeah. It felt right. Good. Doable.

Maverick's voice came through the earpieces they'd acquired from the chopper pilot. "We're inside."

"Ready to rumble," Gabe seconded.

"Copy that," Alex breathed as he turned the brass doorknob and entered ground zero.

Beau maintained an observant cover, scanning the street traffic at his rear and along the dock, Alex's backstop, and everything in between. There'd be no ambush today.

Once inside, he secured the exit door and took a second to acclimate to the dead silence of the place. It had to be soundproofed, it was that still. Which made sense in an eerie, sickening way. A woman known for her depraved cruelty had to keep her victims' screams to a minimum.

"Something's not right," he growled, not that he saw anything out of the ordinary. There wasn't much to see other than the vast empty space between where he and Alex stood to Maverick and Gabe at the far southeastern corner. It was more a feeling of cold hard dread in the pit of his gut than a fact, and Beau's sniper sense was screaming for everyone to 'STOP!'

Alex froze, his head cocked. "Did you hear that?" he asked out of the corner of his mouth.

"A rustle? Yes," Beau whispered, his palm stretched forward for Maverick and Gabe to hold their positions. Might've been the building creaking or a rodent on its creepy patrol. But it also might've been the two-legged kind of rat.

The expansive warehouse that had once held all sizes of watercraft appeared vast, wide, and, shit, empty. The room that passed for an office on the blueprints was an open box of windows that concealed nothing but a cheap metal table, a floor mat, and a single chair. A clock on the wall. Only the concrete floor stretched to where Maverick and Gabe had come to a full stop in the far corner. The floor itself had been poured in ten-by-ten concrete blocks, now covered with a thick layer of dust. Not one footprint anywhere. Something was very off about this picture.

"Where is everyone?" Beau asked his team over their earpieces. Dead silence was not what he'd expected. *And what the fuck am I sensing that I can't see?*

"What are we waiting for?" Maverick asked. "An invitation?"

"Thought we heard something," Alex responded. "Proceed but keep your eyes open. You know the drill. Heads on swivels, guys."

Gliding toward Maverick and Gabe, he moved smoothly and quickly, his pistol on point as he swept along the wall at his right, while Beau headed left. The feeling in his gut persisted. Someone or something was in this building, though he was damned if he knew where they were as exposed as the place was. There was simply nowhere to hide.

Cautiously, Beau did his job. Scanning the arched ceiling, he took in the long metal rafters that bowed upward, their struts like giant arms holding the roof in place. Every twenty feet or so, a massive industrial array of halogen lights hung by chains attached to a pulley system controlled by a lever on the far east wall. Hung low enough to cast enough light had they been turned on, the metal arrays didn't sway, and the chains didn't clank, which meant there was no internal draft at play inside that might have created the noise Beau had heard, damn it. There wasn't one thing the eye couldn't see. Yet acid poured into his gut.

Maverick and Gabe had separated the same as Beau and Alex. Maverick took the far north wall, his pistol cupped in both hands, his back stiff as if he too suspected an ambush. Gabe had headed south along the east wall, headed toward Alex. Disgusted that he'd gotten everything wrong, Beau berated himself. This mission was a waste of time and energy. Where the hell was Montego? He damned well wanted to know.

Until Maverick whispered a quiet, "Son-of-a-bitch," as the floor dropped out from under him.

Gabe bellowed, "No!"

Closer than the others, Beau ran like hell to save his man. Alex and Gabe, too. By the time they got to where Maverick had fallen, they knew they'd been set up. This building was a complex maze of traps, all of them constructed below the surface. They knew because they'd all set off other dust-covered pressure plates as they'd run to Maverick's rescue.

Maverick was in a damned bad way. He'd fallen to his back onto a bed of metal spikes that looked a helluva lot like the infamous punji sticks used by both Viet Cong and American soldiers during the Vietnam Conflict. One pierced his right shoulder below his collarbone, another the left side of his abdomen, and yet another his lower thigh above his right knee. Each an inch thick, they were a brutal way to die.

"Hang on," Alex called down to Maverick even as he barked an emergency 9-1-1 call into his cell.

Hang on, nothing. Beau secured his pistol, measured the distance to where his good buddy lay wheezing and bleeding to death, and down he went.

"Son-of-a-bitch!" Alex bellowed just as Beau crouched to his knees when he landed, flat-footed and—*thank you, Jesus*—not on top of Maverick.

Beau pulled the first-aid kit he always carried in his inside jacket pocket and proceeded to do what Maverick had declared he did best. Save people.

"You sure know how to make an entry," he kidded as he administered the first hypo of pain relief that wasn't nearly enough for the massive injuries Maverick had sustained. Still, he needed to believe he'd live, and by hell, Beau meant him to.

"Yeah, well," hissed out of Maverick's lips along with a spray of bloody spit. "Wasn't how I saw this going down."

"But you've been in worse spots, right? Don't know all the deets, but I know damned well no Marine's smart enough to stay out of trouble, am I right?" Beau kept talking as his fingers and bandaged hand flew from one massive wound to the next. "Jesus H. Christ, are you trying to hold the Guinness World record for sustaining the most multiple spontaneous hemorrhages?" There were so many, and Beau was worried—until a chain dropped alongside him and Gabe touched down next. Then Alex.

"Maverick," Gabe cried as he dropped on his knees at his friend's side. "Shit. I... I... Brother, I..."

While Alex went to work on Maverick's shoulder, Beau thumped Gabe's beefy bicep and handed him a tourniquet before he broke down and made everything worse. Yeah, this was a damned tough break, but Maverick needed positive reinforcement, not weeping and gnashing of teeth for things nobody could change. "You take his thigh. Tie it off. Make it tight. Do what you have to. Cowboy can take it, right?"

Another groan answered as, frantically, Gabe scrambled to obey. All men carried blow-out kits and they'd need every last thing in them, but this was bad.

Maverick clutched Beau's wrist. "Tell China… For me. Tell her…" Only this time there was more blood than saliva in that awful, telling spittle. One of those punji sticks had hit a lung.

"Uh-uh. No way. That's not the way this works, and you damned well know it," Beau chided as he applied his entire supply of QuikClot to the bloody hole in Maverick's side, praying the holes in his back weren't seeping as badly. "I'm not telling China nothing, so get that stupid idea out of your thick, jarhead skull. You want to tell her you love her, then you'd better decide right here and now you're gonna live. Don't pawn important stuff like that off on me. I'd just fuck it up, and you wouldn't want that, would you?"

"Shit. Hurts... like a... mother... fucker."

"What'd you say? You're a motherfucker?" Beau asked, because right then and there, he'd say and do anything to keep this warrior alive and talking. He'd never had a real friend before. Yeah, Pickett had taken him in, but he'd never once been someone Beau could confide in. But Maverick... *Jesus, don't let him die. He's got a wife and a kid. You want someone, take me. I've always been expendable.*

By the time the first responders arrived, Maverick's pulse was weak and thready, and Beau knew chances were damned slim that this man—this brother—would live the day, Goddammit. Yet neither he, Alex, nor Gabe quit working on their brother for one second.

Nor could Beau shut up. "Always wanted a brother. All those days on the run, all those nights in the sewer, always wondered what it'd be like to run with a buddy at my side. Never had one, though. Wasn't that lucky."

Beau doffed his jacket because he needed bandages more than he needed his shirt. Tossing his jacket aside, he ripped his shirt off and over his head. Biting the collar, he jerked the material in half with his good hand, while still compressing the wound in Maverick's gut as much as he could with his other hand, all while working around that damned metal spike. What had looked like galvanized steel from up above was actually pitted, rusted shit up close. Damn Montego to Hell for her cruelty. What if some runaway kid had wandered into this place and triggered her traps? Jesus, what made people so fuckin' bloodthirsty?

Beau worked fast and efficiently, his wounded hand now pressed firmly over his good, as he struggled to staunch the red stream oozing from Maverick's gut.

"I… had…" Maverick breathed. "A… brother… once…"

"Yeah, I remember," Beau told him, his heart breaking for the brotherly love he'd have given everything to have known—just once—in his life. "Darrell was one lucky SOB."

Groaning, Maverick closed his eyes and shook his head. "No. Me. I was... lucky... one…" The breath wheezed out of him, and his body went slack.

"Fuck, no!" Karma was such a bitch!

Gabe scrambled alongside, growling as Alex began careful chest compressions. "Not happening buddy," Gabe told his brother in arms. "I'm not losing one more friend, so—"

Maverick gasped, and—*thank you, Jesus!*

Beau dashed tears off his cheeks.

So did Gabe as he sputtered, "Oh, damn! That was close."

"Brothers," Beau hissed as sweat stung his eyes and ran down his nose. Might've been tears. Could've been blood for all he cared about himself right then and there. His heart pounded so hard, he didn't care what he said next. "Breathe, damn you, Maverick. You're the only brother I've got, and I'm not letting you go! So breathe, you asshole!"

There! He'd said it, and he'd meant it! Let the whole fuckin' world know! Beau Jennings finally had a brother, and he meant to keep him!

"Take it easy," Alex muttered.

"I am," Beau shot back at his boss, the very man known for losing his temper in just as colorful, cursing ways. "This is me, taking it easy, Boss." *When I'm really about to lose my fuckin' cool!*

Gabe sat back on his haunches, visibly shaken, his fingertips fluttering on his massive thighs. "Back off, Beau. He's breathing again. Shit, he's really breathing."

"Yeah, well, this isn't over yet," Beau ordered as steadily as he could. Gabe wasn't the only one whose fingers were shaking.

When the call came from above that the first responders had arrived, Alex climbed back up top to assist. It still took too damned long for the fire department to stretch their ladders across the labyrinth of sprung and yet to be sprung traps. After one brave medic finally dropped into the hole and administered a hypo, Maverick finally breathed easier. The medic also initiated an IV drip, taped an oxygen mask to Maverick's face, then taped the IV bag to his chest in preparation for transport.

It seemed like hours until Beau and Gabe were told to stand back while the good guys slowly lifted Maverick, along with his rack of spikes, up from the hole. It had to be done. The spikes could only be removed once Maverick was in surgery with a team of skilled miracle workers. Thankfully, they weren't part of the floor. Even now, it was like watching one of those horror movies where Frankenstein lay bound to a metal frame while being electrocuted. Shit, the things that go through a guy's mind when it feels like he's losing his whole world.

"Easy, damn it," Alex growled when one corner of Maverick's awkward contraption snagged the lip of the hole. The bizarre scene vanished when the medics carefully swung Maverick out of view, no doubt to a waiting gurney. Beau wasn't worried with Alex up there running the show. He'd make sure everyone treated Maverick right.

At last, another team of eager firemen turned their efforts on the two men still in the hole. Beau allowed a hand up, make that a rope up, but only after they'd lifted Gabe to safety. Once on top, he was met with a horror show. What he'd thought was a stable floor had changed into a checkerboard labyrinth of solid floor panels mixed with gaping holes where the pressure plates had been. Some holes were traps, some were earthen pits where Montego had imprisoned her victims.

Scores of FBI SWAT, police officers, and various other emergency personnel were carefully scouring the building, setting up barriers over the dangerous traps, and triggering any other pressures plates they found. It looked like the entire National Guard was on site, too. By that time, portable floors, the kind the Army used when setting up remote camps, were laid out at intervals, providing a crisscross of stable walkways throughout the warehouse.

"Shit, you've been busy," Beau told his boss.

Alex merely growled like that was a no-brainer. He jerked his head at the huddled mass of men who looked like concentration camp survivors seated in rows of fold up chairs near the office. All male. All gaunt and emaciated.

"Shit. Are they—? Were they—?"

Alex nodded grimly. "Montego's victims? Yes. Aaron Pope's the tall blond on the back row. The one who won't look me in the eye."

"Of course not. He's not the same person he was the last time you saw him. Were they in the pits?"

"Yes. Watch your step. We're not sure we've located all the pressure plates yet."

"How'd she—?"

"There's a trap door in the office floor. Stairs under the mat. The cells downstairs are connected."

Beau couldn't take his eyes off those poor men. "Damn, how many?"

"Nineteen," Alex muttered darkly. "The FBI and paramedics are questioning them, trying to get a handle on the scope of Montego's operation. They found her wood chipper. Another table. Another body. Body parts..."

Unbelievable. "How'd these guys survive?"

"They did what she told them to," Alex replied, an odd pitch to his tone.

Beau quirked at sharper look at his boss. "What aren't you telling me?"

Alex minced no words. "China called and—son-of-a-bitch, Beau. McKenna's been taken."

Beau took off running. He had one mission left. End Montego or die trying. Today!

Chapter Forty-Nine

She woke with her head spinning and a bright light in her face, blinding her. Restrained again, this time in a chair instead of on her bed, McKenna swallowed hard, the wires at her wrist and ankles biting with every move she made.

"You're awake."

That voice. Lifting her head, she came face to face with one of the few women McKenna had ever confided in. "Margo?"

The friendly office assistant was gone. A coldhearted person stared back at McKenna. "No. I'm Bambi. Your mother's sister and your aunt, not that you ever cared."

"I was a kid," McKenna whispered. *How could this be?*

"No, you were a slut and a liar. And before you lie your way out of it again, let me tell you a few things about your mom."

Until then, McKenna had never noticed how smooth the skin on Margo's neck was, instead of thin and wrinkly like many women her age. How perfectly coifed her hair always was. And if those tiny lines around her hairline meant anything, how much plastic surgery she'd had done. "You don't look like my mom."

Margo traced her index finger along her eyebrow. "That was the plan. One of us had to get close enough to stop you. I volunteered and here I am."

"Stop me from what?"

"Spreading lies about Aurora, what else?"

"Let me get this straight. You, Daisy, Minnie, Alice, and Wendy—all my mother's sisters—my aunts—are in on this?" She dreaded the answer. "Is my grandmother, too? Does she know what you're doing?"

That earned her another coldblooded sneer, and for an instant, Margo looked just like Daisy. All she needed was a thick, heavy braid and a snakeskin tattoo. "Your grandmother died a long time ago. Did you think we'd let you and that bastard you call Daddy get away with hurting our sister?"

What on earth was this woman talking about? "Get away with what? Trying to help Mom?"

CRACK! Margo's right hand flashed out, knocking McKenna's head to the side with a vicious slap. "You call what you did help? You killed her!"

Now you sound just like Mom. McKenna shook the blow off and spat a mouthful of blood to the side. That was an unexpectedly harsh response to an innocent question, but lesson learned. *Dad's right. Mom's sisters are crazy.*

Margo leaned forward. "I loved Aurora. We all did, and we were happy before she left, Mom, me, and the girls. But Aurora had to marry that… that animal, and then we lost her. We tried to tell her he was no good for her, but she stopped calling after they eloped. We never knew where she was. He kept moving her from state to state and—"

"Uh-uh. Mom and Dad never eloped. They had a nice wedding and a reception. I've seen the dress Dad bought for her and the wedding album with all their pictures. Mom showed it to me all the time. She said Dad was her prince and she was his princess. We never lived anywhere but on Fig

Street." McKenna forced herself to breathe evenly as she struggled to keep up with the wild story she was hearing for the first time. "We never moved when I was a kid. Not once. Even after Mom went into the hospital, Dad wouldn't ever leave her. Ask him."

"It wasn't a hospital!" Spit flew off Margo's lips, she shrieked so loud. "It was an insane asylum, and you're the one who put her there!"

"No, I didn't." McKenna swallowed hard. Of all the family history she'd just shared, the only takeaway Margo heard was about the hospital. She was Aurora all over again. She had selective hearing, too.

McKenna kept an eye on her one-time friend's quick hands and her large rings. Margo's hands were much larger now that she had time to notice. Those were why McKenna felt as if she'd been hit with a brick.

"You're right," she said softly. "It wasn't a hospital. It was an assisted living home for the criminally insane. After the way Mom abused me, and after her psych tests, the state put her somewhere safe where she couldn't hurt herself." *Or me.* "Dad took me to visit Mom until she screamed at him and made him stop." *Because like you, she also called me a liar and a slut—before she beat the shit out of me and locked me in a closet.* "But there were no bars on any of her windows, and she had the best rooms Dad could afford. A nice living room. A walkout patio. The best medical help. Counseling."

True, there was a fence to keep the residents from walking away from the private facility, and the staff made certain Aurora couldn't leave the premises. But Sanders sold everything he'd owned back then to make sure she received the best care. If anyone suffered, it was him and the daughter

Aurora had assaulted. They were the ones who'd lived in a two-bedroom flat.

"Liar!" Margo spat, her cheeks flushed bright red. "He killed her for the insurance! Anyone with half a brain knows that!"

McKenna knew better than to argue. The sad truth was that the only life insurance policy Sanders had on Aurora denied claims based on death by suicide. Which was what he'd wanted, and why he'd had the contract written with that specific wording. Money meant nothing to him. If he couldn't have his happy family, he refused to profit from her death.

"So what now?" McKenna asked quietly. "Are you going to cut me up with a wire like Daisy did? Is that all my family's good for, killing each other?"

Jumping to her feet, Margo leaned into McKenna, one hand on each armrest until they were nose to nose. "No, child," she whispered, her lips so close and her breath so noxious that McKenna turned her face to escape it. "This isn't about killing you. This is about revenge. An eye for an eye. A pound of flesh for a pound of flesh. I'm here to finish what Daisy and Minnie started."

So I am going to die. Yet even as that truth registered, McKenna recalled a lost detail from her night of terror. Like Daisy's breath, Margo's breath smelled of anise. Though McKenna doubted that distinct odor had less to do with black licorice and more with paregoric, the camphorated tincture of opium. *Just. Like. Aurora's.*

Which begged the question, why? At one time, paregoric was commonly sold over the counter. Lazy mothers used it on their children for outright sedation when they wanted to spend a peaceful day at the club. Its overuse and misuse led to stricter controls, and today most physicians avoided prescribing it. Had Grandmother Lynch relied on this drug while raising her daughters? It made sense, especially if they'd all inherited the same mental issues as Sanders believed they had. What mother wouldn't sedate a house full of unstable children?

Yet McKenna was no longer sure just mental illness plagued these women. She'd been a child when her mother died. She'd believed everything Sanders said. For the first time, McKenna wanted to know more about her mother's family. Were they so poor that they couldn't afford psychiatric help? Who was giving them paregoric? But mostly, how could they be unstable while she, Aurora's child, was not?

"But I believed in you, Margo." McKenna purposely used the name of her friend instead of her would-be killer. "I've worked with you for months. We went to lunch together. I thought we connected. I even requested that you handle all my patients. I thought we were friends."

"Which was exactly what I wanted you to think, child." Margo stroked the cheek she'd slapped, then gritted her teeth and pinched it. Hard. "Don't ever call me Margo again."

McKenna held her breath as her eyes watered, conditioned now to expect only the worst from her mother's siblings. And to think this insane person had been around tender little babies and toddlers all this time. Another memory intruded. *Where's Shelby?* "The woman with me. You didn't hurt her, did you?" McKenna asked as she shook her aunt's cruel grip off.

Wiping her fingers on her pants as if she'd soiled them by touching McKenna, Bambi scoffed. "Don't worry. That blonde bimbo didn't feel a thing."

For the first time, McKenna noticed the holster on Bambi's hip. "You killed her?"

"Just stunned her. I don't need anyone else to deal with."

"But how'd you get on Maverick's ranch?" Where were China's hired hands, X and Z? Were they dead too?

"Stop with the questions!" Bambi yelled. "I have a job to do."

"And that is...?" McKenna prompted, hoping whatever lay in store for her, it would go quicker than what Daisy had done.

Her aunt rolled her eyes and shook her head as if she were dealing with an idiot. "That's for me to know and you to find out." A sinister chuckle growled out of her, like one of those hellhounds in the movies right before it jumped out of its skin and ate you alive.

"Wait," McKenna asked before things got more out of hand, her poor heart pounding in her chest. "D-don't you want to know what Mom used to say about you?"

Bambi cocked her head, one brow spiked. "What?"

"She told me..." *Think fast, McKenna, and it had better be good.* "She told me that... that of all her sisters, she liked you best. That you were the smart one. That you were different. Kind and loving. Was she wrong?"

A truly evil smile slithered over Bambi's cold, harsh features. "Liar. Aurora wasn't that nice."

True.

Chapter Fifty

By the time Beau made it back across the highway to the helicopter, he knew Shelby had gone down while trying to protect McKenna, and that Shelby had only been tasered. She'd survive. He knew because Alex dogged him every step of the way, barking at Gabe to stay with Maverick while Alex had another of his pilots fly their wives into the District hospital where Maverick was being taken.

"Hurry," Alex growled as he jerked the chopper's side door open and climbed inside, "and tell me where the hell we're going."

"On it, Boss," Beau said as he jumped on board, fastened his safety harness, then snapped open McKenna's laptop and hacked into Maverick's security system as he adeptly secured his headphones. Whoever'd taken McKenna would soon be revealed. That was the plan. Find the woman Shelby vaguely remembered talking with McKenna before she'd gone down. Had to be Montego. Then waste her ass. Up close and personal, that was how Beau saw this going down. He'd show that bitch no mercy. With a double tap, she'd be on her way to Hell where she belonged, and at last this nightmare would be over.

Drawing on every last bit of patience he possessed—which wasn't much on a good day—Beau worked the keyboard, wishing he had all ten digits instead of five and a bandaged hammer. That was all his left hand was good for. His once severed finger no longer throbbed, and he wasn't sure he needed it anymore. Like the sewer rat he was and always would be, he'd already adapted.

Focusing on the security camera views from the rear of the ranch house where the abduction went down, Beau zeroed in on the face of the woman who'd confronted McKenna. "Who the hell is this?" He held the laptop up so Alex could see the monitor. "You know her?"

Alex barely glanced at the screen. "No. Send it to all TEAM agents and Howie Prince. Maybe one of them knows."

Beau hadn't thought of that. Seconds after he forwarded the image, Alex's cell buzzed. He activated the radio link between his phone and the headsets. "Stewart. Speak."

"Alex, that's Margo Heller's picture," Kelsey informed him. "Doc Fitz's assistant. What's going on?"

Alex spared Beau an evil brow. "Want to bet Heller's the Lynch sister Howie can't find?"

"Let me check." Securing the data he'd already collected on the women, Beau ran a facial scan and came up with twelve markers that matched Heller to Minnie and Daisy despite their apparent dissimilarities. Plastic surgery couldn't conceal everything. "Bambi Lynch. She's been working with McKenna all this time?" How was that even possible?

"Find her," Alex ordered curtly, then as nice as you please, told Kelsey, "I'll be home late tonight, sweetheart."

"You'd better be," Kelsey answered. "I just heard about Maverick."

Alex grunted, but by then, Beau was circumventing yet another secure city system and hooking into every available traffic camera within a ten-mile radius of Maverick's ranch. Zeroing down on those with the strongest signals, he backed the pre-recorded coverage to the approximate timeframe of McKenna's abduction. From there, he zoned in on a cream-colored Toyota sedan that had recently approached the ranch. There was no way to enhance the footage enough to be certain McKenna was in the car when it left the ranch, so he tracked the vehicle until it turned onto a road, unfortunately, without cam coverage.

Bringing up a satellite view of the area, he mapped the long dirt road to the only structure at the end of it. Impatiently, he passed the coordinates to Alex and told him, "Get those to the pilot. Do it now! He needs to land the second we arrive, or he'll be looking for a new job."

Alex spared him an evil look even as he passed the information forward. "When this is over, *Junior Agent,* you and I will discuss how the chain of command works in my team."

Beau licked his upper lip. *Oh yeah. Your team.* He swallowed hard and nodded. Where once he would've argued, or worse, come back swinging, now he accepted the rebuke and offered a reluctant, "Sorry, Boss. I, um, get carried away."

Alex huffed. "Forget it. Just wish we were hunting Montego instead of the Lynch sisters."

"Me, too," Beau said, his foot tapping out every lost second that he wasn't watching this new threat unfold behind a rifle scope. Two holsters on a one-armed man still meant squat. "We've been looking for the wrong woman from the start."

"Not true. The real Catalina's still out there. You've just been preoccupied."

The view of the District at this altitude was tremendous, but Beau's mind was on McKenna. All this time, there'd been six women he should've been targeting. If not for his failed intelligence gathering and lousy memory, which everyone seemed to have forgiven him for, everyone that is, but him, McKenna would be safe. This was his fault.

Preoccupied with his cell, Alex said, "Lee and Adam have a lead on Montego."

"The real Montego? Where the f-f-f-f… I mean…" *Shit.* "Where is she?"

"Back in my neighborhood like you predicted. They've got her holed up in one of the new homes near the bridge over the river."

Finally. But damn. Beau wanted to be the one to take her in. Make that, kill her.

"Is she alone?" *Or is she busy hacking off another guy's finger?*

"Don't know. They haven't gotten inside yet. Sheriff Prince is on the scene. She's armed but she's not getting away this time."

'But I want to be the one to end her. I'm the one she hurt, not them.'

"Let it go," Alex muttered as if he'd read Beau's mind. "McKenna's worth a million Montegos."

Which was the first time Beau heard what Alex didn't say. Kelsey meant more to Alex than anything else, maybe even more than The TEAM. Somehow, that insight helped.

"You're right," he admitted.

Canting his head, Alex sent him *that* look. "When we land we'll still be a mile or so from the farmhouse. Justin'll drop us far enough out that we won't raise suspicion. But we're going in hot. You take point. You know the rules. No collateral damage. We do this quick and—"

"We do this right," Beau finished.

"Damned straight."

The LZ ended up being dead center of a farmer's meticulously plowed field, one click west of the deserted farmhouse, where, oh by the way, that Toyota sedan sat parked on the far side of the home, away from the road. The pilot touched down, and in seconds, Beau and Alex were boots on the ground and running for the house.

Beau ran between the furrows, careful not to put his big feet on any of the tender sprouts breaking through the soil. Farmers were part of that group of hard-working people he respected. This day wasn't about making trouble for the little guy just because he owned a field.

The farmhouse itself was a leftover relic from the forties or fifties, maybe earlier. Its clapboard siding was weathered and gray, not a speck of paint on them. What had once been an asphalt-shingled roof now revealed the bare skeleton of roof joists. There was no glass in the window panes. A string of straggly cottonwoods and overgrown shrubbery allowed Beau and Alex to get close to the home without being seen. With their backs against the western wall, Alex ordered Beau to breach the rear entry, while he took the main.

Beau nodded his agreement but paused when he nearly stumbled over a storm cellar at the rear northwest corner. Interesting. Every type of weed, thistle, and Virginia creeper in the state concealed the rest of the derelict stone foundation.

Yet these two slanted doors were both clear of debris, in fact, looked downright tidy. Someone had recently accessed those doors.

Dropping to one knee, he examined the fresh prints leading up to the door. Definite heel marks from a woman's dress shoe, another from an athletic sole. Not a boot. Lighter tread marks. Most likely not left by a male. Males tended to be heavier. Their feet bigger.

"Got a situation back here, Boss," Beau whispered into his mic. "Located an exterior cellar door. Looks used recently. I've got fresh shoe impressions. Also recent. More than one set."

"Copy that," came back to him, then a huff, and, "I'm inside. Watch your step. The floor's not stable. Not sure the roof is, either."

"I'm blocking the cellar doors, just in case," Beau said as he slid the dried-up, fractured piece of two-by-four he'd found in the weeds through the two door handles to prevent escape. With Alex already inside, he hustled up the back steps and entered the deserted home.

With his index finger raised to his lips, Alex stared across the cavernous hole in what had once been the kitchen floor. Antique appliances still lined the wall on one side, a rusted enamel sink and a sideboard lined the other.

Beau cocked his head, listening to the sounds of the relic. The quiet creak of aged lumber against framework and beams. The breeze whistling through the space between the slatted siding and the open roof. The rustle of leaves, insects, or vermin inside the home.

Whoever lived here had left in a hurry. Dusty knickknacks still lined the kitchen window over the sink, though all were on their sides. Tattered remnants of curtains hung from the curtain rod. Hell, a picture of the Last Supper still hung on the grimy wall. Wallpaper with roses that had once been red or pink instead of gray, barely showed through the dirt that had blown in over the years.

All walls were water-stained. Debris from the roof and upper level now lay in a jumbled mess in the basement, which meant the storm cellar had been built separately from the rest of the home. Better yet, the cellar was now accessible only through the double doors out back. The barricaded doors. Margo Heller, aka Bambi Lynch, had painted herself into a corner. Sweet.

"We've got her, Boss," Beau murmured. "She's trapped."

Muted voices lifted up from the recesses of the cellar, but no specific words were discernible. It definitely sounded like two women arguing. Beau canted his head, listening for McKenna's voice.

Alex signaled for him to circle back outside.

Beau nodded, message received, and quickly returned outside to the cellar doors.

"On my mark," Alex murmured over his earpiece. "Three…"

Quietly, Beau slid the two-by-four out of the handles.
"Two…"

Beau secured his pistol in the holster under his left arm in order to grip the right door handle and…

"One."

He flung the door open, quickly retrieved his pistol from its holster, and dropped down the rickety steps onto an earthen floor ten feet below. Automatically, his weapon zeroed down on two women. McKenna sat with her arms restrained behind her back on a chair positioned behind a flood lamp, her face lit with shock to see him. The other woman jumped up from the stool in front of McKenna.

"It's over, Lynch," Beau bellowed, his arms outstretched as the laser dot from his scope targeted her forehead.

At the same precise time as he shouted, Alex landed silently in a crouch at the far side of the earthen room, his pistol up and also trained on the scene.

As if sensing Beau's intention to distract Lynch, McKenna screamed, "Don't shoot her!"

"Why not?" he yelled back to make Lynch think he was the only one she had to deal with. She had yet to glance Alex's way. *Smart move, Boss.*

"Because she's sick just like my mom was. She needs help. Please, Beau, give her a—"

For that McKenna earned a vicious slap from Lynch that left a stream of blood trickling out of her mouth. "I am not sick, and neither was Aurora!"

"Do that again, bitch, and I'll drop you where you stand," Beau promised the older woman. He didn't need two hands to make that wish come true.

"Oh yeah, well take one more step, dumbass, and this place goes up in smoke," Lynch promised him right back, her voice shrill as a detonator appeared in her left hand. "Did you think I came down here without a backup plan? You're as dumb as Sanders!"

"So you're ready to die for what you believe? About Aurora and Sanders? About McKenna? Who by the way, was just a little girl when her mother went Mommy Dearest on her, whipped her, and stuffed her in a fucking closet." Beau took a step forward, his gaze flitting over Lynch's shoulder to his silent partner in the shadows.

Still unaware of Alex, McKenna whined, "Don't, Beau. Please, don't."

"Won't if I can help it, baby," Beau promised as he put another boot sideways to the ground, drawing closer. Drawing Lynch's attention to him, away from McKenna and Alex.

"Ha! That's what he calls you? Baby? You're no baby. You're Sanders kid, a bitch!"

Without taking her eyes off Beau, Lynch slapped McKenna again while she aimed the detonator in her other hand like a pistol to keep him at bay.

She still didn't realize Alex was also in the room, though still secreted in the dark and as silent as Death itself. Most criminals would've been more than a little worried about Beau's scope marking their foreheads. They might've put their hands up and begged to be taken into custody instead of shot. The laser dot all by itself was an overwhelmingly successful law enforcement tool. The promise of death got most idiots to reconsider their plans.

It didn't seem to work on Lynch.

"Please, Beau," McKenna pleaded. "Bambi's my aunt. My mom's sister and—"

Alex took two silent steps forward, put his pistol to the back of Lynch's head, and skillfully assumed control of the detonator. He grunted, then tossed it at Beau. "It's a TV remote." At which point he jerked Lynch to her knees while Beau ran to McKenna.

"How many times am I going to have to save you from yourself?" he chided.

Breathing hard, she flung herself into his arms the moment her hands were free. "How many times are you going to run away from me?"

She had him there, but now was not the time for that discussion. He nodded, his weapon still in his right hand against her back, while he circled his wounded hand around her shoulders to hold her steady. "Deep breath. It's over," he said even as he kept an eye on the crazy woman in the room.

Bambi Lynch started laughing then. A hysterical, demented cackle that lifted chills up Beau's spine. "It's not over. It's just begun! Here! Now! You don't know what you've done, you stupid, stupid men!"

Beau looked at Alex. Alex looked at Beau. Like highly trained covert operators the world over, an uncanny glimmer of awareness flashed between them. This was a trap. Not wasting another second, Beau tossed McKenna over his shoulders in a fireman's hold and ran for the exit.

He made it to the top step, when—*BLAM!* A flaming vortex of fire and percussion blew him and McKenna out of the cellar and twenty feet across the yard. In the violent maelstrom that ensued, Beau ended on top of McKenna, thank you Jesus. He'd twisted his body and ended shielding her head within the crook of his neck, shoulder, and bicep. She was the important one. She had to live.

Shards of twisted lumber rained down, hammering them like a bizarre wind from hell. With fire and brimstone. With Death. Smoke seared his eyes and nose, and still he hunkered over McKenna, determined that she would walk away from this catastrophe. This was why he'd been born, for this singular moment and the supreme task of saving this one woman. She was the giver of life. It seemed a fair trade-off. A sinner for a saint.

A jolting burn pierced his left side, pinning him to the ground, and still Beau took the brunt of what followed the explosion. By then his ears rang. His nose bled. Possibly his eyes were bleeding, too. Either that or he was bawling his eyes out. But if life had taught Beau Jennings anything, it was that he was no quitter. He held fast, and he held true to the only one who mattered in this diabolical nightmare. It sure as hell wasn't Lynch. Not Alex, either. Only the woman who saved children.

At last, the dragon's breath behind him abated, and things stopped falling out of the sky. Beau lifted his head with a groan, needing to see how or if his boss and Lynch had survived. Only Alex lay just feet away, his hands covering the back of his head. He sent Beau one of those tough guy chin nods that he was okay. But there was no sign of Bambi Lynch. *Damn. What a shame.*

Sweating like a beast with a new kind of pain to deal with, Beau dipped his grimy forehead to McKenna's. "You okay, baby?"

She craned her neck to see beyond him, then placed both palms to his chest and tried to shove him up and off. "My aunt. You see her? Did she make it out?"

"Not so fast," he growled, the flaming burn in his side a hundred times worse than waking up to a severed finger.

"You're bleeding!"

Like he didn't know? "Happens," he told her easily, sure this was the end of the road for him.

Jesus, it had been a long day. Whatever shrapnel nailed Beau's back and dug into his side hurt, like a mother. Nausea climbed up his throat at what his body endured. Shadows danced at his peripheral, threatening to take him down with them. Back to Hell. That was where he belonged. In Hell with Bambi Lynch, her insane sisters, and hopefully, that witch Montego.

'Jesus,' he prayed. *'Please let the guys on my team kill her today. She really needs to die.'*

"Help!" McKenna cried out, half-holding Beau, half-pushing out from beneath him. "Alex, help!"

"Son-of-a-bitch," Alex hissed quietly as he scrambled to his feet and knelt over his wingman yet again. "You took a damned big splinter to your back, Beau. It went through you like a spear. Hold still. Help's on its way." He didn't sound too good, his voice winded and raw. But he sounded a helluva lot better than Beau felt.

"Save McKenna," he told his boss, losing blood and his grip on her.

It was odd, though. She hadn't yet asked after her Aunt Bambi, which meant she knew. Her aunt was gone. But even as he lay dying, Beau found McKenna's loss impossibly— sad. Jesus, could anyone in this crazy, mixed-up world ever have enough family? Was the loss of just one aunt or uncle— just one little sister or a baby brother—ever acceptable? Beau didn't think so. Which was why Maverick and every last man and woman on The TEAM had to live.

"I'm here, Beau," McKenna sobbed as, out from under him now, she tenderly eased his head onto her lap.

Even that sweet gesture hurt like a mother. Yet face down and in excruciating pain, he couldn't have been happier. This was the way a warrior died. In his woman's arms. After he'd saved her. Not that Beau deserved her. He knew that for a fact he deserved no such thing.

McKenna was never meant to end up with him. She was light and goodness and so much more. He was just one of those avenging angel types. As evil as the Devil. Born to wander, but never to rest. Here today. Gone tomorrow...

"Don't go," she begged, her tears raining down. "Don't leave me again. You promised."

He reached one hand—his good hand—to the top of her thigh one last time. Intertwining her fingers with his, she leaned over and kissed the side of his sweaty head. That was nice. Would've been nicer if he'd been face-up and could've kissed her sweet lips one last time. Not happening. He was shoving off for Valhalla.

"Always meant to tell you," he whispered, losing touch with the feeling in his left arm. Then his legs. "Always loved you… green eyes."

"Beau! Beau!"

Chapter Fifty-One

"She's still alive?" Beau asked. *Un-frickin'-believable.*

"Yeah, well…" A disgruntled Connor stretched one long leg out in front of him, his eyes on the floor. "Don't worry. We'll get Montego now that the Lynch sisters are out of our way."

He and Gabe had filled every bit of the spare space in the private hospital room with Starbucks cups and bags of breakfast junk food Beau wasn't supposed to eat—but most certainly did. Usually, these guys were two long-legged, trash-talking, calorie eating machines. His kind of people. But both were particularly glum today.

Once more consigned to GWU, Beau had spent the last hour listening to how Connor, Gabe, Lee, and Izza had been duped into thinking Catalina Montego had set up camp inside that half-finished mansion near Alex's place. Instead, some homeless gal had been paid to dress like Catalina, to distract and mislead The TEAM. Imagine her shock and awe when Izza Maher stormed the place and ended the charade with the business end of her rifle.

Which meant psycho-witch Montego was still on the loose. Probably laughing her guts out while she stalked yet another unwitting, male victim or watched The TEAM chase their tails. Alex and his agents had been brought low by one woman with a helluva grudge, and apparently, unlimited financing. Hell hath no fury and all that rot.

But Beau still wasn't convinced Montego's current crime spree had anything to do with her brother's death. Not after seeing the victims she'd housed in the hidden cells of that nasty warehouse. The nineteen survivors who'd fallen for the black widow spider were traumatized basket cases now. All were malnourished and ill. Every last one had been tortured, either by Montego or by each other, and all had a long struggle back to normalcy ahead of them.

Interestingly, the FBI had also located an amazingly gruesome array of freezers in her basement of horrors. Talk about one bat-shit crazy woman. Just as she'd done in Congressman Ringer's home, each freezer held plastic containers of forensic evidence that would take the FBI months to analyze. Maybe years. All were labeled in bold block letters with individual men's names and dates beneath the word LOVER. Apparently in Catalina's book, love really had to hurt.

For now, Maverick still roomed down the hall from Beau's room, which was a definite win/win. When folks came to visit Maverick, most stopped by to check on Beau, too. Even a handsome older couple from Ohio, Wade and Cadence Maverick, had stopped by for a quick, albeit intensely emotional visit.

Beau thought he was safe until Maverick's mother sat timidly at the edge of his bed and said 'thank you'. But when she leaned over and carefully tugged him into her arms like his fake parents had never, ever done. Jesus. The needy little kid inside Beau lost it. He closed his eyes and just held on.

"You saved my boy," Maverick's mom had cried, her tears damp and hot on his cheek, the desperate crush of her matronly arms around him the best thank-you he'd ever received. Because she was a real mom. A good mom. And Maverick was one lucky SOB. She didn't need to say anything more, but then she'd ended with, "Thank you so very much, Mr. Jennings. I'll never forget you. I don't know what I'd've done if… How I'd've gotten through the rest of my life without…"

It was all Beau could do to not break down and bawl like a baby. If he'd let Maverick die, life would've been mighty bleak for this incredibly sweet mother and father. They would've lost both their children, and Beau understood the level of hell to that kind of devastation.

Yet not once had he thought of Maverick's family when he'd done what he did. He hadn't thought of China or Kyrie, either, and he should have. Because Jesus, those people were important to Maverick, more important than Beau would ever be. But in the middle of that godawful nightmare, he'd honestly only thought of himself. That he couldn't—Just. Could. Not!—lose the first brother he'd ever had. Didn't that make him a selfish bastard?

Yet sitting there with Cadence Carson while teary-eyed Wade Carson looked on, and knowing that he'd saved Maverick's folks from the despair he'd lived with since he'd lost AJ? Knowing that Kyrie and China didn't have to wake up every morning without the husband and father they loved, make that adored? Yeah. For sure, Beau was no hero. But after all was said and done, he was good enough.

"My pleasure," he'd told Maverick's mother when she'd finally let go of him.

By then his eyes had been shimmering plenty, too.

"So what's next?" Beau asked Connor now, needing details.

"We regroup. Rethink what we thought we knew, and we go after Montego again."

"Only this time..." Gabe slanted a hesitant look Beau's way. "You do know you're off the case, right?"

"Yeah, yeah," Beau waved his one good hand dismissively. "Alex said something about me taking some well-earned R&R." Precisely what Beau was not good at doing.

But this time he just might do as he was told. He was after all, physically attached to some bright, shiny torture device hooked up to his bed frame, one that kept his new and freshly bandaged hand elevated, the attached finger in question restrained. The recently installed metal pins and rods in that hand also kept him from getting dressed and taking off like he had before.

The catheter under his sheets wasn't much fun, either. Neither were the monitors at the head of his bed that the nurses fiddled with around the clock. But after emergency surgery to extract one helluva splinter from his extreme lower back, Beau figured he was lucky to be alive. The damned thing had barely missed one of his kidneys.

Not to mention that once Dr. Decker and Dr. Fitzgerald put their pointed little heads together, his war for independence was lost. Joining their forces, Alex Stewart had posted guards, like Gabe and Connor, to *'visit'* and otherwise ensure that this *'junior agent'* stayed put this time. Normally, that sort of treatment would've made Beau fighting mad, but he was learning what it meant to be part of The TEAM. Damned if it wasn't—nice.

Not like Beau had any place to go besides his empty apartment, that while good enough, hadn't been more than a clean place to chill. Bottom line, his world had changed, and he was changing with it. He'd finally ceased fighting the war within himself. He wasn't an army of one. Had in fact never been one. And that was okay. *All's well that ends well, and all that crap.*

Cocking his good arm behind his head, Beau asked his all too subdued teammates, "So where is she now? Do we, umm, do you guys know?"

"Seth spotted her in Havana," Connor answered quietly. "He's due home in the next day or so. Hope he's got good intel."

"We could use some," Gabe added.

"Havana, huh?" Beau raised his eyebrows. "You guys sure that wasn't another fake Montego?"

Connor shrugged. "Not sure of anything right now. This op's been crazy from day one."

"You've got that right. There were too many crazy women," Beau replied.

"Makes you wonder if it's nature or nurture," Gabe mused as he scratched the day's scruff under his chin and kicked his long legs out in front of him.

"Both," Alex said as he opened the door, his other arm around his wife. "Montego's parents were depraved murderers. No doubt Catalina and Roland witnessed plenty growing up. You slackers mind if we join the party?"

"Come on in," Beau replied easily. "Sorry I can't get up, ma'am," he told Kelsey as he sent his boss an evil glare. "For some reason, I'm not allowed to leave."

Alex grunted like he couldn't care less, which was par for the course. Gabe and Connor however, popped to their feet and transferred their garbage to the waste can to clear a seat for Kelsey as quickly as they could.

"Guys, relax," she told them. "We're not staying. Just wanted to check in and see how you're doing."

Beau eyed her suspiciously. Both she and Alex were wearing black, him in a suit and she in a simple A-line dress with black heels. There was something she wasn't saying. "Be better when I'm back on my feet, but Doc Fitz says I have to stay put if I want to keep my finger."

"I'm surprised it's still attached after all you put it through," she said.

Connor chuffed. "So's Doc Decker."

Beau looked at his heavily bandaged left hand. For now, it was numb, but supposedly responding well. But if it ever came down to losing a finger, a hand, or hell, his leg to save McKenna, she'd win every time.

"So where are you guys headed?" he asked.

"Dempsey's viewing is tonight," Kelsey murmured.

"When's the funeral?" Beau had to know.

"No funeral," Alex said grimly. "Just a celebration of life, which you won't attend if you know what's good for you."

'We'll see about that,' Beau thought as he gave Alex his chin like he concurred with that stupid order.

Alex cleared his throat. "I heard back from the Army."

This ought to be good. "And?"

"And you've earned a full and honorable discharge, Special Operator Jennings. No reduction in rank. No loss of seniority or benefits. The case has been officially dismissed."

Kelsey smiled. "Isn't that great?"

Beau's throat went dry at how much his boss had done for him these last few days. "I, ah, don't know what to say."

Alex shook his head. "Forget it. It's my job to take care of you screwballs. But before we leave…"

He reached behind Kelsey and opened the door to a frail Latino woman with an even frailer Latino gentleman at her side. The woman wore a light pink blouse over tan twill pants. The man's outfit consisted of faded jeans, a worn western style shirt, a light gray cowboy hat, and a fancy tooled leather belt, complete with a silver buckle. Both were around fifty. But my hell, they looked like a puff of air would blow them over.

"Beau Jennings, I'd like you to meet Rubio and Esperanza Villanueva. Essie for short."

"Evening," Beau said as he eyed the strangers. Yet, there was something familiar about them. Something that called out for him to remember. He motioned them to come in. "It's kind of crowded in here, but please—"

The woman's fingers flew to her mouth. "It is him."

Beau swallowed hard at the tremor in a voice that sounded damned familiar. "I'm who?"

"It's you. My son," she breathed, those slender fingers now fluttering at the center of her chest. "Do you see it, Rube? His eyes. The way his lips move. The shape of his eyes. It is him. I know it is. I'm sure."

The gentleman's dark brown eyes brimmed. He wiped a hand over his weathered, wrinkled brow, then took his cowboy hat off, and—

The planet jerked to a full stop. *Damn. It can't be...*

Beau cocked his head, not ready to believe in miracles, but finding it hard to catch his breath. Truly afraid to believe that a hardass like Alex could pull off two miracles in one day, an honorable discharge, and whatever this was. But that older gentleman standing there twisting his hat in his hands could've passed for Beau's older brother. Same skin tone. Same piercing dark eyes. Same—Jesus Christ—same everything.

Had Hell officially frozen over? "You know me?" Beau asked, seeking the truth in tired, mellow eyes that looked so much like his. Jesus, even the way this guy cocked his head and blinked as if he needed to clear his vision was oh, so familiar.

He bobbed his head as he pressed a sharp crease in that cowboy hat. "A father never forgets the child he lost," he said, his voice cracking.

Chills swarmed up the back of Beau's neck as suspicion gave way to suppressed anger. "Why?" he croaked, daring to believe this was true.

The woman's head canted like she didn't understand. "Why what, my little one?"

And that was enough.

"I'm not your little one!" Beau blasted her and the old guy for all the pain and suffering they'd left him to endure. "Why the fuck did you give me away? What'd I ever do that was so bad you didn't want me?"

With tears in her eyes, she flew to his bedside and reached for him, but didn't touch him. "Oh no, no, no. I did not give you away. It wasn't like that. Your father and I have searched many years for you."

Rubio nodded silently at her side, that crease pressed as sharp as a blade. "Do not curse us before you know what happened. It was not our fault. Someone stole you."

"Then how?" Beau ground out. "How do you know I'm your kid? Cuz I'm sure as hell not feeling it. Not after all this time. Not after the crappy life I've had. It's been years!"

Alex stepped forward. "DNA, Beau," he said evenly. "I located them in Mexico City after they took one of those ancestry tests that are so popular right now. I've checked out their story. You were stolen out of the back seat of their truck at a rest stop in Nevada, when they traveled north to work the apple orchards in eastern Washington. As illegals, they had no way to locate you. Nobody at the rest stop saw anything. But trust me, Essie and Rubio are telling you the truth. They did all they could, even contacted the authorities, but there were no leads. No way to track you or to know who took you. No way to get you back."

Bass and Fidget stole me? Why? Beau stared through his tears, ashamed at his ugly outburst, but so damned sick at heart. All these years wasted. All that time gone. And through every last sucking day of it all, he'd had parents who'd truly wanted him. Who still did. They were here, weren't they?

"You named me Beau," he said, not asked. Here was the test. He was sure Benjamin Beau had always been his name, though Bass had called him everything but.

With her fingers clenched at her side, Essie's head bobbed. Man, with all those tears in her eyes, they were the exact dark chocolate caramel as his.

But it was the gentleman beside her, who claimed to be his father, who spoke. "That is not entirely true. We named you Benjamin Beauregard after your grandfathers. Beau for short, but none of that matters. I can prove you are my son." Tipping forward as if he had a bad back or something, he pulled a tattered folded document out of his rear pocket. "Here. This is your birth certificate, Mr. Jennings. Look at it if that is who you really are, then tell me you are not mine."

Beau did just that, snapping what looked like an aged document out of this convincing man's fingers. His own eyes were plenty blurry, but he'd been fooled before. And yet…

The yellowed sheet of paper did look authentic.

That was the great seal of Mexico in the upper left corner.

The name of the civil registry judge did look authentic.

The date of birth wasn't right, but that made sense. How would Bass or Fidget have known when he'd been born? Yet that was his name under the heading 'Recorded Data'. Those were Rubio's and Esperanza's names on the lines. *Villanueva, huh?*

Rubio stepped forward, his head bare and a hint of something Beau could relate to in his eyes. Anger. "Why do you not believe me? Why are you still so angry, my son? We have waited long for this day."

Essie's fist went to her clenched lips. "You do not remember us," she whispered, her voice no more than a raspy breath. "You... you do not need us."

But Rubio had just used a term Beau had craved all his life. Not just son, but *my son*. To hear it now and said with such sorrowful conviction ripped the scabs off the blistered, aching holes in Beau's heart. *My son* declared an intimate knowledge and an ownership. It declared fatherly possession of what had been lost. Goddamn, it declared love.

"It's not that. It's just" —he swallowed hard, finally convinced and in need of apologizing— "it's just that all these years…" *Jesus, how do I say this?* "I thought…" *Just spit it out.* "I thought you gave me up because you didn't want me."

Those last, few, pitiful words came out like a pointed accusation. Out there in the universe somewhere, Kelsey's sob caught. Alex cleared his throat. Connor and Gabe were silent.

"I thought, I don't know, that I did something wrong to make you… to make you…" Beau never got the rest of that false childhood assumption—*to make you stop loving me*—out of his mouth.

With a heartrending cry that pierced every last chamber in his heart, Essie reached out and circled his hard head into her soft, warm embrace. Crying unabashedly, she kissed the top of his head while she rocked him and cried, "Mi bebé. Mi pobre bebé!"

My baby. My poor baby.

And Beau let her. Like a damned two-year-old, he let her, because this—this!—was what he'd missed every day of his miserable life as the worthless son of Bass Jennings. This connection. These arms. This sensation of being valued and treasured. Of being loved.

Reaching up with his one good hand, wishing to Jesus he had two, Beau clutched his mother's quaking shoulder while her tears fell on him like rain. Blessing him like only a mother—a real mother—could ever do. Sobbing and crying, and that was proof enough. Fidget had never cried over him, not once. Over herself, yes. An addict living with Bass Jennings had plenty reasons to cry.

But this woman pressing him against her body now—like she wanted him back inside of her heart—like she was absorbing him even as big as he was—like he'd always been her little boy and no one would ever take him from her again—was hurting as much as Beau. No one could fake this kind of anguish.

"I'm sorry," he cried as he held his mother for the first time in his memory.

"No, no, no! Not sorry, not you. I have you now. You are come back to me." Without letting him go, she crossed herself and murmured, "Gracias Jesús. Muchas gracias," into his hair.

To which Beau heartily agreed. *Yes, Jesus. Thank you, thank you, so damned much.*

Closing his eyes, he took a deep breath and let his weary soul fill with the lovely fragrance he vaguely recalled from long ago. Rosewater. His mother's unique scent and the smell of home. Windows too long shuttered in the forgotten reaches of his heart reopened. Memories of sunny apple fields. Baskets of red, ripe fruit. Clusters of purple and green grapes. Dusty truck rides over bumpy gravel roads and fields. Giggling. Smiling for no reason other than he was a happy kid, and at long last, he was loved.

"Ma," he choked out, then corrected himself. "Mi Madre…" Those words his heart knew. He'd said them before. "Mi Mama," he savored, then nodded at his father to

come join the huddle with a ragged, "Mi Padre. Papa. Dad."
My real Dad.

Essie stepped aside, giving Rubio access to his son for
the first time in years. And Damn! Real men didn't cry, yet
when his father jerked him into his arms and squeezed the life
out of him, Beau sobbed. Sons aren't men. Not really. Inside,
they're needy little buggers who just want their moms and
dads, and Beau was that very lost, needy little kid who'd
finally been found.

When at last he lifted his teary face from the dampened
folds of his father's shirt, the room was empty except for him
and his parents. And that was a good thing. Beau had some
catching up to do.

Dragging his wrist across his face, still putting on a brave
front, he motioned for Rubio to pull the hospital chairs closer
to the bed. "Sit," he told his mom and dad.

And stay. Please, please stay.

Chapter Fifty-Two

"Did I miss it?" McKenna asked as she ran toward Beau's room, where it looked like a TEAM convention was in process. "I couldn't get away."

Alex stood there with his arm around Kelsey, who had her face in both hands against his chest. Connor and Gabe just looked awkward, like they didn't know what to say or do.

"Rubio and Essie arrived early. I couldn't make them wait to see their son," Alex answered.

"No, of course not." But darn. McKenna wanted to be with Beau when he met his parents for the first time. That had to have been hard on him.

"I'm sure he'd like you to join him now," Kelsey added, wiping her teary eyes as she stepped away from Alex.

"Are you okay?" McKenna asked.

"Yes, but that was some reunion. All this time..." Kelsey's voice trailed away.

Gabe blew out a whistle. "All this time is right."

"What I just heard in there explains a lot. All this time, I thought he was just an ass...." Connor choked on his unfortunate word choice, then auto-corrected, "Ass-tronomically big jerk."

"Good save," Gabe snorted as he punched Connor's bicep.

"How did he take it?" McKenna needed to know before she wandered into the lion's den. Beau could be unpredictable, and this was such an—astronomically big event in his life.

Alex inclined his head at the closed door. "Go find out."

"But first," McKenna said when her hand hit the doorknob. "How's Mother?"

"Dempsey's viewing is tonight," Alex replied. "Her celebration of life is tomorrow."

"I can't make it tonight, but I'll be there tomorrow."

"We'll all be there," Connor added. "My kids, too. They loved Dempsey."

"Thank you, guys," Kelsey said as she wiped the corner of her eye again. "Mother's always kept so much of her life and problems to herself. I'm sure she'll appreciate the support."

Connor cocked his head, the sparkle in his blue eyes gone. "She's always had it. She's like Beau, she just didn't know it."

"And now she will," Alex said as if that solved everything. "Damned hard way to figure it out, though. Are we still on for early this afternoon?" he asked McKenna.

"I'll be there if you're still willing." Offhandedly, China had mentioned how much McKenna wanted to learn to shoot, but now she wasn't so sure. Once Alex heard that, he'd scheduled time at the range. She'd rather wait for Beau, but she was committed now.

"I'll see all of you later then." And with that, McKenna slipped out of the hall and into Beau's room.

His eyes lit up the second he spotted her. "McKenna! Come meet my mom and dad. And I've got older brothers.

Robert lives in Houston, Mateo and Diego in Southern California. They're coming to see me!"

Her eyes teared up at the genuine glow in his heretofore grumpy eyes, that, *oh, my goodness, look just like his dad's.*

"Mr. and Mrs. Villanueva," she said as she extended her hand to the teary older couple sitting on the edge of the bed. "I am so, so happy to meet you."

Later that same day…

"Again!"

Sucking in a deep breath, McKenna narrowed down on the target Alex had just sent down range to the thousand-yard line. *Damn, he really thinks I can hit that tiny little red circle from here?* Steadying her trembling arm while relaxing her grip—less recoil that way—she closed her left eye and—

"Both eyes open!" her personal drill sergeant barked, reminding her yet again that snipers didn't flinch when their rounds fired. Apparently, they weren't supposed to close one eye to narrow down on their target, either. Situational awareness. It was all about situational awareness, and a decent shooter needed both eyes open for that.

Sniffing at Alex's continual badgering, McKenna straightened her spine and sucked it up. It was no wonder Beau cursed like he did. She too felt an f-bomb waiting to explode off her tongue. McKenna rolled one shoulder, not perturbed with Alex but also not quite sure she could ever perform to his high standards. The man was an intimidating beast of a teacher.

"Easy," Alex ordered from where he stood a few feet to her right and to her rear where no expelled shells could hit him. Not that one would dare. He was made of stern, intimidating stone. Even if an empty shell did strike him, it'd probably turn to dust.

'I can do this,' she thought as gently, but with calculated precision, she squeezed the trigger—just like he'd told her—and, whew! Killed that target, dead center. The darn thing barely fluttered, and she was thankful she didn't have to calculate distance and windage. Yet.

"Again," he ordered crisply.

"As you wish," McKenna whispered as she obeyed and squeezed the trigger of her very own precision-crafted SIG Saur Mosquito. Okay, so it was only a .22 LR, and ten percent smaller than its big brother, the P226, which Alex fully intended her to shoot. But this weapon was more than enough for now, and to be honest, it frightened her when he'd first placed it in her hand—loaded—and told her it was hers.

When she'd told Alex she didn't want it, that she was afraid of it, that guns killed people, he'd sharply cut her off with a curt, exasperated, "No, they don't. Get that through your head right now. Guns are tools like matches, axes, steak knives, and cars. Yes, they can all be used to kill people, but it's the idiot behind them that does the killing. You can ban all the weapons in the world, and a murderer will still find a way to end a life."

Well, alrighty then. McKenna honestly hadn't considered that perspective.

"Empty the entire clip this time," he barked. "Stop holding back. Don't be afraid of your firearm. Chin up, not down. Look your target in the eye."

McKenna did, though every round she fired didn't quite strike the bulls-eye. A couple had the nerve to go wide, darn them. Swallowing hard, she ejected the magazine and laid the pistol on its side on her shooting stand, barrel pointed down range, before she turned to Alex and asked, "How was that?" *Pretty darn good if I do say so myself.*

He stood with his legs spread, his back erect, and a rangefinder lifted to his eyes. "You missed three out of ten," he said without so much as a glance her way. "You can do better. Stop over-compensating. Load up. Do it again."

Honestly, the man cut her no slack, but if this was how Beau became an expert sniper, so be it. She reloaded the magazines she'd just emptied, then set two aside while she slapped one home. Took a deep breath. Maintained correct posture. Cupped her left hand under her right so both cradled the SIG's grip. Bit her lip because, damn, Alex was intimidating the hell out of her! Looked that damned bulls-eye in the—eye. Lined up the target just beyond the reticle, then…

Repeat. Repeat. Repeat. She did it until the magazines she'd just reloaded were empty, then she did it all over again. After an hour of reloading and killing every target Alex sent down range, McKenna finally grew more confident. Not cocky, but more certain of herself and the extremely lethal firearm in her hands.

The pistol itself wasn't hard to shoot or scary once she'd practiced enough. Over and over, she ejected spent magazines, cleared the occasional jammed round, and trained her wandering index finger to stay clear of the trigger until she'd sighted in and was ready to blast another bulls-eye.

But McKenna also learned another gun safety rule. Backstops were extremely important and a vital consideration she'd never, well, considered. But every single discharged round went somewhere, and if that somewhere was into a neighbor's house or yard or, heaven forbid, his head—yeah. Not good. A thoughtless shooter could unintentionally kill someone. A child. Or a dog. It happened every day, and she didn't want to ever be that careless person.

"Rules of engagement, McKenna," Alex had explained. "A good sniper never forgets precisely where he is, where his target stands, or what's behind that target. We don't kill innocent people just to *'get our man,'* and we don't shoot into crowds like those idiots on TV." He'd layered sarcasm aplenty on those last words. "That's not who we are or how we work. We're not trained killers or assassins. We're honorable men and women who've stepped up to do a dirty job no one else has the balls for. At the close of every day, we sleep well because we've done our best, and the world's safer because of us."

"Understood," she'd told him as she drilled the final paper target—a zombie rat—right through its one, bright red eye. *There, take that.*

"Good enough," Alex growled. "Put your gear away. Now you'll learn how to disassemble and clean your pistol. A clean weapon is a safe weapon. If you take care of it, it'll take care of you."

"Good enough, nothing. I did damned good today," she shot back at him as she ejected the magazine, racked the slide to ensure all cartridges were accounted for, slid the trigger guard through the open breach, and replaced her now empty firearm in its protective storage case. Just like she'd been taught.

He canted his head, a gentler light in those silvery blues. "For a novice, yes. You did okay. For self-defense, no. Tomorrow you upgrade to the type of weapon I carry, a P226. It's heavier and has full take down power. At the end of the day, you'll be—"

"What caliber?" she snapped. Hey, if he could dish it out, so could she.

"Semi-auto, 9mm Luger," he snapped right back. "It weighs in empty at thirty-four point four ounces. The weapon you fired today is based on the P226, which is why you started with a Mosquito. I babied you. I wanted you to get the feel of the weapon you're going to carry the rest of your life. It's important to make your pistol part of you. It's not a baseball bat. It's not a piano. And it's not something to play with. The second you wrap your fingers around the grip, it's your soul and your heart on the line every time you squeeze that trigger. Understood?"

Humbled at his fervor, McKenna nodded, sorry she'd poked him when she should've been serious. Man, the guy was a beast when it came to gun safety.

"You want pink?"

She blinked, not sure what he meant by that offhanded and extremely sarcastic question. "Excuse me, pink what?"

"Your weapon. Would you prefer a pink one?"

Why did she feel like this was a test question? "Why would I want a pink gun?" That sounded like Alex thought she was an airheaded Barbie doll who wanted a pretty toy instead of a deadly firearm for self-protection.

"So that's a no?"

"Of course that's a no. Little kids don't need the mixed signals that kind of weapon would surely send. Guns have killed enough children, damn it. They're not toys to play with, so why make them cute and pink?"

His eyes narrowed as if she'd finally said something he respected. "Just asking. Now let's clean that weapon of yours."

She followed Beau's testy lord and master off the indoor range to his monster-sized black GMC pickup, her weapon stored and her gun case in hand.

"Your place or mine?" Alex asked as he hit the ignition, and his diesel-powered vehicle rumbled and rattled to life.

"For?" she asked as she tucked her gear behind the passenger seat and climbed aboard.

"I never clean my weapons here. It's easier at home. Less equipment to haul."

That made sense. "I'm staying at China and Maverick's for now," McKenna admitted as she buckled her seatbelt.

"Oh?"

"Yes, I couldn't go back to my place, and China offered, so yes. I'm sure she won't mind."

Alex performed a careful K-turn and cranked the wheel, headed for the freeway. "Does Beau know I'm teaching you to shoot?"

"He knows I wanted to learn, but with him in the hospital, I didn't want to wait any longer."

"Good decision," Alex replied, his tone still gruff but with a hint of admiration seeping into it. "People need to be able to rely on themselves. Glad you're staying with the Carsons. I hear you've got a pet."

That made McKenna smile. "One of Kyrie's motherless kittens, yes."

"Now that the rest of your aunts are in jail, I've got a proposal for you. But I want you to think about it before you give me an answer."

She cocked her head, wondering what this formidable powerbroker could ever want with a pediatrician. "And that is?"

He shot her a quick glance out of the corner of his eye. "I want you to work for me. Libby Houston's got her own practice now, and Harley's wife Judy is always ready to lend a hand when one of the guys gets hurt. But I need someone on staff. Every day. Interested?"

Harley's wife, Judy Mortimer was more than a good sport. A dynamic bundle of redheaded energy, McKenna knew plenty about the emergency room triage nurse. Judy ran a tight ship at the hospital, and she also had a way of running The TEAM whenever they gathered for picnics, dinners, or events as simple as one of the baby's baptisms. The woman was a strong enough alpha that she gave Alex a run for his money.

"That depends," McKenna murmured. "Is Beau still employed with you?" *Because if you fire him, I'll never work for you.*

Alex nodded, his eyes on the hectic traffic. "Sure, why wouldn't he be?"

"Just curious," McKenna answered. "Do you have extra space in your building for a doctor's office? An exam room or two? X-ray equipment? Things like that?"

He nodded. "Your office and exam rooms would be in the lower level alongside the gym and Zack's PT area."

"He handles physical therapy?" That was a surprise.

"Sports medicine," Alex clarified. "It's a sideline. He and David Tao keep us in shape."

That explained The TEAM's incredible physiques. "Let me think about it. I'd really like to talk with Beau before I commit."

A smile creased Alex's lip. "Then you don't know."

"Know what?"

"I've recommended Beau for the Medal of Honor."

Her jaw dropped. "Really?"

She'd never seen this side of Alex. He looked positively—sweet. "I'm not saying he'll get it, and to be honest, it's a long, drawn-out approval process. We won't know for years, but I've spoken with his state senator and his previous CO, and..." The truck accelerated onto the interstate. "They're both solidly behind the idea."

"Why are you doing all this?" McKenna had to know.

Alex shot her a stern look. "Because I take care of my people."

Which wasn't precisely true. Alex didn't just take care of his people. He took care of the world.

Chapter Fifty-Three

Finally. Home again.

"You want anything before we scram?" Connor asked. "Another bottled water? Pizza? I could call in an order for you?"

"Nah," Beau replied as he perched gingerly on the edge of his recliner. He'd dressed in the clean clothes Connor had been good enough to retrieve from his apartment for the ride home. A pair of old ragged jeans, an OD Army t-shirt, and boots. But the walk from Connor's SUV on the front curb to this modest living room was longer than Beau remembered.

Both Connor and Izza were in their TEAM apparel, simple black polos with the gold TEAM logo high on the left of their chest. Black work boots and jeans. Their ever-present gear bags, backpacks, and holsters. Beau's severed finger was now successfully healing, but the recent wound in his back still hurt like a mother. Stubbornly, he'd refused the pain meds the hospital wanted to send home with him. The plethora of side effects those kinds of meds came with wasn't worth the trouble.

"Man, you like white or what?" Connor asked as he scanned Beau's apartment with its solid white walls, carpet, and furniture. "Feels like winter wonderland in here."

"Yeah. White. It's clean," Beau replied. *And it's pure. Just the way I like it.*

After living in the sewers and tunnels and streets of Las Vegas most of his childhood, white soothed his ragged nerves at the end of the day. It wasn't just clean, it was untouched. Undefiled. Like Superman's fortress of solitude, this apartment was more chapel than combat zone. And Beau intended to keep it that way.

"This place reminds me of a temple," Izza said quietly, her big, brown eyes extra wide as she took in the only decoration on the walls, the simple gold-framed painting of Jesus H. Christ hanging beside the gun safe in the mostly empty dining room. The one of Him with a cream-colored robe pulled over His head and shoulders. The one with Him smiling, like He knew precisely who you were, but He liked you anyway. "You Catholic?"

He shook his head at his one and only Latino girlfriend. "Nah, but I know a guy."

"Oh, yeah?" She jerked her head at the picture behind her, asking without words. *Him?*

"Yeah," Beau admitted quietly. *Him.* He was by far no example of the Lord's best work, but Beau knew what he felt the few times he'd prayed. He'd been a believer in the Man Upstairs since he'd popped in on that Army chaplain years ago. Not that for the life of him that he could recall why he'd made that singular visit, but yeah. Sinners and saints and all that stuff.

Beau knew now why Connor loved Izza. These two kids were a study in walking, talking romance. Everything they did, they seemed to do in sync and in perfect rhythm. Like they were made for each other. Izza was every bit the covert operator Connor was, but she came with feminine intuition and other womanly benefits men just didn't have.

Once she decided she liked you, you became family, and she stepped up to take care of you. Like right damned now. Since the moment Beau manned up and apologized for being an ass, Izza had wholeheartedly adopted him. Not only had she and Connor brought him home from the hospital, but Connor said she'd filled Beau's refrigerator with ready-to-heat containers of enchiladas, tamales, and this fantastic Spanish rice you had to taste to believe. His mouth salivated thinking about it. She'd sneaked some into the hospital for him, and yes, it was that good.

That simple kindness all by itself humbled Beau. Husbands with wives were lucky SOBs. They didn't realize the power of a home cooked meal.

Izza cocked her head, her bouncing ponytail lying still on her back. "You're a good guy, you know that, Jennings?"

"No, I'm not."

Snorting—Izza's very masculine way of proving she was always right—she leveled her fist and punched his bicep a good one. "Wise up, asshole. If I say you're good, you're good enough."

"If you say so." Beau grimaced, feigning that she'd actually hurt him, when there was no way in hell a tiny thing like her could. Being good enough for Izza was a big deal, but it felt odd verbally sparring with the woman he'd once believed he'd had no use for. Izza was something else. Totally devoted to that blonde, surfer-boy sniper waiting at the door for her, the one with an I-am-so-whipped grin on his tanned face, she'd still made room in her *familia* for a guy like—*me*.

Connor opened the door, his boot tapping impatiently. "Time to go, babe. The kids are waiting."

And that was another thing. These two special operators had children! Yeah. Deep in the corner of his shriveled heart, Beau hated them because, well, they had everything he wanted.

"See ya later, Unco Bo-Bo," Izza said airily as she headed for the door.

Yeah. He was never going to live that one down.

"Be smart for a change," she taunted. "Do what the doc said. Get some rest."

"Call if you need anything," Connor ordered, stabbing his index finger at Beau in warning. "I mean anything. You're not far from Mark and Libby's new place, and Taylor's just fifteen minutes in the other direction. We live just as close, so don't be shy. Got it?"

"Trust me, he's not shy," McKenna said as she peered around the doorframe, the sparkle in her pretty green eyes the best part of Beau's day.

His heart climbed up his throat and damned near choked him. How had she known where he lived? But mostly— Damn, what a sight.

Izza jerked her chin at Beau. "Hey, McKenna. You showed up just in time. Want to explain to this bad boy how recuperation works? You know, that whole rest, rest, and more rest concept we can't seem to get through his hard head?"

"Army guys," Connor chuffed. "Come on, Izza. CMIR. CMIR."

Beau hadn't heard that acronym before, but whatever secret code these two shared, it got Izza's attention. That cocky little street fighter blushed.

"Only for you, babe," she said as, without a backward glance, the door closed on her and Connor. Beau was pretty sure he heard giggling and an ass getting slapped out there in the hall, though there was no way to know if that ass belonged to Izza or Connor.

"Damn, those two have it bad for each other," McKenna moaned. "Have you noticed that about your team, Agent Jennings?"

Oh, now she's getting formal with me. "Come here," Beau told her.

She stood across the room from him with her hands cupping her very curvaceous hips. "I mean, really? Alex and Kelsey can barely keep their hands off each other when they think no one is looking, and have you seen Zack and Mei Lennox when they're together?" She rolled her eyes and fanned herself. "Talk about hot, hot, hot. Those two can burn an ice factory down."

Beau crooked a finger and repeated, "Come here."

She shrugged her shoulders. "And David and Nancy Tao? They've got seven kids—seven! How do they keep the romance alive?"

"Come. Here," he said with more authority, pointing to the floor at his feet and wanting her on her knees. Okay, maybe not on her knees, but definitely straddling his knee or bent over it, he wasn't picky.

"Then there's Maverick and China. I'm not kidding you, the minute he came home—"

"McKenna!"

She had the nerve to shake her pretty little head, which sent a cascade of golden, reddish curls spilling over her shoulder, and a rush of hot, molten lava straight to his manhood. "Did you want something?"

"Do. Not did," he told her, still indicating the floor between his knees.

"Me?" she asked, all innocent and clueless—not.

"You," he growled, his blood on fire for the one person in the world who held any power over him.

Losing the coy routine, she came straight to him, but dropped to her knees instead of climbing onto his lap. Snuggled between his thighs, she wrapped her arms very carefully around his waist and pressed her cheek to his chest, which put her breasts on his belly. What a sublime moment. "Sorry, but I had an emergency, and couldn't get away this morning. But why aren't you at the hospital where you should be?"

"First things first. What emergency?"

"One of my favorite patients. Sweet little Walter. The chemo and radiation haven't worked, and he's not strong enough for a bone marrow transplant. Even if he were, we've run out of time." She raked her fingers over her forehead and through those silken tresses, smoothing them away from her face, her voice soft and sad against him.

"How old is he?"

"Three and a half," she replied, then sighed in frustration. "Kids always tell you they're so many years old and always a half, like they can't wait to grow up and do all the things big kids do. Only Walter..." Her voice trailed away. "What's sad is his parents won't accept the oncologist's or my opinion. They want to pursue every last option, and I don't blame them. I would, too. But Walter's at the point where all those experimental procedures amount to torture. I know they don't want to hear that their son is dying, but…" She shook her head. "I hate this part of my profession."

"I can understand why," he murmured, stroking her upper arms. "Which hospital's he at?"

"Children's National."

He took hold of her jaw, his still bandaged and very useless hammer hand in her gorgeous raspberry blonde hair as he drew her to his mouth, needing to comfort her. "Missed you, baby."

McKenna melted against him and took command of his mouth. That kiss ignited into a full body press. With his blood pounding in his veins, he dragged her onto his lap. Not straddling him, but ladylike with her legs still together. Any straddling to be done was up to her.

But fingers were everywhere. His. Hers. Their teeth clashed as their tongues made wild, slick love. This was all he wanted. This woman. This moment. "I've got a bed in the next room," he muttered around her wet, luscious lips.

"I'm thinking this is a bad idea," she breathed into his open mouth. "You're still recovering and—"

That earned her a soft slap on her ass. "I'll be the judge of that."

She sighed, and that was the answer Beau needed. Groaning, because he was in pain he'd never admit to, he lifted to his feet with McKenna in his arms. "I'm taking you to bed, so speak now if you're opposed to the idea."

Wrapping her arms around his neck, she tucked her head under his chin and murmured, "Lead on."

Chapter Fifty-Four

"More," McKenna urged as Beau sank into her rigid body, this insertion not as painful as the first time they'd made love. The second they'd retreated to his bedroom, they'd stripped each other bare. Yes, she'd been a virgin until that moment back at Maverick and China's ranch, and yes, she and Beau had had a quick, but terse discussion about her failure to share that pertinent detail the first time they'd made love.

He'd been so shocked to learn he was her first, she'd almost felt guilty for not telling him sooner. But that first time had happened so quickly, and right now, he was balls deep in make-up sex and forgiving her. The man was a gentle giant in the art of lovemaking, so worried he'd hurt her that his callused fingertips barely scraped over her sensitized nipples. He held her as carefully as a one-handed man could, his left forearm alongside her head as his hips thrust forward.

Loving the intimacy of his rugged body sliding over hers, she threaded her fingers into his lush, dark hair, cupped the back of his head, and drew him closer. Tighter. Like that was in any way possible. In truth, she strived to be as careful of his bandaged wounds as he was of her entire body, but she needed more. More thrust. More power. Just more, damn it.

All this cautious lovemaking was getting her nowhere, and she'd been on the verge way too long. It was time to take control before the friction between them turned painful and before Beau succumbed to his weakened condition. Grunting, she bucked him onto his side, then eased him onto his back before she climbed aboard and straddled his hips. "Is that okay? Am I hurting you?"

A truly beautiful smile blossomed over his handsome, rugged face, lighting those beautiful eyes up like a homing beacon in a dark and dangerous night. The man really was pretty in a rugged, sexy way. "Baby, everything you do is okay, and no, you're not hurting me."

He wiggled his hips, adjusting his position until he was once more breaching her very feminine defenses. "I like you right where you are," he growled, his voice so throaty that her heart skipped a beat in anticipation.

Lost in the tangy scent of his masculine body, she dropped to his lips and sucked the lower one between her teeth. Tugging at him to open up and give her what she wanted. Rubbing her chin against the exquisite scrape of his whiskers. His hands smoothed down her back to cup her ass, and she was certain his left hand had just squeezed just as hard as his right.

"You're getting stronger," she murmured as she trailed kisses from his cheek to his forehead, then stopped with her breasts poised over his mouth. With one sure lunge forward, his good hand slid up her bare ribcage to assist his mouth. Ever so gently, he squeezed, then consumed the tip of it.

"Yes, there," she mewled, her stomach tightening as he suckled, lighting the explosive link between her breasts and her needy, quivering core.

"You're dripping wet," he growled.

"Always. For you." She lifted just enough to impale herself, taking him into her body to his hilt. "Ah," she ground out as the burgeoning pleasure of this coming together seared her from the inside out.

"You like the top," he noticed.

"I love you," she clarified, her eyes closed tightly as the sweetest fire roared up her spine and— "Yessssss!" she hissed, her toes stuck into the mattress, launching her soul heavenward. The very foundation of the world exploded into fireworks. Stars! Her body turned into one giant feminine muscle that propelled her into the universe, her heart breaking at the sublime pleasure of mating with this once-in-her-lifetime, oh, so yummy male.

Beau arched into the pillow and roared, his long, callused fingers cupping her full breasts as he joined her in her—their—release. Panting and sweating from the ecstasy, she tipped her forehead to his chest and licked up the delicious canyon between his massive pecs. Loving the salty, sultry, musky scent of his skin. "Hmmm. Let's do it again."

Still breathing hard, he moaned, his fingertips fluttering over her backside. "I wasn't too rough, was I?"

A giggle escaped. "Like you would ever hurt me."

He cupped her ass in both hands, and a spark of worry for his still-healing finger flittered through her very satisfied mind but was lost to the overwhelming pleasantness of the moment. This was so worth waiting for.

At last, she settled comfortably to his right side, tucked in under his good arm, her head on his shoulder, and his bandaged hand on his pillow where she couldn't bump it.

"Did you mean what you said?" he asked quietly, his chin up and his gaze on the ceiling.

Startled at the timidity behind that question, McKenna lifted to one elbow to see him better. "Did I mean what?"

His hand slid to her waist, but his gaze seemed fixated on something overhead. He shrugged, not answering, and just that fast, she knew. He couldn't look at her, wouldn't. Yet he wanted to know if she really loved him. If she would keep him.

There was still a lost child looking out of this handsome rugged warrior. Expecting another rebuff. Already prepared for rejection. Maybe ready to shove off before she tossed him aside. Like she'd ever let him go now…

Ah-ah. Not happening. Slyly, she licked her fingertips, then scrubbed them over his magnificent chest, taking extra time to moisten his nipples. Resting her chin on the back of that same hand, she blew on those unsuspecting flat discs, thrilled when they puckered in response.

"Did you mean what *you* said?" she asked instead of answering.

Still not meeting her gaze, his brows slammed together as he grunted, "What'd I say?"

Slowly, she let her fingers slide down his centerline. Taking firm hold of him, she said, "I'm pretty sure you just told me you love me. Maybe not with words, but with your entire, sexy body, and with all the times you risked your life to protect mine. Am I right? Huh? I am, huh?"

Tension hissed out of him like a balloon that had been filled to bursting. Yet he shrugged, not admitting. Not denying.

McKenna scooted up until her breasts lay on that magnificent chest, yet she still maintained possession of his now hardening manhood. "Say it for me, Beau. Come on. I know you can do it. You love me. Say it," she teased, turning this confrontation into a lover's game instead of a power struggle.

She didn't really need to hear those three words. She already knew. He'd proven his rough brand of love these last weeks. In the ways he'd protected her. In the ways he'd nearly died for her. Yes, a few of those times he'd deserted her, but every time he'd only left for the purest of reasons. What woman tossed that kind of courage away just because of a few missing words?

Instead of tapping her toes like some prima donna, she dipped her lips to his chest and kissed a trail up the strong muscles of his neck to his scruffy chin. Over that chin, until she angled her head and took his stubborn mouth by storm. Licking him. Nibbling those defiant, full lips. Loving the sweet-salty taste of the man she loved with every beat of her heart. Breathing him into her soul like she was, her willing body amped up and was ready to go again.

His left arm shifted over his eyes, still hiding. Still not trusting. And that was okay. Baby steps. This lonely man who'd fought the world all his life, loved her, and she knew it.

"I love you, Beau," she told him sincerely, needing to pour her heart into him the only way she could. "I love you for your courageous heart, and, news flash, I'm never letting you go. Not today. Not next year. Not. Ever. If you let me, I'd move in with you tomorrow. If you'd rather not, I'll stay at China's, and I'll understand. Because it doesn't matter to me where we live, as long as I get to live for you. Because…" She tapped her fingertips over his heart. "I already do."

Wide manly palms smoothed up her spine until he squeezed her against him. McKenna was very sure there were tears in his eyes. That was why he refused to look at her. Pressing her lips to the hollow of his throat, she gave this tender, broken warrior what he needed to live. She gave him herself... over and over again.

A man's not much without the woman of his heart at his side. The right woman. How well Beau knew. Lying in his bed with McKenna softly snoring in his arms, he knew damned well he was half of a whole, but not the better half. Yet with this woman beside him and with his real parents now safe and sound with Alex and Kelsey, for the first time in his life, Beau felt like more than just a tossed out, broken piece of garbage.

Turned out he wasn't Bass Jennings' guttersnipe after all. *Thank you, Jesus!* He was Benjamin Beauregard Villanueva, the son of a proud, hard-working man and the best mother ever. Come morning, Beau meant to legally change his name. And with that proud new name, he meant to ask Maverick how the hell a dumb Army guy should propose to a fine upstanding woman like McKenna without making an ass of himself. She deserved nothing but the best, and Beau meant to be that man. He wasn't nothing, damn it. He was good enough. Complete. Finally home from the battle of a lifetime.

His pulse throbbed every time he looked down into her lovely, innocent face as she snuggled tightly against him. The white sheets and comforter flowed like a cloud around her. Lifting one crimson-blonde tangle, it curled instantly around his finger, just like she'd done with her long legs when they'd made love. Like a sweet seductive vine, she'd intertwined her fingers and legs with his, her heart and her soul as well. Like a warm ray of the purest sunshine. Like the holiest kind of celestial love. She'd seeped into the dark depths of him and shone light where none had been in a very long time. But the very best part? She had loved him when he was as close to gutter trash as any man could get.

There were no words to describe how much he adored her. Was the Grand Canyon big? Was the Pacific deep? The tidal wave of love welling inside of him was that immeasurable, that deep and that wide. Maybe wider.

The enormity of her declaration had humbled him. He couldn't have looked into those pretty green eyes then if he'd tried. Who was he that Jesus had sent this heavenly angel into his wretched cesspool of a life? Who indeed...

Pressing a tender kiss to the satin expanse of her forehead, Beau locked his heart against the violence of his past. Bass Jennings would scourge him with a cat-o-nine tails no more. Never again would that bastard have the power to take one blessed thing away from the child he'd kidnapped.

It was time to start over. To be the better man Beau knew he could be. To let go of the lies he'd dragged with him every dogged step of his days. All except sweet Almond Joy. Her memory alone he would keep. He would cling to.

"I love you, baby," he told McKenna from the deepest depth of his broken heart. That had to be how she'd sneaked into his life. Through all those cracks and crevices. All those breaks. Past the lies and ambushes. "I'll never hurt you, and I'll never leave you again unless you're in harm's way. I'll spend the rest of my life in your service, foremost and forever. I promise."

Arching her back, she pushed her breasts into his hands as a tiny smile tweaked the corner of her mouth. "Okay," she breathed drowsily.

He wasn't sure if she'd heard what he'd said, or if she meant what she'd said. Didn't matter. He finally had what he wanted, and this courageous woman had given it to him. Forgiveness. Trust. Her innocence and her love. The rest of her life.

Chapter Fifty-Five

Beau watched McKenna sidle into the pew alongside China and Kyrie. She'd gone ahead of him into the crowded chapel to make sure they'd have room to sit together for the commencement of Dempsey's celebration of life, whatever that was.

Once McKenna nodded back at him, he began his arduous trek forward. It shouldn't be this difficult. He'd been hurt worse before. Maybe it was the accumulation of injuries. Whatever. He walked like an old man. Past Harley, Judy, and their two boys. Past Adam and Shannon and their little guy. Then past the Stewarts. "Hi!" Lexie whispered loudly when she saw him.

Beau nodded silently at her quick smile despite Alex's disapproving head shake. Man, that guy could chill an iceberg. Well, let him be pissed. Mother needed her entire team here today.

"I saved two places," Kyrie was whispering to McKenna as Beau approached. "Isn't Beau coming?"

"Probably not," China answered, then frowned over McKenna's shoulder. "What are *you* doing out of bed, Agent Jennings?" she hissed. "You shouldn't be here."

Cautiously, Beau lowered his butt alongside his future bride. Backs could heal, but Mother's broken heart would not. "Please. It's Villanueva if you don't mind, Miss China. And

I'm here to honor my friend." He tipped his head to Kyrie. "How's the kitten business?"

Kyrie beamed, reaching past her grouchy mother for his hand. "I'm so happy you're here. You scared the heebie-jeebies outta me! Thought I'd never see you again."

When her pretty eyes brimmed, Beau swiped a quick hand over his face to keep from bawling with her. *Holy fu... um, heck.* Most folks didn't miss a guy like him, much less admit it out loud. Yet the mental shifts he had to make for these kinds of emotional displays were kind of—nice. He shook the tips of her outstretched fingers and told her, "I'm too tough to die. You're not rid of me yet."

"I don't want to get rid of you!" she replied enthusiastically.

"But you should be home," China insisted as—

Damned if Maverick didn't pick that moment to limp stiffly, albeit leaning heavily on a cane, into the other end of the pew. Breathing hard, he took up residence alongside Kyrie.

"Dad! You came!" she cried as she wrapped her arms around him.

"Of course," he growled, wincing as he bowed his chin to the top of her head. Pale and sweating, he'd dressed all in black from his slacks and button-up shirt to his suede vest. But man, he looked like shit.

Beau spiked a brow at the dumbass. Maverick had no business being there. Yet he offered a crooked grimace, then tipped two fingers to his forehead in a silent salute that clearly said, *'We're both dumbasses.'*

Well, yeah.

"God, give me strength," China muttered even as Maverick stretched his arm along the back of the pew, reaching for his wife. "I'm surrounded by men whose ears are obviously painted on!"

Beau noticed she still interlocked her fingers with Maverick's, though. He took the hint. While Kyrie leaned backward into her parents' embrace, he put his good arm around McKenna and whispered, "Thanks for not giving me crap about coming."

"Like I could stop you," she muttered.

How Beau wanted to kiss that sassy mouth, but now was not the time. The minister had just taken the pulpit, and her lips were still swollen from last night. "You could've tried," he said as he buried his nose in her hair and teased her earlobe with his tongue.

She turned to look up at him. "I'm just glad you didn't fall walking in. When this is over, we're going straight back to your place, and I'm putting you to bed."

"Promise?"

Sparks flashed in those pretty emerald greens. "You're not funny," she hissed.

"I'm kind of funny."

Her brows turned into an impressive V. "No. You're not. Nothing but bed rest until Dr. Decker okays you for light duty. Understood?" She was using her stern doctor voice on him and damn. That was kind of hot.

"Yes, ma'am." He nuzzled her ear and loving the way her eyes changed from mellow green to brittle emeralds when she thought she was being drill sergeant tough. To be honest, McKenna didn't have a mean bone in her body. He'd checked.

Dempsey's celebration of life ended up being a simple affair, where everyone mingled and told what stories they could about her and Mother. Boxes of tissues were passed, and tears were shed, but at the end of the event, The TEAM, a rowdy construct of hard-assed, badass friends dressed in slacks and compassion, surrounded her. With Alex on her left and her companion Justice on her right, the day finally proved too much. She buried her perfectly composed face in her elegantly manicured fingertips and fell apart.

Beau had never seen so many hard men tear up. Some brushed their emotions away. Some just stared at the ceiling. But this team of warriors had Mother's six, and at last, she knew it.

"I don't know what to say," she murmured when she could finally speak. "I've been so foolish. All this time..."

Sweet Ember Dennison ducked past Alex and grabbed hold, squeezing Mother hard. "You don't have to say anything. Just know we love you, and we're here for you, Sasha. Always have been. Always will be."

Mother cried as she clung to Ember while poor Justice patted her back. Hell, everyone cried. Losing a child was hard, and a couple of these folks had also lost a child. Even Beau.

Due to their injuries, he and Maverick had been planted on the front pew in the chapel while everyone else gathered around Mother. Beyond the group of friends, a magnificent oil painting of sweet, innocent Dempsey presided over the gathering, the urn with her remains off to one side, a magnificent arrangement of white roses to the other. One single red rose stood out against all that white. Brave and bright and true.

Beau looked up into the angelic face of that childlike young woman. Dempsey looked so much like AJ. How he missed his sister.

A rough clap on his shoulder turned him around and there was Maverick still at his side, wiping a hand over his face, and obviously fighting his emotions. "Don't," he told Beau, his voice ragged and tight. "Just don't."

Don't what?

Oh. That. Beau swallowed hard, instantly understanding what Maverick meant, but could not say. As tough as it was, the ones they'd lost would always be with them. AJ and Darrell were part of what made Beau and Maverick who they were today. But Jesus, it was a heavy load to bear, and watching Mother go through the same awful thing, offering useless condolences that would never—ever—fill the hole in her heart... Just. Plain. Sucked.

"I need to talk to you," Beau said, gulping down his pain and grief. Forcing it back.

"Sure." Maverick sniffed and inclined his head. He had to be operating on sheer willpower by now. "What's up, bro?"

Damn. *Bro.* Beau cleared his throat, then swallowed hard before he could meet Maverick's tender gaze. If only he had been this guy's real brother, things could've been so different. But he wasn't. And wasn't it odd to be jealous of a dead man for that unique honor? He coughed, not sure now was the best time or place for this discussion but needing the distraction before he fell apart.

"I, umm..." Beau cleared his throat, hopefully for the last time. Oh, what the hell. Maverick might as well know. "I'm going to ask McKenna to, umm..."

Talk about feeling stupid. Hell, he'd never once asked for directions or any man's advice, yet here he was, trusting Maverick with something intimately private and confidential. Trusting him not to be the ass Beau knew he could be. To be that older, possibly wiser, brother. Summoning his last ounce of courage, Beau blurted, "I want to ask McKenna to marry me."

"Yeah?" Maverick bit out as he nodded encouragingly. "And?"

His eye color changed from deep, angry to a more golden hue, but Jesus, was he tearing up? It was weird how Maverick had just morphed into something—someone—else. Someone Beau had no experience with. *So, this is what it feels like to be a brother.* He swallowed hard at this strange new camaraderie warming the airwaves between him and the guy called Cowboy.

Jesus, how do I say this? "Ah, how'd you ask China, I mean…" Beau scrubbed his good hand over his hard head. "Did you take her dancing or something before you popped the question? Wine and dine her? Or what? How's a guy do that?"

A tiny smile eased the creases in Maverick's tired face. "You do know McKenna wants you to take her to Belize, right?"

Oh, yeah. That. "She told China?" *Duh, and China told you.*

"Women talk, so yeah. McKenna's never been out of the country, but she's adventurous. You ever thought of whisking her off to Belize and dancing under the stars with her?"

Precisely what McKenna had asked once upon a time. Guess women did a lot of talking. "That's a good idea," Beau admitted.

"Hey, you don't have to be Gene Kelly or Fred Astaire. It's not rocket science, Beau. Just make her happy. Give her something to smile about every morning. Tell her a joke. Surprise her with flowers once in a while. Find out what makes her happy. If it's horses, buy her a horse. If it's a baby, give her a baby. Make love with her every night. Never let her go." Maverick shrugged. "Least that's what I do."

Beau knuckle-bumped his teammate. "You're all right for an old guy."

"You're not so bad yourself," Maverick replied, a wistful glimmer in his eye, "for an asshole."

Beau grinned at the brotherly insult. But it was time to go before McKenna put a halt to his plans. Gingerly, he eased to his feet, holding his back, and trying not to make a scene. Sitting down was easy. Getting up was not.

"Where are you going now?"

Beau grunted in pain for thinking he was in any way up for this next mission. "Got some place to be," he said, then tipped his head and quietly told Maverick everything.

"Really? He's leaving tonight? You're sure?"

Beau nodded solemnly. "That's what the nurse said."

"Then I'll go with you," Maverick growled as he lifted unsteadily to his feet.

"Are you sure?" Beau had to ask.

"Hell, yeah," Maverick replied, his voice hoarse and uncommonly low—like a growl. "This is what we do, isn't it?"

"It is," Beau agreed as he eyed China, who was deep in conversation with Kelsey. "But won't she be mad?"

"Which is why I'm not going to tell her. Yet."

Well, okay then. Like two old soldiers, Beau and Maverick inched to the rear of the chapel. This was a better plan anyway, leaving with an accomplice. To anyone watching, like sharp-eyed Alex, they probably looked like two old codgers helping each other totter to the restroom. No one would suspect a thing…

Chapter Fifty-Six

"Have you seen that husband of mine?" China asked, her blue eyes bright with barely restrained anger. "Anywhere? I can't seem to find him."

McKenna scanned the dwindling crowd, her gaze instantly on the front pew where only minutes ago, she'd spied Beau and Maverick talking instead of arguing. How rare was that? "He was with Beau a minute ago." Maybe longer. Come to think of it, she hadn't seen either of them for ten, twenty minutes. "They can't have gone far as slow as they're moving."

"Humph," China grumbled, her dander up. "I am so tired of those two. If I have to hobble that man of mine—"

"Mom," Kyrie murmured, her cell in her hand. "Dad says don't worry. He and Beau had something they had to do tonight. They'll be okay."

"Where is he?" China snapped the cell out of Kyrie's hand. "Cowboy? What the hell—?"

McKenna's toes were tapping. How could Beau leave her today of all days? That man!

"Oh. Okay then. Yes, I'll be right there," China whispered, then handed the cell to McKenna. "Beau wants to talk with you."

And he was going to get such an earful! "You'd better not have left this chapel," she told him in no uncertain terms, looking down the center aisle for that man.

"Jesus, I love it when you're pissed at me," rumbled over the connection.

"Then you're going to adore me when I get my hands on you."

"Already do. But listen—"

"Where are you?"

"Children's National."

McKenna's anger fizzled. "Excuse me? You're…? Why?"

"Because this brave little soldier needs an honor guard," Beau replied quietly, his voice gone low and rumbly. "Don't worry. Maverick and I will see that Walter isn't alone when he passes. We'll take especially good care of him."

"Walter?" she asked just to be clear. "Where are his parents?"

"They're out in the hall arguing. I think they're finally accepting the truth. This little guy's barely breathing. If you hurry—"

"I'll be right there." McKenna handed the cell to Kyrie. "I have to tell Mother goodbye. Then—"

"We're with you," China said. "Let's go."

It took them a full hour to get to Children's National, park the car, and run up to Walter's room. His parents, JoBeth and Rodney Wrigley waited in the hall. Devastated. Their hopes crushed by reality.

"I hate you," JoBeth cried even as she wrapped her arms around McKenna. "He's dying. He's really dying."

"She's only saying that because you're right, Doc Fitz. We should've listened to you," Rodney explained. Both handsome professionals with law degrees, they made a stunningly sad couple. Rodney had once played for the Philadelphia Eagles. A handsome black American, he'd gone from tackle football to the courtroom, and he'd done well. "We just couldn't let him go," he said, his voice tight as he glanced at his son's closed door. "We thought if we never gave up hope…"

McKenna returned the desperate, passionate hug from the little boy's mother as she told Walter's broken father, "I'm so sorry. This was never about being right. I was only trying to prepare you for all scenarios."

"We should've listened," he said as he dashed his tears away.

JoBeth pulled away from McKenna and fell into her husband's open arms. With her mocha coloring and his much darker skin, they were a fairytale couple come to life. Except for tonight when their hearts were breaking.

"I don't really hate you, Doc Fitz," JoBeth murmured even as she burrowed under her husband's chin. "It's just this damned cancer. Right now, I hate everything, but not you. Not really."

"I understand. Please join me?" McKenna asked before she palmed the door to Walter's room open.

And there they were, two weary warriors, Beau and Maverick. If she lived to be a hundred, McKenna would never forget the resolute determination etched on their exhausted, but rugged, handsome faces while they sat at Walter's bedside.

China and Kyrie went to Maverick. McKenna went to Beau. "You really can't help yourself, can you? You have to protect people, don't you? It's the way you're made, isn't it?" McKenna asked as she cupped his jaw.

Beau lifted a solemn gaze to hers, his eyes bleary, his lips thin and tight as he leaned into her hand. "We need to talk," he ground out as he kissed the center of her palm. "Not now, but tonight. For sure. After you take me home. Promise. Don't let me fall asleep. There's things I need to tell you."

Leaning into him and wishing they had more time to do just that, she pressed a kiss to his forehead. "Promise. Let me check on Walter now."

"I love you, woman," Beau ground out before she stepped away, his voice ragged with grief.

And there it was, the truth finally spoken. The truth she'd seen shining in his eyes so many times during these past few days. He didn't see himself as a gentle, giving man. Yet he was, always put himself between Death and the victims it stalked. Only tonight, Death would win, and it was wrecking him.

"I love you, too," she told him truly.

Slowly, McKenna left him to join JoBeth and Rodney at their son's side. Walter's readouts were grim. Once a bouncy toddler, his fragile skeletal frame now labored with every shallow breath. It wouldn't be long now. "Would you like to be alone with him?" she asked his parents.

Rodney shook his head. "No, ma'am. I want these men at Walter's side when he goes. Your husband prayed with us. He asked Jesus to keep us stronger than a Ranger, and—" His voice broke.

"And more stubborn than jarheads," JoBeth continued, her fingers skimming over what was left of Walter's thin hair. Her sad eyes filled with a mother's undying love for the weary little soldier at her hands. "Thank you for sending your man to us in these final minutes. My baby's been fighting this battle for so long."

McKenna glanced over their shoulders to Beau. *My husband? My man?* "I didn't send him. It's just the way he's made." *And I love him because of it.*

Beau's black eyes glistened back at her, but not once did he blink. There it was again, that subtle shift in the universe that told her he'd make such a good father. That he deserved the sweet love of a child, and that even now, his heart was breaking at the loss of another little one.

Yes, denying motherhood had always been the safest course for McKenna, at least, that was what she'd once thought. Never having a child neatly avoided the deadly, pain-filled traps of love and loss and grief. It avoided the harsh realities of what her own mother had put her through. If you never had a baby, you never stood to hurt it or lose it, right?

Wrong. At last she understood. If you never had a child, you never knew the tender mercies of living with your heart outside your body. The grace of falling in love with that child's father every single day for the rest of your life.

Suddenly, McKenna didn't want safe. She wanted to make that gentle, grumpy man over there, the one with the sheen of tears in his perpetually angry eyes—happy. After what he'd missed in his own life, after all he'd suffered, he deserved the family he'd always craved. And she wanted to be the one who gave it to him, to see his face when she placed a squirming, wet newborn infant in his callused hands. She wanted to be there when his heart broke from nothing but the sheer joy and love and happiness of fatherhood.

Yes, McKenna had known her share of trouble, but she'd also known the infinite, loving care of her father. Beau had had no one, but she'd had Sanders Fitzgerald in her corner every day. And the love of that one humble, hard-working man had made all the difference.

Beau groaned, and in the split-second it took for McKenna to glance at him, then back to Walter, the monitor sent a steady beep to heaven that it had gained another angel.

McKenna turned the noise-makers off. The nurses would soon dash in to assist Walter's parents. The chaplain was most likely already waiting outside or on his way. Even in death, there was a process to smooth the way for all concerned.

JoBeth choked as she gathered her son up from the pillow, pressed him to her heart and sobbed. Rodney gathered his sad family into his arms while grief jerked out of him.

McKenna looked at Beau, who sat with his head bowed. Maverick sat stone-faced next to him, his hand in the middle of Beau's back. Poor Kyrie outright bawled. Tears streaked China's face.

It was time to go home.

Chapter Fifty-Seven

Beau sat still and quiet in the back seat of the Uber driver's car, his fist raised to his mouth, chewing on his knuckle. He'd gone from his room in the hospital this morning to a somber celebration of life, then to the quiet passing of a cancer-ridden child. All in one day. Jesus, he felt like an old, old man. Too crippled to stay on his feet and utterly useless when it came to saving kids. Not Dempsey. Not Walter. Not AJ. What the fuck good was he?

McKenna's soft and warm fingertips fluttering on his knee pulled him out of his mood. Beau didn't know how it worked, but when she looked into his eyes, she seemed to see past what others saw. She connected with him on some primal level, where souls didn't have to define themselves or explain why and who they were. They could just hold hands and understand each other without words and feelings getting in the way. They could just be.

He pulled his gaze off the traffic passing by in a blur that he really wasn't seeing and back to her pretty face. Even now, she radiated a calmness he didn't understand. He wanted to hit something, to scream and curse and rail at the total unfairness of Death and Life, and he wanted an answer to the ancient question of why some kids got it good while others got nothing. Why some floated through life with a silver spoon between their lips, while others got shit on, fucked, and died early. Just once, it'd be nice if someone—*Someone! I'm talking to you, Jesus*—leveled the playing field for little kids and puppies, for kittens and old people. Just once, it'd be nice if there were no headlines about child abuse, animal neglect, or murder on the morning news.

Yet with one soft touch, McKenna had tapped into that mountain of rage, and he wasn't so, so angry anymore. Not calm yet. But manageable.

Lifting that slender hand to his mouth, he kissed her knuckles. No words. Just a kiss. If he lived to be a tired old man, which wasn't likely in his chosen profession, he'd never stop needing the taste of her on his lips and the gentle touch of her fingers.

Before long, they were inside his apartment. Not in bed. Not naked. Instead, she'd slid out of her shoes and sat in the center of his couch, her knees curled up and waiting for him to join her.

Beau left his shoes at the front door alongside hers and nestled in behind her. He needed McKenna inside his arms for this next revelation. Yeah. He was a sucker for the downtrodden, the innocent and the helpless. Always had been. Always would be. It was time she knew why.

"I hope you know how much I love you," she murmured as she ducked her head and kissed his hand.

"I don't understand why. I'm not a good guy," he began softly.

"Yes, you—"

"Shush. Hear me out." Beau held on tight with his nose in the back of her neck, breathing in the feminine scent of her skin as he began at the beginning. He'd never told anyone. He'd nearly told Maverick. He needed to tell McKenna. "I'm sorry if it's not what you want to hear, but it's true. I'm not who you think I am. I've done things to survive that I'm not proud of."

She nestled her back to his front. "I know better but go on. Tell me your worst."

Jesus, he loved this feisty woman. "I hit the streets when I was just a kid, but there's more." The day it all began rolled over him like a fiery sandstorm in Iraq. "I had a sister. AJ, short for Almond Joy."

"Your parents named her after a candy bar?"

He nodded. "Druggies' brains don't work like yours and mine. Don't even know if Fidget was my mom's real name, but it fit her. Especially when she needed to score. Of course, now I know she wasn't my real mom. Not that it matters anymore, but, yeah. Almond Joy. I didn't know then, but Bass and Fidget Jennings stole me. Guess Fidget wanted a baby, so Bass probably grabbed the first one he came across. Lucky me."

McKenna's fingers curled around his wrists, careful of his bandaged left hand as she crossed them over her chest.

Beau blew out a belly full of air. "Anyway, I'm pretty sure he hated me on sight. Never went a day without getting slapped or the shit kicked out of me, spat on, or yelled at by that asshole. Sorry, I didn't mean to—"

McKenna growled. "Stop apologizing. He *was* an asshole. Was Fidget as cruel?"

"Fidget? Nah. She was the most passive person in the world. Just took whatever Bass doled out."

"She never protected you?"

"She never stood a chance," Beau murmured. "Fidget was as powerless as me and AJ. Drugs. That's all she cared about. She let him do whatever he wanted as long as he hooked her up."

McKenna shook her head, her body tense against his, and Beau couldn't help himself. He kissed her neck and held her, so damned thankful for her anger at his lying parents. Yeah, they failed miserably in the child-rearing department, but he'd never hated Fidget the way he did Bass. Fidget didn't have a mean bone in her body. But Bass was a stone-cold killer.

"Everything changed when Fidget came home with AJ." That was the day Beau stopped caring about the abuse or the name-calling. AJ was the one and only oasis in the shit storm called his life. Tiny and perfect, she'd needed him then as much as he'd needed her. "I used to stand guard over her cardboard box baby bed—"

McKenna twisted to glare at him, her eyes wide and her dander up. "A cardboard box! Really?"

"Shhhhh. My story. Just listen. Then you can decide if you want to stay. But yeah, I slept under the kitchen table. When she was tiny, she slept in her box on the table." Absentmindedly, he scratched his fingers through his hair, remembering the itch of lice and ringworm. "They didn't want her to get bit, so they kept her off the floor. There's fleas and bugs and rats in Vegas. But me—" *I was fair game.*

"Jesus," McKenna hissed, her rage an exquisite thing of beauty to watch unfold. The green in her eyes flashed with an internal fire, and her lips pinched. Even her grip on his arms clenched tighter. It brought tears to his eyes. McKenna would've been such a good mom for AJ.

"Anyway, I used to stand guard over her box, you know, not because they'd ever hurt her, but because I couldn't take my eyes off her. I think I fell in love with AJ at first sight. Everything about her was tiny and perfect. Her little fingernails. Her lips. Her eyebrows. You could barely see her lashes because her hair was light gold, but even they were perfect. Curled like tiny butterfly wings. She was like a miracle, you know, sent from heaven to me." *So clean. So pink. So pretty. So mine.*

"Jesus knows I loved her," he told McKenna, his nose still in her hair. "She was skinny and blonde, no more than a puff of air in one of those receiving blankets she came home in. She wrinkled her nose when she slept. She fussed. The way she passed gas with an adorable grunt always made me smile. I was proud of her, you know? She was my own Christmas angel. The one who genuinely smiled at me just because I was there."

McKenna had gone still in his arms, holding her breath.

"Anyway…" He closed his eyes, struggling to swallow. "She was already sick when they brought her home. I didn't know it then, but she'd been born addicted to the crap Fidget used. AJ screamed and cried for months. That made Bass mad enough to stay away, not like we missed him. But he started drinking more. Always had a bottle of some rotgut within reach. He got meaner. Accused me of pinching his little girl to make her cry. Told me to stay clear of her."

His little girl. But never my little boy. Why that still hurt, Beau would never understand, but it did. Then and now.

"Did you?" McKenna asked. "Stay away from AJ?"

"No, but I got sneakier. Used to hide in the alley and wait until he left. Then I'd circle the house to make sure he was really gone before I went back inside." Beau ran his good hand over his head. "Used to rock that stupid cardboard box for hours until she wore herself out crying."

"Where was Fidget during all this? Didn't she care for her?"

"Not sure she could by then."

"So who changed AJ's diapers and fed her and—? You did that, didn't you?"

He shrugged. It was no big deal. "Someone had to."

"Oh, Beau," McKenna breathed.

Yes, most days he was the one to change AJ's diaper and keep her clean. So what? He did her laundry too, because he loved AJ more than he loved himself. That was what big brothers did. He'd fixed plenty of baby bottles over her short two years of life, too. The little thing had to eat, and Fidget was usually oblivious.

"Then one day she opened her pretty blue eyes and stopped crying. Just like that, the sun came out." Beau could still feel that tiny little angel's head under his chin when her wretched sobs had turned into soft murmurs, like she knew she was safe with her big brother. In that instant, she'd made all the misery and every last beating bearable. Hell, he'd endure them and more for just one more day with her.

"Anyway..." He cleared his throat. "Bass sent me for more candles. Told me to bring back a propane tank if I could steal one. I wasn't there when it happened. Only know they were screaming at each other when I got home. Thought Bass was mad because I didn't get a tank like he told me to, but then..." Once again bile filled his gut, and Beau didn't want to go on.

'Do you know what you did?'

'This is your fault, you bitch! Not mine! You gave it to her!'

'I didn't mean to. I hate you!'

'Never should've believed a word outta your lying mouth! You're no mother! You're nothing but a sack-of-shit whore!'

Jesus, they hadn't even picked AJ up to comfort her. They didn't even try to keep her breathing. Just hurled ugly accusations and promised to kill each other.

And so on...

And so on...

Until it was too late.

"I think Fidget put the wrong powder in AJ's baby bottle," Beau finally whispered. "That's all that made sense. She didn't mean it, just finally decided to get out of bed and take care of her daughter, and... Yeah. She gave my little sister heroin. Once I cleared the front door, I dropped the bag and ran to AJ, but by then she was barely breathing. Jerking, you know. Drooling." He stretched his fingers and splayed them, remembering how AJ had wrapped her entire, sweaty little hand around his index finger, her blue eyes begging him to save her. Whimpering. Her tiny chest caving in more and more with every seizure until...

Beau shook his head, not sure why he'd started this horrendous trip down memory lane. McKenna didn't need to hear this godawful story, and he didn't need to relive it. He knew damned well how it ended.

Yet McKenna nestled in closer, pressed her back flat against him while she curled his hands once more around her. Tighter. Not pushing away. Just absorbing his information overload. "Don't stop now," she whispered.

Beau nodded, the hell kicked out of him all over again. "So yeah." He swallowed hard, wishing he could get his heart to climb back down his throat where it belonged. "Bass grabs me up and slams me up against the doorjamb in the kitchen. Starts screaming it was my fault. That I did it. That he never should've let me in. That I wasn't his kid. Like I didn't already know."

No fuckin' shit. By then, Beau had figured that truth out all by himself. Else why was his skin so much darker than AJ's? Than Bass's and Fidget's? Why was his hair black, while theirs was blond? Why'd his old man slap him around and call him so many mean names Beau couldn't bear to remember even today? Yeah. A kid in that house grew up with more questions than answers. And a helluva lot more scars.

Beau always knew he didn't belong in that house. Never had. He hadn't even belonged in his mostly Hispanic neighborhood, which hadn't seemed right or fair. Everyone there was poor, yet even the kids he looked like had no use for the shithead son of Bass Jennings. It didn't help that more than a few of their mothers worked for his old man. That he slapped them around as regularly as he did Beau. But never AJ. That was the one and only thing Bass Jennings ever did right. Like Fidget and Beau, he'd loved sweet little Almond Joy. An angel named after a candy bar.

"Then what happened?" McKenna asked as she turned sideways on his lap.

"Then he dragged off his belt and cursed the day I was born. After he whipped me, he dragged me over to the kitchen table. He lit the candles I brought home. Four of them." Beau tried to joke it off. "Glad I didn't steal more."

McKenna gasped, her shoulders lifted, cringing. "He tortured you?" Her green eyes begged Beau not to confirm that awful truth.

Beau didn't want her pity, but McKenna needed to stay with him because she knew and wanted him, not because she pitied him.

Her palms cupped his chin, her fingers holding his head, forcing him to look at her. "Deep breaths," she told him in her doctor-voice. "Focus on me, Beau. Breathe, baby, just breathe." Smart woman. She'd used his words. "We're here in your immaculate apartment, which I have to tell you, is quite an amazing accomplishment considering your gender, your job, and your childhood."

"I like white," he said simply, fighting the urge to break down like a sissy jarhead. But looking into her clear, green eyes, it was hard to remember the reject he was. There was no doubt glimmering there, not an iota of disbelief. Only trust. Only love.

His diaphragm relaxed enough to finally draw in a complete breath. "Someone must've called 9-1-1 because all at once, the police showed up. The paramedics, too. All the neighbors were standing on the street. He threw me out the back door and into the alley behind the house before he let anyone come in, though. Told me to start running, that he'd make sure everyone knew I killed AJ. Said it wouldn't matter what I said. Once he talked to the cops, he'd make sure they hunted me down. That if they didn't find me, he'd kill me if he ever saw me again."

"So you ran?"

"I had to. Didn't stop until I joined the Army. Not sure I've stopped yet." *Not sure I can.*

"Where is this asshole?" McKenna demanded sharply. "Didn't Alex say Bass Jennings is in prison? We need to pay that son-of-a-bitch a visit!"

Jesus, just when Beau thought he couldn't love this woman more, he realized that he could. "Doesn't matter. I know the truth now. Alex gave me a copy of his findings. Can you believe he had me investigated?" The man thoroughly amazed Beau. Such an ass. Such a jarhead. Such a damned good—friend.

"According to the Vegas ME, Fidget died the same night AJ did, both from heroin overdoses. Either Bass made her shoot up or she did it to kill herself. No one will ever know for sure, but that's how I think it went down. Fidget was tired of living anyway. I know I was."

"No," McKenna cried, her eyes swimming. "Don't ever say that. Ever! My mother killed herself and—"

He bumped his forehead to hers. "I'm sorry. That wasn't what I meant. But life was so damned hard. You just don't know."

"I wish I'd known you then," she said, her hand gently cupping his cheek. "Me and Dad would've taken you in and fed you and loved you and—"

He closed his eyes at the thought of having had another little blonde girl in his life during those dark days. Maybe he'd be someone else now if he'd been so fortunate.

McKenna inclined her head to his. "I'm never leaving you, Beau Villanueva," she said, using her very stern doctor voice this time. "News flash. As your doctor, I prescribe one McKenna Fitzgerald to be taken at bedtime for the next ten days. Another one every morning."

"Just ten?" The next question tumbled off his treacherous lips. "How about the rest of your life?" He could almost hear Maverick's voice in the back of his head saying, '*Way to go, dumbass.*'

McKenna's head canted, and all that lush, gold hair tumbled over Beau's arm like his own private waterfall. "Are you asking me what I think you are?"

He nodded. "I can't breathe without you, McKenna, and I don't want to. I know this isn't Belize, but I'll take you there, and I'll dance under the stars with you, and I'll do anything to make you happy. Only... Take a chance on me? Marry me?"

She answered the same way sweet little AJ did. With one arm hooked over his neck and her ear pressed against his heart, she simply sighed and replied, "Yes."

Beau tipped her chin up and covered her mouth with his as he swallowed her kindness to hide his tears. There was still more to tell, but it could wait. He had a woman to love, and he needed her more than anything. Even more than his ghosts.

Chapter Fifty-Eight

Alex drove to Massachusetts alone, not wanting to burden Kelsey with yet another drama for which there was no sure conclusion. He'd asked another agent to join him, but Seth McCray hadn't gotten in from Cuba yet. He'd promised to hook up with Alex if his connections fell as scheduled. But he'd run into weather delays at his layover in Florida, and Alex wasn't sure he'd make it. That was life for you. Shit happened.

With the remaining Lynch sisters in jail and Catalina—for now—out of the country, things had calmed down in Virginia. The TEAM was back to business as usual, and most agents were once again on covert ops. Maverick and Beau were still on extended leave. Mother too. She and Justice were somewhere in the Pacific. The TEAM wives were back to their regularly scheduled programs, which as far as Kelsey was concerned revolved around Lexie.

At the moment, Alex sat across from a man he barely recognized: Aaron Pope. Gone was the good-looking former NBA star with the cocky buzzcut, lightning reflexes, and quick smile. In his stead, a broken, twitchy man sat at the kitchen table between them, thumping his thigh with what remained of his left hand, though he probably didn't realize what he was doing.

Gaunt and too thin for his tall, lanky frame, Aaron was under house arrest at his parents' home in Boston. He stood to go to prison for his crimes, and he knew it. He'd been formally charged and was complicit in more than a few of Catalina Montego's vicious assaults on young military men along the East Coast. Dressed in a simple white t-shirt that accentuated his skeletal frame, Aaron had yet to make eye contact that lasted more than a fleeting tenth of a second. Had yet to acknowledge Alex. But this meeting had to happen. For both their sakes.

Instead of his normal business suit, Alex came to this meeting in the accepted casual wear of his crew, jeans and The TEAM's black polo. But after all the years he'd spent searching for Aaron, Alex had no idea what to say. The man across from him was a complete stranger.

So he began at the beginning. "Do you remember me?"

Aaron's head bobbed, but as he had all along, he avoided eye contact. *The coward.* "Yeah. You're Alex. Thought you were my buddy? My friend?"

"I was. I am." *Look at me, damn you.*

Aaron sneered, his gaze still flitting everywhere but to Alex. "Then where you been all this time, huh?"

"Looking for you," Alex answered evenly as he reached into the briefcase at his feet and tugged out the stack of file folders. Each thicker than the last, he'd stuffed these files with one investigative research after another and dozens of dead-end leads. Sliding them across the table, he said, "Been looking for years."

Aaron's Adam's apple bobbed, a sharp blade in his too thin neck as he fingered the papers that spilled out of the folders. The man resembled Ichabod Crane in Washington

Irving's *"The Legend of Sleepy Hollow."* Except Aaron was much thinner than Irving's gangly hero, and all four fingers on his left hand had been reduced to one-knuckle stumps.

"Where have you been all this time?" Alex asked even as he winced at the brutal evidence of Montego's sadism.

"Around," came back to him with an indifferent grunt.

Alex called bullshit. "What'd she do? Pay you to abduct those other men or did you get to sleep with her when you were her good little boy?"

At last. Angry, pissed off eye contact. Finally, there was the man Alex remembered, Aaron's eyes gray and mean and sparking with rage.

So Alex fed the fire. Leaning into the table, he snarled, "I asked you a question, Marine."

A tic started in Aaron's clenched jaw. His nostril's flared and Alex squared his shoulders, prepared for war. But as quickly as the storm manifested, it died. Aaron slumped back in his chair. "You think I wanted this? You think I stayed with her because I liked what she did to us?"

"I think you had a duty to escape, you asshole, but you didn't!" There was only one way to get through to this broken man, and Alex intended to get there.

"Yeah, well fuck you! You have no idea what I lived through!"

"Then enlighten the whole world how tough things were for you! You joined the Corps, you pussy-whipped reject! They didn't come looking for you. Why don't you tell me what was so important that you stayed with a psychotic bitch like Catalina Montego?"

"Because of them! Us! That's why!"

Not good enough. "Because of who, damn it?"

"My men! The other guys! None of us had a choice! Once we woke up from whatever crap she poisoned us with, it was either do what she wanted or watch her mutilate us. Some guy. Some kid. Shit, Alex! She took everything. Our clothes. Our Pride. And when one of us disobeyed or broke, we all paid!" Aaron scraped his remaining fingers over his thinning hair, tearing long scratches into his scalp, forehead, and down to his cheeks. "She made sure we paid in blood. If she didn't take a finger, she took other b-body parts. And if any of us tried to escape..." A sob wrenched out of his throat. "God. We went into the w-w-wood chipper."

Aaron's peculiar choice of referring to himself as *'we'* indicated how thoroughly he identified with Montego's other victims. He and his brothers had melded into a collective 'we' to survive. He'd witnessed utter depravity that ensured the collective endured. He'd been caught in a vicious circle. It was no wonder he hadn't escaped.

Alex swallowed the bile creeping up the back of his throat. He would have done the same thing. For the first time, he stretched his arm across the table and extended a hand to his friend. "She attacked my TEAM," he said more gently. "We never would've found you if she hadn't come after me through one of my guys."

"Wh-what'd she do?"

"She left a severed finger in a hotel room. Said she knew where I lived, and if I gave her what she wanted, I could have the rest of *'him'*. At that time, I thought she meant you. Turns out she'd already kidnapped one of my agents. It was his finger."

Aaron blinked. "Really? You thought of m-me?"

Alex nodded. "Your parents aren't the only ones who've been looking for you."

That seemed to get through to Aaron. "You keep saying guys and agents. You run an insurance agency or something?"

Honest mistake. Alex shook his head, not breaking eye contact. "I own a covert surveillance company that goes after bitches like Montego and assholes like her brother. Sometimes we get paid to end people like them. Sometimes we just do it because it's the right thing to do."

Aaron ran what remained of his left hand under his nose, then swiped that same hand on his pants. "What'd, umm, *you* do to piss her off?"

"Sent a couple of my guys into Cuba after her brother. One of them killed Roland in the tunnels under the Presidio Modelo."

"I been there," Aaron whispered, his eyes gone wide with what had to be horrific memories. "It's an awful place, that tunnel. You… you say Roland's dead?" It was hard not to miss the timid note of hope in his voice. "For real? He's… d-dead?"

"And the women and children he stole and assaulted are back home with their families. Every single one of them. They're alive. He's not."

Aaron leaned forward. Listening. "When'd that happen?"

"Almost a month ago."

"Whoa," he murmured, his gaze flitting to the left and the right, blinking like he was trying to figure things out. "That's when she went crazy. Shit. She killed three of us in one night. Ground us up. Kept screaming and crying, howling, you know? Throwing everything that wasn't nailed down into her chipper. Like a banshee or something."

"More like a raving lunatic." Alex kept his palm raised and his fingers extended, just in case. But so far Aaron hadn't given any indication he'd seen the gesture or knew what to do with it.

"Wh-who?" Aaron asked, his voice gone soft. "Who's the lucky SOB what killed him? He still have all his digits?"

A quiet knock at the kitchen door interrupted as Aaron's father peered in. An older, gray-haired gentleman in wire-rimmed glasses, he looked like a weary version of Pinocchio's father, Geppetto. "Your friend's here." Bruce Pope said. "Should I show him in?"

"Thank you, yes," Alex replied as he withdrew his hand.

Aaron ducked both his hands under the table then. His face fell, and his lashes came down. Damn it. Eye contact was an integral part of this meeting. Alex regretted the loss of it.

"You okay, son?" Bruce asked, his brows pinched with worry for his boy.

"Yeah, Dad," Aaron answered with venom, though he didn't look his father in the eye, either. "Fine. I'm fuckin' fine, same as I was last time you asked."

Bruce sent Alex a fatherly look of exasperation as Seth McCray angled his bulky frame through the doorway and took the empty chair alongside Aaron.

Instantly, Aaron shifted his chair to the other end of the table, glancing sideways at Seth. Furtive. Like a kid who was afraid of being slapped or touched.

"Whew!" Seth exclaimed, his face tanned and his hair bleached from the sun. "Would've been here sooner, Boss, but traffic out of Logan's a bitch." Logan International

Airport, Boston, Mass. "They screwed up my rental. Ended up with an Uber driver."

"Glad you could make it," Alex replied. "Just wanted you to confirm that Roland Montego can't hurt anyone anymore."

"Who's asking?"

"Us," Aaron said quietly, his eyes fixed to the table and his hands still hidden beneath it.

Seth kicked back and extended one long leg under the table. "And us would be...?" There was a day Seth had been nearly as broken as Aaron. If anyone could reach Aaron, Alex hoped he could.

Aaron stared at Alex. "Used to be USMC Corporal Aaron Pope."

"You still are USMC Corporal Aaron Pope." Alex offered with a nod of encouragement.

"Damn, Boss. Another jarhead?" Seth blew out a soft whistle. "You keep a hiring quota or something?"

Alex chuckled at the implication that he might have hired more of his USMC brethren over others. Which he had. But once a Marine, always a Marine.

Seth turned to Aaron. "I've been hearing bits and pieces of the op that went down around here. You're the man Alex has been searching years for." He stuck out his hand. "Good to meet you, Aaron Pope."

Aaron jerked back. "D-d-d-d-don't touch us."

Understanding creased Seth's brow. "You were abducted, weren't you? She tortured you."

"We're free now," Aaron declared though his chin quivered when he spoke.

"Damned straight you're free. She's in Cuba again, but her ugly-assed brother's dead, and you're still here. Sounds like one helluva win to me."

"Are you sure?"

"Hell, yeah," Seth replied. "I'm not one to brag about killing a guy, but Roland Montego had a bullet coming, and by hell, I'm the lucky bastard who delivered it. Speaking of delivery, you like pizza?"

Alex nearly grinned. He hadn't seen that not-so-subtle segue coming.

Aaron nodded, his eyes furtively seeking contact with Seth. "Umm, yeah. Haven't had it in y-y-years, but…" His head bobbed. "Yeah. Used to like it. A lot. With icy cold beer."

"What kinda beer?" Seth asked, his head cocked and his brows pinched. "Not that imported shit, right?"

Alex leaned back into his chair, finally at ease as he watched Seth handle Aaron like a pro.

"N-no, no," Aaron sputtered. "Shit, no. They still make Sam Adams? That's what I like. Sam Adams Boston Ale or any ale. Just c-c-cold. It'd be nice if it was cold."

"Great. Then plan on poker, pizza, and a case of icy cold Sam Adams tonight," Seth declared, his legs stretched under the table, his eyes as bright and as healthy as Alex had never seen him. Since he'd married Devereaux Shepherd, Seth was a different man. "How about I call some of the guys, and we'll throw down here with you tonight. You good with that?"

"Shhhhh… sure," Aaron replied. And suddenly, he lifted both hands out from under the table. Four stubs, what were left of fingers that had once been so long he'd easily palmed regulation-sized basketballs, now curled over his right hand. "But what if I can't hold onto the c-c-cards?"

Seth noticed the sadistic result of Montego's vicious reign, the glint of shock and sympathy a quick flash in his eyes before he covered it up. "Then I guess we'll just have to trust you not to cheat."

Aaron made a noise like he was choking, but damned if tears didn't well in his eyes. He had no way of knowing it, but he'd just met the indomitable spirit behind The TEAM. Oozing confidence and reliability, Seth was proof of the magic of brotherhood, the very thing Aaron desperately needed whether he knew it or not. Just like that it happened. One brother reached out to save another, and that was all it took.

"You staying, Boss?" Seth asked, his eyes bright as a crooked smile stole over his sly mouth.

"I'm here, aren't I?"

"Yes," Aaron said quietly as he looked directly at Alex. "You are here. Thanks for coming. It's sure good to see you."

Epilogue

"Hit the damned thing!"

"Stop teaching my baby to swear," McKenna called out even as the babe within her womb leaped.

Beau spun Isabelle Esperanza—Baby Essie for short—in a wide circle, her arms spread like a miniature airplane as she tried one more time to nail the pink donkey piñata Grandpa Rubio had gifted her with for her first birthday. She didn't need a blindfold. The plastic baseball bat in her chubby little hand had yet to come close to making contact with *'el burro.'*

Grinning, Beau dipped her low to the ground, then tossed her high over his head and told her, "Go, baby! Go!"

Essie squealed, and McKenna's heart took a snapshot of this perfect moment in time. The giggling angel suspended in midair. The radiant smile on her handsome husband's gorgeous tanned face. The gleam of sunshine on his thick, dark hair, and the ever-present light in his chocolate brown eyes.

There was a time those eyes hadn't known the grace of a smile, but those days were gone. The tender love of the child who'd just landed in his arms, beaming up at him like he was her world, had changed Beau.

He no longer cursed everyone who crossed his path, and McKenna couldn't remember the last f-bomb he'd dropped. Out of the blue, he'd signed up for anger management classes shortly after they'd married. He was more vocal about praying, though he usually only addressed Christ. Something he still hadn't disclosed linked him to the second deity in the Christian Godhead.

Whatever it was, Beau had an almost personal relationship with Jesus. Come to find out, he hadn't been using His name in vain as much as relying on Him. Kind of like calling in an airstrike when all else failed during combat. McKenna suspected Beau viewed the Lord as just another PJ dropping in to save the day. It was a comforting piece to the puzzle that was Benjamin Beauregard Villanueva.

And yes, he'd repainted and re-carpeted, in crystal white no less, the entire house. It was a difficult color scheme to maintain with a messy toddler just learning to walk. But the cleanliness and the uncluttered feel of all that white was important to Beau.

As were the simplified furnishings he and McKenna had carefully selected. He'd adamantly rejected the concept of a dining room, something she suspected had to do with how he came to have a shorter, but still useful, baby finger. Instead, he'd turned that room with sliding glass doors off their kitchen into an indoor patio, complete with Adirondack chairs, a toddler-sized swing set for Essie, and a cat loft for Manny, the fluffy orange tabby McKenna had adopted from Kyrie. The lazy feline now lounged in comfort with his adopted sibling, Sid.

In the shade of the lofty honey locust beside the house, Sanders Fitzgerald and Rubio sat chatting like two loving grandfathers with the same stars in their eyes. Two cold beers and a plate of gingerbread cookies sat on the table between them. It turned out Sanders had kept a secret from McKenna, too. It all came to a head the day he'd called the police station to warn her that, *'There's a lot you don't know, princess. Whatever you do, don't come looking for me!'*

He'd set her straight as soon as they'd reunited after Bambi had tried to kill her and ended up killing herself. Point blank. He'd no more than grabbed her into his arms when he'd blurted, "You're adopted. I'm sorry, Princess. I should've told you a long time ago, but you never asked, and I just couldn't bring myself to hurt you more than you already were. Blame me, not your mother. It was my fault. She couldn't get pregnant, and she knew I wanted a family, so we adopted you as an infant, and… and…"

He'd broken down then, with McKenna still holding *'her dad'* and wondering what the hell just happened.

"I'm adopted?" Which actually made sense of all the loose ends in her life. Her mother. Her aunts. Her maternal grandmother. Why she didn't suffer the same mental illness. That was what always worried her the most, that one day she'd fall off the deep end and hurt the tiny patients in her care. Being told she'd been adopted was actually a relief. Of sorts.

But by then, Sanders had been a mess, he'd cried so hard. "Are you disappointed?" he'd asked, which her heart interpreted to mean, *'Do you still love me?'*

So yes, she forgave him on the spot. "Adoption doesn't change what I feel about you. You'll always be my first love, and I know you've always loved me," she told him sincerely. "It doesn't change anything, except now I can look for my birth parents. Who knows? Maybe they've been looking for me like Rubio and Essie searched all of Beau's life for him."

Which made Sanders cry harder.

"I love you, Dad," she told him. "Forever and ever."

To which he replied, "Amen, Princess. Amen."

Fast forward to now, with Baby Essie chortling as she bounced against her father's belly for that elusive more. It was like watching a gentle giant with his tiny elfin princess, the way Beau cradled her protectively into his chest. The way he closed his eyes every time he kissed the mass of thick, dark brown curls on the top of her head. The way he looked across their yard, his sharp sniper eyes always searching for McKenna. The man was simply made to protect the people he cherished. His love and devotion for sweet little Almond Joy had programmed him early in life to be the man he was today. And McKenna had never felt more cherished.

Once their gazes locked onto each other, she melted. Her heart hammered, and her breath caught. No woman on earth had it better than she did. And McKenna had it bad—for him.

She blew him a kiss while Grandma Essie tsked and wiped her hands on her apron as she settled to the picnic table with McKenna. "He treats that little girl like she's a boy. I tell him to be more careful, but my son is so strong. I know he will not drop that baby, but I worry. The way that son of mine handles his daughter is too much for this old heart some days. It's good this next little one is a boy, si?"

"Shhhhh, Mama V. I haven't told him we're having a son yet," McKenna whispered as she joined hands with Beau's mother and nodded toward the sexy man under discussion.

But Karma had a way of making even impossible dreams come true. Grandma Essie and Grandpa Rubio had moved into the quaint mother-in-law bungalow just off the lavish home Beau had bought for his new family. His brothers had all arrived for McKenna's wedding to their brother, and what a day that was. All four boys were physical works of art, fit for a gallery and a private showing. But Beau outshone his three brothers in height, sheer muscle mass, and that rugged, bad-boy sex appeal that he wore as easily as an old shirt.

Their initial meeting had been awkward, but by then, McKenna was six months pregnant with Baby Essie. One look at her belly and the brothers swarmed Beau with congratulations, clapped his back, hugged him, and promised to always be there for him.

Diego in particular. As the oldest, he'd been charged with making sure Baby Beau stayed safe at the rest stop that fateful day. When Bass took Beau, Diego's screams alerted Rubio and Essie. But by the time they'd run back to the truck, Beau was gone. Diego still had nightmares. Once he had his arms around Beau, he broke down. Robert and Mateo fell apart, too. Like the loving brothers they were, they'd never forgotten Beau. They'd blamed themselves for failing him.

That reunion was another Kodak moment McKenna would never forget, the Villanueva family huddled together in tears with Beau smack in the center of all that love. Right where he belonged.

Then Mother surprised the life out of Beau, when she sent another one-of-a-kind wedding present from the Pacific island where she was taking an extended leave of absence. She never said how she came to find it, but McKenna suspected the original came from the Las Vegas investigator she'd hired. It was a magnificent oil painting, on canvas. Almond Joy's pretty face now hung in the family room surrounded by Baby Essie's pictures. Whoever had snapped the image had caught AJ with her thumb in her mouth. Her blue eyes were smiling straight into the camera. Despite the dark shadows under those eyes, she looked angelic and happy. The artist Mother had hired to do the painting managed to make AJ look ethereal, as if she truly were Beau's angel baby.

Overwhelmed, he'd dropped to his knees the moment he saw his first true love again. McKenna knelt with him, then took him into her arms and they'd cried together. Sad tears. Happy tears. They cried a lot these days.

"You need to rest," Grandma Essie reminded McKenna, patting her hand like she did when she worried. And Beau's mother always worried.

"I will. Later. But I don't think I've ever seen him happier," McKenna confessed as she found her grinning prince marching toward her with sweet Baby Essie high on his shoulder. "I'm so happy that you and Rubio accepted our invitation to live with us. I know this is a long way from Mexico, but you've made Beau happy, and that's all I want."

Grandma Essie wiped a tear. "It is all I want as well. You have such a beautiful baby."

McKenna agreed. Baby Essie was the cutest little girl in the world. There was no doubt about that. But Beau was...

Totally.

Utterly.

Beautiful.

The End

Thank you for reading Beau's story!

Be sure to check out the rest of the guys and gals from The TEAM in Irish Winters' series: *In the Company of Snipers*

Other Irish Winters' books/series

King of Hearts, Deuces Wild Series, #1

Joker Joker, Deuces Wild Series, #2

One-Eyed Jack, Deuces Wild Series, #3

Smoke, Hearts and Ashes Series, *#1*

Ash, Hearts and Ashes Series, #2

Angel, An SOBs Novel, #1

Coming soon

Assassin, An SOBs Novel, #2

Ace, Deuces Wild Series, #4

YOU ARE THE KEY TO THIS BOOK'S SUCCESS!

Please tell other readers why you liked Beau and McKenna's story by leaving an honest review at the retail site where you purchased it. Recommend it to your friends. Lend it. Most of all, enjoy it!

The best way to keep up with my new releases, giveaways, and actionable intel is to sign up for my spam-free newsletter at IrishWinters.com.

About the Author

Irish Winters

...is a best-selling author who, when she isn't writing, dabbles in poetry, grandchildren, and rarely—as in extremely rarely—the kitchen. More prone to be outdoors than in, she grew up the quintessential tomboy on a dairy farm in rural Wisconsin, spent her teenage years in the Pacific Northwest, but calls the Wasatch Mountains of Northern Utah, home. For now. She believes in making everyday count for something, and follows the wise admonition of her mother to, "Look out the window and see something!"

Connect with Irish online:
On Facebook:https:/www.facebook.com/author.irishwinters
On Twitter: https://twitter.com/irishwinters1
Or at www.IrishWinters.com